TIME AND PLACE

Alan Sheridan read English at Cambridge, then spent five years in Paris as assistant at the Lycées Henri IV and Condorcet. His first novel, *Vacation*, was published in 1972, his *Michel Foucault: The Will to Truth* in 1980. His widely acclaimed biography, *André Gide: A Life in the Present*, appeared in 1998. He has translated over fifty books, including works by Sartre, Lacan, Foucault, Robbe-Grillet and Pinget.

Pro Petro, non Anglus sed angelus

TIME AND PLACE

Alan Sheridan

Alan

Scribner

First published in Great Britain by Scribner, 2003
This edition published by Scribner, 2004
An imprint of Simon & Schuster UK Ltd
A Viacom Company

1 3 5 7 9 10 8 6 4 2

Simon & Schuster UK Ltd
Africa House
64–78 Kingsway
London WC2B 6AH

www.simonsays.co.uk

Simon & Schuster Australia
Sydney

A CIP catalogue record for this book is available
from the British Library

ISBN 0 7432 3195 3

Typeset by M Rules
Printed and bound in Great Britain
by Cox & Wyman Ltd, Reading, Berks

To all those who . . .

Responsum est, quod Angli
vocarentur. At ille: 'Bene,' inquit,
'nam angelicam habent faciem,
et tales angelorum in coelis decet
esse coheredes.'
                    Papa Gregorius Magnus.
Bede, Historia Ecclesiastica

They announced that they were
called Angles. 'It is well,' he said,
for they have the faces of angels,
and such should be the co-heirs
of the angels of heaven.']

Author's Note

This is, very largely, a true story. I have made use of diaries and notebooks given me by a relation of mine, Mark Sheridan (1880–1969), dating from 1903 to 1912. I have tried as far as possible to keep within the perspective of those years. Any lack of resemblance between real persons and fictional characters bearing their names is to be attributed to the limitations of my knowledge and the consequent exercise of my imagination.

The days have long since gone when a London publishing house could turn down André Gide's *La Porte étroite* on the grounds that nobody who wanted to read the book would be unable to do so in the original. So, for the benefit of those without French, I have included footnotes containing translations of French words and passages, as well as other pieces of information.

I should like to thank the one-time Arts Council of Great Britain and the one-time Wolverhampton Polytechnic for two years spent as a Creative Writing Fellow.

1907: Berlin

'The rest . . . is . . . silence.' Mr Tree's elongated, no longer youthful figure draped itself down the steps leading up to the throne. I was standing a few yards away, upstage right, trying to look concerned, but not so much as to distract attention – I was, after all, no more than a mute attendant lord. Basil Gill, whose voice was almost as beautiful as his face, brought things to an end:

> Now cracks a noble heart. – Good night, sweet prince:
> And flights of angels sing thee to thy rest!

Adolf Schmidt lifted his baton and the orchestra in the pit played the final section of George Henschel's score. Curtain. For that is how *Hamlet* ended in those days: like an Italian opera, with the prince's death and angelic choir off-stage. No Fortinbras, no return to a healthier, if mediocre normality.

Hamlet must be the longest part in Shakespeare. When he is not addressing his father's ghost, begging him, at length, to speak, spinning out studentish witticisms with Rosencrantz and Guildenstern, lecturing actors on how to do their job, engaging in metaphysical debate with gravediggers, Hamlet is delivering long speeches to himself. Many an actor must have felt relief that thereafter the rest *was* silence.

As the curtain fell, I looked across at Esmond; to certain

wicked-tongued members of the cast, who delighted in inventing nicknames for everybody, he was Rosamund, now abbreviated to Rose; on the programme, he appeared as

Rosencrantz .... E. Egerton Hine

Rosencrantz and Guildenstern had already met their deaths in England, of course. But now, disguised behind a beard, Esmond was, like me, a silent courtier, as were three of our young friends, John Cooke Beresford, Alfred Goddard and Robert Atkins, who, clean-shaven, had earlier appeared as Guildenstern, Bernardo and Marcellus, respectively. With Shakespeare's large casts, the beard was an essential tool of economy.

Tree, too, was wearing a beard, one of the few Hamlets to do so — this in the interest of textual accuracy, for does not Hamlet say: 'Plucks off my beard and blows it in my face'? Though it had no doubt occurred to Tree that a young beard could help disguise an old face: at fifty-three, he could hardly pass as a contemporary of my nineteen-year-old Esmond at Wittenberg University. Only a few years younger than her husband, Mrs Tree would have had no such aid had she decided to play Ophelia once again: that role now fell to their daughter, Viola, 'the Twig' to us, then a mere twenty-two.

The time and the place? Late in the evening of 17 April 1907, on the stage of the Neues Königliches Opern-Theater, Berlin. Earlier in the year, during the run of *Antony and Cleopatra*, a summons had come from the German Emperor to take the production to Berlin. With his usual foolhardy generosity, Tree offered to take five more productions, thus affording the Berlin public a broader view of English theatre at its best. None of us, except Tree himself, who was half-German and spent his summers at Marienbad, had seen Berlin before. I had been through it twice, but seen nothing of the city itself. With their usual efficiency, the Germans had worked out a system whereby, whatever direction one entered and left their capital, one did not have to leave a station. Berlin was like a gigantic points system in which the stations were arranged in a circle, linked to one another by rail. I had never even had to leave my train: I arrived in Berlin at one station, moved on round the northern suburbs and left by another. The last time I had done this was in 1905 when, with my parents, I returned to London after spending a year with them in St Petersburg, where my father was then Secretary of Embassy. The year before, I had also gone through Berlin, on my way not to the Russian, but to the Chinese capital, where I was born.

1904: London–Peking

'On arriving in Moscow by a morning train, Levin had put up
at the house of his elder half-brother, Koznishev . . .'

No sooner had I picked up my book and begun Chapter VII
than I put it down again and looked out of the window. It was
not that I was finding the book boring or the view any less
boring than usual – had it not been for a fall of snow
overnight, the landscape outside would no doubt have looked
no different from the desolate North European plain that
stretched across Germany, Poland and Russia proper. No, it
was the mention of Moscow and the train that gave me pause:
the day before, I too had arrived in Moscow by a morning
train.

After several hours spent wandering around the half-dozen
cathedrals in the Kremlin, interrupted by luncheon at an hotel
on Theatre Square, I boarded the 'Trans-Siberian Express' at
the splendid Kursk station. The 'Express', I was to learn,
moved at the same leisurely pace as an English country train
linking one village with another. It never exceeded twenty
miles per hour and, when confronted by the gentle slope of the
Urals, dropped to fifteen. Not that, inside, the Trans-Siberian
had anything of the English country train about it. The carriages were wider than those of Western Europe and still
wider than the British ones, longer, taller and considerably
better appointed than either. The five carriages consisted of

one for luggage and staff quarters, next to the engine, followed by another for the *'wagon restoran'*, one first-class carriage (painted blue-black) and two second-class ones (painted mustard yellow). There seemed to be little difference between the two classes, other than the attribution of four, rather than two, passengers per compartment. This did give the second-class compartments a more 'Russian' character, that is, an air of total confusion: bedding, tables, open suitcases, fur coats, kettles covered every inch of space not occupied by the passengers' behinds. Whenever I passed such a compartment, the occupants always seemed to be playing cards and smoking cigarettes. At the end of each carriage was a stove, with a pile of wood beside it. The fire-tender, who gave you a military salute as you passed, spent his time going from one stove to another. There were also a bathroom, an exercise-room (equipped with stationary bicycle and other such wonders) and lavatories (one of which could be used for photographic work, an odd facility, given that for most of the journey there was nothing of interest to photograph). One entered the first-class compartment in the middle and found oneself in a saloon, comfortably furnished with sofas, armchairs and tables. There was a piano, with sheet music provided. Church and State looked down impassively from the walls under the species of an icon, its oil lamp glowing behind its red glass, and a photograph of Tsar Nicholas, flanked by more functional wall lights. A bookcase contained volumes in French, German and English, as well as Russian. Chess, draughts and other table games were provided. Beyond the curtain at either end of the saloon corridors led to the compartments. These, too, were furnished to a high standard, wood-panelled, with proper full curtains, detachable tables for meals or card games and a pillar-standard electric lamp as well as delicate glass-shaded wall lamps. The heating was controlled by a lever, with thermometers inside and outside the windows, showing alarming discrepancies. A bell summoned a waiter from the dining-car or, at night, an attendant to make the bed. The seat of the banquette folded out to form a large, comfortable double bed – another could be formed by folding up the back of the banquette over the first. The cost of all this relative luxury, over the 4000 miles and eleven days from Moscow to the Chinese border was only £10. It had cost as much to travel, less comfortably, from London to Moscow, half the distance, in three days. The meals, too, were reasonably priced. By comparison, the hot baths seemed expensive at three roubles (six shillings).

First-class passengers were usually expected to share a compartment, so I was relieved to see that I was left in splendid isolation. This, I felt sure, I owed to an impressive-looking letter of recommendation from the Russian Foreign Ministry, accorded either as a privilege of my quasi-diplomatic status or as a security measure in time of war, my nationality making me an ally of Russia's enemy, Japan. In the dining-car and saloon I encountered some of my fellow-travellers, and felt even more pleased that I had been left to myself. They seemed, for the most part, to be Russian officials or army officers, none accompanied by a wife. I later discovered that we also counted among our number a German journalist, who turned out to have some French and some English, but nothing very interesting in the way of conversation, and a French fur trader, whose observations never rose above the most banal and whose company I ceased to cultivate.

Three weeks before, I had left Paris and the home that had been mine since my arrival from China at the age of ten. In a little over a year I had watched my beloved Dumollard grandparents die, one after the other. After handling the sale of the apartment in the rue de Vaugirard, I spent a week or two with my Sheridan grandmother in London. I could, of course, have stayed with her, but I decided to join my parents in Peking. I was interested to see again a city that I had not seen for fourteen years and which still haunted my imagination. It was, too, an opportunity to live for a while with my parents: I had seen little of them in recent years. After eight weeks, I would accompany them to St Petersburg, where my father was being seconded to the British Embassy.

Paris had accustomed me to a certain facility in what the French call, charmingly, if with a touch of euphemism, *aventures amoureuses*. Grief, I found, did nothing to abate sexual desire: while living at my grandparents' I had kept a room at an hotel in the rue Cujas. My eight weeks in Peking would, I felt sure, be spent chastely, or at least unadventurously. Would St Petersburg prove any better? If not, I could always return sooner rather than later to London or Paris. Meanwhile, over the next few weeks, I would be alone on a train, enjoying the unusual privilege of a compartment to myself. Since my fellow passengers could be eliminated at a glance, I was left with the staff as the only possible source of adventure. On my first day, however, the waiters did not seem to offer any more hope than the passengers: they were all shaven-headed Mongols of uncertain age. I later learnt that they were Tartars and that many of their fellows were to be found in the best St Petersburg restaurants. With familiarity, I was able to distinguish between them; there were three in all, serving variously in dining-car, saloon and compartments. Next morning, at breakfast, I was served by a newcomer, a young man in his early twenties, more than acceptable, whom I assumed to be Russian. I congratulated him on his excellent French.

'*Mais je suis Français,*' he replied, with mingled outrage and amusement, the second undermining any seriousness in the first. He then complimented me on my French.

'*Mais je suis moitié-Français,*' I replied, imitating his tone.

'*Ah!*' he said, '*Monsieur a bien l'air anglais pourtant.*'

'*Mais je suis moitié-Anglais,*' I said, with a laugh.

'*Ah, bon. Et maintenant vous êtes en train –*' he paused to savour his own wit – '*de traverser la Russie.*'[1]

He was called François. I asked him how he had ended up on the Trans-Siberian. It was a long story. I said that he must tell me about it some time. I retired to my compartment and *Anna Karenin.*

Just before lunch, Moscow and railway trains cropped up again. If one insists on reading long Russian novels on long Russian train journeys, one should not be surprised by such coincidences. I had reached the point when Anna arrives in Moscow from Petersburg and learns that a man has just thrown himself under the train and been killed. 'Oh, how horrible! Oh, Anna, if you had seen it! Oh, how horrible!' says her brother, Oblonsky, who has come to meet her. But Anna herself did not see it and we learn little of her reaction. All she says is: 'It is a bad omen.' Ten days, 4000 miles and 700 pages later, I had forgotten the incident on the Moscow platform, as Tolstoy intended that I should. So it came as quite a shock when, approaching the Russian–Chinese frontier at Mandshuriya, I read:

> And all at once she thought of the man crushed by the train the day she had first met Vronsky, and she knew what she had to do. With a rapid, light step she went down the steps that led from the tank to the rails and

1 'But I *am* French!' 'But I'm half French.' 'But Monsieur looks very English.' 'But I'm half English.' 'I see. And now you're [in a train] crossing Russia.' *En train de* is a French locution corresponding to the English continuous present.

stopped quite near the approaching train. She looked at the lower part of the carriages, at the screws and chains, and the tall cast-iron wheel of the first carriage slowly moving up, and trying to measure the middle between the front and back wheels, and the very minute when that middle point would be opposite her.

'There,' she said to herself, looking into the shadow of the carriage, at the sand and coal-dust which covered the sleepers – 'there, in the very middle, and I will punish him and escape from everyone and from myself.'

She tried to fling herself below the wheels of the first carriage as it reached her; but the red bag which she tried to drop out of her hand delayed her, and she was too late; she missed the moment. She had to wait for the next carriage. A feeling such as she had known when about to take the first plunge in bathing came upon her, and she crossed herself. That familiar gesture brought back into her soul a whole series of girlish and childish memories, and suddenly the darkness that had covered everything for her was torn apart, and life rose up before her for an instant with all its bright past joys. But she did not take her eyes from the wheels of the second carriage. And exactly at the moment when the space between the wheels came opposite her, she dropped the red bag, and drawing her head back into her shoulders, fell on her hands under the carriage, and lightly, as though she would rise again at once, dropped on to her knees. And at the same instant she was terror-stricken at what she was doing. 'Where am I? What am I doing? What for?' She tried to get up, to drop backwards; but something huge and merciless struck her on the head and rolled her on her back. 'Lord, forgive me all!' she said . . . And the light by which she had read the book filled with troubles, falsehoods, sorrow, and evil, flared up more brightly than ever before, lighted up for her all that had been in darkness, flickered, began to grow dim, and was quenched for ever.

So the railway train had been not only the means of shifting characters between Moscow, Petersburg and their country estates, an up-to-date piece of stage machinery for scene changes, but a machine from which the tragic god rescued the heroine, not from death, but from life, a life that had the reality and unreality of a book.

In the dining-car, one could take the *obeid*, or Russian *table d'hôte*, costing one and a quarter roubles (half-a-crown),[1] or eat more expensively *à la carte*, in a more international, French-inspired way. On my first night on the train, I was still feeling the effects of my meal in Moscow, so ate lightly *à la carte*. At luncheon the following day, I felt that I ought to essay the *obeid*. I called François over and asked him, as a fellow-Frenchman, for his opinion of the *obeid*.

'*Il y a ceux qui aiment ça, vous savez,*' he replied, with an obvious lack of enthusiasm. '*Il y a aussi ceux qui trouvent ça un peu lourd. C'est consistant, hein.*'[2]

Looking around me, I could see that everyone seemed to have opted for the *obeid*. Despite François's hints that it was not universally loved, that I might even find it on the heavy side, I decided to risk it. He placed a small glass and a bottle of vodka on my table, followed a few seconds later by a selection of cold meats, sardine-like fish and beluga caviar, with black rye bread and butter. These – and the vodka – were then

1 Two shillings and sixpence – ⅛ of a pound.
2 'Some people like it, but others find it a bit heavy. It is rather substantial, you know.'

replaced by a large bowl of cabbage soup, to which was added a spoonful of thick sour cream. François then helpfully explained that the large pieces of meat floating in the soup were to be removed and eaten separately, with mustard. I decided to leave the meat. At this point I ordered half a bottle of Russian red wine, to accompany the roast partridge with cranberries. An *apfelstrudel* type of apple pie was followed by cheese. I then retired to the saloon, where I found an exuberant group of Russian military men playing cards, amid clouds of smoke. When I had finished my coffee, I retreated to my compartment, where, after reading a few more pages of Tolstoy, I dozed off.

That evening, François awaited me in the *wagon restoran*. He asked me if I had recovered from the *obeid*. I made a gesture implying that it had been something of an effort. With gentle commiseration, he reminded me that he had warned me.

'*Peut-être Monsieur voudrait quelque chose de plus léger ce soir.*'[1] I ordered an *omelette aux champignons*, with salad, followed by fresh fruit. Later, I tended to avoid the *obeid* and eat in a lighter, more familiar manner.

François was all attention. He had the Parisian's quick-wittedness, lightness of touch, coquettish desire to please – or to impress. He was dark of hair and skin, slim, of average height, slightly effeminate and, I thought, a year or two younger than I: precisely the type with which I had my greatest – and easiest – successes. I would not have passed him over on the boulevards of Paris, let alone on a railway train speeding in the direction of the Ural Mountains. No time would be wasted: we both knew the rules of the game. Everything would proceed smoothly. As he was serving me coffee and a very

---

1 'Perhaps Monsieur would care for something a little lighter this evening.'

generous brandy, his smile became more than usually complicit. Very quietly, I asked him if he would care to come and *'prendre un verre'*[1] before going to bed. Normally, such an invitation would have been unthinkable.

'Avec plaisir,' he murmured, without batting an eyelid. He then gave a broad grin. He warned me that his *service* did not end until eleven thirty. *'Ça ne sera pas trop tard pour vous?'*

'Non, non, pas du tout. Vous connaissez le numéro de ma porte?'

'Bien sûr!'[2]

At eleven, I pressed the bell labelled *'Konduktor'*. A uniformed attendant appeared, standing at the salute. *'Spate'* (sleep), I said, and he dug out the bedclothes and transformed the seat into a bed. *'Spacoine notche!'* (good night), he said, saluting, and left. Half an hour later there was another knock on the door: there was François, still in uniform, bearing a tray, with glasses, a bottle of Ayala champagne and various delicacies involving caviar. I was wearing nothing but a dressing-gown.

'Vous aimez le champagne, j'espère.' I assured him that I did. I sat on the bed, while he busied himself with it. He sat down beside me. *'À la vôtre!'* he said, holding up his glass to be clinked.

'À la tienne!' I responded. Thereafter we said *'tu'*[3]. We talked, like a couple of exiled Parisians, of Paris. In a few minutes, he had told me the story of his life. His parents lived near the Bastille. He had done his apprenticeship at the Hôtel du Rhin, on the place Vendôme. Until he made up his mind to

1 'Have a drink.'
2 'With pleasure . . . It won't be too late for you?' 'No, no, not at all. You know the number of my compartment?' 'Of course.'
3 'You like champagne, I hope . . . Your health!' 'And yours!' – the shift from *'votre'* to *'tienne'* marked a shift from the polite to the intimate mode.

see the world, he had spent his entire life in Paris. Serge, the train's *chef de cuisine*, who was half-French and half-Russian, was a good friend: they had been working together at the same hotel. When Serge decided to go back to Russia, he persuaded François to join him with the International Sleeping Car Company. When their six-month contract was up, Serge hoped to get a job at one of the big Petersburg hotels; François thought that he would go back to Paris.

Our knees were touching. I put my hand on his thigh and he fell into my arms. We kissed excitedly. By this time, my dressing-gown was wide open; he had not had time to remove so much as his tie. He knelt down and took my cock in his mouth. We stood up and undressed. He got down on his knees again, licking, biting, taking in as much as he could. I lifted him up, moved him down on to the bed, where he lay, stretched out on his belly. Kneeling up between his parted legs, I performed the necessary lubrication. I entered him without difficulty, then lay down over him, my left hand lightly caressing the silky smoothness of his throat, my right hand on his cock. It was nearly three weeks since my last *aventure*. Then it had been just such a young Frenchman in my hotel in the rue Cujas: the same dark, slightly curly hair, the same slim body, the same smooth, flawless dark skin.

If I were not deliberately seeking variation, it was generally thus. Had most of us, I sometimes wondered, concluded that this was the best way of doing things? There were those who took the initiative and lay on their backs, their knees raised, a position that, while obviously passive, seemed less abandoned, less trusting. Though I found it slightly less satisfactory, if only in the matter of penetrating movement, it had the advantage of offering a view of the other's face, presuming that the face added to one's pleasure, rather than detracting from it. There was also a certain pleasure in looking into the other's eyes as one thrust one's way in and out of his body, especially when he was new and particularly attractive. Then there was the pleasure to be found when the other shut his eyes and his mouth opened in pleasure, mingled with slight pain.

I had never made love on a train before. The sexual act is trochaic in rhythm, an accented syllable, followed by an unaccented one, as it were; it would have been impossible to synchronize this rhythm with that of a train, which is a near anapaest, three (not two) unaccented syllables followed by an accented one. Yet it was difficult to ignore such an insistent rhythm. Nevertheless I came with indecent haste. Staying inside him, I moved with him on to our left sides and finished him off. Afterwards, we chatted for a few minutes, drank more champagne. He then said that he was very tired and would have to leave me. If I liked, he would come back tomorrow night – but he would see me before then. He got dressed and left as he had come, minus the tray and its contents.

Next morning, I woke to find that we had stopped at a station, to the accompaniment of a great deal of noise – much shouting, banging of doors, hitting of metal on metal. I looked at my watch, which was still on Moscow time: it was six thirty. I went back, fitfully, to sleep. These stops, I later realized, were not to allow passengers to leave or board the train – no one did – but were to do with its maintenance: the loading on of wood or coal, the checking of the wheels and other mechanical parts, changes in the crew. The kitchen staff remained on the train from Moscow to Irkutsk, but the others, from the engine driver down, slept not on the train, but at various stations along the route and were replaced each day.

I appeared in the dining-room for breakfast. François came over at once, looking very severe, very official:

'*Bonjour, Monsieur. Monsieur a bien dormi?*' His face then broke into a grin.

'*Et toi? Tu as bien dormi?*'[1] I murmured.

From then on, whenever he served me at table, he alternated between a mode of exaggerated formality and intimacy.

Outside, nothing had changed from the day before: the snow-covered plain stretched absolutely flat to the horizon. The monotony would be broken by the occasional appearance of a group of houses or a wooden windmill in the middle distance. The sun was already into view, on the south side of the train, sending up dazzling light from the snow. At lunchtime, I felt the sun's heat through the double windows, despite the very low temperature outside.

That night, as arranged, François came to my compartment again. On leaving, he said that he would not be *disponible*[2] the following night but, if I liked, he could come the night after that. I said that I should look forward to his next visit.

By next morning, the train was entering more interesting country, winding between hills or along a small stream. Once we actually entered a tunnel, the first of very few encountered on the journey. About noon, we reached Zlatoust, a township near the highest point. For once, I decided to don my greatcoat, gloves and the fur hat I had bought in Moscow and brave the temperature outside. Standing around were groups of bearded, sheepskinned figures. Fur-capped mechanics, carrying wrenches and hammers, moved from carriage to carriage, tightening bolts and testing wheels. In addition to the variously uniformed attendants were soldiers, standing to attention against the white, wooden station house: they were to be seen at every stop along the route. At first, bundled up in

1 'Good morning, Monsieur. Monsieur slept well?' 'What about you? Did you sleep well?'
2 Available.

my clothes, I didn't feel the cold as I walked up to the end of the platform. Then, suddenly, as I turned, a gust of wind slashed my face. The thermometer by the station door showed a temperature of minus thirty-eight on the Réaumur scale, which is similar to the centigrade scale used in France. It suddenly felt much colder and, after a few minutes standing by the stove in the first-class waiting-room, I retreated to the enveloping warmth of the train. Putting my bare hands to my face, I tried to bring my anaesthetized cheeks to life. Outside, an official clanged the big bronze bell once, then, after a short pause, twice. The other passengers climbed back into their carriages.

The train set off again, winding its way round hills or cutting between them. We passed a stone pyramid, bearing the words 'Europa' and 'Asia', which marks the boundary between the two continents. We began the descent to Cheliabinsk, which we reached about five o'clock. The dense pine woods thinned out into scattered clumps of birches. By this time, I was sitting over tea in the *wagon restoran*. Outside, the telegraph poles clicked past between the sagging wires, the only sign of life being the twinkling lanterns at the track-guards' huts. Before long one of the waiters turned on the lights and drew the curtains.

The next day, Sunday, the landscape outside began to change: trees and fenced fields appeared, and scattered houses with smoke rising from chimneys. We crossed what seemed like an endless bridge. The train slackened to a crawl. Spires and gilt domes rose above the dark wooden houses. *Droshkies* and carts were passing in the streets. There were even people – the first I had seen anywhere but on the train or in railway stations. We appeared to be leaving the town, without stopping, when we arrived at the station, Omsk. I went out on to the platform for a breath of freezing air and a quick stroll up and down. I noted that many of the faces on the platform were 'oriental' in appearance: perhaps we were in Tartary already. After our noisy twenty-minute stop, we moved off into the dark wilderness. That night, as arranged, I received a visit from François.

Monday was as uneventful as Sunday: as night fell, we arrived, not this time at Omsk, but at Ob. Do such words, I wondered, little more than grunts, signify anything other than the towns they name? At ten forty there was the familiar knock on the door: François delivering champagne. With repetition had come a lessening of passion, a more leisurely progress, greater variation. Afterwards François would chatter on about this and that – about other members of the staff, other passengers. His favourite epithet, for either category, was *'agaçant'*, only slightly stronger than 'irritating', though made to sound much more extreme. As he was getting dressed, he asked me, as he had two nights before, if I would mind if he did not call on me the following night, but, this time, adding that he would pass by with a little present, *'comme remplaçant'*, this said with an unambiguous smile. Then, in order to make matters absolutely clear, he added:

'S'il te plaît, je le laisserai avec toi, hein?'[1] My relations with François entailed no sentimental element whatever: he possessed a clarity of vision in such matters that I have found nowhere so highly developed as in Paris and François was above all a Parisian. Such an attitude to *'l'amour'*, by which is meant sex, something 'done', rather than fallen into, has the effect of maximizing pleasure and reducing heartache to a minimum. If one believes that what the 'romantic' English and Germans call 'love' or *'Liebe'* is not an illusion to be

1 'As a replacement . . . If you like the look of him, I'll leave him with you, uh?'

shattered, but a feeling that can survive change, then the 'classicist' Frenchman may be missing something. Your typical Parisian has no truck with 'sincerity'. His love-making always has a histrionic element to it: he is not aware of this, any more than he is aware of the artificiality of the unvarying formulas he exchanges in everyday social intercourse. François liked me, found me attractive; I gave him what he wanted and he was pleased to give me what I wanted by way of exchange. Apart from our bodies, we had little else to exchange: François realized this and accepted it completely. He also had a very clear idea of the degree of attractiveness I found in him and accepted that too. It was therefore the most natural thing in the world that he should '*rendre service*' to two of his acquaintances by introducing them.

The following evening, François arrived at his usual time, accompanied by his *remplaçant*, a tall, slim, fair-haired, grey-eyed youth.

'*Je te présente Dmitri.*' The young man worked in the kitchens, which would explain why I had never set eyes on him before. He was nineteen, Russian and spoke not a word of any other language. '*Il te plâit?*' I grinned and nodded. '*Bon, je vous laisse alors. Je suis sûr qu'il te donnera satisfaction,*'[1] said François, with a self-satisfied smirk, and left.

Since his arrival, Dmitri had never stopped smiling. He gestured to the champagne they had brought, as if following instructions. I nodded and grinned back. He could not have provided a greater contrast to François, not only in looks, but in manner. He was gawky, clumsy even, probably slow-witted and, of course, said nothing. There was nothing effeminate about him, but he exuded what I can only call intense

1 'This is Dmitri . . . You like him? . . . I'm sure you'll find him quite satisfactory.'

tenderness. I put my hand around the back of his neck and he lay his head on my shoulder. I found the impossibility of verbal communication strangely exciting. I undressed him, revealing his white body and his white, fairly large cock, entirely sheathed in its foreskin, rising erect from its lake of almost grey pubic hair. In every move we made, he required an instruction, not, as I was to realize, because he lacked experience, but because he considered that it was my job to give orders, his to obey them. At no point did a single sound, not so much as a sigh, escape his lips. I took my pleasure on his silent person and my pleasure was far greater than any that I had had with François. I hoped that the pleasure had also been his, but I had no way of knowing. Afterwards, still smiling, he got dressed. Not knowing whether to give him money or not, I played safe and thrust a ten-rouble coin into his hand. It was probably what he earned in a week. A look of horror crossed his face and he moved his left hand back and forth in violent disapproval. It was the first time a smile had been absent from his face. I took him in my arms, kissed him and folded both my hands over the hand holding the coin. Interpreting this as an order, assuming no doubt that this was customary in the far-off land from which I came, he put the coin in his pocket. The smile returned and, still smiling, he left.

Next morning, we were climbing hilly, wooded country. I went up to the observation tower, reached by stairs at the rear of the carriage. That evening, I received my fifth and last visit from François. The following evening we would arrive in Irkutsk, where this section of the line terminated and where most of us, passengers and staff, would spend the night. I had already arranged to stay at the Hôtel Métropole, apparently the best of a very bad job in that sorry town. I suggested that he join me at my hotel, but he explained that it would be too complicated: he and his fellows would be staying at railway quarters near the station, before rejoining their train on the return journey to Moscow, whereas the entire town and its hotels were on the other side of a very wide river. I took my leave of François, thanking him for being such a good *compagnon de route*.[1] By the way, he said, you seem to have been quite a success with Dmitri. Tell him, I said, that he is a very nice boy.

It had gone 11 p.m. when our train pulled slowly up to the station house. White-aproned porters, with peaked hats and big numbered arm-tags invaded the carriage. One of them seized my luggage and ran with it into the crowd outside. I did my best to follow him. The platform was swarming with passengers, officials shouting instructions and the usual soldiers. We made our way into the crowded, smoke-filled first-class waiting-room. The porter then went off to the luggage van with the document that stated my claim to two trunks. At one end of the room was a bar serving drinks and refreshments: these, apparently, were free of charge. I ordered a vodka and picked up a few bits and pieces to eat. After about a quarter of an hour, the porter reappeared with my trunks on a cart, piled on to them the rest of my luggage and motioned to me to follow him. Outside, we were met by a long line of sleighs. François had advised me not to pay more than one rouble. He had omitted to tell me whether that was for one sleigh or for the two that I and my luggage would need. The first driver encountered demanded three roubles per sleigh. We finally agreed on some compromise figure. We set off across the bridge over the wide, frozen Angara River and entered what was, as far as I could see in the gloom, one of the poor quarters of the town. In time the deserted streets of wooden shacks gave way to two-storey whitewashed houses and wider streets.

1 Travelling companion.

At the Hôtel Métropole, my luggage was seized enthusiastically by porters. I paid the sleigh driver and went inside. I showed the receptionist the booking document bearing my name. He brushed it aside and I followed him up what may once have been a broad, impressive staircase, but now looked dingy and ill cared for, its red carpet threadbare in places. With a great flourish of keys, he opened a door and pressed a switch. Glancing up at the big cluster of dimly lit globes of the ceiling lamp, I entered a room as wide, as high and half as long as many an hotel ballroom. He opened another door and led me into another room almost as big as the first, with a forlorn-looking washstand in one corner and a screen across another.

'*Mais le lit*, the bed?' I asked. He led me over to the screen, folded it back and revealed a wooden platform-like structure, with a dirty-looking straw mattress rolled up at one end.

'You desire bed things?' he enquired.

'Yes,' I said.

'One moment,' he said and disappeared. Meanwhile, the porters silently deposited their load and departed with their tips. The receptionist returned, accompanied by some underling bearing bedclothes.

'Passport, please, for police.' With this and his own, larger tip, he bowed and left.

I returned to the first room and looked around. The furniture had seen the best of its time. There was an enormous oak desk, with its own drop-lamp, a big, none-too-strong-looking sofa and half a dozen armchairs around a dining-table, whose polished surface was scarred by innumerable rings, left presumably from hot glasses. There were a few hunting prints on the walls and, high up in one corner, a little icon with its own light. The presence of electricity in such a place was surprising. The room was very warm, but with no apparent source of heat, no stove, no radiator, no grill. I then noticed that one corner was rounded off in porcelain, very hot to the touch. Further investigation revealed that this was one quarter of a stove, another quarter being in an adjacent room, the remaining half in the corridor, from which it was fed.

I decided to order a nightcap. I looked around for a bell: there was none. I went back downstairs. Intrigued by the sound of revelling, I traced it to the dining-room, where, through the haze of cigarette smoke, I could make out a mass of what I took to be carousing army officers. I retreated to the hall.

'No bell,' I said, with gesture, and ordered a brandy.

'You want, you shout, we bring,' I was informed. This would explain all the shouting I had heard in the corridor earlier. I went back to my rooms. Five minutes later, the door opened without any warning knock and an ancient retainer appeared bearing a glass and a bottle of some Russian concoction, half of which had already been consumed. It turned out to be no worse than cheap cognac.

It was ten days since I had gone to sleep without the rhythmic, gently percussive accompaniment of steel wheel on steel rail. This was now replaced by a low rumbling of voices from below, punctuated by unexpected, louder bursts of jollity. When this eventually ceased, the sudden silence opened up like a vast void, itself a distraction from sleep.

I was woken by shouting in the corridor. No, this was not the last drunken revellers going to bed, but the establishment going about its early morning business. I decided to have breakfast at the station – the railway buffets were generally of a good standard – and left the hotel in good time for the train. As we crossed the interminable bridge, I looked back at Irkutsk and was startled to see the great Byzantine mass of a cathedral soaring above what had earlier seemed like some outpost in the American Wild West. Below, a dark line of traffic was making its way along the frozen river.

At the station, it was as if all the peasants from miles around were forcing their way on to the platform to catch the daily train to Baikal. Though it was not due to leave for another three-quarters of an hour, the long train, with its additional third-class carriages painted green, was already waiting for us. After laying claim to my compartment and installing my luggage, I retreated to the relative quiet of the first-class waiting-room for breakfast.

The train left promptly at ten thirty. My travelling companion turned out to be one of the army officers I had seen earlier in the waiting-room.

'*Deutsch?*'

'*Englisch*,' I replied, to his evident disappointment, but he continued to pour out several sentences in what appeared to be fluent German.

'I don't speak German,' I protested, but he clearly did not understand English. '*Parlez-vous français?*' I asked.

He made a gesture to mean 'very little', then pointed to my book, which I handed to him.

'*Ah, Anglais lire Tolstoy?*' he exclaimed in amazement. '*Moi non lire Tolstoy*,' he continued, in approximate French that he made to sound like German. '*Tolstoy non bon. Homme dangereux. Socialiste*,'[1] and he tapped his head with a finger to signify that Tolstoy was not only dangerous and a socialist, but also mad, though he himself had not read any of his works. A much better writer, he said, was X, whom I had never heard of and whose name I instantly forgot – much better stories, he said. After a few more such exchanges, he seemed willing to let

1 'English read Tolstoy? . . . I no read Tolstoy. Tolstoy not good. Dangerous man. Socialist.'

me return to my book or to staring silently out of the window: as the train wound its way up and down the smaller hills and around the larger ones, the scenery took on a new variety. This journey of some forty odd miles took nearly four hours.

It was to be another few years before the railway had engineered the forty tunnels and as many cuttings and bridges that took it round the perilously steep coastline at the southernmost end of Lake Baikal, thus creating a continuous rail line from Moscow to Vladivostok. At this time passengers still had to be conveyed across what is the deepest inland lake in the world. Unfortunately, the lake is frozen for half the year, down to a depth of three feet, so the journey was made in one of two ice-breaker ferries, built, they proudly proclaimed, in England, by Armstrong's of Elswick. For a short time, I went up on deck. As the vessel moved slowly, but unwaveringly through the ice, it threw up spirals of powdered ice that glittered in the last rays of the sun. On either side of us, mountains reared up precipitously, wooded at their lower reaches, topped by snow that merged imperceptibly into mist and cloud. Behind us, a splendid red ball of a sun cast pools of blood across the ice. Unable to bear the cold any longer, I went down into the cabin and tried to warm myself up with a couple of vodkas. The crossing took nearly five hours, some of which I whiled away over dinner.

It was late in the evening when we joined our waiting train, which, though no worse than most trains in England or France, lacked the extra luxury of the Moscow–Irkutsk train. The food, too, was less good and, before long, I was missing not only François's visits, but also the handiwork of his friend Serge. To my relief, however, I discovered that, for the remaining two nights on Russian territory, I was to have the compartment to myself once again. In the evening of the second day, we arrived at Mandshuriya, the frontier-station between Russia and Manchuria, nominally at least Chinese territory, where all our belongings were examined by the customs. The following evening, we arrived at Kharbin's gigantic *art nouveau* station, where I left the Trans-Siberian, which went on to Vladivostok, and changed on to the (Russian-owned) Chinese Eastern Railway.

Two days later, I was at Tientsin, from which, fourteen years before, we had embarked on the ship that took us to Shanghai, on the first part of our voyage to England. I could not but wonder at the marvel of engineering that had reduced the journey between London and Peking from about nine weeks, almost entirely at sea, to about two, almost entirely over land. The train journey from Tientsin to Peking would now take a few hours. I remembered the five-day, pre-railway journey by house-boat along the circuitous river, followed by a day in the notorious 'Peking cart'. My heartbeat began to quicken as I caught my first glimpse of the southern wall of the Chinese City. Somewhere short of there, I presumed, would be the station: it seemed inconceivable that the railway would be allowed inside the walls of Peking itself. But, to my astonishment, the train approached the Yung ting Mên, the central gateway, or, rather the gap where the gate had stood until the ending of the siege of the Legation Quarter in 1900, swerved to the right and entered through another hole that had been made in the wall. It passed the Temple of Heaven, then continued round the inside of the wall until it reached the Ch'ién Mên, the central gateway to the Tartar City. There, at the station, Mother and some servants from the Legation were waiting. A short rick-shaw ride – the Legation Quarter was only on the other side of the wall – brought us to my old home.

1880–90: China

My father was in his last year at Cambridge when he took it into his head to join the Chinese Consular Service. The first hurdle was the Chinese language, one of the most difficult for a European. In those days, the new King's College in the Strand was the only British university with a Chair of Chinese. So, for two years, he attended the special training courses in Chinese provided there for aspirant 'student interpreters'. It was during this period that he met my mother. In the spring of 1877, Caroline Dumollard, a French girl with dark hair and pale green eyes, was staying with her elder sister, Jacqueline, who was married to John Payne, wine-merchant. If not love at first sight, it was love after the first few thousand words. Almost certainly they conversed in English. Westminster School had left my father with quite adequate French, but his future wife's English came more naturally: her father was himself half English. My father passed his examinations and, with four other successful applicants, was appointed to the Chinese Consular Service. In June 1878, he and my mother were married in the *mairie* of the sixth *arrondissement* in Paris – a church wedding was out of the question in the anti-clerical Dumollard family. Student interpreters did not usually marry: only after ten years or more in the service could they support a wife and family. Fortunately, my father had private means of his own and so, two months later, they set sail for China.

It was there, in Peking, that I was born, on 24 April 1880: to my subsequent annoyance, I had missed sharing my birthday with Shakespeare by a day. I was christened Mark in the Legation chapel. The year before, my brother, Matthew, had been born. My father was once asked whether the next addition to the family, if a boy, would be called Luke. 'Of course,' he replied, 'and the one after that John. If we have to have saints in the family, let them at least be writers.' As it happened there were to be no more 'evangelists'. By naming my brother and me as he did, my father was following the Chinese practice of calling one's children by generically linked names. This is unusual in English, though there is no reason why English parents should not call their children Jasper, Pearl and Ruby, say, or Violet, Lily and Rose. My father was not a religious man. He viewed all claims to truth with mingled interest and disbelief. What are usually regarded as the larger questions of life he preferred to leave in decent obscurity. By education a Classicist, he was a Hellenized Roman at heart: sceptical, urbane, even-tempered. A smile was never far from his lips; he seldom laughed. I do not remember him getting excited about anything. The role of consul in China must have attracted him as being the nearest thing to that of some provincial administrator during the more relaxed, less aggressive phase of the Roman *imperium*.

The China of those years was weak, badly governed, corrupt, a fossilized society, ignorant of the barbarian world outside, yet convinced of its superiority in all things. Nature, in the shape of drought and flood, assisted by warlords and landlords whose power must have seemed scarcely less arbitrary, brought misery and premature death to millions of its people. At the spiritual, if not geographical centre of the empire, sealed off from reality by mental barriers as impenetrable as the three-fold walls that protected its Forbidden City, was Kuang

Hsu, the fourteen-year-old boy Emperor, revered and wor-
shipped as the 'Son of Heaven', the 'Lord of Ten Thousand
Years', the 'Buddha of the Present Day'. But the real ruler of
the empire was his aunt, the Empress Dowager Tz'u Hsi. She
had begun her career as one of twenty-eight Manchu recruits
to the harem of the Emperor Hsien Feng. At the age of
twenty-six, by a combination of astuteness and ruthlessness,
she had become an absolute ruler of enormous power. She also
succeeded, in a country financially ruined several times over, to
amass an immense personal fortune. During the Sino-Japanese
war of 1894–5 she consulted the manager of the Hong-kong
and Shanghai Bank in Peking about transmitting to London a
nest-egg of some £8 million in gold and silver bullion. But if
the Court existed in isolation from the country it governed, the
foreigners in Peking were no less isolated from their Chinese
hosts. This state of affairs was to some degree imposed on the
diplomats by the Chinese. The eleven Legations were grouped
in an enclave about three-quarters of a mile square in the
Tartar City, where the foreigners had their own shops, banks,
hotels, churches, club, sports ground.

After five years' service in Peking, my father was due for
leave. So, in June 1883, we set sail for England. The next
twelve months were spent with my grandparents in London
and Paris. On our return to China we moved to Shanghai,
where it was usual for the student interpreters to undergo
some legal training at the Supreme Consular Court. This was
made necessary by the peculiar conditions prevailing in China,
where a consul's duties involved political and judicial, as well
as commercial responsibilities. This situation arose from the
unique position of the half-dozen 'Treaty Ports', foisted on the
unwilling Chinese by Europeans determined to exploit the
immense commercial potential of the country. In those days of
Free Trade and Empire, the unimpeded access of commerce to

every part of the world was regarded as a law of nature. To seek to obstruct freedom of trade was as perverse and unnatural as it was wicked and ungodly to refuse free access to the bearers of the Word of God. By the time my father arrived in China, these ports had large foreign populations, which had set up miniature European towns, with their own law enforcement. Europeans rarely stirred beyond the foreign settlements; for them, 'Shanghai' was a modern European city, with its busy waterfront, the Bund, where the great banking and commercial houses of the world faced out proudly to the sea, its broad, tree-lined, asphalted roads, its large European-style houses set in spacious gardens.

My earliest memory of China is of a visit to the native city shortly before we left Shanghai. I would be about five and a half at the time. One evening, my father announced that the following afternoon we would go into 'Chinatown'. I caused great amusement by asking if we would be going there in a big ship. I was going through one of those periods in childhood when only one thing is of any real interest: at that time it happened to be ships. To my intense annoyance I remembered nothing of the two great sea voyages I had made at the age of three. Father went to the sideboard and took out a plate, belonging to one of the white and blue sets. 'No, we're going in a carriage and we're going to see this!' he announced with the triumphant air of a magician who can materialize anything he pleases. It was as if he had just said to himself, 'Now, let me see! What shall I bring before their eyes tomorrow?' and had chosen to bring the Willow Pattern to life. It never occurred to me that it might be the other way round, that the Old Tea House in Shanghai might be the original, rather than a manifestation, of the Willow Pattern.

All morning my brother had been filling my head with the weirdest notions as to what went on behind those city walls.

He had not exactly been in the native city himself, though he had accompanied my father on a walk around the top of the wall where, at a convenient remove from the swarming, evil-smelling life below, Europeans would often go for a stroll. At last the moment had come. We climbed up into the carriage and set off. We careered along the Bund at breakneck speed, my father pointing out whatever he imagined would be of interest to us: the huge beturbaned Sikh policemen or the Parsees with their curious, high, cylindrical hats. We turned off the Bund, down a long, narrow street and through the French concession. We arrived at the city wall and dismounted. Here we had to leave our carriage behind and continue our exploration on foot, for not even a rick-shaw could be manoeuvred through the narrow alleyways. I still remember the shock I felt as we plunged into the low, dark, stinking tunnel through the wall. Within a few hundred yards one passed from a familiar world of modern buildings and clean streets to the sort of conditions that must have prevailed in medieval London. My reaction was one of mingled fascination and disgust, terror and wonder. Beggars were everywhere, cripples with grotesque and unusual deformities, hucksters crying wares of every imaginable kind. I remember being carried on Father's shoulders through narrow passages, flanked by a jumbled mass of multi-coloured street signs, riding half-proudly, half-apprehensively, through the throng of yellow faces, pigtails and blue cotton. Suddenly, the narrow crack of light overhead broadened out into the full expanse of the sky. Father set me down on my own feet. We were in the Bird Market: here, the shouts of salesmen and customers were augmented by the cheepings and twitterings coming from thousands of cages. At the sight of so many birds in one place I succumbed to a fit of hopeless, hysterical giggling. Further on we came to a lake.

'Now,' said Father, 'what's that? Where have you seen that before?' I stared dumbly at the water and at the rather ram-shackle wooden structure in its midst. 'No, it's not really like the picture on the plate, is it?'

We crossed one of the zigzag wooden bridges to the tea-house itself, where we all sat down among the tea-drinking, smoking, gossiping crowd. I was very disappointed. I had studied the plate in the morning and expected to be con-fronted by an exact replica of it. Father, it seemed, had not done a very good job or, worse still, had merely been teasing – perhaps there was no real connection between the picture on the plates at home and the scene before me. Later, he told us the story of the Willow Pattern and the truth began to dawn on me.

Koong-shee was the daughter of a wealthy mandarin and loved Chang, her father's secretary. The mandarin, who wished his daughter to marry a wealthy suitor, forbade the marriage, and shut his daughter up in the house which, in the pattern, appears to the left of the temple. From her prison, Koong-shee watched the willow tree blossom and pined for her beloved. Chang managed to communicate with her by means of writing enclosed in a small coconut shell to which a tiny sail was attached. One day, disguised, Chang entered the mandarin's garden and rescued Koong-shee. The three fig-ures on the bridge represent Koong-shee with a distaff, Chang carrying a box of jewels and the mandarin following with a whip. The lovers escaped and lived happily together in Chang's house on a distant island until, after many years, the outraged suitor tracked them down and set fire to their house, while the lovers were inside. From the ashes, their two spirits rose in the form of two doves. Gradually, as the details of the Willow Pattern were pointed out, my imagination effected a kind of compromise between what I had seen that afternoon and the picture spread out before me. The two images came together, the remembered reality yielding shape to the monochrome lines on the plate and the variegated hues of the Old Tea House replacing the cold, unrelieved blue and white of the Willow Pattern.

The next major event in my life came a few months later when Father was transferred to Canton (and promoted to the rank of Second-Class Assistant). By the time the great day came, I had a clear idea of the journey we were to take and the kind of ships we would be sailing in. But it was a humble launch we boarded on the Shanghai wharf that cold January morning. This was because we would be travelling not in one of the steamers that served almost the entire Chinese coast, but in one of the P & O ocean liners that set out from Shanghai and called in at Hong-kong en route for London: these liners were too large to reach Shanghai proper and were obliged to lie anchored at Woo-fung, twelve miles away at the mouth of the river. After much delay, we finally boarded the great P & O mail. I looked up from the foot of the gangway and there was the ship, looming over me, dark, immense, far larger than I thought possible, clouds of black smoke coming out of its enormously wide funnel. Once I was aboard, the ship ceased, in a sense, to be a ship at all. It was too large, too all-enveloping for me to take in, an unfathomable warren of corridors and stairs, treacherously similar to one another.

After breakfast on the sixth day, we went up on deck as we entered the enormous mouth of the Canton river. The sunlight was already strong, but a light mist still lay over the water, not quite concealing the hills of innumerable small islands. We swung round into the expanse of water known as Hong-kong road that divides Hong-kong island from the mainland. There before us lay the harbour, filled with every conceivable kind of vessel, from ocean-going liners to fragile little sampans. There was even a British battleship at anchor.

Next morning, we boarded the steamer that was to take us to our new home ninety-five miles up river. For about three hours, we moved through the quiet waters of the estuary, which is between fifteen and twenty miles wide. Then, suddenly, the river narrowed. More and more boats appeared, until the water was so full of them that there seemed hardly room for us to get through the forest of masts and bunting. Over all clambered swarms of half-naked coolies, chattering traders, singing girls and sailors.

We were met by one of Father's future colleagues and our future first boy, Mak. A boat was selected for us and we set out for our new home on Shameen, a small island occupied exclusively by the British and French communities. When bought by the two European governments from the Chinese it was nothing more than a sand-bank, which is what 'shameen' means. Were it not for its proximity to the mainland and the view of the river, with its unmistakably Chinese life, you might have thought you were in southern Europe – the houses had an Italian air about them.

Canton was still a medieval city. The walls, which had survived virtually intact from the eleventh century, were pierced by sixteen gates, which were shut at sundown. The streets were long, winding, very narrow, never more than twelve feet wide on the ground, the roofs almost touching overhead. Before the open shop fronts hung a mass of brilliantly coloured signboards, each proclaiming the name of the owner and the kind of goods sold. The streets often contained shops of one kind only, so you might see the same shoe, musical instrument or hat painted on a whole row of signboards. There were some strange sights to be seen in the food shops: dried rats, dogs' flesh, ducks' bills, birds' nests, lizards, tortoises, owls, storks – all for human consumption. The streets bore curious names, which Father translated for us on our walks through the city: Bright Cloud Street, Street of One Hundred Grandsons, Street of the Ascending Dragon.

Matthew and I usually accompanied our parents when they went on a shopping expedition into the city to buy blue china, ivory carvings, silk or jade. On presenting ourselves at the entrance of some shop we would bow to the master, receive his chin-chin in return, then take a seat in the inner shop. There we would be given tiny cups of tea. Father would then state what he was looking for and various articles would be brought for inspection. The master of the shop would name his price. 'No can, too muchee money,' Father would expostulate good-humouredly and offer half; the bargaining proceeded on its way of compromise. Despite his mastery of Mandarin, the entire discussion was conducted in 'pidgin', the highly sim-plified form of English developed by Chinese in their commercial contacts with Europeans, 'pidgin' being the way Chinese pronounce the word 'business'. In southern China, the vast majority of the population spoke only Cantonese, which would be incomprehensible to a Chinaman from the North; Mandarin was spoken only by officials and literati. I never got over the feeling that there was something childish and comical about 'pidgin' and when we saw Father, with per-fectly straight face, deliver himself of this baby-talk for all the world as if he were addressing a committee meeting, Matthew and I found it hard to restrain our giggles. All this while Mother would say nothing, but sit quietly in the background, at a respectful distance, ignored by all. When the tea was brought, Father was offered the first cup, Matthew the second, I the third, Mother the last. The ordered, hierarchized cere-mony never altered: men preceded women, age youth.

Our house was near the western end of the island. It had

two storeys, with two verandas at the back, looking out across a garden to the Bund and the river beyond. The front of the house gave directly on to the grass walk, shaded with overhanging banyan trees, that ran the entire length of the settlement. From our windows we could see the boats, their double sails rearing up over the treetops, like huge, dark brown butterfly wings. The front door opened on to a large, high hall, with marble paving and pillars. To the left was the drawing-room, which ran the whole depth of the house from front to back and had windows on three sides. To the right was my father's study and a dining-room. Upstairs were four bedrooms. The kitchen and servants' quarters were housed in a low range of buildings joined to the house on the dining-room side. We always had three or four servants, which might suggest either extravagance or considerable means. In fact, neither was the case. If my mother had tried to run the house without servants, it would certainly have cost more. Any European trying to buy food, coal and the other necessities of life would pay several times over what it would cost a native Chinese – and servants were extremely cheap. Having decided on servants, one appointed a 'first boy' or housekeeper. From then on, one handed oneself over to the Chinese domestic system. It was a system that worked very efficiently, providing one did not try to interfere with it. A weekly sum of money, to cover all household expenditure, including wages, was agreed between master and 'first boy', who then assumed full charge. The mistress of the house was allowed a measure of freedom, but a complicated body of 'custom' made certain that she had as little as possible. Depending on the size of the household and his estimation of the master's status, the first boy decided how many other 'boys' were to be employed. The first boy never did any 'manual' work at all: his role was entirely supervisory. No servant would take orders from anyone but him.

One conveyed one's wishes, in pidgin, to him and he spoke in Cantonese to those in his charge.

Mother was more than content to leave the running of her household to someone else. But she also had no great love of 'visiting' the other similarly placed Shameen ladies. In interests and temperament, she was remarkably similar to my father. With her we began to pick up French almost as soon as we learnt to speak English. We could read and write in both languages at an early age. We read the fairy tales of the brothers Grimm and Hans Andersen in English, and those of Perrault and the *Thousand and One Nights* in French. But my mother was not content to be an excellent teacher: she never ceased to be a student. Three mornings a week, a Chinese teacher arrived to give her lessons.

From the time we learnt to speak to the time we left China, my brother and I learnt far more than less fortunate children who had been forced to go to school. Yet the time spent at study was less than that spent by most children under the rigid order of the classroom. We had no timetable, no fixed hours, no organized 'play-time'. There was really no distinction for us between work and play. Because we were not subjected to unnatural discipline for most of the day, we did not know what it was to feel the need to run wild. Learning itself was a pleasure. Undoubtedly, the fact that our teacher was our mother had much to do with the speed with which we learnt. Our 'lessons' were held indoors, in the drawing-room or in Father's study or, when the weather was warm, outside on the veranda or in the garden. But our 'education' spilled out to fill the whole day and, when Father returned in the evening, it would begin all over again: 'Well, what have you learnt today?' Then, to our great amusement, he would turn the tables on Mother and quiz her on her Chinese lesson.

But there would be days, many days, when nothing in the

way of study in the strict sense was done. Wherever Mother went, we went with her. Occasionally, we called for tea on one of the wives of the Anglo-French colony. Much more fun was a visit to one of our Chinese acquaintances. Once we were invited, with some European friends and their children, to the house of a Mr Howqua, a rich mandarin. What struck me most on entering the house was the impression of coolness, contrasting so strongly with the narrow, airless streets outside. Many things from childhood are remembered as being much bigger, much taller, than they seem to the revisiting adult, but a house such as Mr Howqua's occupied many acres of land, and the impression of space was as real to any adult. Chinese buildings spread themselves outwards, rather than upwards and in thin strips, rather than in solid masses, the houses surrounding the gardens rather than the reverse. For about an hour we were shown over the enormous property, moving through an alternating series of rooms and gardens. We were then shown to seats in the huge hall where, at one end, a group of musicians was already playing: beating drums, clashing cymbals and blowing various wind instruments. One of the players then performed a series of tricks with his cymbals, spinning one of them on the end of a stick, which he stuck on his chest, face and neck. His last trick was the best. He picked up what looked like a long folded paper umbrella and, having caused it to spin at great speed, a sudden explosion was heard: the umbrella disappeared and a lamp with a light in it took its place.

Eventually, our hostess came in and announced that dinner was about to be served. But before we could eat, what seemed like an interminable time elapsed while the ladies sorted out the order in which they should be seated. Apparently, this went on at every meal among Chinese ladies, each insisting that another take precedence. What seemed particularly absurd to the European mind was that etiquette was so strict and defined in China that there was never any doubt as to the order in which the ladies would eventually seat themselves, but it was customary to show this affected humility before accepting the honour. The meal began, like many a European dinner, with soup, not one soup, however, but some twenty or so: bird's nest soup, shark's fin soup, seaweed soup and so on. Then a sweet soup was served, accompanied by sweet cakes. But to confound any hopes that the meal might be drawing to a close, meats and soup continued to be served in endless variety. We children had long since stopped sampling these dishes, but our poor mother felt obliged, out of politeness, to taste each one, compliment it and only then let it pass.

The contrast could not have been greater between those Chinese and European women, each, despite their good will, disapproving somewhat, certainly uncomprehending, of the other, yet evidently fascinated. The large-boned, sometimes ample figures of the consular women, with their serious, kindly faces, a little stiff in their concern to set a good example, and their delicate, gorgeously dressed, doll-like hostesses, their hair decorated with flowers and lacquered into fantastic shapes, their lips painted vermilion, rouge on their cheeks and by the side of their eyebrows, forever chattering and giggling. We were amused to see these childlike, very feminine creatures suddenly produce long pipes, which their *amahs* (maids) proceeded to stuff and light for them. They would take a couple of puffs and hand the pipes back to their *amahs* to hold. Indeed these Chinese women were utterly dependent on their *amahs*. When they sat down at table, the *amahs* would take up their places behind their mistresses, waiting upon them as if they were helpless infants. Then, when it was time to leave, the ladies jumped up on to their *amahs'* backs and were thus carried to their covered chairs. These well-to-do women, who had had their feet 'bound' from infancy, could hardly take a few steps without tottering and leaning on their maids for support. The 'binding' of female children's feet certainly provided a graphic instance of how 'superiority' is often expressed in human societies by dependence on 'inferiors'.

A few weeks after we arrived in Canton, in mid-February, the celebrations of the Chinese New Year took place. Salvoes of fire-crackers were constantly let off throughout the last night of the old year. Another festival, much celebrated in Canton, was that in honour of the Tu-ti, or earth gods. This occurs in early March, only a few weeks after the New Year. We were invited to a Chinese gentleman's house to see a display of fireworks. We were seated in the garden, facing a large pool, my father, my brother and I in one group with the men, my mother in another, with the women. Throughout the evening there was no communication between the two groups. In the China of those days the sexes were so segregated in public that a father would not like to be seen with his daughter in the streets, or a husband with his wife. On the other side of the pool stood the family theatre, with its carved, lacquered roof. It was in front of this building that the fireworks were let off. In one set piece a man mounted a horse, fell from the animal and lay beside it. Out of one piece fell strings of pagodas; from another innumerable lanterns were suspended. Each of these set pieces ended in a dazzling display of gold and silver fire. It was almost midnight when our convoy of chairs left our host's house and proceeded along the dark streets, lit only by the lanterns of every size and shape that hung outside the shops and houses, down to the river bank and over the bridge to Shameen.

One morning in the spring of our last year in Canton, we were in the middle of our lessons when the sky grew suddenly dark, lightning flashed, followed at once by thunder claps.

Sheets of rain beat at the windows. Suddenly, there was a great rushing sound. Mak burst in and announced, 'Oh, Mississi, typhoon!' He hurried us under the stairs. The front door had been wrenched off its hinges and was hanging in place only by the lock. The semicircular window above it had shattered and the floor was littered with broken glass. The typhoon did not last more than about ten minutes. When the danger had passed, we went out to investigate. The banyan trees in front of the house had been snapped off at the trunk and lay scattered around. An iron lamp-post had been bent double. A mass of débris was being driven up the river. Yachts had been blown on their side and smaller craft had been sent crashing against one another. The only vessel left standing in anything like a normal state was a large English steamer. As we walked through Shameen we saw the devastation that had been wrought upon the settlement. The hurricane had swept across it in that corkscrew movement peculiar to whirlwinds. Yet, such is the capricious character of a whirlwind, one building could be flattened, the one next to it untouched. Across on the mainland, whole streets of houses had been reduced to rubble.

We had been in Canton for some two and a half years, when Father was informed that he would be moved back to the Legation, in Peking, with promotion to First-Class Assistant. We sailed back down the Pearl River one splendid August morning in 1888. Ten days later, we were entering the narrow mouth of the Peiho River. On either side stood huge, forbidding-looking fortresses, solid cubes of stone, grey as the muddy water that separated them. The same grey extended for miles over the flat, barren land behind, broken only by thousands of little burial mounds, each marked by a red plaque. No greater contrast with our beloved Pearl River could be imagined. By evening we reached Tientsin, where we ate and spent the night. Next day, we were on board our houseboat with a second boat behind it to accommodate our boy, cook, boatmen and luggage.

Given the meandering nature of the river, our sail often proved to be an unreliable source of power. One minute we were sailing north-east; a bend and we turned south, then south-west; suddenly a sharp curve brought us half round the compass again. In fact, Matthew and I spent much of our journey on land: we would jump off the boat on to the shore, take a leisurely short-cut and await the arrival of our floating house. We reached Tungchow on the morning of the fifth day. There, amid the noise and confusion of a Chinese harbour, we found the carts that had been sent from Peking to meet us. The so-called 'Peking cart' consisted of a box about four feet long and about three feet wide with an arched roof. The whole was supported on a pair of iron-covered wooden wheels and drawn by a mule or pony. It was in such conveyances that we travelled the last dozen or so miles of our journey. At the time of its construction by the Mings, five hundred years ago, this causeway had probably been the greatest work of its kind in existence. It extended in an almost straight line from Tungchow to the eastern gate of the capital and consisted of stone blocks quarried from the Western Hills, laid on a bed of earth raised above the surrounding plain. The blocks averaged eight by three feet in size and were about two inches thick but, not having been touched since the day they had been laid, they stuck up at every conceivable angle. So the springless carts – no springs would have survived such treatment for ten minutes – lurched around, occasionally getting stuck in a rut or even overturning completely. As well as the Peking carts, there were sedan chairs, wheelbarrows, laden donkeys and packhorses, and strings of long-haired, reddish-brown camels, with huge fur muffs around their legs and manes like lions, fastidiously picked their way along.

Open countryside gave way to the eastern suburbs. At the end of the roadway the huge grey walls of the capital rose up out of the dust and haze. A dark tunnel brought us inside the Chinese City, with the walls of the Tartar City looming over us on our right. We entered what was known to all the foreign residents as Legation Street, then unpaved and deep in mud or dust, depending on the season. Father pointed out to us the splendid French Legation on the right, the German Legation on the left and, further on, to the right, the Japanese Legation. We arrived at the gates of the British Legation, which was to be our home for the next two years.

This was not as bleak as it may sound, for those gates led not into a massive building, but into a large park, planted with trees and shrubs. Originally an imperial property, it was given by the Emperor K'ang Hsi to one of his thirty-three sons. In 1860, the impoverished owner leased it to the British government in perpetuity for an annual rent of 1500 taels (about £500). It was not a single building, but a series of pavilions and temples spreading out from the original house, now the Minister's residence. The rest of us lived in more modest buildings, dotted about the grounds, built in more or less Western style.

A few days after our arrival, Father took Matthew and me along to meet the Minister. The approach to his magnificent Chinese palace was impressive enough: the forecourt was flanked on each side by a pavilion, supported by huge, vermilion-painted wooden pillars and surmounted by a tiled, tent-like roof with intricately carved eaves painted in red, green, blue and gold. We were shown into the huge reception-hall, popularly known as 'the Queen's room', on account of the life-sized portrait of Queen Victoria that hung there. We were then conducted to the Minister's private study. I don't know what I expected, but the sight of Sir John Walsham – a rather small, slight, middle-aged man with grey moustache and sideburns and mild-looking, shy, grey eyes – came as a great disappointment. He smiled feebly at my brother and me.

'Ah!' he said, with the forced, opaque humour of an adult who wishes children well, but does not know how best to express his benevolence. 'Our two apostles and future Trinitarians!' This allusion to our names and future Cambridge college – of which both Sir John and my father were members – was lost on us. The Minister's next words were no more reassuring, though obviously intended to be. 'Haven't we met before? At the Paris embassy, I think.' Matthew and I looked at one another and nearly started giggling. Father did not help matters by exclaiming: 'Obviously there are no limits to the powers of a Minister Plenipotentiary!' Apparently, before coming to Peking, Walsham had held the titular rank of minister plenipotentiary in Paris during the prolonged absence of the ambassador. His tenure at this post had coincided with our visit to Paris six years before.

Matthew and I wasted no time in exploring the Legation grounds. We lived in a house next to that of the Chinese Secretary, Mr Hillier. A couple of minutes' run from our house were the fives court, the bowling alley, a converted Chinese pavilion – containing a billiard-room, a reading-room and a small theatre – and, behind this, the students' quarters. There were usually four or five student interpreters at the Legation and they all lived in a two-storey Italianate building, with colonnaded veranda and balcony. Each of them had his own bedroom and sitting-room, but otherwise they lived a very communal existence, eating, studying and relaxing together. This 'studentish' mode of life greatly appealed to us and we spent much of our leisure time with them, trying to compete with them in the bowling alley, watching them play fives and just sitting around chatting in front of their common-room stove or on the veranda when the weather was warmer. They would talk about books they were reading, tell hilarious stories of their dealings with the Chinese, gossip about their fellow Europeans, practise their Chinese on one another and talk endlessly of England. They accepted us on equal terms, even though we did not drink beer or smoke pipes.

I became particularly friendly with one of the student interpreters, Edward Werner. Instead of being 'sent south' at the end of his two years' training in Chinese, he had been asked to stay on at the Legation chancellery. Perhaps because he had already been in Peking for two years when the other students arrived and had already finished his initial training, perhaps because of his naturally serious, retiring temperament, perhaps even because he had already acquired what was to be a life-long aversion to alcohol and tobacco, he tended to keep to himself. As I got to know him better I learnt that one of the reasons why he usually kept to his study at evenings and week-ends was that he had already embarked on his researches into early Chinese civilization for a volume in Herbert Spencer's series, *Descriptive Sociology*, which was finally published in 1910. I would often go up to his rooms and discuss the books he had lent me. I was already plundering my father's considerable library; Werner's now provided an alternative source. One after another I was reading the novels of Scott, Dickens and Thackeray.

On my tenth birthday Werner gave me a copy of Palgrave's *Golden Treasury*. This came as a revelation to me: hitherto the experience of literature had seemed a very haphazard affair, subject to the accidents of one's own discoveries or the recommendations of others. Suddenly I discovered the possibility of a more systematic study. Not only did Palgrave's little volume seem to contain poems by all the great poets I knew but, I presumed, every English poet worth reading would be represented there. I soon discovered that it had one serious drawback: it stopped short at Shelley's 'Music, when soft voices die . . .' Despite his fulsome references to the Poet Laureate and the dedication of his anthology to Tennyson's friend Hallam, Palgrave appeared to believe that a poet had to be dead before being worthy of inclusion in his Treasury. I still have that copy of *The Golden Treasury*, but I have to confess that it is inextricably associated in my mind with something that struck me when I first opened the book and continued to puzzle me for long afterwards. On the title page was a line drawing of a naked youth, sitting on a rock playing a small pipe. A dog, crouching at his feet, was looking up at him and a bird was perched on the overarching branch of a tree. I could not understand why the boy was sitting on that rock with no clothes on. I was not familiar as yet with the eroticized conventions of Western art. Yet that figure must have had some subliminal effect on me, since I never thought fit to ask anyone who the boy was – which, given my unbounded curiosity about all things, I would normally have done – and why he was naked. It was as if I expected to be met with 'Who toldest thou that he is naked?' Many years later, in a bookshop, I caught sight of the familiar green cloth binding and gold tooling. Unwittingly I turned to the title page and saw that the boy with the pipe had gone. In the intervening years someone in the Oxford University Press had been told that the young god Pan was naked. The Greco-Victorian trinity of *paidos*, *eros* and *poesis* was no longer considered fit for the impressionable eyes of youth.

Matthew and I were now having Chinese lessons with a Mr Sung, so we were able to practise the language with the student interpreters. They spent two hours each morning and

two more in the afternoon with their Chinese tutor. Their
course of study, based on Sir Thomas Wade's *Tzu-erh Chi* or
'Colloquial Course', was supervised by the Assistant Chinese
Secretary who, in our second year, was John Jordan, later to
become one of our best and longest-serving ministers in
Peking.

The students became great friends and Mother often
invited them round to the house for tea on Sunday afternoons.
Then, one day, just before Christmas, a letter was delivered to
our house addressed in Chinese characters to Yu lao-yeh and
Ma lao-yeh. Mother, who discovered the letter, was quite mys-
tified and put it to one side. When Father returned for tiffin,
he examined the envelope, read out the names and looked
puzzled.

'Ah, don't you see?' he suddenly exclaimed. 'It's for
Matthew and Mark.'

Once grasped, the explanation was simple. When con-
fronted by English names the Chinese were in the habit of
adapting them to their own notion of suitability. This entailed
selecting a syllable from the name, if possible the first, and
finding its nearest Chinese equivalent. To this they added lao-
yeh, which simply meant Mr. Thus Mr Coverdale would
become Ko lao-yeh and Mr Palmer, say, would be Pa lao-yeh.
Now, since we were children, my brother and I were referred
to by our Christian names, and both happened to begin with
the same sound – at least to a Chinese ear. So the sender of the
letter had obviously decided to use the first part of my name
and the second of my brother's. Thus Mark and Matthew
became 'Ma' and 'Yu'.

'So,' said Father, handing me the letter, 'You'd better see
what it says.' I slit open the envelope and took out a piece of
thin vermilion-coloured paper. On it were seven columns of
Chinese characters. 'Well, what does it say?'

My eye roamed over the paper desperately looking for some character that I could recognize.

'Day . . . Your Honour . . . Invitation . . .' I murmured.

'Here,' said Matthew, 'let me see.' He made out a few more words. We looked at one another and laughed.

'Well,' said my father, 'a year's fees to Sung lao-yeh and that's all you can come up with! Let's have a look.' He adopted a most serious, dignified attitude, then, with a slight Chinese accent, read out his translation:

> Yu lao-yeh and Ma lao-yeh for their exalted considera-
> tion
> On many occasions you have bestowed a refection upon
> us
> For many days we have been desirous of returning your
> hospitality
> On behalf of my friends and colleagues I invite
> Your honours on the fifth day of the next moon at the *yin*
> hour to occupy seats in our humble cottage that we
> may fill our cups and chat the while
> Pi Ha and Keh my honoured friends earnestly hope that
> on that day
> My lords will lay aside their work and move their jew-
> elled persons thither
> This he hopes and thus sends a note with the salutation
> of Wen Eh-wah.

Father placed the paper on the table and, moving his finger down the column, commented on the text, the formation of the characters, the origin of some of the periphrases and other such fine points. The columns were of varying heights, a practice known as 'respectful raising of characters', by which every reference to the person addressed requires the beginning of a new column with his name, which is raised two characters above the previous line. If the reference is to a mutual friend or superior, his character enjoys 'single elevation'; on the other hand, where the parents of the recipient are alluded to, an elevation of three spaces is called for. The '*yin* hour' is the period between 5 p.m. and 7 p.m. As Father was making his painstaking, scholarly commentary on the letter, my impatience grew and grew.

'Yes,' I burst out at last, 'but who's it from?'

'Oh, sorry,' said my father, 'I thought you knew. Why it's your friend Wen Eh-wah!'

'But I don't have a friend . . .'

'Turn it round,' my father said. 'Eh-wah Wen . . . Edward . . .'

'Werner!' I burst out. 'Of course!'

'And his colleagues Pi, Ha and Keh?'

'Pitzipios, Hampden and Ker!' Matthew and I shouted in chorus. What we were being invited to was a Christmas dinner with wild fowl bought from Mongol tribesmen, who would shoot them in the mountains, keep them in ice and bring them down to Peking to sell in the market they held every year on a piece of land behind the Legation and a plum pudding ordered from Tientsin in October before the Peiho froze.

Peking was already the capital of the small state of Yen in the fifth century BC, but it was not raised to the rank of Imperial capital until after the conquest of the 'Kin' Tartars, or 'Golden Horde'. With the Mongol conquest of 1215 under Genghis-Khan, it was again reduced to the rank of a provincial capital. But in 1264, Peking was restored to Imperial status by his grandson Kubla-Khan, Marco Polo's great patron, who built the city we know today. Like any child reading the *Travels* of Marco Polo, I had followed the Venetian merchant's son from

the city of St Mark across Asia to the territories of the Grand
Khan. But few could have read his description of Kubla
Khan's city while actually sitting within its walls. In basic
plan, nothing had changed in six hundred years. Its twenty-
five square miles are of a peculiar shape: a square, some four
miles on each side, is extended, to the south, by a rectangle
five miles wide and two miles deep. The former, the Tartar or
Manchu City, was the citadel of a race of conquerors; the
latter, the Chinese or Native City, a sort of vast outer courtyard for the use of their subjects. The Tartar City is itself a
nest of cities. At its centre lies the Forbidden City, about one
mile square, containing the imperial palaces. No one lived
there except the Emperor himself, the imperial ladies and the
eunuchs. Ministers and officials of the highest rank were only
admitted by special authorization. Around the Forbidden City
is the Imperial City, the seat of government, almost two miles
square, with its own high wall.

Marco Polo had the advantage of me in that he knew those
parts of the city now closed to foreigners – the Forbidden
City itself, of course, but also much of the Imperial City and
the innumerable imperial properties. It was not until my
return to China after the Revolution of 1912 that I was able to
appreciate the true glories of Peking. In the meantime, the
best view was to be obtained from the top of the Ch'ién Mên.
Father took us there a week or two after our arrival. It was
Marco Polo illustrated in three dimensions. There were things
of interest on every side, but it was really for the view northwards that one climbed to the top of the Ch'ién Mên. In the
foreground was a stone-flagged square known as the Ch'i P'an
Chieh, or Chess Board Street. In 1421, the great Ming
Emperor Yung Lo, who was responsible for much of the
building in Peking, turned this area into a gigantic chequer-
board, on which scholars could indulge in one of their

favourite games, Wei Ch'i, a form of draughts played with black and white counters on 324 squares. Beyond were the pink walls of the Imperial City and the T'ien an Mên (Gate of Heavenly Peace). Rising behind this gate one could see the five towers of the huge Wu Mên, the main entrance to the Forbidden City, and a sea of gleaming yellow-tiled roofs. To the west of the Forbidden City and extending for two miles from the southern to the northern walls of the Imperial City were the three great lakes. The farthest of these, Péi Hai or Northern Lake, was famous for its lotuses and it was surrounded by a wooded park. This had been the pleasure ground of Kubla Khan.

We arrived in Peking in late September, a pleasant time of year there. It felt distinctly cooler than in Canton, but it was dry and sunny. This weather continued well into the winter, giving the city its characteristically sharp light, though getting progressively colder, especially at night. For much of the winter Matthew and I – often with two or three of the students – spent many happy hours skating up and down what was grandly called the 'Imperial Canal', but was in fact a broad ditch that ran down the middle of the street opposite the Legation. Sometimes we went with the students on an expedition out to the grounds of the ruined Summer Palace. There we would skate on the frozen lake or, in warmer weather, play, read and picnic among the ruins.

Summer in Peking can be unbearably hot, with temperatures remaining around forty degrees centigrade for weeks on end. So, from early June to late August, the entire Legation Quarter forsook the city's dusty streets and airless rooms and took to the Western Hills. There, in the temples dotted along the slopes, accommodation could be rented for the season. A skeleton staff would remain on in the Legation, but during the summer much of the consular business was conducted from

the Minister's temple. Since the monks provided little in the
way of furniture and no food, movement of even one modest
household and its servants from the city to the hills required a
caravan of impressive proportions. Anything up to twenty
carts would be loaded with mattresses and bedding, mosquito
curtains, chairs, tables, rugs, clothes, books. Kitchens would be
stripped of their contents and the entire population of the
poultry-yard packed up, ducks and hens clacking and cackling
in their coops and baskets. Even a cow and her calf would join
the procession to the Pa ta ch'u or Eight Temples, situated on
a terraced hillside some ten miles west of the capital.

Early on the morning of our departure, the *mafoo* arrived
with his coolies, donkeys and carts and, under the stern eye of
Lu, our first boy, everything we thought we might need for the
next three months or so was packed and loaded. With mounting excitement we watched the procession wind its way out of
the Legation grounds. For nine months we had not left the city
walls and only occasionally ventured outside the Legation. A
carefree summer in the fresh air of the hills awaited us. An
hour after the servants had left with all our possessions, we
ourselves set off, accompanied by one of the boys, who had
stayed behind to travel with us. Mother was carried in a chair
by four coolies; the rest of us rode donkeys. After a few hours
we reached the foot of the gorge. We then took the winding
stone path that connected the eight temples. For much of the
way, the path ran beside a mountain torrent, shaded by huge
trees. It was a relief to enter this cool, green cavern after three
hours on a dusty, sun-drenched country road. Our temple,
the Hsiang Chieh Ssu, or Temple of the Fragrant World, was
the sixth. It was very large, with an impressive *p'ai lou* or arch-
way, and several courts, one leading into another. After tiffin
we set off to visit the students who, as we knew, were already
installed in two temples down at Tai Pei Ssu, or Temple of

Great Sorrow. We found them sitting on a terrace, looking out across the plain, smoking their pipes and chatting, much as they did back in Peking.

And so the long hot summer days were taken up with idling, reading, chatting with the students, even, by way of a change, sitting in on their Chinese lessons. Sometimes, when the heat got unbearable, we bathed in a small pool that had formed in the stream that coursed down the hillside, next to their temple. We would explore the hillside on foot or, farther afield, on mule back, accompanied by Mother or one of the students.

One evening, as we were sitting on one of the temple terraces, Father suddenly said: 'You know, about this time next year, I'll be due for a furlough. Now, as far as you boys are concerned, this comes at a good moment. Your mother and I have been giving quite a lot of thought lately to your future – your education and so on. In a year or two, it'll be time for you to go to school. I think you'll find it will make a pleasant change. You'll be with lads of your own age, make friends . . . and you're both bright lads, so you'll have no problem keeping up with the others. So the question arises: where will you go to school?' He paused, looked at us both and smiled.

'Will we have to go away to school, to boarding school?' Matthew asked.

'No, no, I don't think so. Your mother and I will be travelling around a bit, but mainly we'll be staying with your grandparents in London and Paris.' He smiled at Mother. 'Mainly Paris, in fact. Your mother and I thought you should go to some small private place first, then go on to one of the *lycées* in the Latin Quarter. Then, just to make sure you don't both turn into Frenchmen completely, you could go on to Cambridge. In this way, you'll get the best of both worlds. Anyway, nothing has to be decided now and if you do have some eccentric taste for cold showers and caning we can always find you a good English boarding school.'

We both giggled nervously. Then, suddenly, a thought struck me. 'But what happens when you and Mummy have to come back to China?'

Mother got up from her chair, came over and took my hand.

'*Pauvre chéri!*' she said tenderly, looking me straight in the eyes. 'A few years is a very long time at your age – but by that time Pépé and Mémé Dumollard will have become like a second mother and father. Yes, we will have to come back to China, because Papa's work must come first, but sometimes I shall come and spend the summer with you.'

'Anyway,' Father added, 'we thought it might be a good idea if you started having your lessons in French. I'll ask Monsignor Favier if he has a priest to spare who could come and give you a couple of hours every morning.'

So, soon after our return to Peking, we were visited every morning by Père Morrissot, one of the French Lazarist fathers from the Pei T'ang, or Northern Cathedral. We were very surprised on the first day to see what we were led to believe was a French priest arrive dressed as a Chinaman. Over a plain, loose-fitting, cassock-like garment, he wore a sleeveless tunic of pale yellow silk decorated with stylized flowers and birds, which assorted oddly with his full black beard. On his head he wore a *calotte* of two shades of blue velvet. Père Morrissot later explained that ever since the Jesuits had first arrived in China it had been the custom of the Catholic clergy to wear Chinese dress. At first, they had adopted the dress of Buddhist monks, until they realized that this brought them more derision than respect. They were then advised to dress as literati, which had the required effect on the native population.

It was odd, at first, construing Latin into French, rather

than English, but we already had a good grasp of Latin and were bilingual in French and English. All that was needed was time to put the two together. This problem did not arise with Greek, since this was our first introduction to that language. In addition to the two ancient languages, Père Morrissot instructed us in the mysteries of the *dissertation française*, read French poetry with us and generally improved the standard of our written French. At twelve o'clock the Legation bell would strike and we would all go into the dining-room for tiffin, when the conversation would continue in French. Late in the afternoon we prepared the work that Père Morrissot had given us.

My first introduction to something that was to become one of the ruling passions of my life was not particularly auspicious. The custom had grown up for the student interpreters, assisted by other members of the staff, to put on, once a year, some kind of theatrical show. This took place in the little theatre attached to the Legation reading-room, usually around the time of the Chinese New Year, and was attended by members of the staff. I remember very little of either of the two productions I saw. The first must have been some kind of revue, with short sketches, songs and music-hall turns. The second consisted of three one-act plays and all I remember of these was the spectacle of the rather tall, manly Ker playing the part of what, in retrospect, I can only presume was a Parisian *demi-mondaine*. Yet even these creaky confections stirred something deep down within me, something of an instant recognition, a sort of love at first sight.

My real theatrical initiation came later. One day, we all went off to one of the theatres in the Chinese City. Father had gone some way towards preparing us for the event. The shows, he explained, consisted of several short plays performed without a break. The performance began at noon and went on for eight

hours or so. Since he did not expect us to sit still for that length
of time, he proposed that we arrive at about two o'clock and
leave when we had seen enough. This was quite normal: people
wandered in and out of the theatre the whole time. In many
ways the Chinese theatre was like the theatre of Shakespeare's
day. At one end of the hall was an open stage, with no curtain.
At the back, in full view of the audience, was a small band of
musicians. There was no scenery, but a number of conventional means of representation: two bamboo poles with some
calico attached represented a city wall or a gate; a boat was represented by an old man and a girl with an oar moving at a fixed
distance from one another, a chariot by two yellow flags with a
wheel drawn on each, one held in each hand; slowly moving the
hands across the eyes denoted weeping; fireworks indicated the
appearance of a demon, etc. The female parts were played, as in
Shakespeare's day, by men and boys. There were other curious
parallels with Shakespeare's theatre. As in Elizabethan England,
Chinese actors at that time were officially regarded as 'rogues
and vagabonds'. With barbers, they were the only degraded
caste in China, their children being inadmissible to the official
examinations. So, like our King's Men and Lord Chamberlain's
Men, they sought protection from on high. And yet despite – or
perhaps because of – the general moral disapproval of their
profession, every Chinese theatre is adorned with a motto, written in four splendid gold characters, which may be translated
as: 'We hold the mirror up to nature.'

We had a box to ourselves at the back of the theatre. I shall
never forget that first sight of a proper stage: a door was
opened for us, we went in, my father pushed me forward to the
front of the box, and immediately, I became oblivious to
everything except what was taking place out there on the stage.
Two characters – a man, with a full, black beard reaching
down to his waist, and a young woman – were in the middle of

an impassioned dialogue, but I understood hardly a word. In a high, strangulated voice, accompanied by stylized movements and gestures, the woman seemed to be pleading, unsuccessfully, with the man. Other characters came on to the stage, there was a battle – a complicated choreography of the most elegant movements, with the orchestra in full cry – and the play came to an end. Almost at once another play began, then another. As I grew used to seeing a variety of situations played out on the stage, I became more and more aware of my surroundings and the intense *envoûtement*, the magic spell, diminished in intensity. Below us, in the pit, was a swarming, shifting mass of Chinese, who seemed to spend most of their time eating and chatting to one another. After a while, refreshments even appeared on the stage: plainly dressed coolies would come on and casually hand the actors tea.

Our two years in Peking were almost at an end. But we could not leave China, my father said, without setting foot on the Great Wall. So, one bright, crisp September morning, our donkeys, carts, coolies and boys were got ready for our expedition. We reached the ancient city of Sha Ch'eng by about one o'clock. There, outside the old, crumbling city walls, we found a conveniently shady spot by the river and ate the cold tiffin that we had brought with us. After an hour or so, humans refreshed and animals watered, we set off again, reaching our inn at Ch'ang p'ing chou (familiarly known as 'Jumping Joe') well before nightfall.

Next morning, we reached the famous avenue of animals, each carved out of a single block of stone. Pairs of life-size animals – lions, camels, elephants, horses and winged dragons – face each other on either side of the roadway. There are two pairs of each animal, the first sitting, the second standing, each pair being placed about a hundred yards apart. I have a photograph, taken by my father, of me sitting between the two humps of one of the camels. As our ponies approached the first animals, they shied away in terror and took some persuasion to move on. This, it seems, was what usually happened, though the odd horse or pony has been known to approach the first lions with interest, rather than fear.

At the end of this unearthly avenue, the ground drops away to reveal the Ming Tombs nestling at the bottom of a valley. We made our way past persimmon orchards, brilliant with orange fruit, and reached the tomb of Yung Lo, 'The Perfect Ancestor and Literary Emperor'. There we found a shady spot to eat our tiffin and rest. At dusk, we reached Nankow, where we spent the night.

We rose at six, breakfasted and set off for the Great Wall, fourteen miles away. We met strings of camels and scores of mules carrying wool and cotton, hides and grain. There were droves of pigs, bullocks and horses being driven down towards Nankow by Mongolian herdsmen, who trudged along behind them or followed on ponyback. At first the pass was wild and stark, shut in closely by almost perpendicular mountain sides. The bed of the stream that runs down the pass was littered with boulders and our mules picked their way among them. Half-way up the pass we came to a small walled village, where we stopped off at a teahouse.

We dismounted and continued the rest of the way on foot. Then, suddenly, my father called out: '*Voilà la Grande Muraille de Chine!*' And there, indeed, it was: the Wall. We walked on until we reached the stone steps cut in the thickness of the Wall, to one of the small square towers that guard it at regular intervals along its entire length. The tower was roofless, with gaps for windows and doors. On the floor lay a rusty small cannon. At close quarters the Wall itself was not as impressive as I had expected: it was only about twenty feet high and as thick, though the watch-towers rose to a height of some forty feet. What exceeded all my expectations was the sight of that colossal stone serpent, scaling rocks that seemed insurmountable, and would have been without it, dipping down into steep valleys or coiling round obstacles. At this particular stretch it was in fairly good repair, though in parts it was little more than a pile of masonry.

What we call the Great Wall, said Father, is called by the Chinese Wan Li Ch'ang Ch'êng, or Ten Thousand Li Long Wall. Calculating a *li* at one third of a mile, this would give it a length of nearly 3400 miles, though 2500 miles is probably closer to the truth. It was begun in 221 BC and took only twenty years to complete. In addition to over 300,000 troops, all the convicted criminals of the empire were put to work on it. By the time the Wall was completed, a million men had been employed in its construction, many of whom must have died in harness and their corpses thrown into the embankment. According to a popular Chinese saying, it is the longest cemetery in the world. Its ostensible purpose was to protect the empire from the North. In this it signally failed, the Manchus being the last of a line of northern invaders to breach its defences and assume government of the empire. Its true purpose was probably more symbolic than real: symbolic of power, for the man who conceived of the Wall was the same Emperor Ch'in Shi Huang, enemy of scholars, who ordered the burning of all books published prior to his own reign, yet gave his name to the country over which he ruled.

On our way down we overtook an orderly drove of about two hundred pigs. Suddenly Mother exclaimed: '*Regardez! Qu'est-ce qu'ils ont là? Non, ce sont des chaussures! Oh, regardez les jolies chaussures!*'[1] We looked and indeed the pigs each wore

1 'Oh look! What have they got on? No, they're shoes! Oh, just look at their pretty shoes!'

what looked like two pairs of shoes. Each foot of each beast was shod with a leather sock to protect it from the sharp stones. Certainly the spectacle had something laughable about it. The thought of the simple drover tying eight hundred leather socks on to the feet of struggling animals seems as foolish as the building of a two-and-a-half-thousand-mile wall to keep out one's neighbours. Yet not one of those animals seemed tired or footsore; they travelled on at their master's bidding without rebellion. That drover's action was a wonderful instance of the Chinese genius for patience and economy: patience in making and tying on those four hundred pairs of shoes, economy in keeping the feet well, thus enabling his pigs to make their long journey to Peking. Years later Matthew and I had only to say *'Regardez les jolies chaussures!'* and we would collapse in uncontrollable laughter. This would usually happen on a Paris street at the expense of some poor woman who happened to cross our path.

Our Peking days were nearly over. Strangely, I remember little of those last days. I do remember being photographed, in various combinations with my family and our 'boys'. As so often with records, whether written or pictorial, the photographs have usurped the place of memory, excluding whatever is not to be found within their confines. Thus if I try to remember the courtyard or drawing-room of our Legation house, what I see is the image of my photographs, no more. I cannot remember what was on the side of the room behind the camera, yet I can remember quite clearly my bedroom, of which I have no photograph. There is a photograph of Matthew and me standing side by side on the steps leading into the drawing-room from the courtyard, but it is taken at such a distance that it is more a photograph of the courtyard than of us: in so far as our faces are visible at all, we look like small boys usually look when being photographed, serious, vulnerable, unformed. The two figures remind me of nothing; they might as well be strangers. But the sight of that expanse of matting on the floor makes my knees wrinkle at the tactile memory of its dry roughness. Off-centre is a small Chinese carved lacquer table, on it a miniature tree in a porcelain bowl. There are other small tables, bearing other such trees in pots, and a large vase on a mahogany stand. The chairs are all of cane, mostly upholstered. Suffusing everything is that long-vanished light of old photographs: it is that, rather than this or that detail, this chair or that vase, that sets something, somewhere inside me, vibrating gently in harmony. I remember warm afternoons when it was cooler there than anywhere else in the house, sitting reading on one of those chairs, or going in there in the evenings, before going to bed, when the grown-ups were sitting in the soft, feeble light from the lantern. There is another photograph, of Mother, Matthew and me, taken in our drawing-room, showing its cluttered mixture of Chinese and European furniture. Mother is standing behind us, a slight, elegant figure in a long white dress, her arms around our shoulders. But some of my favourite photographs are of our 'boys'. One of all four, standing stiffly, their arms hanging loose at their sides, again on the steps leading into the drawing-room, in descending order, moving from right to left, wearing their white uniforms. Another, in close-up, is one of Liu, our 'second boy', also seen from behind, with his hair unbraided, a magnificent torrent of black hair about a foot wide reaching down to the back of his knees.

My farewell to Peking was not a tearful affair: I was far too excited at the prospect of seeing London and Paris. Our line of carts began the first leg of our journey, enacting in reverse the scene of our arrival two years before. At Shanghai, we said goodbye to Edward Werner, who had been travelling with us: he had just been promoted and was 'going south'. We promised to write to one another, comparing notes about London and Canton.

We boarded the great P & O liner, the *Peshawar*. For the next seven weeks or so, that huge floating hotel was to be our home. The eternal movement of the sea and the constant drone of the screw never let us forget that we were on board a ship at sea. But the P & O company had done its utmost to make us feel that we were in some luxurious hotel on land. Our cabins – Matthew and I shared one, our parents another – were smaller than comparable hotel bedrooms would have been and we had a round port-hole rather than square windows, but they were well furnished and carpeted, while the bathrooms, with their mahogany panelling, baths carved out of marble, huge mirrors and excellent plumbing, were more luxurious and better appointed than anything I had seen in my life before. Below deck, hardly any of the basic steel structure of the ship was visible. Stairs and corridors were of polished oak and, at least in the 'First Saloon' areas, carpeted. The music-room was panelled in oak, with stained-glass windows and skylights, velvet curtains and all the rich furnishings of a Victorian drawing-room.

On our third morning, we awoke to find ourselves in Hong-kong harbour, having berthed during the night. After breakfast, we went on land to see the sights. Hong-kong afforded us our last glimpse of China. In the early evening Matthew and I watched the coal being brought aboard by twenty or thirty negroes – these were the 'Seedies' or East Africans who worked as *aguallahs* (engine-room ratings) on all the P & O ships. Though without them the ship would not have moved at all, they were usually out of sight of the passengers. In addition to the 'Seedies', there was another group of men essential to the running of the ship, the *lascars* or East Indians. They were the servants of this floating hotel:

they worked in the kitchens, cleaned the rooms, scrubbed the decks and, not least, activated the *punkahs*, or fans, by pulling on the end of a rope. Their uniform consisted of dark-blue embroidered tunics, about knee-length, over white trousers. They wore bright red cloths around their waists and brimless caps, wound round with red material. They were usually barefoot. Like the 'Seedies', the *lascars* were always Muslims and could be seen, at sundown, performing their religious duties.

After three weeks at sea, we steamed into the enormous bay that makes Bombay one of the finest harbours in the world. Soon the white buildings of the city could be seen, dazzling in the reflected sunlight. It was a bright, hot Sunday morning and the esplanade was filled with strolling people, Indian as well as British, the Indian women being particularly conspicuous in their beautiful, brightly-coloured clothes. The same kind of fashion parade took place every evening between 6 p.m. and sundown, usually to the accompaniment of a military band. Each morning, over the next few days, we explored the city, returning to our hotel for tiffin and siesta – it was far too hot to do anything in the afternoon.

Our voyage was really two voyages, separated by our five days in Bombay. When we returned on board, it was still to the *Peshawar*, but it seemed, in some sense, to be another, smaller ship and the atmosphere on board was quite different. Our ship, which for three weeks or so had seemed so quiet and spacious (it must have had half its cabins unoccupied), suddenly filled up with an influx of home-bound 'Anglo-Indians'. The drawing-room was forever filled with mothers, *amahs* and their puling infants, the saloon dominated by red-faced, moustachioed majors discussing this or that expedition to the Khyber Pass. Suddenly the mornings were taken over with games organized by a small group of very formidable ladies.

Actually, Matthew and I didn't mind this way of passing the time, so we were soon initiated into the mysteries of slinging the monkey (in which the men had to walk upside down on their hands, their feet tied to a rope), egg and spoon races, 'Are you there?' and deck quoits. Meanwhile other women were organizing the daily 'sweep', which consisted of guessing the number of knots in the ship's daily run. But by far the most popular sporting activity was the afternoon cricket match. The fact of playing in sides – officers v passengers, married v single, Anglo-Indians v the rest, First v Second Saloon passengers and, most popular of all, ladies v gentlemen – probably added to the excitement. To offset the unfair advantage enjoyed by the gentlemen, the ladies not only acted as umpires, but also felt free to change the rules of the game at any time. Thus a particular ball might be challenged on the grounds that the batswoman had not been ready at the time or that it was a 'practice ball', or simply that it was 'too fast'. More balls, which were manufactured by the ship's crew, disappeared overboard during ladies v gentlemen matches than during all the others, as a result, not of the greater relative prowess of the batsmen in these matches, but rather of the greater waywardness of the lady bowlers. Not, I should say, that Matthew and I were any better than many of the women, to the disgust of the Indian Army men, who could scarcely conceive that two young Englishmen of our age should be so inexpert in the national sport.

In the evening, chess, draughts and whist were played in the saloons. Occasionally, too, there were concerts, which consisted of short pieces played on the piano, songs, 'recitations' of comic verse. One officer, 'blacked up' like a 'nigger minstrel', sang to his own banjo accompaniment. Once a week there was a dance, which Matthew and I did not attend and, on two occasions, fancy dress balls, in which the prizes were given to Mrs X as 'Britannia', Miss Y as 'A Swiss Girl', or Mr Z as 'A Scarecrow'.

We proceeded up the Red Sea, which was as smooth as a lake and of the deepest blue. We missed the sea breezes that had made our passage through the Indian Ocean and Arabian Sea bearable and even, on occasion, pleasant. What little wind there was came straight off the desert, dry and burning hot. We reached Suez and entered Dr de Lesseps's marvel of engineering, which had done so much to alleviate the discomfort and inconvenience of crossing this most trying part of the globe.

It was with some relief that we sailed into the Mediterranean. This was to be the pleasantest part of the voyage: the weather warm, but not too stifling, the sea calm. One bright, beautiful morning we steamed into Brindisi. This beautiful old town on the Adriatic coast of Italy had been a port in early Roman times, the terminus of the Appian Way. The obscure Roman poet Pacuvius was born there, Father told us, and Rome's greatest poet, Virgil, died there. We would have been far happier to spend a few days there than at some of our other ports of call. As it was, we had only the rest of the day to inspect the city. But the P & O line had to construct its timetables on strictly utilitarian lines, without reference to the tastes of North European aesthetes. Unlike Aden, Port Said and Valetta, Brindisi was not a coaling station. Indeed, if one looked at the map, it was difficult to see why ships travelling between Port Said and Malta would go there at all, especially as it was the only port of call on our voyage that was not in some sense or other a British possession. The explanation lay in the P & O Co's responsibilities towards Her Majesty's mails. As the *Peshawar* lifted anchor at Brindisi, a special express train was leaving with all the ship's London-bound mail and those of our fellow passengers who had chosen the

quicker, overland route to London in preference to eleven
more days at sea.

On a cold, drear Monday morning, in Plymouth Sound,
we caught our first glimpse of England. It was drizzling. On
the evening of the following day, we arrived in the Royal
Albert dock. After much delay and some confusion, we got
ourselves and our luggage into a couple of hired carriages and
set off, in the dark, through the East End of London. I
remember little of that journey, perhaps because I could see so
little. I remember Father pointing out the new electric lights
on the Victoria Embankment and craning to look out of the
carriage window at the face of Big Ben. A few minutes later we
arrived at Smith Square.

1904: Peking–St Petersburg

That was one arrival: from a China that had been my home all of my first ten years to the exotic, mythical world of England and London. Now, fourteen years later, I was arriving back in the country and city of my early childhood. Along that short journey in a rick-shaw from the Ch'ién Mên station to the Legation – and during walks that I took on subsequent days – my heart pounded with a strange excitement as the memories came flooding back, minute visual memories that had never surfaced since I had left Peking, precise memories of a particular roof, a particular patch of wall, a particular window. But, scattered among those visual objects that caused me such emotion, were scores of others, in themselves no less memorable, that I did not remember at all: that roof, but not that one. Then there was the new to be discovered, or rather the even older heart of Peking, the Imperial City, which I had never seen and, within that, the City, still Forbidden in name, but no longer forbidden to foreigners of importance.

Since the beginning of the year, 1904, Russia and Japan had been at war. During my weeks in Peking I learnt more about the present political situation and why Father was being sent to St Petersburg. Japan was now everyone's favourite foreign power, everyone's, that is, except Russia's and China's. Thirty years before, Japan had turned unflinchingly to the modern world of democracy and industrialization: in the name of the Mikado, the long-powerless Emperor, a coalition of businessmen, intellectuals and soldiers had deposed the arch-conservative Shogun, or hereditary prime minister, thus ushering in a revolution in the guise of a restoration. In 1894, a war broke out between China and Japan over conflicting claims to Korea, which had received its written language, its culture and its religion from China, but was now semi-independent of her. Civil disturbances and a breakdown in political authority gave the Japanese their opportunity. Posing as the guarantors of Korea's independence, they sent in an army to restore order. To go with all its other modernizing programmes, Japan had learnt to speak the language of international diplomacy: not only was she defending her small neighbour against Chinese tyranny, she would also raise Korea to the status of a modern nation. Japan's invasion would bring not only 'peace', but also 'progress'. The Chinese replied in lordly, antiquated fashion, referring to the Japanese by the pejorative term *Wojen*, 'dwarfs'. A Chinese army was dispatched and the mighty Chinese navy, twice the size of the Japanese, brought into action. But the ill-led, ill-disciplined, ill-equipped Chinese were no match for the Japanese modern war machine. In under a year the Chinese suffered their greatest humiliation in a century that had been an uninterrupted series of humiliations at the hands of foreign powers. This time the humiliation was all the greater in that it was at the hands of a smaller, Asian neighbour. Korea was declared wholly independent of China, which was forced to cede the island of Formosa[1] to Japan and pay indemnities amounting to £35 million.

Now Russia had decided to act on China's weakness and Japan's evident aspirations in the Far East. In order to have a

1 Now called Taiwan.

Pacific port free of ice throughout the year, she had obtained a lease on Port Arthur from China. This had now been linked up with the Trans-Siberian railway, facilitating the transport of troops and equipment. Led by the so-called 'Boxer' societies and with the connivance of the Empress Dowager, anti-foreign feeling swept China. In 1900, this culminated in the attack on the Legation Quarter in Peking. The German Minister, Baron von Ketteler was killed. The British Legation was fortified and over two hundred foreign nationals took refuge there for several months, before relief came at the hands of an international expeditionary force. The Court fled and the allies occupied the city. A peace was signed in September 1901 by which China was forced to pay indemnities of £6 million. The British Minister, Sir Claude Macdonald, and his exhausted staff departed for well-earned leave. A new Minister, Sir Ernest Satow, was transferred from Tokyo, where he had also been Minister. He took with him his Secretary of Legation, my father. Satow, a quiet, withdrawn scholar, had risen from the ranks of the student interpreters, but chosen to go to Japan rather than to China. After twenty years in Japan, he spent ten years heading various British Legations elsewhere. But he was an orientalist, rather than a professional diplomat; indeed he had become the foremost Japanese specialist in the service of the British government and it was inevitable that one day he would return to head the British Legation in Tokyo. My father was on closer personal terms with Satow than he had been with any other of his superiors. Even in the few months that I was in Peking I, too, became a good friend: there was an unspoken understanding between this lovable man in his late fifties and me. I knew what it was and I think he did too: he was a bachelor and, I felt sure, a member of the 'fraternity'.

Now more than ever concerned about the rise of Japanese

influence, Russia sent troops into Korea. England and Japan, which had formed a defensive alliance, protested. The Japanese proposed an agreement with Russia whereby the integrity of China and Korea, and Japan's interest in Korea and Russia's in Manchuria, would be respected. Russia refused and, in February 1904, Japan withdrew her minister from St Petersburg. Three days later, the Japanese laid siege to the Russian fleet in Port Arthur, sinking several ships. There was serious concern that the bungling, short-sighted Russian government might indulge in one too many provocations and bring Great Britain into the conflict. This might lead to a war between the European great powers, despite the close blood ties between the Russian, German and English royal families. Germany, on the lookout for territorial gain and envious of British sea power, had close links with Russia. France, which now had treaties with both Russia and Great Britain, would probably remain neutral, for the time being at least: if a defeat of Russia and Germany looked likely, France might come in on the British side, hoping thereby to regain Alsace-Lorraine. But, although Russia might well be defeated in the Far East, there was no hope of England, with no conscript army, defeating the combined forces of Russia and Germany without the French. Apart from certain elements in the Russian, German and Japanese governments, nobody wanted war: the danger was that greed, suspicion and sheer incompetence might bring the great powers into one. Diplomacy was more than ever England's best weapon and, suddenly, St Petersburg was the most important post in her Diplomatic Service. The Foreign Office acted swiftly. The elderly Ambassador, Sir Charles Scott, was retired and Charles Hardinge, Under-Secretary of State at the Foreign Office, was knighted and appointed in his place.

I stayed in Peking for only twelve weeks, before retracing, in reverse, most of my journey on the Trans-Siberian. This time, it was to be a very different journey. It was May, not February. The snow had retreated to the upper reaches of the moun- tains; below, the earth had turned from white to green. There was more daylight, of course, and men were working in the fields. We crossed Lake Baikal in half the time it had taken to cut through several inches of ice. This time, too, I was with my parents and, though I had my own compartment, to which I retreated at night, there were to be no nocturnal visitors, no François, no Dmitri. In that area, Peking had not shone kindly on me either. For all I knew, the Imperial Court might have been a hotbed of Uranism[1], with veritable harems of male concubines, but my room for manoeuvre was limited and I would not have known how to use it had it not been. What, I wondered, would St Petersburg offer *de ce côté-là*?[2]

We arrived one morning at the Moskovsky Voksal, the Moscow station. Father, who had already begun instructing himself in Russian, explained that the word for 'railway sta- tion' was derived from 'Vauxhall': it seems that the railway junction situated a mile from our London house had so impressed Russian visitors that it became a metonym for all railway stations. Outside, three Embassy carriages were wait- ing for us and our luggage. We embarked on an immensely long, broad avenue that stretched into the distance in an absolutely straight line. This was the celebrated Nevsky Prospekt. At its end, glowing in the bright sunlight, was a tall, slim, golden spire. As we got closer, I saw that the spire was surmounted, not by a cross, but by a golden ship, which

1 A term used at the time for 'homosexuality'. Though identified with Aphrodite (Venus), Urania, 'the Heavenly one', represented the passion of love in its nobler aspect. She was also the muse of astronomy, her symbols being a globe and a rod.
2 In that direction.

served as a weather vane: the building was not a church, but the Admiralty, the tallest and most imposing of the city's government buildings. Then, as we turned right, there was the Winter Palace, in all its splendour of ochre, white and gold. A short drive along the quay brought us to the British Embassy, a huge, almost square building, with blood-red stucco walls. Built in the eighteenth century as a town house, it had been the Austrian Embassy before being taken over by the British. Inside, the Embassy was decorated in heavy palatial style. The grand staircase, from the main entrance, swept up through the building in scarlet and white. Our rooms were at the back, overlooking a huge open square, the Marsovo Pole, which, unlike its Parisian namesake, the Champs de Mars, was still used for military exercises. In the spring, I had a splendid view from my room of the great military parades, when the various household regiments could be distinguished not only by their different uniforms, but also by their different coloured mounts (black for the Horse Guards, chestnut for the Chevalier Guards, dapple grey for the Gatchina Hussars). Our drawing-room and dining-room were on the first floor, our bedrooms on the mezzanine below. Our meals were served in our own dining-room, but prepared in the Embassy kitchens, under the expert eye of the French *chef de cuisine*, Monsieur Zamboni.

The day after our arrival, we were invited to dinner by the Ambassador, Sir Charles Hardinge. He was no stranger to St Petersburg: he had only left it the year before, after five years as Secretary of Embassy. In the closing weeks of 1903, Hardinge had seen my father at the Foreign Office and arranged for him to join him, on secondment, in St Petersburg, in charge of relations with China and Japan. He was given the title of Secretary of Embassy, normally the 'No. 2' post. However, there already was a Secretary of Embassy, Cecil

Spring Rice; he remained the Ambassador's deputy and was given the title of Counsellor. He and his wife Florence, a young kinswoman of the Duke of Devonshire, were also there in the splendid oval dining-room. In the course of the evening all kinds of connections emerged between us. I already knew that the Ambassador and my parents were old friends. Sir Charles had served for three years in Paris as Head of Chancery under Lord Dufferin, my father's third cousin. Sir Charles then told us that he had been born in Dufferin Lodge, in Highgate, a house that his father had leased from Lord Dufferin.

'Of course, he had my job here for a couple of years – twenty, twenty-five years ago. I had my first post under him, too, you know. Constantinople. Wonderful boss. Four wonderful years there. Lots of sailing. Dufferin was a splendid sailor. Had an extraordinary yacht – built to his own specifications, all the controls under his hands, like a piano.' Then, suddenly, he turned to me and asked: 'And how's your brother getting on in Tangiers?' I said that I had been there to see him last year and he seemed very happy. 'Yes,' he went on, 'good man, Arthur Nicolson.' (Arthur Nicolson was the Minister at Tangiers.) 'He was with me at Constantinople.' Then, turning to my father: 'Of course, he's a relation of yours, too, isn't he?'

'Yes. He's Dufferin's nephew.'

The conversation shifted from Constantinople to Cambridge: the connections proliferated. Three of the four men around the table were 'Trinitarians' – Cecil Spring Rice had broken with family tradition by going to Oxford. Spring Rice had also met my father, a dozen years before, in Peking, when he accompanied Lord Curzon, his exact contemporary at Eton and Balliol, then Under-Secretary of State for India and future Viceroy, on a tour of China. By the end of the evening, it was borne in on me how, through friendships formed at school and university, followed by the 'musical chairs' of appointments, the world-wide diplomatic service was actually a very 'small world', almost a 'club'. This impression deepened when I got to know the rest of the Embassy staff. One of the Second Secretaries, Hermann Norman, was, like the Ambassador, an Etonian and Trinitarian. (He was also, I suspected, a member of the 'fraternity'.) There were at least two other Etonians on the staff, the two Third Secretaries: Viscount Cranley, who had been replaced as attaché at Tangiers by my brother Matthew and whom I was to see again three years later at the Berlin Embassy, and Viscount Errington.

The Service no doubt has its share of the mediocre and the wildly eccentric, but I am always struck how the better diplomats fall into two broad types, the 'soldier' and the 'scholar'. The Ambassador and his 'No. 2' were good examples of this. Sir Charles, a man in his middle forties, of rather military appearance, bearing and manner, was a 'soldier': he was, in fact, a general's son. There was a straight, honest look in his grey-blue eyes. He claimed to have spent most of his time at Cambridge on the playing-field, but he was a highly intelligent, even subtle diplomat. He wasted neither time nor words. He could see straight through a complicated situation and take the necessary decision. He gained the respect and, more importantly, the trust of the host nation. Spring Rice, a real 'scholar', could not have provided a greater contrast: shortish, slight of build, with an almost delicate face; shy, rapidly moving eyes; a sensuous, well-shaped mouth, emitting a softly spoken stream of beautifully constructed sentences, to the accompaniment of quick, nervous movements of the hands. I soon discovered that he wrote poetry. Duckworth had just published a volume of Persian love lyrics that he had translated with the help of his Persian teacher. Indeed there was something very felinely 'Persian' about him. His fair, neatly clipped moustache – at that time all men of a certain age, actors apart, wore moustaches – failed to give his face a properly 'masculine' finish.

Three mornings a week, my mother and I had Russian lessons with a plump, bespectacled, middle-aged lady who looked, in equal proportions, either stern or warmly smiling. The Cyrillic alphabet held no terrors for me, since, of the twenty-one Russian letters, twelve were the same as in Greek and two more almost so. My poor mother, who had no Greek, took longer to master her Cyrillic, though eight of the letters are the same in our Latin alphabet. Indeed there is the odd Russian word that happens to look like one of ours. Mother used to turn this to comic effect. Suddenly she would say something like: '*Voilà un pectopah!*' or '*Il faut aller au kacca.*' '*Pectopah*' is the Cyrillic spelling for '*restoran*', restaurant, and means nothing in French (or English), but sounds rather ridiculous. Transliterated, '*kacca*' becomes '*kassa*', *caisse* or cash-desk, though, untransliterated, it sounds like '*caca*', a French child's word for '*merde*'.

During our first few weeks in St Petersburg, we took advantage of the fine weather to explore the city. Like London and Paris, Petersburg had its trams and omnibuses, both horse-drawn – in 1904 neither electricity nor petrol-engine had yet reached the public transport system and private motor-cars were seldom seen. There were also steamers that moved slowly up, down and across the Neva and smaller steam-boats, like Venice's *vaporetti*, plying their trade along the other waterways. Then there were the various horse-drawn carriages for hire, from the four-seater *kareta* or carriage and pair to the very Russian *droshkies*, with their characteristic arched harness which, at a pinch, seated two passengers, and were the only things in the city ever to be seen moving at great speed. But our first expedition was on foot: we crossed Troitsky Most (Trinity Bridge), which spanned the Bolshaya (Great) Neva from just outside the Embassy to the Fortress of St Peter and St Paul, the historical heart of the city. The newest of the city's bridges, it was also its longest, almost three times the length of Westminster Bridge. The Fortress, a very Russian sort of Bastille, is really a walled citadel, though smaller than Moscow's Kremlin. It was built, in three months, in 1703. Not content with working to their deaths thousands of forced labourers, fifteen years later Peter had his disobedient son tortured and executed there. Yet at its midst there rises, incongruously, the very Western spire of its cathedral, the tallest building in the city and one of the tallest in Russia, surmounted, not just by a cross, but by an angel bearing a cross twenty-three feet high, spire, angel and cross all gilded. When I looked out of any of the windows at the front of the Embassy, there it was, gleaming in whatever sunlight it could catch, unless swathed in fog and hidden from view.

One hot summer evening, we crossed Trinity Bridge again, this time not on foot, but in one of the Embassy's carriages, with Father and the Spring Rices. We passed the Peter and Paul Fortress, crossing the large island known colloquially as the Petrograd Side and, after another bridge, arrived at Kameni Island. On that occasion, we went not to one of the many villas to which the city's richer citizens retreated in the summer, but to one of the island's open-air restaurants. There we spent a few hours, in a garden surrounded by trees and, as dish followed dish, we were regaled by a band of Russian musicians to an endless stream of pieces, in turn sentimental, martial-sounding or comic. As the eerie light sky of the northern summer night gradually darkened, the lanterns and oil lamps came into their own; the birds stopped wheeling overhead and the ducks squawking.

On other days, Mother and I set out early for one of the imperial palaces: Tsarskoye Selo, Oranienbaum, Peterhof. In St Petersburg, Peter the Great tried to combine the beauties of Paris, Venice and Amsterdam on the uninhabited swamps of the Neva; Peterhof was an attempt to rival Versailles. The Great Palace stands on a hill, forty feet above sea level and the most dramatic approach would have been from the sea. Having landed at the tiny harbour, the imperial guests would have been conveyed along a canal, flanked on each side by vertical jets of water. For that brief half mile, their breadth of vision confined by the row of tall pine trees on either side, their eyes would have been transfixed by the vision ahead: Peter's Versailles, seemingly floating on a wall of water. At the end of the canal, they would reach a semi-circular pool with, at its centre, a gilded statue of Samson, grappling with a lion, from whose jaws a jet of water shoots up to a great height. Behind it, another fountain rises up, its spent water flowing down marble steps into the straight end of the pool. At each side are the twin flights of the Grand Cascade, each step flanked by a pair of gilded statues. When the fountains are turned off, these steps might seem to lead up to the Palace; in fact, they provide courses for more water issuing from more jets, one on each side of each step. At one's point of arrival, the Palace seems almost to disappear behind the wall of water on which it had earlier seemed to float.

That, at least, is my imagined *mise-en-scène*. For seven years, Peter would have watched the realization of the vision that he and Leblond, his French architect, had conjured up. He had only five more years to enjoy it, dying, from syphilis, in 1725, aged fifty-three. In 1904, nobody, not even the Tsar of All the Russias, arrived in such dramatic style. Nicholas II may have clung to the power that autocracy brought him, but he cared not at all for its theatrical trappings, preferring, when at Peterhof, to repair, not to the Grand Palace, but to the Villa Alexandria, a mile away in the grounds. There like Marie Antoinette acting out the life of a shepherdess in her Versailles *hameau*, he and his family could pretend to be an ordinary bourgeois family enjoying the summer holidays.

Our twenty-mile drive by *kareta* along the coast road of Neva Bay took us about three hours. We arrived, like everybody else, on the other, southern side of the Palace. We could, I suppose, have arranged to leave the main road at some point and arrive near the beginning of the canal, completing the rest of the journey on foot. But, to enjoy the miracle of water and light, this would have to have been in the afternoon, when the fountains were turned on, leaving little time to see the wonders of palace and park.

We followed our guide from the Portrait Room (with its 328 portraits of girls and young women), to the First Chinese Room, the Divan Room, the Cabinet, the Cavalier Room, the Blue Guest Chamber, etc., each crammed with furniture of monotonous exquisiteness and paintings of little artistic interest. After a light luncheon at the Hôtel Samson, we hired a carriage and spent an agreeable hour or two driving round the English Park and its English Ponds, arriving at the more 'methodized' nature of the Lower Park in time for the *jeux d'eau*. Also there, jutting out to sea, is Peter's own Dutch-style retreat, Monplaisir. From the terrace we, like Peter himself, could survey his achievements: to the north, the coast of Finland, which he had seized from the Swedes; to the west, his naval fortress of Kronstadt, guarding Neva Bay from the sea; to the east, his new capital, created by imperial *fiat*. With the sunlight still playing on the waters of the Grand Cascade, our *izvoshtchik* (cabby) took us off to the Novi Peterhof Station, where we caught a train back to Petersburg.

From the Embassy, St Petersburg seemed, like London and

Paris, to be built on either side of a river. In fact, the city is built on several islands, separated by various branches of the river and canals, the Bolshaya Neva being only the widest. One of the charms of Petersburg is its waterways. It is always more agreeable to walk through a city beside water. This is especially so in the case of Petersburg, where rivers and canals bend and curve, in contrast to its long, straight streets. In Paris, Haussmann's boulevards and avenues are also long and straight, running roughshod over the twists and turns of the city's medieval streets. But Peter had no such obstacles to sweep away: he simply started afresh on a drained swamp and moved his capital there. His *prospekti*, perspectives, were primarily for the display of military might: soldiers are always more impressive when marching in a straight line. Haussmann's (Napoleon III's) rebuilding of Paris was also military in intention: to get the army as quickly as possible into any rebellious quarter. But the average sensual Frenchman has more pressing needs than military *gloire*: the boulevards were planted with trees, dotted with cafés and became the territory of the *flâneur* and his *aventures*. No such subversion was allowed to undermine Peter's *prospekti*: they impress, but they do not evoke pleasure, and they remain treeless. Happily for the humbler human, the city's waterways avoid an imposed geometry, allowing him to saunter more pleasurably. In summer, their waters cool the air, their trees give shelter from the sun; in winter, their shifting direction provides more protection from icy blasts than long, straight streets. At all times, water and trees provide a fluid, shifting counterpoint to the unchanging, man-made beauties of buildings. To a greater degree than treeless streets, they respond to subtle changes of light and atmosphere, from season to season, from one time of day to another. As the trees lose their leaves in October, the dappled light and shade turn to a uniformly lighter tone. But the most dramatic change occurs a month later when the dark waters freeze over, turning into a dazzling white. Petersburgers are no longer transported along their ways in motor-boats or confined to the quays, but take to them on skates. Then, even the omnibuses, tramcars and private cabs abandon their wheels for runners and a new carriage, the majestic three-horse troika, appears. As we were to discover, one of the compensations for the seemingly endless Petersburg winter is to be pulled around the splendid, snow-covered city, enveloped in one's furs, by one, two or three horses, bells a-jingling.

I never had occasion to use the longest and widest of the waterways, the Obvodni Canal, because it is also the most southerly, far away from the city centre, but the other three were my favoured routes across the city. The next, in size and position, is the broad, stately Fontanka. A tributary of the Bolshaya Neva, it begins near the Embassy, on the eastern side of the Letny Sad, or Summer Garden, whose lake and fountains it supplies with water, hence its name, 'Little Fountain'. It embraces the most elegant part of the city and is lined by many of its most palatial town houses, none more so than the long, colonnaded, cream-coloured Anichkov Palace; built in the 1740s by the Empress Elizabeth for a lover, it is now the winter residence of the Dowager-Empress Marie Feodorovna. It is best seen from the Anichkov Bridge, where at each corner stands a colossal bronze statue of a man training a horse. One day I walked the entire length of the Fontanka, from the Summer Garden to the point at which it rejoins the Bolshaya Neva some five miles later. Over the last mile or so, the river takes on a quite different character. Here tall, dingy apartment blocks or warehouses, rather than stately town houses, line its quays. Here the once prosperous, but now elderly live side by side with those who were never or ever would be prosperous. Here the river here is filled with all manner of boats, all employed in some commercial activity or other. Commerce, in its humblest, most hopeless forms is everywhere: on every bridge some old woman sells ginger bread, apples or *kvas*, the slightly alcoholic liquor distilled from rye bread.

The Moyka, narrower, less stately, less immediately imposing than the Fontanka, has its own slightly melancholy, at times even gloomy, charm. It branches off from the Fontanka at the southern end of the Summer Garden and joins the Bolshaya Neva three miles further on. Of the four watercourses it is the one closest to the Neva and therefore the shortest. Between the Fontanka and the Moyka, lies my favourite of all, the narrow, sinuous Yekaterininsky Canal. The more these rivers and canals bend and curve, the more dramatic can be the views of buildings. The bridges, too, provide a never failing source of pleasure and none has more charming bridges than the Yekaterininsky. My particular favourites were a pair of suspension bridges. The Bank Bridge, opposite the Imperial Bank, in a bend in the canal, is a graceful curve of wrought iron at each end of which is a pair of griffins with huge gilded wings, the suspension cables emerging from their mouths. The Lions Bridge, whose suspension cables come from the mouths of two pairs of stone lions with wavy manes, crosses the canal near Theatre Square and the Marie (Mariinsky) Theatre.

After a few weeks, my peripateticism took on a more purposive character. It soon became evident that Petersburg was not as richly endowed with public conveniences as Paris or London. That was one problem. For what it was worth, Herr Baedeker listed only three *kloseti*: inside the General Post Office, in the Alexander Garden and in the square opposite Nicholas station. There were certainly more, but even these would have escaped my attention without his guidance. Then there was the problem of what to do when one was in them. In every country, these institutions have taken on a complicated body of custom, codes of etiquette, restrictive laws, enforced or ignored, a varying capacity to arouse embarrassment. *Différents pays, différentes moeurs.* If, in a foreign country, one is to use them for any but the purpose for which they were intended, this ethical lore surrounding them must be acquired. I found that, in this regard, the Russians differ from both the English and the French. Like the French, they have none of the Englishman's sense of shame and embarrassment, none of his circumspection. At a time when one could not walk out into a street without seeing a soldier or a policeman, when spies were everywhere and political censorship absolute, no one seemed to care a fig for others' sexual *mores*. All young men, it seemed, engaged in sexual acts with each other or, if poor, were willing to sell themselves to the older and richer. Unlike in Paris or London, however, there are few obvious effeminates. Nor have they the superficial, easy-come-easy-go attitude of the Parisians, who would call it realism; in their friendliness, the Petersburgers are more like Londoners. Yet, even in their friendliness, there is a difference. The friendliness of the Englishman often takes time to emerge; he does not wear it on his sleeve. With the Russian, it arrives, in massive quantities, from the outset. One feels at once the warmth of his broad smile; in no time at all, he is telling you the story of his life and listening to yours with bated breath. He is your friend for life: two weeks later, of course, he may have forgotten about you entirely.

The English have produced the most advanced, most elaborate public lavatories. They are often underground, which lends them a certain infernal, lugubrious atmosphere. Much manufactured porcelain, tiling, copper, brass and mahogany is expended on them. There is often an attendant on the premises. Everything is wrapped in an embarrassed pretence that something is taking place quite other than what is actually taking place: those men standing at their stalls, with their serious, preoccupied, almost dignified air, seeming to avoid others' gazes, might be bank clerks at their desks, adding up endless rows of figures. Some of this may be accounted for by a national puritanical shame at the ways of the human body, but there is also the real danger presented in such places by plain-clothes police. If contact is made, it is made surreptitiously, with a look that might just be read as an invitation to meet outside. There, a few words may be exchanged, a certain trust established, and these serious-looking bank clerks may turn into animated, amusing conversationalists.

Of the various forms of 'convenience' provided by cities of my acquaintance, my preference goes to the Parisian *pissoirs* or *pissotières*, politely (and wittily) referred to as *'vespasiennes'*, after the Roman emperor Vespasian, who introduced a tax on urinals; more colloquially, and almost as wittily, they are known to those who frequent them as *'tasses'*, cups, on account of their shape and liquid associations. These circular constructions of black-painted sheet-metal, perforated by patterns of small holes, are a familiar feature of the Parisian boulevards. In contrast to their heavy English counterparts, they are a triumph of style over substance. They do not provide all the facilities of a public lavatory, but are simply urinals. In contrast to their English counterparts, they are not hidden underground, but unashamedly on view in the street; no one can fail to notice the pairs of shoes and trouser bottoms as he – or she – passes. They have three standing places set at an oblique angle to one another, the most coveted being the middle one; here one doubles one's chances and is less exposed to the (usually good-natured) expostulations of those waiting outside. Our apartment in the rue de Vaugirard was a mere three hundred yards from three such *vespasiennes* – outside the Lycée Saint-Louis in the Boul' Mich', at the place de l'Odéon and outside the Jardin du Luxembourg – with the same distance between each of them. Five minutes' walk brings one to another three – at Cluny, the place Saint-Sulpice and Saint-Germain-des-Prés. There is a quite shameless, amiable, tolerant *cameraderie* among the *habitués* of any particular route, for most of them pass the time walking from one to another. One recognizes one's fellow *habitués*, nods acknowledgement, risks a '*Bonsoir!*' Inside, a look or a smile at one's 'neighbour' is enough to get him to join one outside, when he will say something like '*Tu connais un endroit?*' or '*On peut aller chez toi?*'[1] If my new acquaintance did not live in an hotel room, we could easily find one. Paris is a city of easy virtue: she sees no good reason to stop people getting into each other's beds.

The Summer Garden, perhaps the most beautiful garden in Petersburg, had the particular advantage of being almost next to the Embassy. Originally laid out by Leblond, in the manner of Versailles, its most remarkable feature was a series of fountains, with statuary depicting scenes from Aesop's Fables. In 1777, a flood swept across the park, uprooting trees and destroying the fountains. Catherine the Great had the park redesigned *à l'anglaise*; the avenues of elms and beeches were decorated by some two hundred statues by Venetian artists of the early eighteenth century. About eighty of them still remain. In October, I was amused to see that the statues were all covered with wooden boxes, like so many upturned coffins, to protect them from the frost; they are not exposed again until late April. Behind Peter the Great's Summer Palace are

1 'Do you know anywhere? . . . Can we go to your place?'

two elegant neo-classical pavilions, known as the Tea House
and the Coffee House. At the southern end of the park is a
lake, a veritable *lac des cygnes*. There, during those warm
summer afternoons, I would while away an hour or two sitting
on a bench, reading and observing the passing scene. At first
sight, the Summer Garden did not seem to offer much hope.
To begin with, a medal-bedecked soldier stood to attention
before Felten's splendid wrought-iron gates, his task to forbid
entrance to anyone who did not come up to the required
sartorial standards: anyone wearing peasant costume or work-
men's overalls, anyone who showed any sign of earning a
living with his hands, would be turned away. Children had to
be accompanied by a responsible adult or at least by a uniformed 'nanny'. There was little evidence of Uranians on the
prowl, yet the long metal edifice discreetly hidden behind trees
did seem to be frequented.

During the short Petersburg summer, my wanderings were
unusually pleasant – and unusually propitious. For some
weeks, and especially during the midsummer 'white nights',
when the sky never seems to grow dark and an eerie half-light
persists after the sun has set, Petersburgers are transformed
into Carnival Latins. All is *tempo allegro*, Nods and Becks and
wreathèd Smiles.[1] So urgent is desire that it no longer matters
that no one has anywhere to go: a covering of bushes is enough
to hide one's nakedness. My great discovery was the
Tavrichesky Garden, the large, park-like grounds of the
Tauride Palace, which turned out to be the favoured meeting
place of the city's Uranians. I stumbled on it by chance. One
afternoon, I decided to visit the Smolni Convent, whose dazzling blue and white cathedral, with its five black and gilded
onion domes, rises majestically above all the other buildings

1 With brisk movement. The quotation is from Milton's poem 'L'Allegro'.

around it and is clearly visible from the Embassy two miles or so to the east. On my way back, I decided to explore the Tavrichesky Garden. It was early evening when I entered the park by the southern gates, though still quite light. As I walked up the path, I noticed men sitting alone on benches. Invariably, they gave me a searching, if sometimes furtive look as I passed. My heart was beginning to pound in that insistent way it always did when sexual excitement was in the air. The men were of all kinds and all ages. Many were well dressed, many not; there were ordinary soldiers in uniform, presumably there for the rent, but no officers, or at least not in uniform. I branched off to the right and came to a large, irregularly shaped pond. I followed the path around it. Suddenly, in addition to the odd man sitting on a bench, there were figures standing in small groups among the trees, almost hidden from view by bushes. I wandered slowly over to one such group and was greeted at first by a barrier of men in long greatcoats. I grinned with embarrassment and the group opened up again to reveal open flies and exposed cocks. I followed suit and was soon being fondled by all and sundry. When one man, of a certain age, unattractive, to me at least, got down on his knees in front of me, I cravenly stepped back, did up my flies and left the group – there were, after all, others to explore. I was not the only one on the move: groups dissolved and formed, gained and lost members with great frequency. In one such group I found a youngish man bent over another's cock, while being fucked by a third, the rest standing around playing with themselves and each other, their eyes glued on the scene before them. The *fouteur*, to use the Marquis de Sade's term, then withdrew and I was invited to take his place. I came in no time at all and left the group. Slowly, I made my way out of the park and back to the Embassy. Over the next few weeks, I returned several times to the Tavrichesky Garden.

1890–99: Paris

My initiation into the mysteries of the 'Gents' or 'public convenience', as we euphemistically call it in England, occurred in my nineteenth year. I was sitting alone in the drawing-room at Smith Square; the tea things still lay on the table beside me. My grandparents were both out and, apart from Mrs Chapman and the maid, I was alone in the house. Matthew was up at Cambridge, for his first term. I had been there myself a few weeks before taking 'Little Go', or the Previous Examination. I had been well prepared: like Matthew, the year before, I had spent several weeks at a 'crammer's' in Bloomsbury, revising my mathematics and learning how to turn Latin and Greek into English and vice versa, rather than into and out of French, as I had learnt to do at my *lycée*. I had just heard that I had been offered a place in College. It was the first time I had been in London at this time of year and my school days were now over.

I got up and went over to the window. Outside, in the crisp autumn air, reddish sunlight was bathing the west end of St John's Church. Suddenly, without knowing why, I decided to go out for a walk. Again with no particular end in view, I found myself crossing Lambeth Bridge, into that strange world, so near, yet so entirely unknown to me, of the 'Surrey side'. I passed Lambeth Palace[1] and soon came to an imposing

---

1 The residence of the Archbishop of Canterbury.

classical pile, which I glimpsed behind its huge gates. This, I later learnt, was the Bethlehem Lunatic Asylum,[1] popularly known as Bedlam, since the days when it was situated in the East End. I walked on for about another mile, arriving at a white, classical church, probably dating from the early years of the century. It was, I noted, dedicated to St Mark. However, my present need was more immediate than anything a church could satisfy. At the cross-roads was a 'Gents': I descended the stone steps to the cool, aqueous underworld. Not until I had fully relieved myself did I look around: a young man was standing at a stall on the other side. He turned round as I did. He was older than I, by five years or so; medium-brown hair, medium-brown eyes. With hindsight and experience, I would have added: 'unremarkable, but acceptable'. He waved his erection at me. My own took no time to reach its full dimensions and I showed it to him. He did himself up and came over to me. Staring at it as he moved my foreskin back and forth, he said: 'I don't suppose you have anywhere to go?'

'No, have you?'

'No.'

'Come in here,' and he pushed me into one of the cubicles and locked the door behind us. My heart was pounding with fear and excitement, though I had no precise notion of the danger that I ran – from criminals or police. He took off his coat, hung it on the hook, dropped his braces and trousers, and sat down on the seat, pulling me towards him. He unfastened the top of my trousers – my fly-buttons were still undone – and, standing there awkwardly, I held up my shirt. He just sat there, open-mouthed, staring at it. He then moved me towards him and started licking the end and putting the shaft between his teeth.

1 Now the Imperial War Museum.

'Beautiful cock!' he said, as if in a dream and, grasping the base in his left hand, put as much of it in his mouth as he could. I began thrusting it in and out, while he masturbated himself. In no time at all, I had come in his mouth. To my astonishment, he did not spit it out, but swallowed it. A second later, he came.

'You go first,' he said. 'I'll come up later. Don't wait for me. Goodbye.'

I noticed that he spoke in a way that was half-way between 'cockney' and 'polite': afterwards, when I went over the whole incident in my mind, I decided that he was probably some sort of clerk or shop-assistant. I could only have been down there five minutes. I went back up into the street, my heart still pounding, walked over to the park nearby and sat on a bench, trying to recover my composure. It was as if I were still in a state of shock, or as if I were still regaining normal consciousness after a delirious episode. Then I remembered the word he had used: cock. So that's what they called the *membrum virile* in colloquial English. In French, I knew, *le sexe* was also called *queue* (tail) or *bitte* (bitt or bollard), but I had no idea what their English equivalent was. After a while, I went back into the street and began retracing my steps home. Half-way up Kennington Road, I hailed a passing number 54 omnibus which, I knew, passed along Millbank.

On the way back, my thoughts returned to what had happened. Could such things take place just below the surface of a London street, in that strange twilight world that was neither private nor public? Above, fully clothed people had been going about their business, obeying all manner of unwritten rules as to what one did and did not do, oblivious to what was taking place a few feet below ground. Unknown to them, I had exposed my nakedness to someone I had not been introduced to or would ever be introduced to and, with scarcely a word exchanged between us, indulged in the sort of act that many believed should be performed only by a man and a woman, duly sanctified by church and state, after a long period of betrothal, in the privacy of their bedchamber.

My first intimations of such things had occurred three years before, when the echoes of the Wilde trials reached the French newspapers. But what, in that spring of 1895, did I, a fifteen-year-old schoolboy glean of the Wilde affair? Very little. Nothing was ever said in my presence on the matter, but clearly the grown-ups in a liberal, literary circle must have talked about it among themselves. Their reaction would have been one of horror at the very notion of a man's being brought to court at all for 'acts of indecency' committed in private with willing adults, let alone sending him to prison for it. I was left to learn what I could through the words used in the newspapers. The English press had clearly decided to say as little as possible on the matter. *The Times* confined its attentions to short, inconspicuous accounts under its 'Courts' column, as if the Wilde affair were merely part of business as usual at the Old Bailey. Some of the French newspapers were more forthcoming, but the *Figaro* provided little information about the trials and seemed more concerned to condemn the entire 'aestheticist' movement as a danger to public morals. Indeed it was in an editorial in the *Figaro* entitled 'Aesthetes' that I learnt of the Wilde affair in the first place. 'Oscar Wilde,' I learnt, 'was arrested yesterday for a crime against morals.' I had no idea what that could mean. How could the terms *crîme* and *moeurs* be brought together? Had Wilde been running an unauthorized brothel in his spare time? The article ended: 'So we must ask our aesthetes to restrain themselves. We forgive them Ibsen, though with some difficulty. We are even prepared to put up with Sudermann for the sake of peace. But we should be revolted at the equivalent of Mr Wilde.' I still knew more about the aesthetic and moral prejudices of the *Figaro* editorial writer than I did about Wilde's offence. *Le Temps* moved me closer to understanding. It spoke of 'Oscar Wilde's relations with a number of younger men who were friends of his though belonging to a lower social rank'. What, I wondered, was wrong with that? It seemed rather a mark in Wilde's favour. Then I learnt that one of the co-defendants was 'a provider of young men . . . well known to the police'. Money or cigarette cases had been given to some of the boys thus 'provided'. When taxed with this Wilde had declared: 'I prefer the pleasure of talking to a young man for an hour even to the pleasure of being questioned in a Criminal Court!' Young men, usually male prostitutes, gave evidence. One said how, after an expensive dinner, he had spent the night with Wilde in a room at the Savoy Hotel and that he 'had never committed any immoral act before meeting Mr Wilde'. At the end of the first Wilde trial, the *Figaro* editorialist was fulminating once more. He spoke of 'revolting details' (without providing them) and expressed the hope that 'English society, certain levels of which are seriously gangrened, will be purged of certain individuals who shall remain nameless'. I was beginning to understand: there was a kind of sexual activity that could take place between men. It probably consisted of what some schoolboys did to one another (I had not yet reached the stage of imagining anything further). Certain men do not grow out of this practice and, since they are few in number, are obliged to pay young men to do it with them. I felt neither attraction nor repulsion at the idea, but the response of certain people seemed quite disproportionate.

Wilde spent most of the last eighteen months of his life in hotels not a mile from my grandparents' apartment, but I was in Paris very little at that time, since I went up to Cambridge in October 1899. Wilde died at the Hôtel d'Alsace on 25

November 1900, destitute, almost friendless. He was forty-six.
Douglas lives on, publishing every so often a new article on
the subject, sometimes repeating himself, sometimes contra-
dicting himself, yet steadfastly maintaining that he has never
indulged in homosexual acts, either with Wilde or with anyone
else. If society were constituted differently, several score
Arabs, Cockneys and Wykehamists could no doubt sue him
for libel on that account. Yet in an article published in *La
Revue Blanche* a year after the trial Douglas berated England
in general and his father in particular for hypocrisy. He went
on to point out that the second Wilde trial was forced upon
Asquith, the Home Secretary, for purely political reasons. If,
given the state of national feeling, Wilde were let off with
an acquittal, the Liberal government would be swept from
office. So we have the situation, both tragic and farcical, of a
government led by the former lover of the Marquess of
Queensberry's eldest son, Lord Rosebery, including a Home
Secretary who was 'an old friend of Oscar Wilde', trying to
save itself by accusing that same Wilde of committing
immoral acts with the Marquess of Queensberry's youngest
son. In the public schools, Douglas continues, 'Greek love' is
so general that only the physically disfavoured have to live
without it. At Oxford, homosexuality is commonest of all
among the athletes. 'A large majority of our future legislators,
lawyers, judges, officers, diplomats will, at least for part of
their lives, have been sodomites.' One quarter of mankind's
intellectual heroes, he goes on, were definitely sodomites and
probably a good proportion of the rest. Yet, somehow, if
Douglas's later declarations are to be believed, this handsome
young lord, the future friend of Oscar Wilde, managed to
escape this prevailing mass of homosexuality. By the time I
read that article in *La Revue Blanche*, my thinking on the
question was more informed, but I still felt unable to speak

either to Pépé or to my brother about it. Pépé would have taken me to one side, looked me straight in the eye and given me a long lecture covering the subject from Plato to Oscar Wilde, but actually telling me little that I did not already know; Matthew would have disposed of the matter in a few, contemptuous words based on neither experience nor thought. The summer following the trial I very nearly plucked up courage to speak to Grandfather Sheridan about it: after all, he was a man of liberal outlook, a doctor and had known Wilde. In the end, I did not do so: I had a deep distrust of the capacity of words to convey the information that I sought. The affair did have one benefit, however: it certainly brought the whole question of Greek love, Uranism, homosexuality, as it was variously called, out into the open – or at least into the press. I now learnt that it was not confined to a few retarded men, but something rather more like a secret, but widespread and influential religion. It was a 'purer', 'higher', 'more disinterested' form of love than that of ordinary men and women. It was the love of an *élite* that embraced many of the greatest minds that had ever lived. I even read Plato's *Symposium* in the Greek, with the help of a crib. It was to be some time, however, before I could see the connection between this 'religion' and whatever it was that Oscar Wilde and his companion had done one night in a room in the Savoy Hotel. Occasionally, this attention in the press took a curious form. In another number of *La Revue Blanche* I noticed the headline: BAYREUTH ET L'HO-MOSEXUALITÉ. I could hardly believe my eyes. What followed was the translation of an article published in a German review. It began by quoting an advertisement from a German periodical: 'Wanted young man, Protestant, very good family, to go on a fine excursion to the Tyrol, with a companion (foreign). Required qualifications: pleasing exterior, polished manners, enthusiastic character. Write Numa, *poste restante*, Bayreuth.

Enclose photograph, which will be returned.' 'Numa', the article explained, was the pseudonym of C. H. Ulrichs, author of
a number of apologias for 'homo-eroticism', which it went on
to link with *Parsifal* on the grounds that the hero belongs to a
knightly order, shows no sensual desire for Elisabeth and
leaves as mysteriously as he came.

I imagined that I knew a great deal about the world and its
ways. I had already concluded, with Aristotle, that *ethos*, or
what the Romans called *mores*, was not some universal moral
imperative, but the customs, the practices of the *polis*, the city.
Having spent my childhood in a country that had very different customs to those of Europe and lived in two European
countries that often had different views as to what correct
behaviour was, while belonging entirely to neither, I was peculiarly aware of the relativity of moral codes; for me, they were
like different languages, something that one could employ or
not, as one wished. I had not, like the young men I was to
meet in a year's time, led a life totally protected by home and
school, practising a religion that permeated both. I felt little or
no shame about sexual matters, but had had little or no experience of them. Yet that episode in Kennington had come to
me, out of the blue, like a blinding revelation, undermining all
that I thought I knew. What other arcane mysteries were yet to
be revealed? The initiation into human knowledge provided by
the Lycée Henri-IV, culminating in the final year's *classe de
philosophie*, had not prepared me for that. Was what had happened a mere chance occurrence, unlikely to be repeated?
Could such a thing happen in Cambridge? Perhaps, I vainly
hoped, undergraduates who became close friends did such
things to one another. It seemed unlikely: how could young
gentlemen who knew one another socially open up such secrets
to one another? Perhaps they had done such things at their
boarding schools and some of them continued the habit at

university with those who had shared their intimacy at school. Over the next few weeks, I made a few desultory visits to 'conveniences' when I was in the West End – the one in Leicester Square and the one in the Charing Cross Road, near the National Portrait Gallery. Just before Christmas, I even made a pilgrimage back to St Mark's, Kennington. I stood there a full quarter of an hour, but nothing remotely interesting turned up. I concluded that a rare combination of fortuitous circumstances was required to produce such an event.

After Christmas, I returned to the rue de Vaugirard in the knowledge that I had before me six months of idleness to enjoy the delights of Paris. As the weeks went by, I came to look with renewed curiosity at those vaguely 'oriental', not inelegant constructions on the boulevards. So far I had done nothing to explore the possibilities they might offer, partly because I did not feel free to leave the apartment at all hours for no apparent reason. I had to have some good excuse to hand. There were certain times of the day when I might meet a friend: I could not plausibly leave the apartment at ten o'clock of an evening, let us say, and return an hour later.

Then, one hot June evening, I was walking home when I arrived at the place de l'Odéon. I paused outside the *vespasienne*: one place, on the left, was free. I entered. My neighbour in the middle made his presence felt at once. He looked a few years older than I, with dark brown hair and eyes. He looked down at my erection, then up at my face for reassurance that he could go further. He began to stroke it gently. After a while, he indicated with a movement of the head that I should join him outside.

'*Bonsoir!*' he said, in a rather sibilant, caressing way. '*Tu viens chez moi?*' The interrogative was only just perceptible.

'*Je n'ai pas beaucoup de temps,*' I protested lamely. He brushed aside my objection with a smile:

'*Ça ne fait rien! J'habite tout près.*' We walked up the rue
Monsieur-le-Prince, crossed the Boul' Mich' and entered the
rue Cujas. A few doors up on the left, we came to an hotel. I
hesitated. '*Viens!*' he said peremptorily. '*Il n'y a rien à craindre.
Il est comme nous, l'hôtelier.*'[1] Submissively, I followed.

'*Bonsoir, Albert!*' he called to someone behind a half-open
door.

'*Bonsoir, Claude!*' a cheery voice answered.

It was my second 'experience', the first in a room with a
bed. Claude began to undress at once then, seeing that I just
stood there as if mesmerized, began to undress me. With the
same celerity he went to work on my body, his mouth arriving,
in no time at all, on my cock. I have no idea whether he followed the same routine with everyone he picked up and
brought back to his hotel room, but, on that occasion, it was
the best course of action. Had he begun *adagio molto*,[2] with
much caressing and kissing, I am sure that I should have lost
all my lust. He lay on his back, manoeuvred me into the
required position, kneeling up in front of him and, after more
frantic manipulation and mouthing, opened wide his legs and
drew me towards him.

'*Vas-y . . . doucement. Ne me fais pas mal avec ce monstre!*' So
completely innocent was I in the matter and so anxious not to
hurt him that the 'monster' was soon transformed into a
pygmy. I apologized profusely. '*Oh, ne t'en fais pas! Ça arrive,
tu sais.*' Then, after a while: '*Quel âge as-tu?*' I told him that I
was eighteen. '*Ah, tu n'est qu'un débutant!*'[3] he said gently. He

1 'You're coming to my place?' 'I haven't much time.' 'Never mind. I live
very near here . . . Come on . . . There's nothing to be afraid of. He's one of
us, the hotel owner.'
2 Very slowly.
3 'OK now, but take it easy. Don't hurt me with that big thing . . . Oh, don't
worry. It does happen, you know . . . Ah, you're just a beginner!'

resumed his attentions on my cock and, within a few minutes,
I came – he had already finished himself off. I left soon
afterwards.

When, after going down from university, I went back to live
with my grandparents in Paris, I was much more expert in these
matters. I became an *habitué* of the *tasses*. Before long I realized
that my success would be all the greater if I had somewhere to
take the young men I met there. I thought of the hotel in the rue
Cujas and took a room there expressly for the purpose.

In France, much is made of a young man's eighteenth
birthday. For me, the advent of my *dix-huit ans* was a day of
miraculous happiness. It was a Sunday. I woke to find that,
after weeks of dreary weather, when a grey pall had seldom let
sunlight through, when it seemed to be raining as often as
not, the skies had cleared and the sun was pouring down on
Paris. Summer seemed to have sprung fully-armed from the
head of winter. I woke to find myself the centre of every possible attention. Beside my place on the breakfast table were
presents not only from Matthew, Mémé and Pépé, but also a
parcel from Japan whose arrival had obviously been kept from
me. Inside were letters from my parents, photographs of them
and my present, a Japanese *netsuke*. It was, wrote my father, a
suitable present for a music lover: it represented a *komuso*, a
samurai turned mendicant priest, who travelled the countryside playing a huge flute, held vertically in front of him,
wearing a basket that completely covered his head. It was
carved out of ivory, measured only a few inches high and
dated from the late eighteenth century.

A table had been booked *chez* Lapérouse, a table in the
window overlooking the Seine and the *quais*. As we slowly
walked through the streets of the *quartier latin*, streets so
familiar as to be scarcely remarked on ordinary days, they
seemed transformed, as if all part of some dream that I alone

was dreaming. The others pronounced the meal to be excellent; for me, it was fit for the gods. I had never tasted such exquisite food and wine, though it has to be said that I was only just beginning to appreciate the finer points of both. Two or three hours later, we made our way home: the light had mellowed, but the magic was as potent as ever. We all took a belated siesta and my consciousness found new regions to marvel at as it sank into and out of unconsciousness. That evening, we went to a revival of Dumas *père*'s *Kean ou Désordre et Génie*, an apt choice for a stage-struck Anglo-French young man. And so the day of my *dix-huit ans* ended, to be followed next day by a quite ordinary Monday.

At French *lycées*, at Henri-IV at least, the masters set the tone by treating their pupils as responsible, intelligent adults and the boys respond by treating one another as such. Brute force may have its occasional, surreptitious victory or act of revenge, but it is despised by the vast majority, for whom intelligence is the supreme value. Sport and religion, the twin pillars of the English public school, are totally absent. The masters at Henri-IV tend to be older than in most French *lycées* because they are generally nearing the peak of their academic careers, the next step being a chair at the Sorbonne or the Collège de France.

On my first morning, M. Citoleux, whose task it was to initiate us into the Greek language, began his class with the words: '*Monsieur Renan est mort.*' He made the announcement as if he were privy to some information and we were the first to share it. In fact, Renan had died the day before and the news was all over that morning's newspapers. M. Citoleux then proceeded to deliver what I later realized was a model *epitaphios*, a panegyric in the strict Athenian mode. It is difficult for us at this distance to appreciate what Ernest Renan represented in France at that time. He embodied the kindlier, more 'saintly' aspect of the secular ideal. Of all places the *lycées* were his temples and the *professeurs* his priests. The Church, of course, took a different view and his *Vie de Jésus*, which sought to humanize Christ, had long been on the Index. As a young man, Renan had been destined for the priesthood: as a Sulpician, he had lived in the clergy-house at 50 rue de Vaugirard, which was separated from my grandparents' building only by the narrow rue Férou. That M. Citoleux should spend the best part of our first Greek lesson on Ernest Renan was entirely typical of the man. For him, the Greek world was a living reality and his pedagogic genius lay in making it so for as many of his pupils as would go along with him. For him, Greek was not a matter of learning irregular verbs by rote, but of bringing to life the heroes of Homer and Plutarch, the tragic story of Philip of Macedon and of the Greek democracies. In doing so he taught us more Greek than if he had confined his attention to grammar.

The following year, I came under the aegis of Georges Edon, *'titulaire de la classe de 4ᵉ'* – which means that it fell to him to teach us Greek, Latin and French, or *lettres*, as they are collectively called (in French *lycées*, these three subjects are always taught by the same teacher). Georges Edon had a genuine devotion to his younger pupils: despite his growing renown, he kept the *classe de 4ᵉ* until the end of his days, rather than opt for the intellectually more stimulating higher classes. Our masters at 'H-IV'[1] were as good as one could reasonably expect to find anywhere, but some inevitably stand out in one's memory, either because of the particular qualities of enthusiasm they imparted to their subject or because of some personal eccentricity. M. Edon belonged to the first group. Another was M. Dhômbres, who taught us Roman history in

1 The *lycée*'s colloquial abbreviation, pronounced 'Ash Katr'.

4ᵉ. With him, the Republic, the Senate and the Punic wars came alive: sometimes we would await the next lesson as we might the next instalment of a weekly serial. The following year, in *3ᵉ*, he taught us French history from the Republic to the Second Empire. After those two years with M. Dhômbres, no one could be in any doubt that history repeats itself: in the case of the French Revolution, the repetition was consciously sought by men who no doubt knew as much about their Roman models as M. Dhômbres's most assiduous pupils. M. Dhômbres made it clear that he was no friend of Julius Caesar (nor, therefore, of Bonaparte), but his republican sympathies seldom overcame his sense of impartiality. By a kind of forced antiphrasis (Dhômbres = *d'ombre*), we nicknamed this gifted *lumière 'Lux'*. Sometimes his sense of history could take a more immediate turn. Once, while supervising written work, he caught a pupil staring at him. *'Oui, oui, contemplez-moi,'* he said, *'la beauté s'en va, la laideur reste.'*[1] More memorable perhaps in his person than for his teaching was M. Parnajon, clearly regarded by all as an eccentric. While the other masters all wore very formal dress, dark suits, wing-collars, top hats and gloves, opting, as the temperature rose in June, for a straw hat, M. Parnajon would arrive, with the first hint of summer, in a light alpaca suit and a broad panama. To his pupils, M. Parnajon was known quite simply as 'Panama'. At this point I should admit that it was not long before I was known to my fellow pupils as 'Chéri'. The same fate befell my brother: when differentiation was required between us, we were given, like the Coquelins, the additions *aîné* and *cadet*.[2]

---

1 *Ombre* = shadow, shade; *Lux* (Latin), *lumière* = light – as a noun *Lumière* is used to signify an 'enlightened one', especially one of the adepts of the eighteenth-century cult of reason. 'Yes, yes, observe this face. Beauty vanishes, ugliness remains.'
2 Senior, junior.

The *lycée*'s penultimate form, the *classe de rhétorique*, culminating with the first part of the *bachot*, consists mainly of a concentrated dose of French and Classics. There are always two main teachers, one teaching Latin, the other French and Greek. It is the custom for them to alternate their tasks each year. That year we had Henri Chantavoine for Greek and French. He never appeared to plan his lessons or, if he did, he soon got carried away on an excited, exciting flow of ideas. His personal preference went to the poets and he would quote long extracts, in French or Greek, by heart. He would even bring in contemporary literature, sharing with us his views on the latest Loti or Heredia's sonnets. Aeschylus would lead to Leconte de Lisle, Propertius' Elegies to Sully-Prudhomme. I shall never forget the time he read to us the official account of the trial of André Chénier: it told us more about the French Revolution than hours in the history class could have done. For Latin, we had Paul Monceaux, another gifted teacher who was open to modern things, while making Antiquity seem young, fresh and close. A few years later he left the Lycée to take up the Chair of Latin Literature at the Collège de France.

The secular architects of the French educational system, having banished the teaching of religion from their schools, enthroned philosophy as queen of the sciences and decreed that the final year at the *lycée* should be devoted to its study. We had the extraordinary good fortune to have as our *prof' de philo'* a philosophical original, a man who devoted all his efforts to undermining the academic philosophy of his day and to seeking, through the discipline of philosophy, contact with a real that was not the space-dominated, determinist reality of science, but a real that existed in time and was therefore a constantly changing one. Our philosophy classes did not, of course, consist of Bergsonian philosophy. Nevertheless, while adhering to the syllabus, Henri Bergson's lessons were like no others. In fact, they did not seem like lessons at all, since the teacher did not appear to be teaching. It was as if he were pursuing some internal dialogue with himself, trying to discover what he thought about Plato, Spinoza or Kant. There was no 'playing to the gallery', no histrionics. He sat behind his desk, hands joined, his eyes burning intensely beneath his bushy eyebrows and huge forehead. For one and a half hours he spoke, without notes, quietly, slowly, in a regular, almost musical tone of voice, as if trying to seduce his ideas out into the open. He avoided all jargon, technical terms, obscure words or abstractions. Sometimes he would seem genuinely puzzled and ask us for our opinion. When he addressed us individually he did so with exquisite politeness, our surnames always preceded by a 'Monsieur', as if we were in some fashionable salon. But there was no trace of affectation in this: he seemed to respect the opinion of each and every one of us. Like me he was only half-French: his mother was English and he spent some time every year in England. Ours was the last year Bergson taught at Henri-IV. He had already been appointed to a chair at the Ecole Normale Supérieure. Three years later, at the age of forty-one, he took up a Chair of Philosophy at the Collège de France. This admirable institution is not part of the university, its lectures being open free to the public. There Bergson continues to hold spellbound a public of unique variety, from Society hostesses to anyone who wishes to hear the great man.

1904: St Petersburg

One windy September afternoon, I was looking for books to while away the long winter hours I expected to spend in my rooms. Among my purchases were two recently published philosophical works, both by friends, if, in the case of one of them, one can call one's *lycée* philosophy teacher a friend. It was with enormous pleasure that, browsing through the shelves at Mellier & Co in the Morskaya, I chanced upon a slim volume called *Le Rire* by Henri Bergson. No philosophical work, not even one on laughter, can give much comic delight. Yet the very idea of writing a philosophical work on the subject at all struck me as being in itself funny. I laughed out loud in the shop when I first saw the conjunction of title and author's name. There was, of course, a great deal of *classe de philo'* analysing of terms, but even the expository opening paragraph soon turns into poetry: '*Que signifie le rire? Qu'y a-t-il au fond du risible? Que trouverait-on de commun entre une grimace de pitre, un jeu de mots, un quiproquo de vaudeville, une scène de fine comédie? Quelle distillation nous donnera l'essence, toujours la même, à laquelle tant de produits divers empruntent ou leur indiscrète odeur ou leur parfum délicat?*'[1] If Bergson begins with grace, he ends with beauty. Like all true artists whose

1 'What is the meaning of laughter? What exactly is it that makes us laugh? What do a clown's grimace, a pun, a misunderstanding in a music-hall

work exists in time, he knows the importance of beginnings and endings. I shall try, as best I can, to render the end of *Le Rire*:

And so the waves struggle unceasingly on the surface of the sea, while a profound peace reigns in the lower depths. The waves get in each other's way, crash together, try to regain their balance. White foam, light and gay, follows their shifting contours. Sometimes the incoming tide leaves a little of this foam on the sandy shore. A child playing nearby picks up a handful of it and, a moment later, is surprised to find that he has only a few drops of water in the hollow of his hand, but water that is saltier, much more bitter, than that of the wave that brought it. Laughter is born like that foam. It signals clashes on the surface of social life. It marks out the shifting shape of those disturbances as they occur. It, too, is foam, consisting largely of salt. Like foam, it sparkles. It is born of delight. The philosopher who picks some up to taste it may find, for a small quantity of matter, a certain amount of bitterness.

On the same day I bought Bergson's *Le Rire*, I picked up G. E. Moore's *Principia Ethica* at Watkins's English Bookshop on the Nevsky. It would have been unfair to expect a treatise on ethics to be as entertaining as one on laughter. But, knowing Moore as I did, I would have been surprised to find a single sentence that brought a smile to my lips. Reading *Principia Ethica*, I was instantly carried back to those rooms in Trinity,

sketch or a scene of subtle comedy in the theatre have in common? What distillation will yield the essence of laughter, ever the same, to which so many varied products owe their pungent smell or their delicate scent?'

where young men scarcely out of school, with little experience of life outside school and university, many of them in the grip of passionate friendships that had no other means of expression than looks and words, would sit around the fire in one of their rooms, trying to define 'good in itself', as opposed to 'the good as necessary' (Herbert Spencer's 'naturalism'), 'the good as pleasure' (Mill's Utilitarianism) or 'good as identity with some Supreme Good' (all religion and much metaphysics). The book is dedicated *'doctoribus amicisque Cantabrigiensibus discipulus amicus Cantabrigiensis'* (To Cambridge teachers and friends, by a Cambridge pupil and friend) and the very first sentence of the Preface took me back to Cambridge: 'It appears to me that in Ethics, as in all other philosophical studies, the difficulties and disagreements, of which its history is full, are mainly due to a very simple cause: namely to the attempt to answer questions, without first discovering precisely what question it is you desire to answer.' In my mind's eye, I saw Moore, apparently paying no attention to what was going on around him, suddenly spring to life, leaning forward in his chair, eyes ablaze, letting forth a gasp of astonishment that brought the speaker to an abrupt halt, as if he had just uttered some obscenity, and exclaiming: 'I simply *don't* understand *what* you mean!'

The year before, in Paris, I had read reviews of the book but, such was the turbulence of my life at that time, I never got round to buying it. News of it also reached me from Cambridge friends. From the wilds of Ceylon, a rather bemused Woolf (Leonard) reported an enthusiastic letter from Strachey (Lytton) exulting in the 'wreckage' wrought by the book. Among the 'indiscriminate heap of shattered rubbish', one could glimpse 'the utterly mangled remains of Aristotle, Jesus, Mr Bradley, Kant, Herbert Spencer, Sidgwick and McTaggert'. It is altogether typical of the Cambridge of that time that the last two victims – sharing their place in the wreckage with Jesus and Aristotle – were associates of Moore's at Trinity and another – Mr Bradley – was a *confrère* at the Other Place. It was also typical of Strachey to allow what he regarded as the truth of his statement to be undermined by his irrepressible sense of humour, a quality not possessed by Moore or, for that matter, by many of his disciples.

1899–02: Cambridge

Moore had been the still, not always silent, centre of a small group of my friends at Trinity. This small, delicate-looking man, with his intense, piercing blue eyes and angelic face, had not yet acquired the extreme corpulence that is now his, a dozen or so years later: indeed, in his early undergraduate years, he had been a cox in one of the College boats. He was liked by most people, held in awe by many, loved by some few. He was older than most of us – seven years older than my contemporaries – at an age when even a year makes a quite disproportionate difference. He was not an undergraduate, but neither was he a don. He was the holder of the Prize Fellowship, which lasts for six years: his term expired the year after I went down.

The focus of Moore's influence was a supposedly secret society, the 'Cambridge Conversazione Society', known to its initiates as 'the Society' and to others as 'the Apostles', a singularly inappropriate name for a group that, far from being *apostoli*, 'sent out', stayed resolutely indoors. It was founded in St John's in the 1820s, but was soon dominated by Trinity men, with several members from King's. Two of my friends, Strachey and Sheppard (Jack, of King's), were elected Apostles in my last year; two others, Woolf and Sydney-Turner (Saxon), the following year. I was not supposed to know this, of course, but all 'secret societies' are more permeable than

106

they imagine: it sometimes seemed to me that I had one foot in the Society. At least two others in this group of friends were in a similar position. Stephen (Thoby), a very large, very handsome man nicknamed 'the Goth', was probably found insufficiently intellectual, though he had an uncle who had been a member. Bell (Clive) was not elected either, to his undying chagrin. In his case, the reason was probably that, although his family owed its wealth to coal, Marlborough had turned him into a country gentleman who hunted with the Wiltshire hounds. However well he might hold his own in philosophical discussion, his healthy, ruddy complexion, his air of possessing a self-confidence acquired elsewhere, went against him: he was regarded as not quite 'one of us'.

In my case, the objection was probably that my non-English education had left me bereft of a whole world of reference that they shared. More seriously, having attended a French *lycée*, I had spent my last year at school studying nothing but philosophy. The *classe de philo'* has been praised as the seed-bed of French intellectual excellence and castigated as a mental straitjacket, cutting the educated Frenchman off from the real world. In this respect a true Englishman, I can see both points of view: indeed I would say that both are true. At its best the French *lycée* achieves the first; human shortcomings being what they are, it too often produces the second. We all know Frenchmen who will argue, with great fluency, indeed without pause, almost any position that takes their fancy. What interests such men is not the search after some elusive truth, but the formal game of constructing and demolishing arguments, executed with speed and apparent passion; problems are solved, not by reflection, but by verbal legerdemain, with much play upon words. When I first went up to university I was astonished to find how much silence accompanied intellectual discussion there. It was as if the truth were something that had to be captured by stealth, by subterfuge. There would be much nodding and smiling, as of agreement, followed occasionally by tentative, almost reluctant dissent. When, in my 'French' way, I began analysing arguments with some alacrity, the reaction of others tended to be of mingled admiration and embarrassment, as if, like some *nouveau riche*, I had broken an unspoken social code. None of my friends was reading Moral Science, as philosophy is curiously termed at Cambridge, but all felt qualified to discuss it. My ability to cite Plato, Descartes or Kant was itself a sort of threat to their cosy world.

In my second term, I was invited to tea in Moore's rooms in Neville's Court. Also there were Strachey, Woolf, Sydney-Turner, Anderson (William) and Salter (William). We were all reading Classics. Looking back, it seems obvious that Moore was prospecting for the Society. I talked to him quite a lot, perhaps more than anyone else did. We discovered a shared passion for Wagner: he had not seen anything like as many of the works as I had, but he had the advantage over me that, during the previous Long Vacation, he had been to Bayreuth and had therefore seen *Parsifal*. We then got on to the subject of philosophy and he quizzed me about what precisely I had learnt in the *classe de philo'*. I felt that Moore had taken a fancy to me, but was unsure of how he could get me in his thrall. During my three years at Cambridge, I saw quite a lot of him but, as time went on, I became less and less interested in the kind of discussions that took place when he was present. Life, I already knew, lay elsewhere. I was altogether more mature, experienced in the things that the virginal schoolboys around Moore talked of endlessly, but never did.

For many of them, especially those, like Strachey, less interested in the technicalities of philosophical debate and less gifted in its conduct, the essence of *Principia Ethica* was to be found in the final chapter, 'The Ideal'. Here Moore suddenly declares: 'By far the most valuable things, which we know or can imagine, are certain states of consciousness, which may be roughly described as the pleasures of human intercourse and the enjoyment of beautiful objects.' On the question of 'beautiful objects', Moore admits that his analysis is incomplete: 'it would be necessary to attempt a classification and comparative valuation of all the different forms of beauty'. Such a study belongs to aesthetics and he does not 'propose to attempt any part of this task'. Nevertheless he can pronounce on the subject because there is something that people call beauty and that quality is possessed by objects that people call beautiful. The use of the term 'beauty', to the exclusion of any other, when discussing works of art, struck me as being a peculiar form of puritanism. In a sense, Moore never entirely escaped his puritanical upbringing and his adolescent 'conversion' at the hands of Baptists: his manner of conducting philosophical discourse always struck me as being shaped by the Protestant 'examination of conscience'. Again, for him, being beautiful was a work of art's way, not only of being 'good in itself', but also of 'being saved'. Beauty may be an appropriate term to use of a Ming vase, if one ignores its practical function, but is it really the most appropriate term to use of a Rembrandt self-portrait, let alone, say, *Hamlet* or Beethoven's Fifth Symphony, which Moore himself refers to? What interested me – and Moore never touched on such matters – was the relation between a work's 'shaping', its aesthetic aspects, and the emotions and thoughts that such works give rise to. It was no use, it seemed to me, to discuss such matters in the abstract, yet philosophy, Moore seemed to be saying, could only discuss things when they had been emptied of the contingent and particular, when the work's individual sins had been washed clean in the redeeming blood of abstraction.

If Moore threw no light on aesthetic experience, let alone on works of art themselves, how much more restricted seemed to be his account of 'the pleasures of human intercourse' and 'personal affection'. 'Mental qualities', says Moore, play an important part in the affection one feels for another, but they require such 'corporeal expression' as looks, words, actions. Indeed the appreciation of mental qualities does not, in itself, possess as much value as 'the appreciation of corporeal beauty'. Moore is dimly aware that there exists another world outside the charmed Platonic world of beautiful young men appreciating each other's 'mental qualities' – though his etiolated monologue has none of the cut-and-thrust of real life, the passionate jealousies, sexual activity and scurrilous gossip to be found in Plato's Dialogues. The question of 'human intercourse' is one of 'immense complexity'; much human intercourse may have 'little or no value' or may be 'positively bad'. There are, for instance, such 'great intrinsic evils' as 'cruelty' and 'lasciviousness'. Over and above its conjunction with 'cruelty' and 'great intrinsic evils', the very use of the word 'lasciviousness' gives pause. It is a corruption of the Latin *lascivia*, which primarily means 'playfulness', from *lascivire*, to frolic or run wild. Clearly, the corruption has come about through the Christian take-over, not only of the Romans' *imperium*, but also of their *lingua*. What Moore calls 'lasciviousness' the Romans would have termed *libido*, from which our 'libidinous' comes. But the Romans would have felt none of Moore's evident disgust for it. For them, it would have been closer to what a Frenchman would call *luxe* or *luxure* (the Romans' *luxuria*), a powerful force, physical in origin, that can cause tumult in human lives, but which is the source of one of man's greatest satisfactions, something that should more properly be termed 'sensuality', even 'sexuality'.

Moore's 'puritanism' eats into the very texture of his prose.

Not only is it totally devoid of humour, it also lacks any felicity of expression, any stylistic elegance, any sense of play, any life, all eschewed or beyond his reach, like so many worldly frivolities or lusts of the flesh. His prose is as pejoratively 'prosaic' as the verse of his brother, Thomas Sturge Moore, is 'poetical'. Yet he is not, at heart, a desiccated man; at times, whole surges of emotion well up within him. He is not a bad amateur pianist and singer: I have seen him play Beethoven's *Waldstein* sonata or sing a Schubert song, to his own accompaniment, and emerge with tears pouring down his face, his hands trembling. The music, because it was his own, yet not his own, allowed him to give expression to emotions that would have been crushed had they been entirely his own.

At university I seemed to be surrounded by fellow undergraduates in love. Yet I believe that all these passionate *liaisons* remained, as those who have not read the Dialogues in the original Greek have it, 'Platonic'. By my second year, I was in no doubt as to what I wanted, but had found no one to share either my 'soul' or my body with. I was attracted to none of those in my immediate circle in Trinity and, although, outside it, there were scores of attractive young men on view at all hours of the day, I could see no way of pursuing matters. Looks were exchanged, certainly, but such looks remain ambiguous, especially when one of the parties is unaware of what he is communicating by it. Through Strachey, I met a King's man, John Sheppard, who liked to be called 'Jack'. He was very small, white-haired and rather wizened in appearance; there was already something middle-aged about him, though his face was pretty enough. He pursued me almost as relentlessly as Strachey pursued him. He was an amusing, witty companion and, after the intellectual rigour of my Trinity set, I warmed to his lightness of touch. Eventually, one evening, after supper in his rooms, I gave in. Sitting on a sofa, he laid his head on my lap. I began to get hard and, very soon, his hand was at my flies. As I feared, the sight of his diminutive person on his bed did not fill me with lust. His spirit was very willing, but his flesh was inexperienced. However, to my surprise, and his, I think, I managed to bugger him, at the third attempt. We remained on good terms, but the experience was not repeated.

Through him, I met another King's man and Classicist, Lubbock (Percy). With him, things proceeded more smoothly and, for me at least, more gratifyingly. He had spent much of the previous Long Vacation in Italy and talked appreciatively of the beauties of Florence, Venice, Rome, always managing to blur any distinction between the beauties to be found in gallery and street. Emotionally, he seemed very self-contained, with no trace of sentimentality, and little in the way of sentiment. This sets limits on a relationship, but it can also bring greater freedom. Because one knows that feelings will not be hurt if one moves on to others, or frequents others at the same time, there is less danger of matters coming to a premature end. I ended up in his bed, or he in mine, some half-dozen times over a couple of terms.

On arriving in Cambridge to begin my last year, I took a cab at the station as usual. Just as it passed the new Roman Catholic church, in Regent Street, I noticed a man emerge from the ground – out of a 'Gents' that I had not noticed before. About a week later, as the last light was leaving the sky and that mist, so special to Cambridge winter evenings, was swirling around the gas lamps, I set out on the long trek – in reality, no more than a twenty-minute walk – to the 'Gents' that its *habitués* called 'the Catholic'. As is the way with these institutions, men of all ages came and went. As is also so often the way, those one might desire departed too quickly and too many of those one did not remained too long. I was already

112

familiar enough with 'the Catholic's' sister foundations in Paris to know that everything was a matter of chance. Clearly, the longer one stayed there, the greater one's chances of success, but one could spend two hours there and find nothing. One might also arrive and find Prince Charming awaiting you. Some times are more propitious than others, but the most popular hour guarantees nothing. That first time, I stayed about half an hour and nothing came of it. During that term and the next, I must have gone there thirty times – and ended up, in my rooms, behind a sported oak,[1] with some half-dozen young men.

Early one evening, at the beginning of my last term, walking down Petty Cury, my eye caught the eye of a neatly dressed young man. I'm sure he didn't realize it, but there was an almost hypnotic stare in his eyes, a look that expressed not power, but pleading. Hardly taking his eyes off me, he stopped and made as if he were looking in a shop window. A few yards on, I stopped and looked back at him. His face betrayed no other feeling but that pleading in the eyes, willing me to go back. I went back, smiled and said 'Hello!' He said 'Hello!' back, but did not smile. He was so nervous, he forgot to.

'Excuse me,' I said, lamely. 'Don't you work at Trinity?' I should have been very surprised if he had said that he did, but I couldn't think of anything else to say and I couldn't depend on him to keep the conversation going.

'No,' he said. 'I'm a bank clerk.'

'Oh, perhaps I've seen you in your bank.'

---

1 At Cambridge, undergraduates' rooms have an outer door, known as one's 'oak', leading to a small vestibule. To 'sport' it means to close it, which signifies that one does not wish to be disturbed. If one is 'at home' to visitors, one leaves it open.

'Yes, perhaps you have,' he conceded, without much conviction. 'I work at Foster's Bank.'

Ah, yes, I thought, the Puseyite confection of Gothic arches and tiled mosaics on the corner.

'Look,' I said, 'would you care to join me for a drink? We could go to a pub or we could go back to my rooms if you'd prefer.'

'That would be very nice,' he said, non-committally. I decided that the second would be the better option. 'You're an undergrad at Trinity, aren't you?'

'Yes,' I said. We introduced ourselves and agreed to use our Christian names: he was called Arthur. He was twenty, two years younger than I, of medium height, very slim, with dark brown hair, good-looking in an average kind of way. His only outstanding feature was those eyes which, from their bottomless, dark depths seemed to be saying something that was entirely contradicted by the studied sobriety of clothes and hair, the pinched, uneasy movements of his arms and legs, the careful, hesitant speech. Once past the porter's lodge, I hastened my step, Arthur following obediently at my side. We got to my rooms without anyone I knew seeing us. I banged my 'oak' shut.

'Welcome to my 'umble abode,' I said, dropping into mock-Dickensian in an effort to break the ice.

'Oh, it's very nice,' said Arthur, humourlessly, without giving the room a glance, without taking his eyes off me, as if I might disappear if he did. We were now in my bedroom. I drew him to me. His lips found mine at once and we embarked on what certain novels call 'a long, passionate embrace'. I had never kissed anyone so much before. I drew the curtains and began undressing him, but we soon took to getting out of our own clothes as fast as we could. We kissed again. My hands on his shoulders, I motioned him downwards. He fell at once to his knees, his mouth agape, taking what he could of it into his mouth, releasing it, smothering it with kisses. I led him over to the bed where, after more kissing, I went, briefly, into the *soix-ante-neuf* position. I then knelt up in front of him, my fingers stroking his neck. His thin body, with its soft, smooth skin, its yearning vulnerability, called out to be possessed. He let go of my cock and looked up, his eyes piercing mine.

'I want you to take me,' he said.

After the slightest indication from me, he turned over and lay there obediently, expectantly, as I applied the jelly. I thrust his legs apart with my knees and entered him. He gave a little, fulfilled moan. Had I not stopped, I should have come at once. After nibbling the back of his neck, I resumed and came. Staying inside him, I turned him over on his side: he had already come. We lay on the bed, both happy. I reminded him that I had brought him here under false pretences: would he like a beer? He smiled, for the first time, and said: 'That would be very welcome.'

We dressed, drank our beers and chatted. He would not be able to stay much longer, he explained: his mother would be expecting him back for supper. He lived alone with her in a house in Barnwell. His father was dead and he had two older sisters, both of them married. As we were at the door, making a supreme effort to say it, he said: 'You want to see me again, don't you?'

I said that of course I did: we arranged to meet the following Sunday. I walked with him as far as the end of Jesus Lane. For the rest of that term, I saw Arthur regularly, twice a week, on Sunday afternoons and Thursday evenings. We had little to talk about, but our physical passion survived, diminishing only towards the end. On Sundays, he stayed longer: we filled up the time by lying in bed afterwards and dropping off to sleep. We both knew that the end of term would bring our *liaison* to an end. Fortunately, his body seemed to understand from mine that this would be so and reduced its ardour accordingly. By the time I went down, his mind had also accepted the inevitable.

There were many among my friends who had sworn undying devotion to Cambridge. For them, university meant the realization of an undreamt of freedom to do what they liked doing best. Coming as they did from those prison houses of the growing boy, the public schools, they did not notice all the petty regulations that irked me more and more the longer I stayed there. For them, the obligation to attend chapel on Sundays and three more times during the week, to arrive back at College by 10 p.m., unless one has obtained permission not to do so from one's tutor, to wear one's gown outside College all day on Sunday and after dusk on all other days – which severely curtailed my extramural activities – for them, these were minor inconveniences, as nothing compared with the disciplines they had known at school. For me, they were unconscionable infringements of the liberties of a grown man. Many of my fellow undergraduates had come from homes that offered little in the way of aesthetic and intellectual stimulation; for them, Cambridge was an oasis of such delights. For me, that little county town and university had its charms, but it could not be expected to rival Paris and London in the way of operas, plays and concerts. And so, I decided, it was to the rue de Vaugirard that I should return at the end of my third year.

1904–05: St Petersburg

By the end of August 1904, summer seemed to be over and the 'white nights' a memory. A month later, the magical, all too brief Petersburg autumn had gone in a blaze of golds and crimsons. What we began to speak of as 'the rainy season' began and, like all Petersburgers, we took to wearing galoshes. Suddenly, in two days of high winds, the trees were stripped of their leaves and winter seemed to have arrived overnight. By October, the nights were drawing in, the temperature had dropped sharply and we were now wearing our fur coats and hats. The public gardens were closing earlier and fewer people seemed willing to linger during those magical twilight hours. In Petersburg, I soon discovered, those who interested me – the young – did not have places one could go to. I had a couple of rooms of my own in the Embassy, not too close to my parents', where I could entertain friends. But I had no friends as yet and it was out of the question that I should take back to the Embassy someone I did not know. Spies were everywhere and, as we were to discover a few months after our arrival, we not only had the odd spy on the Embassy pay-roll, but were subject to break-ins by the secret police. One night, after a dinner party, the servants were closing up the rooms, after the Ambassador had gone to bed, when two footmen discovered a man hiding under a sofa in the dining-room. After nearly killing him with a curtain pole, they handed the intruder over, battered and bleeding, to the policeman outside the Embassy. Nothing was heard from the authorities on the matter: the man was undoubtedly a member of the secret police. Spying worked in the opposite direction, too. Soon after the earlier incident, it was found that the Ambassador's dispatch box had been tampered with. Sir Charles was then sent a photograph by our own informant in the secret police of a letter from our Minister in Tokyo that had been taken from the box, photographed and put back again. As Russian losses in the war with Japan increased, the political situation in the country became ever more tense. Strikes and political demonstrations were illegal, but were happening nonetheless. The non-Russian parts of the Empire were getting restive. A few days before we arrived, the Governor of Finland was assassinated – not by some unknown terrorist, but by the son of a Finnish senator, who saw it as his patriotic duty. Then, a few weeks later, the hated Minister of the Interior, Plehve, was assassinated.

So I was already aware of the possible dangers of a British diplomat's son behaving as I was, without inviting *chez moi* young men I had just picked up. Nor were there the kind of cheap, easy-going hotels to be found anywhere in Paris. I was on the point of exploring the *bains russes* or *bani* (Baedeker mentioned only three), when I was initiated into the mysteries of this most Russian of institutions. One afternoon, I entered the *kloseti* in the Summer Garden. There were four men standing there; only one of them – a young man in uniform, about my age – was a possibility. Closer inspection revealed that he was a soldier: this would not be immediately obvious, since half the male population seemed to wear uniforms. In addition to the thousands of soldiers in the city, every kind of servant, all state employees, from the humblest clerk to the most exalted minister, all students, not just schoolboys, had their

own uniforms. But soldier he was: there was always a disproportionate number of soldiers here, usually from the
Pavlovsky barracks nearby. He had the fair hair and grey eyes
of so many Slavs, very slim, with high cheekbones, almost my
height. I went and stood next to him. I looked down at his
erection: his cock was almost as thick as mine, if not so long.
He took one look at my erection, touched it, then buttoned
himself up, gave my arm a little pull and left. I followed him
outside. He did not smile, as most Russians do on meeting.
Rather formally, he held out his hand.

'Ivan Ivanovich.'

'Markus Karolovich.'

'*Deutsch?*'

'*Net, Angliysky.*' The news was received non-committally:
the English – allies of the Japanese – were not popular at this
time. He then said something ending in: '*vash dom*' ('*chez
vous*').

I smiled, apologetically: '*Net.*'

'*Banya,*' he decreed. We would go to the steam-baths. We
crossed the Fontanka at the Panteleimonsky Bridge and
walked down the quay to the next bridge. During our ten-
minute walk to Tzelibyeyev's Baths in the Basseinaya, I
discovered that conversation would be difficult: he had as little
German and French as I had Russian. He did not seem particularly pleased by our meeting; no feeling of friendliness
escaped him; he seemed to have no feelings at all; he was very
unRussian. Several times as we walked to the *banya*, I was on
the point of dropping him. But he was good-looking, in a
straightforward, masculine kind of way – and several weeks
had passed since I had 'made love'. At least we would be in a
public place: no harm could befall me.

At the entrance to the baths, Ivan Ivanovich explained what
we wanted then, turning to me, said:

'*Dva rublee.*' I paid the two roubles – about four shillings. He had asked for a *nomer*, or number, that is, a private room. Our 'room' turned out to be a suite of three rooms: a dressing-room; a bathroom, with a large bath, quite large enough for two; the steam-room proper, with stove and wooden benches arranged around it in a semi-circle, on which one could lie down. In the dressing-room, Ivan began to undress, carefully arranging his clothes in neat piles, without giving me a glance. I undressed, then followed him into the bathroom. In the bath he washed himself methodically; I went through the motions of doing the same. He then let out the soapy water and refilled the bath with fresh water. We got out and he led me to the steam-room. Clearly, he intended getting my money's worth: I began to wonder whether he was interested in me at all. We stood by the stove, sweating profusely. We then lay on the benches. He now began to play with himself, staring at my cock. Then he got up and came and sat on the edge of my bench, still staring, as if he had never seen anyone else's cock before. I played with his. I gently moved his head down on to mine. He did not resist; indeed, I thought that he would stay there all afternoon. I lifted his head to kiss him; he moved his face away. I moved into *soixante-neuf* position, then, after a while, reached for my tube of jelly, which I had secreted in a towel, and started inserting my finger into his hole. He got up, as if shocked to the depths of his being, waving his hands in violent protest. He took the tube and began on me. With some difficulty, I explained, in gestures, that I would let him do it to me if he let me do it to him. With a great show of reluctance, he agreed. I had been in this situation before. I would show goodwill by letting him go first, but not letting him come: if he came, he would not let me enter him. I lay on my back and opened my legs. I lubricated myself and his cock generously. In case he might try and enter in one thrust, I kept my hand

round the base of his cock at first. After a while, I pulled him
out, pushed him on to his back and knelt up in front of him.
With my left hand I lubricated his hole again, then my cock.
Holding him down, my left hand on his right shoulder, I
entered him, slowly, but surely. He was clearly more used to
this than he had let on. I came in a few minutes; he a second or
two later. Reassuming his *sang-froid* – it had never really
deserted him – he moved back to the bath and resumed his
ablutions. Ten minutes later, we were in the street. My first
experience of the kind in St Petersburg had been satisfactory
enough, but curiously unsatisfying. As I was to find out, too,
it was quite untypical.

The other two *bani* mentioned by Baedeker were the
Voronin, on the south quay of the Moyka, not far from St
Isaac's, and the Central Baths, near the Tsarskoye Selo station.
The Central, though the largest of the baths, was, in fact, the
least central and I rarely visited it. My favourite was the
Voronin: it was near, on the one hand, the Military Academy
and the Horseguards' barracks and, on the other, one might
say, the Marie Theatre and the Conservatoire of Music. It
was also a short distance from the *kloseti* in the Alexander
Gardens. In my searches, I could do one of two things: I could
pick up a young man in one of the *kloseti* or parks and take
him to a *nomer* in a *banya*, or I could go straight to a *banya*,
take a *nomer*, then wander around the communal areas until I
found what I wanted. It was, in any case, a time-consuming
business: it always is, in whatever city one finds oneself, if
one is limited in one's tastes. It is as well, therefore, that the
time spent in the preliminaries should be as agreeable as possible. There is much to be said for a system that places its
lavatories above ground, often in gardens, and its *maisons de
rendez-vous* in bath-houses. I later discovered that the attendants in many of the *bani*, or *pays chauds* (hot countries) as

they were called in the argot of Russian Uranian circles, were also available as prostitutes.

Of course, being a Secretary of Embassy's son, I also had access to the opposite end of Russian society. There may have been a war raging on Russian territory, the Russian Pacific fleet may have been defeated by the Japanese at Port Arthur, but that was four thousand miles away: life in the capital continued on its extravagant course. With September came the return of the Court to the Winter Palace. Everyone swore that the receptions given by the Russian Court were on a more magnificent scale than anything to be found anywhere else. I went along with my parents to the first Court ball of the Winter Season. The Russian men were all in full uniform, their ladies covered in jewels. The dancing did not begin until the arrival of the Imperial family. The Emperor and Empress, the Grand Dukes and Duchesses, Ambassadors and their wives then opened proceedings with a mazurka. At midnight, supper was served to the four thousand guests, seated in several rooms. Because we belonged to the diplomatic corps, we had the privilege of eating in the same room as the Imperial family; Sir Charles and Lady Hardinge were even on the same high table as they. A servant in gold lace livery stood behind each guest, the serving of each course being announced by bugle. The food, much of which had been sent, with the flowers, from Paris, was, of course, excellent: as soon as the Imperial family left, other Russians dashed to the tables and made a clean sweep of what remained of it. This was just as well: they would probably not find food like that for a long time to come, for this was only a formal return of the Court. The Tsar had made it clear that he had no desire, in these troubled and, for him, troubling times, to spend any longer than was absolutely necessary in his capital, at the beck and call of his ministers. At the earliest opportunity, the Autocrat of all the Russias would take himself off to Peterhof, where he could escape into the privacy of his family. I now realized why the Imperial couple had looked so glum during their state visit to Paris, eight years before. They had never seen so many people at once: in Russia, they never appeared before their 'people'. In Paris, they were probably quite simply terrified, assuming that at least one member of that regicidal mob would try to kill them. 'But she never smiled!' people repeated for days afterwards of *'la belle czarina'*. The Tsar's disinclination to govern was all the more reprehensible in that Russia had no effective government. There was no office of prime minister and the Imperial ministers never met as a body: each minister dealt with the Emperor separately and the Emperor was not interested in government. Russia was in the extraordinary situation of being an autocracy in which the autocrat was incapable of taking a decision: he usually agreed with the last person he had spoken to, with a consequent confusion of contradictory edicts. Only one of the ministers was truly effective, Witte, the Finance Minister. This ruthless modernizer, of distant Dutch descent, the instigator of the Trans-Siberian railway, had been responsible for the massive foreign investment in the Russian economy. Not surprisingly, the Emperor could not abide him, but knew that things would be far worse without him.

In September the theatres reopened. When we arrived, in June, they had already been closed for a few weeks and St Petersburg has no Summer Season. Whereas English Society descends on London from its country seats in May and expects to be entertained by the best for the next twelve weeks, Russian Society deserts the capital for the summer, in favour of the country, the Black Sea resorts or abroad. My first visit to the theatre was to *Rigoletto* at the Marie, the senior of the three Imperial, state-owned theatres and the one devoted to opera. The evening had a particularly potent, quite magical effect on me. To begin with, the auditorium itself was the most beautiful I had ever seen. I looked out from the box we shared with the Spring Rices, situated about a quarter of the way round the sweep of the second circle. Immediately opposite the stage, occupying the height of two circles of boxes, was that alternative cynosure of neighbouring eyes, the splendid Imperial box. That evening, it was occupied, not by the Tsar, who rarely came here, but, Cecil informed us, by a party that included the Grand Duke Vladimir Alexandrovich. At first, the auditorium seemed as large as that of Covent Garden. In fact, this was an illusion: although it had the same width, its horse-shoe was shallower. But the most obvious difference between the two theatres lay, not in size or shape, but colour. In this they seemed to reflect the seasons at which they were most frequented. If Covent Garden's warm, welcoming red and gold seemed to evoke some ideal summer, the Marie, with its blue and gold, the blue turning the gold almost to silver, recreated within its walls the blue sky, the pale, but brilliantly silvery sun, the ice and snow of the Petersburg winter at its best.

Auditoriums may add magic, but only what comes from the stage can create it. The Marie was less often favoured by the world's great singers than were Covent Garden, the Metropolitan, the Paris Opéra or La Scala, though the singing of the mainly Russian cast was very creditable. What, more than anything else, cast such a magical spell over that evening was, quite simply, that it was six months since I had been in a theatre: my histrionic appetite had been starved for so long. During the two seasons I spent in Petersburg, I saw the usual *Trovatores*, *Figaros*, *Lohengrins* and *Tannhäusers*, as well as such native fare as *The Queen of Spades* and *Eugène Onegin*. Particularly memorable was a revival of the 1902 production of *Götterdämmerung*, with scenery by Alexandre Benoist. But what was an entirely new experience for me was the discovery of ballet. Incidental dances had always been a stock-in-trade of the Paris Opéra, but evenings devoted to ballet alone were rare. At the Marie, ballet took over the whole of Sunday and sometimes Wednesday evenings. In Russia, ballet, which had come from Paris, took root and expanded into an art form in its own right. While preserving that elegant, courtly language of formal gesture, with its original French terminology of *jetées, grandes échappées, entrechats*, it had become a romantic, expressive form of theatre, often based on folk tales. Under a Frenchman, Marius Petipa, the Russian ballet had attained unprecedented excellence, culminating, at the end of the nineteenth century, in a series of masterpieces set to music by Tchaikovsky. In our first Season, we saw a revival of *La Belle au Bois dormant*, with the famed Polish ballerina Matilda Kchessinskaya, one-time mistress of the one-time Tsarevich, now Tsar, as Aurore and Nikolai Legat as her princely saviour. For me, if ballet had a fault, it was that the music was often of inferior quality. By way of compensation, it boasted an array of splendid young men never to be seen on the opera stage.

I saw everything put on at the Marie, but rarely went to any other theatre. Apart from the odd French play at the Michael Theatre, given by visiting companies from Paris, there was little else worth seeing. Had there been plays by some Russian Molière, Schiller or Goldoni, I might have gone to see them, despite my limited command of the language. The truth was that the capital's theatre was in a poor state. The good Russian theatre, as I was soon to discover, was happening in Moscow. But there were very good concerts – in the Conservatoire, in the Hall of Nobles, even in private palaces.

By this time, I had become a good friend of Cecil Spring Rice, or 'Springy', as he was known to his friends. My parents would entertain him and his wife, in our rooms or they us in their apartment in the Sergievskaya. We would meet at receptions, concerts or the Marie Theatre. To my initial surprise, I learnt that they had only been married for a few months: they were obviously on good terms, enjoyed each other's company, but seemed more like old friends than a new *ménage*. In fact, they were old friends: they had met nine years before, in Berlin, where he was Second Secretary and her father, Sir Frank Lascelles, the Ambassador. He moved on to Constantinople, Teheran, Cairo, but kept in touch with the Lascelles family, in Berlin and in England. Then, at the beginning of the year, he proposed. 'She was crazy to accept an old bachelor like me,' he said. He encouraged me to drop in on him in his office and often found time to chat with me for half an hour or so, or he would invite me to join him for a drink before going back to his apartment. Occasionally, for one reason or another, his wife was not free and he would invite me to go to a concert or opera with him. He always acted as if we were in some unspoken conspiracy. The theatre was a passion we shared: one of his regrets about his chosen career was that it had made visits to the London stage so infrequent. At Oxford, he took up amateur dramatics: he appeared in a production of Aeschylus's *Agamemnon*, in which F. R. Benson played Clytemnestra. He told me how, at Eton, he had been befriended by one of the masters and invited to join the 'Saturday evenings' that he held for promising boys at his house. One Christmas, he proposed taking young Spring Rice and his friend Curzon to see Irving's *Hamlet*. Later that year, to the fury of his favourites and disciples, this mentor of youth was dismissed from his post – whereupon he returned to his Fellowship at the sister-foundation in Cambridge.[1]

1 King's College – school and college were both founded by Henry VI.

'Did you happen to come across Oscar Browning when you were up?' 'Springy' asked, giving me a searching, quizzical look. I knew exactly what that look meant: when I was at university, twenty-five years or so after his dismissal from Eton, Oscar Browning had reached the end of his career, now quite the most celebrated, for some most loved, for others most notorious don at King's. As at Eton, he had a special evening when he invited his 'favourites'. I was taken along to one of O.B.'s Sunday evenings by my Old Etonian friend, Percy Lubbock. The corpulent host moved sleekly round his rooms, smiling rather fatuously first at this, then at that young face, his fingers darting everywhere, with quick, searching, but inconsequential movements. Though I had never seen it with my own eyes, it was said that Browning often scattered a sprinkling of handsome sailors and working-class youths among his favoured undergraduates on these occasions. Yet, though he never allowed one to glimpse it, there was a serious, genuinely pedagogical side to O.B. In true Socratic manner, he encouraged his disciples to think the unthinkable, constantly coming out with shocking or unfashionable opinions. In addition to his work in College and the University History Faculty, he also founded and ran the Cambridge Day Training College for future teachers in the state schools. I cannot say that I warmed to him very much, or to his conspicuously frivolous acolytes. I was twenty years old and far too unsure of myself not to feel threatened. They certainly provided a contrast with my own group of friends at Trinity, who might be described as conspicuously unfrivolous, forever quizzing one another about the meaning of their feelings or what it meant to see a chair. I was aware of the shortcomings of both types or, rather, when in the company of the one, my reactions were those of the other. The two groups, I later concluded, had more in common than either realized: both were living on the edges of their bodies, their own and others'. They were, as a friend later put it, 'all talk and no action'.

I was now spending less time in the city's streets and gardens, more in my room reading, with occasional visits to the *bani*. Before long, winter brought another pleasure. Here skating in the open air lasted for months on end, far longer even than at Peking. The Neva itself was not always suitable: the ice floes that sailed majestically on their way to the sea in spring and early winter left the surface in too uneven a state. But I had only to walk out of the Embassy to find myself on the narrow canal that flanked the Summer Garden and led down to the Swan Lake while, on the other side of the Summer Garden, was the Fontanka.

In early December, my friend Maurice Baring turned up in St Petersburg. He was well known to the Embassy staff; he was a close friend of his fellow Etonian Cecil Spring Rice and he was a relation of one of the young Third Secretaries, Richard Baring, Viscount Errington. I had first met Maurice in January 1899, in Paris, at a British Embassy reception; it was his first diplomatic post and, as an unpaid attaché, he was on the bottom rung of the diplomatic ladder. We talked of Cambridge and Trinity, like one who had just been there to one who was about to go there. After a time I noticed that he was talking of Balliol and Oxford. My face must have registered admiration or confusion, because Maurice then gave one of his self-deprecating laughs and said: 'Oh dear, you probably imagine that I've had a brilliant academic career at both universities. It would be truer to say that I have been to neither.' Apparently, he had spent only a year at each, had no degree, had been only 'loosely attached', as he put it, to Trinity and Balliol in turn. As a result, the two colleges, two universities and two cities were inextricably confused in his mind. He could never remember which

I already had an inkling of what my own objects of infatuation might be like and they looked nothing like Maurice, who, with his huge moustache and rapidly balding head, was then what seemed six enormously long years older than I.

At the end of June that year, 1899, I went with Pépé and Mémé to London for the Summer Season. In October, I went up to university and did not see Maurice until the following Easter. Later that year, he left Paris to become Third Secretary at the Copenhagen Legation and I had not seen him since. Over the next week, he brought me up to date with his life. In Copenhagen, he became very friendly with the anglophile Russian ambassador, Count Benckendorff, and his wife. The following year, the Benckendorffs invited him to spend a couple of weeks with them at their country house, at Sosnofka, south of Moscow. It was his first visit to a country that he was to love, rather hopelessly, more than any other. I later realized that he also fell in love with the Benckendorffs' son, Constantine, whose mother fell in love with Maurice, the genial Count remaining beloved of the other three, and they of him. Learning that Count Benckendorff had been appointed ambassador to London from January 1903, he applied to be transferred to the Foreign Office at the same time. He stuck it for six months, then abandoned a career that he now claimed he never cared for. He wanted to be able to write full time. He approached various publishers with the project of translating the works of Dostoievsky into English. The response was always the same: there would be no market for them in England. Yet they were already being translated into French. He then applied to the *Morning Post* with a view to being the newspaper's (unpaid) correspondent for the Russo-Japanese hostilities. He arrived in St Petersburg in April, a couple of months before us and, after taking on a servant, an enormous ex-cavalryman, set off at once for Siberia.

Of his seven months covering the war, he said very little.
With a faraway look in his eye, he spoke of Cossacks bathing
their horses and swimming naked, by the light of a full moon,
like so many centaurs, in a lake covered with pink lotuses.
Once, only once, did he speak of the horrors he had witnessed.
In a battle at Mukden, a town I had been through on the train
to St Petersburg from Peking only six months before, the
Russians had lost 56,000 men. Maurice had witnessed only a
tiny fraction of that statistic, but the images of men shot to
pieces, of men with mangled limbs, of men with scarcely any
face left would remain with him for ever. He had supped full
of horrors. The *Morning Post* had now decided that it no
longer required a war correspondent in Siberia and he was
returning to London.

During the short time he spent in Petersburg, I saw him
every day. I would call on him at the Hôtel d'Angleterre,
opposite St Isaac's, and we would go to the Marie, where a
hand-written invitation awaited him. I was accustomed by
now to the extraordinarily warm welcome Maurice was given
by Russians wherever he went. This was not really surprising.
His charm apart, he was seen by them as an unconditional,
unequivocal friend at a time when Russia had few friends.
During his time as a war correspondent, he had not only failed
to hide his sympathy for the hopelessly inefficient, foolhardy
Russians, but he had spent the whole time with them, never
once going over and seeing how things looked from the van-
tage-point of the Japanese, for whom he had no time at all,
regarding them, with their modern efficiency, as the eastern
counterparts of the Prussians. But, with some of his Russian
friends, his reception was even warmer than usual, more complicit. Clearly, he already had a small circle of like-minded
Russian friends: he never said as much, in so many words –
with Maurice, everything had to be read between the lines –

but I suspected that many of them were 'members of the fraternity'. One such was introduced to me on our last visit to the Marie, as Prince Something Somethingovich. He spoke excellent French: Russians of his class often speak better French than Russian. There was something feline, infinitely smooth, unruffled about him. To me, he was exquisitely attentive, his eyes darting back and forth between Maurice and me, suggesting, by the merest smile, gleam in the eye or pause in his speech, the thought: 'Maurice, *mon cher*, is this your latest, or is he just an acquaintance?' We were invited to join him afterwards: '*une petite réception*' for the company and a few friends would take place on the stage. It was a tantalizing two hours: it was a long time since I had seen so many dazzlingly attractive young men assembled together. They seemed almost interchangeable, like inmates of a harem, but communication with them seemed as difficult for an outsider as it would have been with such persons. Something subtler than armed guards and eunuchs seemed to hold them in thrall. There was much darting of eyes and looks exchanged, but nothing that could be construed as an invitation to pursue. It was as if the eyes of superiors were upon them even here; the iron discipline that reigned in the Imperial Dance School extending to every aspect of their lives. There was another problem, too. I was with Maurice and was constantly being presented to older men who, while eyeing some young ballerina, felt obliged to waste a few minutes exchanging pleasantries with me or, worse, were obviously attracted by me. Towards the end, I did manage to start up a conversation with one of the male dancers and, before being interrupted, give him my card, but nothing came of it.

Maurice proposed that I accompany him to Moscow, where he would be spending a few days before leaving for London. We took the over-night *wagon-lit*, which left about eight in the evening and arrived at about eight next morning. After calling at our hotel, the Dresden, where Maurice always stayed, we set off on our tour of the city. 'My eye and brain may admire Sankt Peterburg,' he said, 'but my heart remains with Moskva.' Maurice appreciated beautiful cities as much as I did and I am sure he would have been a better-informed guide than I to any of them, but what really interested him were people. He had an insatiable appetite for people of all kinds, but especially simple people. He would listen enthralled, for hours, to some peasant recounting some endless anecdote that turned into the story of his miserable existence. He was in love with the Russians because, of all the people he had encountered, they seemed to him to be the most human, in their vices and in their virtues. He venerated the way that they endured, endured their appalling climate and their even more appalling masters, whom they saw as God's representatives on earth. Everything, in the end, was God's will. It was all, he said, in Dostoievsky. He preferred Moscow to Petersburg because, quite simply, it was more Russian. This was evident everywhere, from the Kremlin, that triangular bewalled citadel at its centre, the size and shape of Green Park, with its Arsenal, palaces and cathedrals, to the people in the unpaved streets, half of whom seemed to be wearing different kinds of folk costume.

Round the corner from our hotel was the Art Theatre, the real reason why Maurice had invited me to come with him to Moscow. It was, he said, the theatre of the future, a theatre of real people. He was a friend of the two men, Stanislavsky and Nemirovich-Danchenko, who, five years before, had taken over a very small old theatre, the Ermitage, and turned it into the Hudozhestvenii Teatr, literally, Artistic Theatre. But, two years ago, the Art Theatre moved into a larger building: the gilt, the crystal chandeliers, the velvet seats were removed, the wood panelling of the auditorium was painted olive green, new, angular lamps, with frosted glass shades, were fitted and leather seats installed. The stage machinery and lighting were of the latest. The proscenium was a huge, plain arch, a slightly extended semi-circle that reached almost to the ceiling. The curtain was also unadorned, save for a pair of white birds, seagulls, near the bottom, on either side of the divide: the seagull, the *chaika*, Maurice explained, was the theatre's symbol and the title of one of Anton Chekhov's plays.

That night we were going to see a play called *Vishniovy sad*. A *sad*, I knew from my adventures around Petersburg, was a garden. *Vishniovy?* Ah, yes, cherry.

'Good,' said Maurice. '*The Cherry Garden*. Though perhaps "orchard" might be better than "garden" – Russians have no word for "orchard", they usually say "*fructovi sad*", "fruit garden".'

It was the last of Chekhov's plays – he had died earlier in the year at the age of forty-four. Chekhov was still unknown outside Russia and none of his plays had yet been translated. Even in Russia he was better known as a short-story writer. By appearing to say nothing, said Maurice, Chekhov depicts the whole of Russia, even, one might say, the whole of life.

The curtain parts to reveal a very Russian room: through the tall, rounded windows, one can see that it is early morning and that the cherry trees are in blossom. A man and a woman enter and talk. After a while, another man enters: his boots are squeaking and he drops the bunch of flowers that he is carrying. There are noises off-stage and a party of travellers arrives, led by a lady, with a little dog on a lead. She seems to be the 'principal lady' – her arrival, however, is not met by applause. (At the interval, Maurice told me that she was Olga Knipper, Chekhov's widow.) More characters arrive from time to time: a very old manservant, wearing a top hat, white waistcoat and tails, who is sent off to fetch some *kvas*; a man who, from time to time, seems to imagine that he is playing billiards; a young man wearing spectacles, obviously an *intelligent*, an intellectual, certainly the only person on stage who looked remotely attractive – I assumed he did not wear spectacles off-stage. Everyone talks a lot – especially the lady – and occasionally someone laughs. The act ends and I have not the faintest idea what, if anything, has happened. The second act is much the same as the first, except that it takes place out of doors, at some roadside shrine. A long line of telegraph poles ends in what looks like a small town in the far distance. Many of the same characters talk and the man with the squeaky shoes plays the guitar. In Act III, more happens: we are back in the house, in a different room. There is dance music; I hear familiar French phrases, though pronounced with a heavy Russian accent – *'promenade'*, *'grand-rond balancez'*, *'les cavaliers à genoux et remercier vos dames'*. Couples enter from the ballroom. One of the women performs conjuring tricks but, most of the time, people talk. The last act has the same set as the first. The curtains have gone from the windows, the pictures from the walls; the furniture is stacked up in one corner. There is a pile of suitcases: presumably, the lady and her entourage are leaving. More talk. The sound of an axe striking a tree is heard. The lady and her followers enter. The servants come in and stand in line to take their leave. One of the women says: 'Farewell, old house! Farewell old life!', to which the intellectual responds: 'Hail, new life!' That much I understand. The lady takes up the theme: 'My dear cherry orchard . . . My life, my youth, my life . . . Farewell!' They all leave. We hear doors being locked and carriages moving off. The axe is heard again. Then the old manservant comes in, muttering to himself, then lies down. Repeated blows from the axe are heard. Curtain.

My understanding was not helped by the style of acting: it was of a restrained, unassertive kind that I had not seen before. Sometimes actors spoke with their backs to the audience and everyone carried on acting when someone else was speaking. What it reminded me of more than anything else was the acting of Duse. But Duse, despite her manner, gave the impression, as with all great acting, of immense power, albeit held in reserve. And, whenever I had seen Duse, she had been surrounded by actors who seemed to be existing in a different world from her: her art was so unique to her that it made all those around her look like posturing amateurs. In this company no one stood out: everyone was a Duse, or demi-Duse. But the most extraordinary effect was produced at the end when, to tumultuous applause, the actors failed to appear to take curtain calls, thus expressing their team-spirit and devotion to the author.

Afterwards Maurice took me back-stage to meet the actors. In such situations, actors, especially young ones, are often effusive in their welcome. These Russians, who had been so utterly unlike actors on stage, suddenly turned into actors playing emotional, high-spirited Russians, exuding warmth and sincerity. I do not for a moment question the sincerity of their feelings. They were, after all, actors, now being themselves: on stage they had been actors of consummate art playing, not actors, but a rather silly lady of the provincial gentry and her relations, a thrusting, ambitious estate-manager, neighbours and servants. Stanislavsky invited us to join him and some of the actors for supper at his favourite eating-place, the Slavyansky Bazaar. We left the actors to prepare themselves for their entrance on the stage of the real world and set off on foot, across the vast expanse of the Teatralnaya Ploshchad, or Theatre Square, past the Bolshoy (Grand in name and big in size – it held three thousand, half

as many people again as the Marie in Petersburg) and the Maly
(Little in name, but not, with its thousand seats, so very small).

The Slav Bazaar turned out to be one of Moscow's best
hotels and restaurants: there was nothing particularly 'Slav'
about it, still less anything of the 'bazaar'. We were joined
soon after our arrival by our host and his other guests, all men:
none of the women in the company was with us, not even
Olga Knipper, who had played Mme Ranyevskaya, nor
Stanislavsky's wife, Lilina Petrovna, who had played her
daughter. Stanislavsky was a tall, handsome man of about
forty, with a finely chiselled, fastidious mouth and a deep,
warm, husky voice. He was now without the moustache and
curious rectangle of beard under the lower lip that he had
worn as Gayev, the billiard player. Despite dark, bushy eyebrows, his hair was grey. I also noted the presence of the actor
who had played Trofimov, the *intelligent*. He was now without
spectacles and pallid make-up: I decided that he was attractive.
Whenever I looked at him, he smiled back, but I was not sure
if it meant anything. Afterwards Maurice told me that he was
Vasily Kachalov, the company's most talented young actor.
Earlier in the year, he had been a great success in the company's production of *Julius Caesar*, not, to my surprise, as
Mark Antony, but in the title-role; Stanislavsky himself had
played Brutus. Also there were Ivan Moskvin, who had played
the clumsy young man with squeaky shoes and Aleksandr
Artiom, who had played the old retainer: now looking a
healthy man in his early sixties, not at all a decrepit octo-
genarian. There were two other young men in our group who
had not been in the play. One was a big, burly man, with a
broad, genial face, perhaps a few years older than I. The other,
about my age, was slight of build, with a thin, pretty face and
dark, curly hair; he wore a ring on one of his fingers set with
a huge sapphire. He approached me at once, speaking good

French. He was not, he told me, an actor, just '*un amateur de théâtre*'. '*Mon ami*,' he said, indicating the other man, '*est aussi un grand amateur de théâtre*.'[1] I wondered if this were Russian code for 'Uranian', rather as some people say 'musical' in English. When, later, I sought enlightenment from Maurice, he laughed: 'Not as far as I know, but, yes, they are *friends*,' he said, with emphasis and a knowing look. He then explained to me that Tarasov, the one who had spoken to me, and his friend Baliev were both extremely rich and lived together in a splendid house in Moscow. They were devoted admirers of the Art Theatre and munificent patrons of it.

A large table awaited us in a corner of the splendid dining-room. There were eight of us. Our host sat at the head of the table, with Maurice and me on either side of him. I talked mainly to my charming neighbour, Nikolai Tarasov, since no one else except his friend seemed to have much French or English – though I soon found that Stanislavsky had a smattering of both. Every now and then I noticed that Nikita Baliev would look over towards us, catch what one of us had said, smile at his friend and at me, in a complicit, quite unpossessive way.

At one point, Stanislavsky turned to me and asked: 'You understand much of *Cherry Garden*?' I confessed that I had not: the acting of the company had been too good. He looked puzzled and turned to Maurice for elucidation. 'Ah!' he exclaimed delightedly and put his hand on my arm. '*Excellent!*' In French, I then said that I had found the ending unbearably moving: not so much the chopping down of the cherry trees as the plight of the old man, left, apparently forgotten, in the locked up house. Stanislavsky had listened to me intently, his right hand partly raised. When Maurice offered to

1 'My friend is also a great theatre-lover.'

act as interpreter, Stanislavsky agitated his left hand slightly by
way of refusal, while his right made a gesture that said: '*Voilà!*'

'*Vous comprenez, Anton Pavlovich et moi, nous n'étions jamais
d'accord. Pour moi, La Cerisaie est une tragédie avec des
moments amusants. Pour lui, c'était de la comédie, seulement de la
comédie! C'est amusant, la fin?*'[1]

No, I agreed, in the author's despite, the end was not amusing. What, I asked, was to happen to the old man?

'Ah,' said Stanislavsky, 'what kind of a king does Fortinbras
become? How long are Portia and . . .' He hesitated; I provided
the name. 'Yes, yes, Bassanio. How silly of me to forget – we
did *Shylock* a few years ago. Anyway, how long are Portia and
Bassanio happily married? I don't think we can say. Certainly
Anton Pavlovich didn't know what happened to old Fers!' He
then raised his left hand in the direction of the actor at the
opposite end of the table: 'What does Aleksandr Rodionovich
think?'

Artiom looked seriously into the distance and said: 'I think
he dies.' Then added: 'Playing old men doesn't get easier the
older you get.'

'You see!' said Stanislavsky triumphantly. 'If that isn't
tragedy, Chekhov only just stops short of it. The fact is, they
all assume that old Fers has been taken off to hospital. You
aren't going to tell me that Gayev, or any of those silly, selfish
people would bother to find out what had actually happened to
Fers!' He then turned to me: 'Our young Anglo-French friend
has raised a very important question.'

Our supper came to an end. I noticed that it was nearly
three o'clock in the morning, but then we had not sat down

---

1 'You see, Anton Pavlovich [Chekhov] and I never agreed about this. For
me, *The Cherry Orchard* is a tragedy with some amusing moments. For him,
it was comedy, just comedy! You find the end amusing?'

before midnight. As our party broke up, Tarasov took me to one side and asked me how long I was staying in Moscow. I told him that I intended staying on for a couple of days after Maurice left on Sunday. Would I be free on Monday evening? They would be entertaining a few friends and would be very happy if I could join them. I said that I should be delighted to do so. He gave me his card and we parted.

Next day, we resumed our tour of the Kremlin and Krasnaya Ploshchad (Red Square). That evening, Maurice was calling on a dear friend of his, an elderly lady, and apologized for leaving me to my own devices. We left the hotel together, I saw Maurice into a *droshky* and set off on foot, following the route that we had taken the night before. After wandering around the Teatralnaya Ploshchad, I happened to turn up a side street and found an underground *kloseti*. With beating heart, I descended the steps. I found myself in the longest public lavatory I had ever seen, in any country. It consisted of a gutter on each side, with a sheet of metal rising up the wall to shoulder height. In the dim light, I could make out that it was about half full: clearly, this was an important meeting-place. I moved along between the rows of greatcoats, rejecting first this gap, then that, before alighting beside what looked like a possibility. I already had an erection and had some difficulty getting it out. I knew from my Petersburg experience that I need make no attempt to disguise it: the Russians are a relaxed, tolerant lot where 'private' matters are concerned, even in 'public'. If they are not that way inclined, they will just give you a glance and look away. Once my cock was exposed, my neighbour's hand came off his: average, like his face. I decided not to encourage interest: better to explore other possibilities. I looked around me. The night was yet young and, in any case, even if I found what I wanted, where would we go? Even if I managed to get someone into my room

at this time of night, there was the problem of Maurice. I was
not sure at what time he would be back and, on his return, he
might check whether I was in or not. If I were, I could hardly
refuse to answer his knock. I decided that I would stay in the
locality, have dinner and then review the situation. I went back
to the street and turned right, continuing in the direction I had
come. Then, to my astonishment, some fifty yards on, opposite a church, were the Central Baths. Tempted to enter at once,
and eat afterwards, I hesitated. In the end, I decided that
hunger was the more immediate appetite to be satisfied,
retraced my steps to the Teatralnaya Ploshchad and entered
the Hôtel Continental. Perhaps, I thought, when Maurice
leaves Moscow tomorrow evening, I should move in here,
close to *kloseti* and *banya*.

By the time I had consumed three light courses and half a
bottle of wine, it was ten o'clock. The baths would shut in an
hour's time, so there seemed little point in going there now.
Gnawed as one always is by curiosity, however often the
evidence should dull it, I returned to the underground
Adonisberg. It was even more *mouvementé* than before. I
walked confidently to the far end and took up position in the
last gap. I took it out and stood there as if drunk, oblivious to
my surroundings. Within a few seconds, a hand was upon it.
The face next to me was more than acceptable, but I felt that
it was too late, the situation too complicated, to embark on the
ritual of human exchanges required to bring matters to a more
satisfactory conclusion. The sooner it was over, the sooner I
would be released to go back to the Hôtel Dresden. I half
turned to the figure beside me, opened wide my coat against
prying eyes and, with the lightest touch on the nape of his
neck, he was down on it. I came within a minute or two,
smiled at my 'handmaiden' and left. I took a *droshky* at the
rank in the square. Back at the hotel, I found that Maurice was

already there. We exchanged pleasantries on our respective evenings with, I fancy, more editorial licence on my part than on his. Tomorrow morning, he announced, I had one more duty to perform: I must accompany him to mass at the Uspensky Cathedral.

The Cathedral of the Assumption, as it is also called, was Maurice's choice of the four Kremlin cathedrals (or five, if one includes St Basil's, which lies just outside its walls). I was not, like Maurice, a connoisseur of ecclesiastical drama. Apart from the desultory Sunday services at the Legation chapel in Peking, whose sole aesthetic attraction was the Tudor prose of Prayer Book and Bible, my first contact with a religious rite was being taken by Grandmother Sheridan to Midnight Mass at All Saints' Church, in Margaret Street. Only later did I realize how different such Anglo-Catholic churches were from the usual Anglican ones. Later, when I was about sixteen, I was taken by a friend to Holy Week services at the church of Saint-Gervais in Paris. Apart from the use of Latin, which attracted me greatly, the services there differed little from those at my grandmother's church: they were, if anything, even more splendid to eye and ear. If I say that they were theatrical creations, I intend no disrespect by this: on the contrary, for me it is the highest praise. Only in such superior forms of make-believe as the theatre does one have that sense of losing oneself in something higher, richer, more significant than one's own humdrum existence: and what, after all, is religion but just such a willing suspension of disbelief? We owe our first modern theatre, the 'mystery plays' of the fourteenth century, to the Church from which they emerged. For some thousand years, the mass itself was the only drama available to people. It played a similar role to that of the plays of Aeschylus for the Athenians of the fifth century BC, complete with sacrifice of the god-hero. Indeed, in one sense, the mass went beyond Aeschylus, back to the primitive origins of drama in blood sacrifice, with the participants eating the hero's flesh and drinking his blood, not by *mimesis*,[1] as in the Athenian *theatron*, but literally, by an act of magic performed by the high priest, or so the initiates believe. When I attended a good performance of the *eucharistia*,[2] I felt as though I were communing with the middle period of Western civilization. Maurice probably felt this too, but he also wanted to believe in the literal truth of what he was witnessing, as those around him believed. He was tired of being alone and outside. He wanted to be at one with the communion of all believers. But, having lost one faith, the Protestantism in which he had been brought up, he had not yet found another. At this time, his election lighted, as in much else, on Mother Russia.

It was the first time I had attended an Orthodox service. The first thing I noticed was that there were no seats: the vast square space seemed full and everyone was standing, as one might well do in the presence of the Tsar of the universe. Here the entire audience was reduced to the same level, with no account taken of sort or condition; no hierarchy of stalls and pit; no family names inscribed on pews and churchwardens to conduct you respectfully to them. A duke might stand beside some smelly old *babushka*[3] of the people, going about her private devotions, repeatedly kissing the icon of her favourite saint-intercessor. To my eyes and ears, the service itself differed as much from the Catholic and the usual Anglican rites as they from each other – though perhaps the most immediate similarity with the first and difference from the second was the appeal to the nostrils with that all-

1 Imitation.
2 Eucharist – literally, thanksgiving.
3 Grandmother.

pervasive smell of incense. It also shared with the Catholic the non-participation of the congregation. On the other hand, where it differed from both the others was the sense of a secret rite being performed behind the closed doors of the *iconostasis*,[1] excluding the laity from the priestly sanctuary, where the bloody sacrifice is performed. This, while increasing the sense of the numinous, was, to my mind, an aesthetic loss, though classical tragedy, with its off-stage deaths related by messengers, did no less.

On our way from cathedral to restaurant, I talked to Maurice about the Holy Week services at Saint-Gervais. These began soberly enough, then, in the office of *Tenebrae* on Good Friday; the plainchant was augmented by responses by Palestrina and Victoria, and a *Miserere* by Josquin des Prés. The service began at 4 p.m. and throughout the candles were gradually extinguished until, at the end, the church was in darkness, a masterly piece of *mise-en-scène*. The week came to a musical and liturgical climax with Solemn High Mass on Easter Sunday. Here was the eucharistic drama carried to perfection, all in full view of the congregation. There was the gorgeously clad, hierarchized trio of priests, with their boy attendants, dressed in black and white, all moving according to a strictly laid down choreography; every so often, against the human background of monochrome speech and plainsong, would burst forth the heavenly sunlight of Palestrina's *Missa Papae Marcelli*.

Maurice listened intently, but he was beyond persuasion. 'Perhaps,' he would say every so often. What he said amounted to this: Christendom cannot be accommodated in the church of Saint-Gervais; millions take part in the sacrifice of the Lord's Supper every Sunday; what the Church has to do

1 The solid altar screen decorated with paintings of various saints (icons).

is for them, not for theatre-loving non-believers like you. It was true that what happened at Saint-Gervais was in no sense typical of Catholic practice. The inspiration of what was happening in that Paris church came not from the Church itself, but from a movement in the Parisian musical world, led by the organist Charles Borde and Vincent d'Indy, both pupils of César Franck and devotees of Wagner. Attending those Holy Week services were many members of the literary *avant-garde*, Mallarmé *en tête* – just as he always occupied the same unnumbered, but inviolable seat on Sunday afternoons at the Concerts Lamoureux.

Maurice was leaving Russia indefinitely. No doubt he would be back. After seeing him off at the Alexander Station, I went back to the Hôtel Dresden, collected my things, and moved into a double room at the Hôtel Continental. Overcome by curiosity, I could not help investigating the *kloseti* nearby. Perhaps the Sabbath had taken its toll, but it was less busy than it had been the day before and there was little of interest. I resolved to save myself for whatever might turn up the following day and continued my exploration of the city.

Next day, I spent an hour or so at the Central Baths. It was a rare pleasure to pamper my body knowing that I was relieved of the labours of the chase, that I was there simply to reconnoitre the terrain. I went back to the hotel, informed them that a friend would be arriving late that evening: if my *amis de théâtre* failed to provide me with a companion, then I should end up finding one for myself.

About seven, swathed in fur against the penetrating cold, I took a *droshky* to my friends' house in the northern end of the inner town. On arrival, the gates were opened and a short drive brought us to a medium-sized town house in neo-classical style. I was welcomed inside by an immensely tall young servant, whose hair was so fair it was almost white. He took my coat and hat and showed me to what he called, in French, the *'salle de toilette'*. He then led me upstairs to the drawing-room. There I was met by Nikolai Tarasov: I was struck again by the combination of grace and warmth in his manner. He had warned me that it would be *tenue informelle* and everyone was wearing ordinary suits, but he himself stood out by the addition of an embroidered silk waist-coat. At each end of the long room was a magnificent tiled stove, rising to the ceiling. The furniture – *commodes, secrétaires, fauteuils* – looked for the most part Louis Quinze. Along one side were three large windows, the middle one opening out on to a balcony; on the wall opposite, three tall mirrors; between them, three splendid chandeliers. This glittering wintry ensemble of white and blue, glass and gilt, contrasted with the warm colours of the carpets, which came from the Russian Caucasus.

Another attractive servant appeared with champagne and Nikolai took me over to meet some of his guests. He explained, in French, which they all seemed to understand, that I was half-English and half-French, and that we had met as guests of Stanislavsky. The conversation launched at once on to the subject of the Art Theatre. Nikolai told me how, from the outset, Nikita and he had been fervent admirers of what was being done there; so much so that, when the company went on a tour to Berlin, they decided to follow in its wake. It was there, not in Moscow, that they had met Stanislavsky and become friends.

It seemed that the dining-room at the Slav Bazaar had a sacred significance for the Art Theatre, for it was there, on 22 June 1897, that the actor Stanislavsky and the playwright and drama teacher Nemirovich-Danchenko met to discuss the foundation of a new theatre. Their discussions began at two o'clock, proceeded through luncheon and continued for several hours; they had supper there. At about midnight, Stanislavsky suggested that they continue their discussions at his villa outside Moscow; next morning, they were still deep in talk. The sky had never darkened and the flow of intellectual light had never abated: eighteen hours of discussions had produced the blue-print for what was to become, the following year, the Moscow Art Theatre.

I was intrigued as to how such a company approached Shakespeare. *The Merchant of Venice*, I was told, was part of its first Season in 1898; it brought the company notoriety because Stanislavsky got his actor to play Shylock with a Jewish (German) accent, which was considered demeaning for a classic play. Much more extraordinary was last year's *Julius Caesar*. At the first rehearsal, Stanislavsky declared: 'We are going to act this play as if it were Chekhov.' I asked what that could possibly mean. Various ideas were proposed, none of which made sense to me. I concluded that this was an attempt by Stanislavsky to shake his actors free of any preconceived notions as to how Shakespeare should be played. But the main innovations, it seemed, were in the shift given to the play's politics and in the treatment of the Roman crowd. Shakespeare's humane even-handedness between the two parties was skewed in favour of Brutus and his followers, defenders of the republic, against Mark Antony, the advocate of Caesarean tyranny. The crowd was not an ignorant rabble, played by a dozen identically dressed supernumeraries, but a huge body of citizens, a hundred and fifty in the street scenes of Act I, played largely by amateurs and students, each of whom was given a particular biography – and costume. Among them were priests, soldiers, senators, merchants, craftsmen of every kind; there was even a Syrian belly-dancer. For, said Stanislavsky, there are no such things as small parts, only small actors. The Russian word for 'super' or 'walk-on', *statist*, literally 'one who stands still', was banned. Nevertheless, these individuals did form a crowd, a *demos*; its movements were punctiliously choreographed, not as a single unit, but as a shifting combination of parts, occasionally achieving unity. What was special about the Art Theatre, it seemed to me, was not the scenic realism, which was to be found in the theatres run by Irving, Tree and Sarah Bernhardt, but the extraordinary labour of detail expended on the acting of every member of the company and the sense of the company as an *ensemble*. This was achieved only by months of preparation and rehearsal.

While this conversation had been going on, mainly between Nikolai Tarasov, Nikita Baliev and a third, older man, in his forties, wearing a pince-nez, who smiled at me a great deal, more guests had arrived. All seemed to be attractive young men. I noticed in particular the arrival of two, who could not have been more than eighteen. Both were very good-looking, one strikingly so. He was tall, stood perfectly erect and had a mass of hair the colour of chestnuts. As they came closer, I saw that he had grey-blue eyes, high cheekbones, sensuous, but delicately shaped lips. In repose, his face wore a haughty expression but, as he responded to something said, it became a veritable cinematograph of expressions as one dramatic situation followed another; his companion looked on placidly, smiling gently, his foil. I was consumed with lust. Though, to be honest, had he not been there, I should have been more than happy to have the favours of his rather overcast friend – or, for that matter, of half a dozen of the other guests or any of the servants.

Nikita Baliev must have noticed that my attention had strayed and took me over to meet the new arrivals. My proud *erómenos*[1] was called Jan Zalesky – the 'j' pronounced as in German. His friend was called Sergei, as far as I remember.

1 Greek for 'beloved' (male).

'Jan?' I repeated. '*Vous êtes Russe?*'

'*Pas exactement,*' he said dreamily, as if his mind were elsewhere. His face then came alive, assuming a haughty, almost aggressive expression: '*Je suis Polonais. Et vous, vous êtes Français?*'[1] I explained that I was half-French, half-English. 'Ah, I like the English, but I like the French more. I want to go to Paris. Do you live in Paris?' He giggled.

'No, at the moment I live in Petersburg, but I lived half my childhood in Paris.'

'And the other half in London!' More giggles.

'No,' I admitted, knowing full well what the response would be. 'In China.'

'In China!' The expected giggles mounted. His face lit up in wide-eyed astonishment, as if anyone who looked like me could not possibly have lived in China. By now I felt sure that he was making fun of me. His friend pulled his arm and told him in Russian not to be impolite. I avoided further explanation with another question: 'Are you studying in Moscow?'

'I'm at the Imperial Dramatic School. I'm studying ballet.'

'Ah, like Kschessinskaya, Polish and a ballet dancer.'

'There are many Polish dancers. More in Petersburg than Moscow.'

'And your friend, is he studying ballet too?'

'Yes, but he is Russian. His French is not as good as mine.' They both giggled. Indeed Jan's French was really quite good. His pronunciation was lighter, less emphatic than that of most Russian-speakers. 'And what are you doing in Moscow?'

And so this conversation, at once very ordinary and rather odd, continued. We moved into an adjoining room, where, on one table was laid a display of delicious-looking food of French inspiration with a strong Russian admixture, especially

1 'Are you Russian?' 'Not exactly . . . I am Polish. And you, are you French?'

in the *zakusky* or Russian *hors d'oeuvre*, with several varieties
of caviar. On a larger table, provided with chairs, places were
laid and bottles of wine lay ready. The guests helped themselves to food, then sat where they liked at the table.

One thing struck me particularly: everyone was smiling.
Usually in society people respond in a great variety of ways to
what is said; when they are not responding, they generally
look serious. At first, I thought there must be something
funny about my person that I was not aware of; then I saw that
people were doing it to each other. People were carrying on
perfectly polite conversations on the usual matters, but it was
as if their minds were elsewhere, like actors at the end of a
long run who were scarcely aware of what they were saying
and had forgotten to react to one another in the appropriate
way. It had been evident from the beginning that no ladies
were expected that evening, but only now did I realize that this
was no ordinary assembly of theatre-lovers, of the kind at
which we might be disproportionately represented. Here we
were all members of the fraternity and everyone knew it. It
was the first time I had been in such a gathering. As the
evening wore on, the numbers around the table thinned out. I
asked Jan if he would like to come back with me to my hotel.

'*Bien sûr*,' he replied, with a dazzling smile, and asked me
which hotel I was staying at. I told him. 'Excellent. That is
very near the School – I have to be back for classes in the
morning.' By now there were very few people around the table;
even his friend had disappeared. I suggested that we go soon.
'*Oui, bien sûr*, but first come with me.'

We got up and went out, through the drawing-room, to the
stairs.

'*Viens*,' he said, using the familiar form for the first time.

'*Tu es sûr que . . .?*' I protested weakly.

'*Bien sûr!*' Jan seemed to be sure of everything. Then, to my astonishment, he took my hand and led me up to the floor above. There, all the doors except one, were slightly ajar. He peered inside one room and pulled me inside, leaving the door ajar. We kissed excitedly: I had never before kissed anyone with such excitement. His right hand went to my flies. In no time he was on his knees, plunging it greedily into his mouth. After a while, he stood up.

'*Déshabille-toi*,'[1] he commanded and set about flinging his own clothes on to the floor. We stood there naked, our hands and lips roaming frantically over each other. I was struck by the contrast between his extraordinarily thick, muscular thighs and the rest of his svelte figure: I had never had a ballet dancer's body in my hands before. He had a beautiful cock, well above average in size. I looked around the room: there was a bed, but how could we . . .?

'Don't you think we ought to go to my hotel now?' I asked. '*Bien sûr! Viens!*'

He took me firmly by the hand and led me, in all our erect nakedness, into the lighted landing. There, he paused in front of the room with the shut door.

'*Viens!*' he said. '*N'aie pas peur!*'[2] He turned the handle and we entered.

It was a larger room than the one we had been in and was completely unfurnished, save for some mattresses at one end. In the dim religious light cast by a couple of candles, I could see that we were not alone, nor were we alone in our nakedness. Most of the guests and some of the servants had anticipated us. Our arrival was greeted by smiles all round. Jan fell to his knees in front of me. The others had abandoned their play and gathered round. Was this what actors felt when

1 'Get undressed.'
2 'Of course. Come with me . . . Don't be afraid.'

they were out on stage? Most of our spectators were well endowed, the three servants particularly so; indeed, the extremely tall, extremely thin, extremely fair youth who had greeted me at the door had the most enormous cock I had ever seen. Surely, I thought, no human rectum could possibly accommodate it. After a while, eyes gave way to hands and, in turn, my hands were filled. I pushed Jan's head away and pulled him to his feet: had I not done so, I should have come instantly.

'*J'étais sur le point de jouir,*' I explained.

'*J'espère!*'[1] he said, with a dramatic smile.

I took his hand and guided him to one side, leaving others centre stage. The older man, I noticed, now sans pince-nez as of all his other lendings, fell to his knees before the Nordic colossus, while one of the better-endowed guests, a dark-haired young man, began to fuck the youth. Before long, the other two servants were fucking two of the younger guests, while Jan's friend was being fucked by a handsome fair-haired young man. I reached for one of the containers that looked like huge marble ash-trays and lubricated Jan's hole and my cock. He did not resist: indeed I entered without difficulty. He then bent over and the blond Norseman, now free of attentions, pointed his huge member in the direction of his mouth, which took in as much of it as it could. I came within seconds – I could no longer contain myself. As I extricated myself, I noticed that the older man was bent over in front of one of the servants, while the other was slowly fucking him, to the accompaniment of loud slaps on his right buttock and imprecations in Russian that I did not understand but which, given the assumed tone of voice, I took to be abusive. I also noticed, for the first time, that our hosts were standing together in a

---

1 'I was about to come.' 'I hope so!'

dark corner of the room not, like us, naked, but wearing what looked like dressing-gowns – a variation on *Le Déjeuner sur l'Herbe*.[1] I could only think that they had been there the whole time, spectators in the main of all.

Before long, my erection was back. Jan then took me over to the thin blond giant and indicated that I should enter him. Meanwhile, Jan stood beside us, his right hand on the *membrum immensum*. Staring at the action before him, he began to masturbate himself. My entrance, for such it was, was like no other that I had ever made – or have made since. I did not have to force my way in, as through a dense crowd, nor did I enter in a mighty rush, nor even was it the more usual matter of entering slowly, but determinedly, at some point *reculant pour mieux sauter*.[2] That entrance is best likened to being received at a papal audience. At each new room, the doors would be flung open, then closed behind me; room followed room in this way, some larger, some smaller, until I found myself in the vast audience chamber. At that point, of course, the simile breaks down, for my movements then became a seemingly endless series of retreats and lungings forward. As I finally came, Jan hastened his movements and came too, splashing his sperm on to the youth's monster, still erect, as if to make up for the sperm that never came from it.

Before long, people began to drift away. Jan and I went back to the room where we had left our clothes. When dressed, we went down to the floor below, where, in the dining-room, we found the other guests, helping themselves to food and wine as they stood around. I found it a strange, exhilarating sensation

1 A reference to Manet's painting, 'Lunch on the Grass' (1863), in which fully clothed men are sharing a picnic with a female nude.
2 A common French phrase meaning to indulge in delaying tactics – literally, to step back in order to jump further.

to stand there, wearing my clothes, holding a plate in my hand, talking quietly to Jan, among people with whom, a quarter of an hour before, I had been indulging in multifarious sexual activity.

'Do you still want to come back to my hotel?' I asked Jan.

'*Bien sûr.*'

'I should like you to, but you mustn't feel under any obligation . . .'

'Obligation?' He gave a contemptuous snarl. 'Of course not.'

'Can we give . . . Sergei a lift?'

'Not necessary. He will go with Andrei.' He indicated the young man his friend was talking to. 'Well!' he said, giving his most dazzling smile. 'Let us go!'

Our hosts came over. 'I do hope you enjoyed yourself,' said Baliev, with a wicked smile.

I smiled back and raised my hands. 'You see, I am speechless with gratitude.'

He put his hand gently on my arm. 'But you must come to Moscow again – and come to see us. We shall also, if we may, call on you at Petersburg.'

'Nothing would give me greater pleasure than either,' I said, in diplomat's French, 'though I fear that the New Capital has little to offer in comparison with the Old.'

We walked to the end of the road and took a cab. As we rode down the Rozhdestvenka, Jan sat on his seat like some fairy-tale Tsarevich, more erect than I thought it possible to be, as if acknowledging the acclamations of a crowd.

At the hotel, I ordered a bottle of champagne to be brought to our room. On arrival in the room itself, Jan declared that he was taking a bath. Half an hour later, he emerged from the bathroom, smelling of the *eau-de-cologne* provided by the management.

'A few glasses of champagne and we go to sleep,' he decreed.

Next morning, I awoke to find that fallen angel's face on the pillow beside me. Unusual for me at that hour, the lust had risen within me: I had come to more quickly than usual, jostled into consciousness perhaps by the restless twists and turns of my bedfellow, who seemed to be acting out some dream of *jetées* and *entrechats*. I put my hand down and found that his lower parts at least had achieved consciousness. I reached for the jelly and began lubricating him. I felt no affection for this vain, self-centred creature so unfairly favoured by nature. I did not want to kiss him or to lavish on him any of the other amatory courtesies. I wanted simply to possess him, to force my way into him, to rape him as he lay there, unsuspecting. I turned him over and knelt up between his legs. He muttered a few words of complaint. I roughly pushed his legs apart with my knees and entered him forcefully, moving back and forth with long, rapid thrusts. Fortunately, on account of the previous night's exertions, I took some time to come, thus prolonging my triumph.

'*Oh, quel brute!*' Jan muttered when it was all over and smiled with evident satisfaction. He seemed not in the least put out by my rough handling of his somnolent body, but declined any further attentions to it.

'I shall now go to the bathroom and you will order breakfast, *un petit déjeuner à la française, café au lait et croissants.*'

I rang and did his bidding. I had not, I now realized, been a master at all, not at any stage since I first met him, merely a good servant, anticipating and carrying out my master's wishes.

Over breakfast, he condescended to be charming and talkative. He had known Baliev and Tarasov for about six months. Their 'at homes' usually took place once a month. Sometimes, however, Nikolai was 'indisposed': his health was very weak. Then the *réception* would be postponed. It was always the same, some guests were familiar, others new: last night was better than usual. The hosts, who were devoted to one another, never took part in the 'orgy', always content to look on, *'amateurs de théâtre'*, theatre-lovers who love by show. And who, I asked, was the Giant of the North?

'Ah, il est extraordinaire, n'est-ce pas? Il s'appelle Sven. Il est suédois et vient de Helsingfors, en Finlande. Il ne peut pas jouir, tu sait. Pauvre garçon! Mais enfin, il s'amuse bien.'[1]

During that short speech, Jan's face had traversed a series of dramatic expressions from astonishment, to gravity, to tragic distress and, finally, to a bemused acceptance of life's perplexities. What, I wondered to myself, was the truth of young Sven's condition: could he not come because he was so big, or was his size a result in some way of his impotence? Was he like the eunuchs of old who, I had been told, were not always fat, but sometimes unusually tall? Were they, too, unusually well endowed? Was that the secret of their success in the harem – that they could 'serve' their mistress's pleasure in a way that their masters could not, and with none of the attendant risks?

I walked with Jan to the Imperial Dramatic School, then went straight back to the hotel. I had decided to catch an early train, rather than the *wagon-lit*. I felt as though I had been in Moscow for three weeks rather than three days: I looked forward to ten hours of physical inactivity, spent reading, eating and travelling, in a perfectly straight line, through the flat, snow-covered Russian countryside – and that was how my quite uneventful journey passed. I would, I felt sure, be back

1 'Yes, he's extraordinary, isn't he? He's called Sven. He's Swedish and comes from Helsingfors [now Helsinki], in Finland [at that time a Russian province]. He can't come, you know. Poor boy! Still, he has a good time.'

in Moscow before long. Where, I wondered, were the Petersburg equivalents of Baliev and Tarasov? Maurice was a friend of theirs. Had he, I wondered, ever attended one of their *réceptions*? Even if he had, I should never find out: Maurice was far too discreet to discuss anything of that sort. Perhaps he had never been invited; perhaps he was not considered attractive enough. He often went to the *bani*: was it just that he loved wallowing in sheer Russianness or did he have some darker purpose? It was just the sort of ambiguity he delighted in.

December turned out to be unusually unpleasant: it was normal for the sun to go down at three but, that year, it hardly deigned to put in an appearance at all. Nevertheless the temperature rose, with the result that the snow and ice, unusually for this time of year in Petersburg, began to melt, at least during the day, producing a slush that made it difficult for carriages and trams, either on runners or on wheels. Even the ice covering the Neva began to crack, producing an archipelago of ice-blocks. Fog seemed to hang around for ever.

For me, the view from the Embassy windows was the great image of authority, of its absence rather, in the Russia of that time. The St Peter and St Paul Fortress, the very symbol of the state's authority, was invisible, lost in a cloud of unknowing, just as the Tsar himself was never in his capital and seemed quite unconcerned about matters of state, let alone about the grievances of his people. The Neva, usually rock-solid at this time, was cracking, revealing a dark murkiness below. The very seasons had shifted from their accustomed course: just as spring seemed to have arrived four months before it was due, so something new was stirring in the depths of society. Yet Russia had never been so prosperous. Wealth was no longer the preserve of the nobility; there was now a huge class of *nouveaux riches*. Late in the day, but with intrepid speed,

Russia was undergoing her own industrial revolution. Thanks to investment by state and foreign banks, the economy had been kicked into movement. Huge factories had sprung up around the capital and other cities; half the working population now worked in them. All this had been forced on an unwilling Tsar and a largely reactionary government by the Finance Minister Witte. The labouring class had tasted little of this prosperity: one-time peasants or sons of peasants, they lived in appalling conditions of squalor and overcrowding, often in factory barracks; they were fed in factory canteens, often forced to accept food and clothing in lieu of wages. They had no right to strike and trade unions were illegal. But the disaffection was felt not only by the labouring class, but by virtually everyone. Yet, while foreign observers criticized the Tsar himself, few Russians did, preferring to blame his 'bad advisers'.

Things were not helped by the worsening position of Russia in the war: rather than unite the nation, defeats, like the destruction of much of the fleet at Vladivostok in August, merely increased discontent against the nation's leaders. For a time, the appointment of Prince Mirsky, a moderate, relatively liberal man, as Interior Minister raised people's hopes. In a first, tentative move towards a parliament, he revived the institution of the *zemstvos*, or county councils, elected albeit on a very restricted franchise. In November, a conference of *zemstvo* councillors and liberal gentry met in the capital and formulated a resolution appealing to the government to unite the nation on the basis of a widening of the franchise and freedom of conscience, religion, the press, speech and assembly. At Mirsky's instigation, the Tsar agreed to accept a degree of religious toleration, to relax press censorship and to enlarge the powers of the *zemstvos*. On 14 December, the government issued a communiqué condemning all illegal gatherings and violations of public order, and warning the *zemstvos* not to meddle in matters that were not within their sphere. 'Nothing is working,' Mirsky confessed to Cecil Spring Rice. 'We'll have to build more jails.' He tendered his resignation, but the Tsar refused to accept it. What concessions were made were usually too half-hearted or arrived too late to improve the situation. The promise of change that came with Mirsky's appointment seemed merely to bring the discontent more openly to the surface. There were riots in many of the Empire's provincial capitals, Warsaw, Helsingfors, Baku, Riga. In September, a conference of opposition groups, ranging from Polish and Finnish nationalists, through moderate conservatives and liberals, to several socialist parties, took place in Paris. In Petersburg itself, bands of students carrying red flags could often be seen marching in the streets. On 11 December, one such group was walking down the Nevsky Prospekt when it was joined by thousands of workers. The police arrived on horseback and violently dispersed the demonstrators, slashing them with sabres. Hundreds were injured, many arrested and one student was kicked to death.

Towards the end of the month, Sir Frank Lascelles, our Ambassador in Berlin and Cecil's father-in-law, came to spend a few days in St Petersburg. One evening, after dinner, I stayed with the two ambassadors, 'Springy' and my father over coffee and brandy. The conversation soon got on to the situation in Russia. If there was any disagreement at all among the professional diplomats, it was only a matter of nuance. Sir Charles Hardinge was the least sympathetic to the protesters or, rather, he considered that their grievances should concern a foreign diplomat only in so far as they affected the international situation. He had no sympathy for rebels, but had come to the conclusion that it was time for the Russian autocracy to make whatever concessions were necessary to the maintenance of national and therefore international order. Sir Frank Lascelles agreed, but believed that a rapid move towards parliamentary democracy, led by the Tsar, was the only way of avoiding a violent revolution that might sweep the Tsar away with it. Cecil thought that there was absolutely no chance of that happening, that the Tsar and his government would never agree to more than a fraction of what was required, but thought a full-scale revolution equally impossible; the revolutionaries, being Russian, were as divided and ineffective as the government. Some reforms would be forced on the government; the opposition parties would go on arguing; things would continue as before, with civil unrest breaking out from time to time. In the short term, within a few weeks, it was to look as though Sir Frank's forebodings were justified. In the longer term, however, Cecil was proved right: Russia got some reforms, the danger of revolution passed – and civil unrest continued. A few days later, Sir Frank left, with his daughter and son-in-law, for Berlin, where they were to spend Christmas together. I was to see Sir Frank again, three years later when, to his evident astonishment, I turned up in Berlin, a humble member of Tree's company.

Russian 'Society' – as indeed most of Russian society – had little notion of the dangers facing it. Life in the capital continued unchanged. At the end of December, 'everyone' was talking, not of revolution in the streets, but of a revolution on the stage, brought about by a young woman from America of half-Scottish, half-Irish parentage. She had recently moved to Paris, where she had been taken up by Comtesse Greffühle and her fellow-American, the Princesse Edmond de Polignac, *née* Winifred Singer, the sewing-machine heiress. These two great 'literary hostesses' invited her to dance at their Paris houses, to enormous success.

Isadora Duncan's visit to St Petersburg was at the invitation of the Society for the Prevention of Cruelty to Children. For weeks, excitement had been mounting at the prospect of seeing the American 'barefoot dancer'. I went with my mother to the first performance. Several members of the Imperial family were present at the Assembly of Nobles that evening, together with a glittering array of St Petersburg Society. It was all the more astonishing, then, that, when the dancer appeared, not just barefoot, but largely bare-legged and wearing the scantiest of garments, she was greeted with tumultuous applause. The truth is that there was nothing salacious about the rather plain young woman on the stage, with her sturdy, muscular legs and her serious, rather uninviting expression. Against a blue curtain, on a stage bearing no more than a carpet, a few poplars and classical columns at each side, and a lady at a grand piano, she began to dance to Chopin's Nocturne in E flat. Throughout the whole of that evening, she danced to nothing but Chopin. Each piece was given a very different physical expression. In one, the dancer would run around the stage, making rapid movements with her arms and head; in another, she would move slowly, intently, as if submerged in some inner meditation; in one mazurka, her feet remained still, while the rest of her body mimed poses. Indeed the bare legs and feet, which had made her famous, were less used than her arms and hands. There were some in the audience who dismissed what they had seen as immoral, an insult to the home of ballet, but most people were deeply affected by it. I was at an age when one seeks out the new and challenges the *status quo*. It was a few years before I realized that Isadora Duncan was unique and unrepeatable; that were she to have followers, their dancing would lack her divine spark; that, if one saw her very often, one would tire even of her; that she did not challenge the sort of dance to be seen at the Marie. As it happened, among those who welcomed her most enthusiastically were dancers from the Imperial theatre. The following day she was visited at the Hôtel de l'Europe by Kchessinskaya, the most senior of the Marie's *danseuses*, who invited her to a gala evening, followed by supper at the palace of the Grand Duke Andrei, the father of her infant child.

Three weeks after Isadora Duncan had taken to the Petersburg stage, thousands of protesters took to the Petersburg streets. It was the beginning of what came to be known as 'the 1905 revolution'. I missed the climax and culmination of that 'revolution', which took place in October, some weeks after I had left Russia, but I witnessed at first hand, in the streets of the capital, the extraordinary events of 'Bloody Sunday' that triggered it off. In truth, 'Bloody Sunday' was itself the culmination of a process that had begun with the outbreak of war with Japan. On 2 January, we heard that Port Arthur had fallen to the Japanese. With it went the bulk of the Far Eastern Fleet: 30,000 men were taken prisoner, including eight generals and four admirals. At first the news was suppressed; it then leaked out. Public opinion, which had been deceived for so long by official reports, exploded with fury. Unrest spread, made worse by food shortages. The entire workforce of 12,000 at the Putilov engineering works, in the south-west suburbs, went on strike. The strike soon spread to other factories in the Petersburg suburbs. Within two days, 35,000 workers were on strike and their demands had widened from the reinstatement of four men, whose dismissal had been the original cause of the strike, to a forty-hour week, better wages, medical care, and so on.

For me, that Sunday began like any other: I got up later than usual, took longer than usual over breakfast, sat around in the drawing-room reading. Father, too, was there, reading some papers. We were aware that the political situation of the country was worsening: there was now virtually a general strike in the capital; there were severe food shortages; the previous day, even the street lamps had failed to come on, plunging the city into darkness by about four o'clock. We knew that a march, from the southern, industrial suburbs to the Winter Palace, was planned for that morning; that the authorities had been notified of its peaceful intentions; that its organizers had asked the Tsar to be present to receive from their hands a loyal entreaty to intervene on their behalf. We also knew that the Tsar would not be at the Winter Palace to receive them and that troops had been called in to bar all entry to the centre of the city. As far as we were concerned, this would be just one more instance of the Russian government's incompetence: its reaction would further worsen a deteriorating situation.

Suddenly a manservant rushed in: the Ambassador wanted to see my father at once in the official reception-room. In case I might be of any help, I went along with him. We found Sir Charles at the window, binoculars in hand. He told us that, after morning service at the English church, he had walked back along the Angliskaya Naberezhnaya, the English Quay, and had seen large crowds of people crossing the two bridges from Vasily Ostrov. By the time he reached the Embassy, he could hear the noise of a crowd gathered on the other side of the Troitsky Bridge and went straight up to the first floor for a better view. 'Look,' he said, 'they're trying to cross the bridge.' It was a cold, but beautifully clear, sunny day. On the other side of the bridge, a huge crowd had gathered and was shouting, presumably at the massed infantry and cavalry that were preventing anyone from getting near the bridge. We had been there for ten minutes when shots rang out. The infuriated crowd tried to surge forward; the shooting continued for several minutes, followed by a charge from cavalry, wielding swords.

The Ambassador suggested that some of the younger

members of staff should go out into the streets and find out
what was happening, while he would try and make contact
with members of the government. I said that I should go out
at once; Father said that he would go with me. Thinking to
avoid the crowd of people gathering on the quay, we left the
Embassy by the back gate and made our way down Millionaya
ulitsa – Millionaires' Street, so called on account of its many
large town houses – with the intention of reaching the Winter
Palace. Before very long, we found that we could go no further:
the crowd gradually thickened to the point at which it was
impossible to move forward. We cut down a side street to the
Moyka, continuing along the quay until we reached the
Nevsky Prospekt. There were more crowds there too but,
since there seemed to be no traffic, the immensely wide road
gave enough room to move. We decided to walk in the direction of the Admiralty, but, at the edge of the Alexander
Garden, the crowd became dense once more. People were talking to perfect strangers, asking questions, retailing bits of
information – or rumour.

Over the next few days, the Embassy pieced together the
truth of what had happened. The march had been the idea of
Father Georgei Gapon, a prison chaplain who, the previous
February, had been encouraged by the Ministry of the Interior
to form an 'Assembly of St Petersburg Factory Workers'. This
was not a trade union, which would have been illegal, but an
attempt by the government to channel workers' grievances into
economic demands, away from political activities. As the situation worsened and the government did nothing to alleviate it,
Gapon decided to write a petition that he himself, accompanied
by as many of the strikers as chose to join him, would present
to the Tsar. He was joined by leading members of the Social
Revolutionaries, the 'indigenous' socialist party – at this time
the Marxist Social Democrats were a very small group and its

leader, known as 'Lenin', was in exile in Switzerland. The petition was drawn up. This long, curious document began with expressions of loyalty and appeals to religious conscience: 'We working men of St Petersburg have come to you, our ruler, in search of justice and protection . . . We are not regarded as human beings . . . we are treated like slaves . . . Is this, O sovereign, in accordance with the laws of God, by whose grace you reign?' There followed radical political demands that had clearly come from the Social Revolutionaries: universal compulsory education; freedom of the press, association and conscience; the freeing of political prisoners; a progressive income tax; land reform; an end to the war with Japan.

And so, on that fatal morning of 22 January, about 150,000 men, women and children, in their best Sunday clothes, many of them singing hymns, armed with no more than religious banners and portraits of the Tsar, set out on their five-mile walk along the snow-covered streets from the Putilov works to the Winter Palace. At the head of the march, in full ecclesiastical dress, was Father Gapon, flanked, on one side, by another priest and, on the other, by the Social Revolutionary leader, Pinchas Rutenberg. They got no further than the Narva Gate before they were stopped in their tracks by soldiers barring the way. A company of Cossack cavalry bore down on them, wielding whips with leaded knouts or slashing them with their swords. The terrified crowd dispersed, some of the more determined continuing on their way up side streets. Meanwhile, to the north and east of the city, thousands more had gathered and were walking towards the centre: these were the demonstrators that Sir Charles had seen crossing from Vasily Island and we had seen being shot down at the other end of the Troitsky Bridge. Shots were heard in various parts of the city until midnight.

Next day, an uneasy peace reigned: the crowds had

dispersed, but the troops remained at their posts. It was calculated that up to one thousand people had been killed and many more wounded. Prince Mirsky, the liberal Minister of the Interior, and the Prefect of Police, neither of whom had sanctioned the shootings, resigned. Gapon had disappeared: weeks later, we learnt that he had been spirited away by the police and sent to France, where he stayed, in considerable comfort, for the best part of a year. He certainly had great sympathy for his labouring flock and did his best to bring about a settlement of their grievances, but it is also likely that he was in the pay of the police the whole time. This certainly became the view of the Social Revolutionaries. (A year later, he was seized, brought before a private Social Revolutionary court, presided over by his fellow-marcher Rutenberg, condemned to death and hanged.) The following day, plain-clothes police turned up at the Petersburg branch of the Crédit Lyonnais and demanded that a safe bearing a particular name and number be opened. They seized the contents, a very large sum of money, and left, refusing to sign a receipt. The account was Gapon's and was well known to the police. Nothing in Russia is what it seems.

At the time of 'Bloody Sunday' some 125,000 men and women were on strike in Petersburg. Over the next few weeks, there was a drift back to work; life in the city took on a semblance of normality, but there was a sense in which things would never be the same again. People would not forget what had happened and, even among many people who had never concerned themselves with political matters, there was an awakening to the need for change, not small, unconnected changes wrung out of a reluctant government, but the need to match Russia's undoubted economic progress, with greater social justice and a modern constitutional democracy. In Petersburg, students held meetings, attended by thousands, passed resolutions declaring solidarity with the workers and themselves went on strike. The liberal professions joined in, forming a Union of Unions. As a foreigner and a diplomat's son, I could not become involved in such activities but I, too, had been deeply affected by the events of 'Bloody Sunday'. Hitherto I had 'taken an interest' in political and social matters, regarding myself as a well-informed, right-thinking liberal, but they had held little sway over my emotions.

As the long winter dragged on, as the snow lost its pristine brightness, there were sunless days when the air outside was not exhilaratingly cold and dry, but cold, damp, foggy. It was then that my thoughts went out to Matthew, luxuriating in the English summer of a Moroccan winter. I remembered the few weeks that I had spent with him in the autumn of 1903. At first, Tangiers seemed in no mood to shift the despondency that I felt after taking my final leave of Mémé and Pépé, the rue de Vaugirard and, it seemed, my own past. The Legation building overlooked a cemetery and, all day long, funeral followed funeral, with endless cries of *'La ilaha illa Allah. Mahamed Rasal Allah.'*[1] Fortunately, unlike poor Matthew, I did not have to spend all day in view and earshot of the cemetery. With a population smaller than that of Cambridge, Tangiers had nothing but itself to offer; no theatre, no social life other than that provided by the embassies for each other. Its theatre, its inexhaustible entertainment, was to be found in its streets and gardens.

The gardens proved especially fruitful. I was sure that Matthew did not share my sexual tastes and, given his situation, he would no doubt have had to abstain even if he had. By what divinely thrust on *peripeteia*[2] was Matthew in

1 There is only one God and Mohammed is his prophet.
2 Reversal of fortune, a key term in Aristotle's *Tragedy*.

Tangiers, unable to avail himself of its few, but considerable delights, while I shut myself up in front of my fire in a city that Matthew would have been overjoyed to be in. I arrived in Tangiers quite ignorant of its ways, its *ethos*. I knew that women would be rarely seen in public, and then veiled and guarded. What I knew nothing of, and it took me a few days to understand it, was that the male population had hit upon the obvious solution to the problem: it had sex with itself. All unmarried men – and, I later discovered, many married men, too – had friends to whom they were more devoted than they would be to any woman and with whom they found sexual gratification. Moreover, for a derisory sum, almost all adolescent boys and many young men were willing to sell their favours. This was not done in an overt, obvious way, as with prostitutes in Paris or London. The question of 'payment' arose only towards the end of proceedings and took the most tactful, indirect form. Matters always began with a broad smile. If this was reciprocated, it would be followed by a request to help you carry your bags, or polite questions as to where you came from, how you liked Tangiers, and so on. If the boy was quite young, he might ask if you would like to be his friend. A walk would be proposed. If it were still broad daylight, this might lead to the *bain turque* or further afield to some deserted spot by the seashore; if light was already failing, some bushes in the gardens would provide cover enough. From the two dozen or so encounters that I made in this way, I could already rise to tentative generalizations. The boys were usually called Mohammed, sometimes Ali, occasionally some name I had never heard of and instantly forgot. They always expected to be sucked: they were generally well endowed and assumed that this was what one wanted to do. They often took a little persuading to return the favour: being all circumcized, they regarded my foreskin as a possible harbour of

infection. Indeed they tried to ignore it by leaving it pulled
right back, rather than moving it backwards and forwards.
Few were willing to be fucked. Those who were could be recognized by their obvious femininity of gesture and gait, and
they charged a little more for their services. Had I had the
strength I could have spent the whole of every day indulging
in such pleasures. As it was I cultivated the art of *ejaculatio
retarda*, which might have given offence or led to doubts as to
my virility, were it not being practised by everybody else, with
the same aim in view. In this way, we were able to avoid having
to retire from the field for some hours. Though seldom bringing me the ultimate satisfaction, the gardens of Tangiers, and
the hills and seashore outside the town, in the mild evening
air, provided a paradise of sensual delight compared with the
gloomy hours of time expended, often to little effect, on the
boulevards of Paris.

I spent many of those long winter hours in my room over-
looking the Marsovo Pole reading. Before leaving for London,
Maurice had said: 'You'll never understand Russia till you
read Dostoievsky. If you can't read him in Russian, at least
read him in French.' At Watkins's I did pick up an old copy of
Buried Alive or Ten Years of Penal Servitude in Siberia, by
'Fedor Dostoyeffsky', published by Longman, Green as early
as 1881. But, as Maurice had warned me, nothing more of
Dostoievsky was available in English. At Mellier & Co, the
French proved to be, as usual, more open to foreign literature:
two of his books had been translated into French. *Les Frères
Karamasov* would have to be ordered from Paris, but I was
able to walk off with a three-volume copy of *Le Crîme et le
Châtiment* published by our estimable Paris neighbours of the
rue Garancière, the Librairie Plon. I also bought a copy of
the novel in Russian: when I was feeling studious, I read it as
best I could, using the French translation as a crib. More often,

I got so caught up with the story that I abandoned this haltering *régime* and continued in the French alone.

I read much of the book during a week when I was confined to my room with a bad cold. It was a strange, haunting, long drawn out experience to return, day after day, to a world so different from anything I had ever known, peopled by characters so different from any I had ever read about, let alone known, with anxieties and concerns, feelings and ideas so alien to mine. I could not entirely explain that sense of alienation. There I was, living in the city in which the novel is set; Raskolnikov, its hero, was twenty-three, I twenty-four; he refers to himself as an 'ex-student', which is what I was. Yet I still felt like a stranger in that world, in a way that I had not when reading Tolstoy.

'When you've read *Crime and Punishment*,' said Maurice, 'go and see where Dostoievsky lived when he was writing it. You'll see that a lot of the book takes place around there.' He then jotted down a few addresses and marked them on a map. 'To understand Russia, you must get out, go to parts of the city that never saw the work of Peter the Great and his successors. A few miles from the Winter Palace and you might be in Moscow.' Maurice warned me that the Haymarket district still had some of the character once possessed of its London namesake, a seething mass of humanity desperately bent on survival by means of petty trade, robbery and prostitution. When I came to plan my first Dostoievskian 'pilgrimage', for such it had become in my mind, I was astonished to see that the area where much of the novel takes place was no more than a mile from the most elegant part of the Nevsky Prospekt. Raskolnikov seems to spend much of his time walking up and down and criss-crossing the Yekaterininsky Canal, which he refers to simply as 'the Canal'. Other places are indicated by the initial letter of their name, but they are easy enough to locate.

So, one morning, armed with my Dostoievsky itinerary, I set out. I left the Embassy by the rear entrance and traversed the Field of Mars, past the Pavlovsky Barracks, behind whose splendid pale yellow façade dwelt hundreds of the god's adepts. Avoiding the possible temptations of the Summer Garden, I crossed the Mikhailovsky Bridge, to the Academy of Engineering, where Dostoievsky spent five years training to become a military engineer. On one of his walks, Raskolnikov toys with the idea that the Summer Garden should be extended over the bleak parade ground of the Marsovo Pole to the Mikhailovsky Garden, thus creating a continuous sequence of parks, rather like, though, of course, he does not say so, a miniature version of the royal parks in London. I emerged from the Mikhailovsky Garden at the Church of the Resurrection, more colloquially known by the curious name of the *Khram 'Spasa na krovi'* or Church on Spilled Blood, the blood in question being, not that of the Resurrected Lord, but of the unresurrected Tsar Alexander II: another imperial assassination, this time by Nihilists, in 1881. His son, Alexander III, ordered that a church be built on the exact spot where his father's blood had been shed, which explains why the west end of the church extends partly into the pavement. I was now on the quay of the Yekaterininsky Canal. I passed the side of the Alexander III Museum and the back of the Michael Theatre, crossing the Nevsky Prospekt at the Kazansky Bridge. There, on the right, stood the enormous mass of Kazan Cathedral, modelled on St Peter's in Rome. Fittingly, there is a very military air to this creation of Paul I and, this time, the literary associations are not Dostoievskian, but Tolstoyan. Outside, there are statues of two of the generals of the Napoleonic wars, the Scottish-born Michael Barclay de Tolly and Mikhail Kutuzov, the hero of *War and Peace*. Inside are a hundred banners and eagles captured from

Napoleon's retreating army and the keys of twenty-five captured cities, from Dresden to Rheims.

I continued along the Yekaterininsky Canal, past the
Bankovsky Bridge, with its gilded griffins, to the Kamenny
Bridge. There I turned right up the Gorokhovaya to the
Moyka, where I turned left and continued as far as the
Voznesensky Prospekt. There I tried to locate the courtyard,
'on his left', just before reaching 'the square' (this could only
be Mariiskaya ploshchad) where, under a great stone,
Raskolnikov hides the money-lender's purse and the other
things that he had stolen. But the yard had been built on since
Dostoievsky's day. I continued down as far as the Voznesensky
Bridge, where Raskolnikov, who is himself contemplating suicide, watches a woman throw herself into the Canal, only to be
rescued by a policeman. I crossed the bridge and, turning
right along the quay, followed the sharp bend in the Canal,
past the Lions Bridge, as far as no. 104, where Alyona
Ivanovna, the old money-lender, lived and where Raskolnikov
kills her. Like Dostoievsky's hero, I

> approached an enormous tenement building that over-
> looked the Canal on one side, and —Street on the other.
> This building consisted entirely of tiny apartments and
> was inhabited by all kinds of jobbers and people trying
> to make a living: tailors, locksmiths, cooks, Germans of
> various descriptions, prostitutes, petty clerks and the like.
> People kept darting out of both entrances and through
> both courtyards ... The staircase was dark and
> narrow ...

I retraced my steps along the quay as far as the Kokushkin
Bridge where, crossing the Sadovaya ulitsa, I made a slight
detour to the Yusipov Garden, where Raskolnikov sometimes

walks, before going on to the Syennaya Ploshchad, or Haymarket Square. At the far end of the long rectangular square stands guard the eighteenth-century Church of the Assumption. It is in the middle of this area that Raskolnikov, repenting of his double murder, gets down on his knees and, surrounded by bemused bystanders, kisses 'the dirty earth', for, in Sonya's words, he has 'sinned against it too'. Unfortunately, for my purposes, the *ploshchad* was no longer a bare stretch of 'dirty earth', covered with 'all manner of filth and garbage ... sheeps' eyes, fish tails, crab shells, bits of meat, blood, hay, horse dung', but covered by four iron market halls, in which meat, fish and vegetables were being sold.

I moved round the square, back to the Canal, crossed the Demidov Bridge and doubled back on the other side. There, in one of the buildings, are Sonya Marmeladov's lodgings. Svidrigailov rents a room in the same building, where he eavesdrops on a conversation between Sonya and Raskolnikov. From there, I went up Stolyarni pereulak (Joiners' Lane), where Dostoievsky had lived while writing *Crime and Punishment* and which he used as the model for Raskolnikov's rooming-house. I went into the filthy courtyard of one of the run-down buildings, with their peeling, dirty yellow walls, stared up at the attic windows and tried to imagine Dostoievsky (or Raskolnikov) looking down at me from his

tiny little cell, about six paces long ... it presented a most pitiable aspect with its grimy yellow wallpaper that was everywhere coming off the walls; it was so low-ceilinged that to a person of even slightly above average height it felt claustrophobic, as though one might bang one's head against the plaster at any moment.

I returned to the Voznesensky Prospekt, with the intention of continuing my itinerary, but it was now about two o'clock: I was tired and hungry. I turned off at the Morskaya and hesitated before the Hôtel de France. I resisted the siren calls of its French menu and entered the Malo-Yaroslavetz, a cheap Russian eating-house, next door, where I had a beer and a bite to eat: I owed it to Dostoievsky to 'eat native'. Rested and refreshed, I made for the temporary Dvortzovi Bridge, which consisted of boats lashed together, and crossed over to Vasily Island, not forgetting to turn back, like Raskolnikov, and admire the view of St Isaac's, the dome, covered entirely with gold leaf, rising majestically above the blackened drum of its tower. Reeling about like a disembarked sailor, I set my unsure feet on *terra firma*. I cut into the Island, past the University, to the lodgings of Raskolnikov's student friend Rasumikhin on the far side. I then followed them, across the Malaya Neva at the Tuchkov Bridge, to Petrovsky Park, where, in the heat of a Petersburg July, they would go in search of fresh air. Of course, the novel takes place entirely when the natives are more inclined to spend as much time as possible out of doors. No such weather was at my command on that cold, if sunny February day. So I passed the park and went up what Dostoievsky calls 'the endless –oi Prospekt' (Bolshoi Prospekt). Svidrigailov spends his last night in the Arianopol Hôtel and shoots himself on the corner of Syezhinskaya ulitsa in front of the firetower. I then passed behind the Peter and Paul Fortress, where Dostoievsky was held as a suspected member of the 'Petrashevsky Circle', a literary discussion group of socialist leanings. There he was subjected to a mock execution by firing squad before being transported to a Siberian prison camp. My Dostoievskian 'pilgrimage' now at an end, I closed the rough circle of eight miles or so by crossing Trinity Bridge to the Embassy.

Despite the uncertainties of war, political turmoil and social unrest, Sergei Diaghilev's Exhibition of Historical Russian

Portraits opened in February: indeed, Society would have been horrified if such lowly matters had been allowed to interfere with such a celebration of the Imperial past – and what was to be the social event of the year. Diaghilev had spent three years amassing those three thousand paintings and turning them into an exhibition. The Imperial family had been lavish in its loans, but Diaghilev had also travelled all over Russia and abroad, persuading hundreds of owners to part with their ancestors. The arrangement of the exhibition was strictly chronological, 'dynastic' even: from a full-length portrait, covered by a canopy and surrounded by portraits of his family and courtiers, each reigning monarch dominated his own 'room'. It was an impressive, if rather depressing spectacle. There were a number of *vernissages* before the exhibition was open to the public. On the first of these, the Tsar and his closest relations attended; on the second, nobility and court were invited; my parents and I, with our diplomatic corps invitations, arrived on the third day. I knew that Nikita Baliev and Nikolai Tarasov, whom I had nicknamed, purely for my own use, 'the Young Niks', would also be there. I had already written to them, hinting that I might be going to Moscow in the near future and would very much like to see them again. Nikita replied that they hoped to be in Petersburg for the exhibition: Diaghilev was a good friend of theirs. When I met up with them, I told them how very much I had enjoyed their company in Moscow.

'We enjoyed your company immensely,' said Nikita, placing his hand on my arm. 'We should both be very happy if you could come to one of our *lundis* again – usually the last Monday in the month. Do let us know next time you're in Moscow.'

I said how sorry I was that I had no such friends in Petersburg. They looked at one another and smiled.

'Yes, I suppose we are more *open* in Moscow!' said Nikita.

'Oh, don't imagine that we're typical Muscovites!' said Nikolai. 'But there must be someone we know who could introduce you into the right circles.' He looked enquiringly at his friend.

'There's always Sergei Pavlovich,' said Nikita.

'Sergei . . .?'

'Diaghilev!'

We all three laughed. So he, too. They thought for a moment, then Nikita said:

'Now that the exhibition has opened, he might have a little time to do old friends a good turn. On the other hand, he might try to keep you for himself . . .'

'. . . or see you as a potential rival and keep you out of the way,' Nikolai interrupted, with a flash of his eyes. 'Then there's Sergei's great enemy, Prince Volkonsky . . .'

They giggled, then, seeing my perplexity, Nikita said:

'Oh, you must forgive us. You probably don't know who or what we're talking about. But perhaps this is neither the time nor the place for gossip.'

I asked them if they would have lunch or dinner with me. They said that they were only staying in Petersburg for a few days and would not be able to fit in a further such engagement, but could I call on them at six the following evening?

They took me over to the group around Diaghilev. As we waited, I was presented to several of their acquaintances. At last our turn came. Diaghilev was a handsome young man in his early thirties, with striking dark eyes, a thin moustache and a shock of dark hair with a white streak in it. He gave an impression of power and authority. He welcomed Nikita and Nikolai warmly, like long-lost brothers, then eyed me up and down, with evident expertise. Placing his hand solicitously on Nikolai's arm, he asked him how he had been keeping. Nikolai said that he had been quite well for the last few months and introduced me, saying that he could speak French to me. I congratulated him on the magnificent exhibition; he asked me a few desultory questions about myself, gave me his card and our few minutes' audience was at an end. Was it a mere coincidence, I wondered, that his exhibition took place in the Tauride Palace, of which the Tavrichesky Garden was once the grounds? Was Diaghilev one of the Garden's *habitués*? Ironically, when his celebration of the Russian autocracy ended some months later, the Tauride Palace was used as the seat of the fledgling Russian 'parliament', the Duma.

I turned up at six, at the Hôtel de l'Europe, the following day. In the course of our conversation, I learned more about Diaghilev – and Prince Volkonsky. I knew that Diaghilev was a co-founder of the art review *Mir Iskusstva* (*World of Art*); of Volkonsky I knew nothing. Apparently, the Prince had been Director of Imperial Theatres, a post that gave ultimate responsibility for all five state theatres, the three in Petersburg and the two in Moscow. He knew Diaghilev well – he, too, was 'one of us' – and had contributed to *Mir Iskusstva*. It was therefore quite natural that, when he took charge of the theatres, he should use Diaghilev's talents. Before long, however, Diaghilev was making enemies, especially Kchessinskaya, all-powerful not only on account of her seniority, but also because of her close relations with members of the Imperial family. Matters came to a head over an incident concerning a fine imposed on Kchessinskaya for wearing a costume other than the one prescribed by the producer, Diaghilev. The *prima ballerina* soon got to work: a letter arrived from the Tsar himself instructing Volkonsky to cancel the fine – and sack Diaghilev.

I expressed surprise that the man who had helped found and largely run *Mir Iskusstva* and who had tried to breathe new life into the ballet, should have lavished so much time and energy on an undertaking like the exhibition that we had seen the day before. My Moscow friends agreed, but hinted that the exhibition might be part of some complicated plot of Diaghilev's to curry favour with the authorities and to return to the state theatres at a later date. None of us could have guessed that, in a few years' time, as an independent impresario, Diaghilev would take Paris and London by storm with his extraordinary seasons of opera and ballet. To obtain the services of the cream of the Marie and Bolshoy companies during their long summer closures did, of course, require the goodwill of the authorities.

Meanwhile the government was proving as incapable of making peace as it was of waging war. The Ambassador spent May in London, on leave, but he took the opportunity of urging the British government to strengthen its ties with Japan: this, he believed, would make it easier to persuade the Japanese not to insist on reparations against Russia, the main stumbling-block to peace. Then, in early June, the Russian Baltic Fleet finally arrived in the Far East. Within days, it was completely destroyed by the Japanese at Tsushima. The news reached us at the Embassy long before the Russian public was allowed to know of it. Not only was it the most humiliating defeat so far but, for the first time, St Petersburg Society was immediately affected by the war. Very few of the officers of the *élite* regiments had volunteered for service in Manchuria, but the ships of the Baltic Fleet were full of young men from the greatest families in Russia. As a result, the 'peace party' gained in strength: before long, the Tsar was almost alone in wanting to pursue the war. Cecil was already in London for consultations when, a few weeks later, President Theodore Roosevelt, a personal friend of Cecil's, managed to persuade the combatants to enter into negotiations: a reluctant Tsar appointed Witte his Chief Plenipotentiary.

Spring arrived late that year: there was snow around in the Petersburg streets in May. Then day after day of brilliant sunshine raised the temperature; the ice-floes sailing past the Embassy to the sea became ever smaller. Suddenly, the miracle happened, as it happens every year: in a matter of days, the trees were covered in fresh, pale green leaves. During the winter months, I had continued to frequent the *bani* once or twice a week, usually with some success, though none of those I took to my *nomer* was the equal of young Jan, my Moscow ballet student. I had written to the 'Young Niks', suggesting that I might be coming to Moscow before long. Nikita replied that Nikolai had been rather ill for several weeks and they had had to abandon their *réceptions* for the time being. With the coming of milder weather, I resumed my *promenades à l'aventure*. One afternoon, sitting on a bench in the Alexander Gardens, near the *kloseti*, was a young man who gave me a shy, enquiring look as I approached. I sat down next to him, smiled and said: *'Dobri dyen!'* ('Good afternoon!') I always avoided using the more informal *'Zdravstvute!'* ('Hello!'): given the peculiar character of my slight stammer, the Russian word seemed especially concocted to floor me. He looked about twenty, was very slight of build, had dark curly hair and brown eyes. After a few words, he asked me if I was English. That was unusual: I was invariably taken to be German. Did I work in Petersburg? I explained that my father was 'in business' and that I was staying with my parents for a few months: it was obviously preferable to conceal my father's occupation and where we lived. I asked him if he would like to go somewhere for a drink. He said he knew a good place. It was near the University, on the Island. Did I mind going so far? I was in no hurry, I said.

As we walked along the quay to the Palace Bridge, he told me about himself. He was called Sergei, but he gave me permission to call him by his diminutive, Seriozha. He came from Baku, the Caspian Sea resort. Had I ever been there? I confessed that I had not; he launched into a rhapsody in praise of the Caucasian South in general and of his native city in particular. St Petersburg was, he conceded, the most beautiful city in the world, but it had the worst weather. He was a student in the History and Philology Faculty, the nearest equivalent to reading Classics at Cambridge, there being only three other faculties, Physics and Mathematics, Jurisprudence and Oriental Languages. Like most educated Russians, he spoke good German and passable French; unusually, he had more than a smattering of English. So we used French as our main medium of communication, resorting to Russian or English when difficulties arose. I explained that I was an 'ex-student' and we embarked on a long conversation in which faculties, curricula and university life on the Vasily Ostrov and at Cambridge were compared and contrasted. This led, inevitably, to a discussion of the political situation in Russia: in sympathy with the workers and in favour of constitutional reform, students and staff at the University had declared a strike for the rest of the academic year. He was, he said, broadly in sympathy with the strike. There were some extremists at the University, even a few followers of Lenin and the Social Democrats, but most of the students were, like him, liberals, rather than extremists. Over the past few weeks, I had been struck by how fearless Russians had become when talking politics: only a few months before the subject was taboo among all but trusted friends.

We had a beer at Seriozha's *kafe*. He then asked me if I would like to go back with him to his room. He lived in a rooming-house on the other side of the Island, near the Tuchkov Bridge, close to where Raskolnikov's friend Rasumikhin lived. His room was small and dingy, with little more than a bed, a table and a chair in it. I could not but compare it to my rooms in Trinity but, as in Dostoievsky's day, this was how a 'student' lived; an English undergraduate was not a 'student', but a young gentleman and the College servants treated him as such.

Seriozha was not what might be called a handsome young man, but I found him attractive enough. I also liked him and enjoyed having a friend with whom I could discuss subjects of common interest. I was not sure, on that first afternoon, how he was inclined sexually. On arrival, he offered me the chair and a glass of vodka, and removed himself to the bed. After a decent interval, in mid-sentence and without invitation, I joined him on the bed. I finished the first glass of vodka and put my left arm around his small, bony shoulders. He gave me a look that might be described as anxious compliance. I sensed, correctly as it turned out, that we were in uncharted waters.

Almost my entire sexual experience had emerged from unambiguous situations: even when making approaches to a waiter on the Trans-Siberian or picking up a youth in Tangiers, the situation was clearly understood on both sides. Only in Cambridge, with fellow undergraduates, had I ever been in any doubt as to the outcome. Despite the obvious differences, I was taken back to the uncertainties of my own university days. Then, too, nothing could be more natural than to continue a conversation in one's rooms, though, at Cambridge, we should not have got to the bed so quickly; indeed the transition from study to bedroom was never easy. Perhaps I had misread his friendly, but shy invitation; perhaps he knew not man; perhaps he did just want to go on talking, or was simply being hospitable. If one wishes to go further in such circumstances, there are two possible strategies: the approach direct and the approach indirect. The approach indirect would mean that the arm around the shoulder might be followed by a kiss. With members of the opposite sex, this is no doubt the approach to be adopted in all cases. With men, the approach direct is generally the more effective. I took his hand and placed it on the flies of my trousers, then put my hand on his thigh. He felt my erection and by the time I had reached his flies, he had one too. He put his head on my chest and lay there, as if in fear and wonder. I undid my flies for him, took out my cock and, with my left hand around the nape of his neck, brought his mouth towards it: I guessed that he had never done such a thing before.

The room was on the top floor and overlooked a courtyard. I got up and went to the window: as far as I could see, there was no *vis-à-vis*. I drew the curtains all the same. I pulled Seriozha to his feet and started to undress him, undressing myself the while. His body was small, thin, almost girlish, his cock in proportion to the rest. When we were both naked, I finally kissed him. He seemed to enjoy it. It was not that he needed encouragement: he was simply inexperienced. I pushed him down on to his knees: he seemed to like that, too, more and more. I lifted him up, took him back to the bed and got into *soixante-neuf* position. Before long, I opened the small tube of petroleum jelly, which I always took out with me on my excursions, and set to work on his hole. When he realized what was happening, he moved my hand away. I looked up and said: '*Harasho*' ('it's all right'). He looked disconsolate. '*Je ne peux pas*,'[1] he said. I kissed him. We returned to *soixante-neuf* and finished each other off.

Some days later, I went back to his room on the Island. Thereafter, I went back about once a week. Each time, I tried again, always with the same result: the disconsolate look, the

1 'I can't.'

same word, *'impossible'*. I would not have kept trying were it
not obvious that nothing would have pleased him more. I
assured him that there was nothing abnormal about him: most
people found it difficult at first. I explained the technique to
adopt: relax, trust me to go no further than he could take and
to press outward, as if trying to shit. On the fourth occasion,
I got inside, but it hurt him so much I had to give up. The following two occasions, I did not even try. Then, one afternoon,
he himself suggested that we try again. He was more relaxed.
He smothered his cries in the pillow, but he let me keep going.
The barrier had been broken. After a few movements, I came.
I stayed inside him, rolled him on to his side and made him
come. By my next visit, he was a creature transformed. His
tenseness, his nervousness were gone; gone was the sorrowful
face; he smiled and smiled; his hands were all over me.

During those weeks, we did not spend all our time together
lying on his bed. We went for walks. We went to the Hermitage
and the Russian Museum. We went to a few concerts in the
Assembly of Nobles. I took Seriozha to the Marie Theatre,
which he had never been to before, but I bought cheaper seats
than I should normally have done, because I knew that he did
not have any formal evening clothes. When the weather got
warmer, we would often cross over the Tuchkov Bridge to the
Petrovsky Park, as Raskolnikov did. Over the weeks, my
Russian improved, as did his French and English.

In May, Maurice wrote to say that he was re-entering the
employ of the *Morning Post*, not as war correspondent, but as
theatre critic. Eleonora Duse was coming to London for a six-
week season at the Waldorf Theatre. There were also to be
two French visitors that Season – Réjane would be at Terry's
for three weeks and Coquelin *aîné* would be at the
Shaftesbury – and they, too, would come under Maurice's
jurisdiction. His letter had reawakened in me a great nostalgia

for London, in particular for the endless offerings of its theatrical Season. In Petersburg, not content with closing throughout Lent, which is longer here than in the West, the theatres shut up shop throughout the three summer months. I knew that, before long, perhaps in a few months, my father's secondment to the Russian capital would end and my parents would return to Peking. I had decided that I should not accompany them, but go back to London, to my grandmother and Smith Square. There, perhaps, I should try to 'live' a little less and write a little more. Perhaps something would eventually come of my scribblings. Perhaps, one day, when, like Maurice, I had passed my thirtieth birthday, I, too, might be considered sage enough to become a dramatic critic. But I knew, too, that Maurice was a good friend of Oliver Borthwick, the son of Lord Glenesk, the proprietor of the *Morning Post*, and I had no such connection. Moreover, Maurice already had a few publications to his credit: in June, a signed copy of his latest, *With the Russians in Manchuria*, arrived in the post. A few weeks later, Maurice wrote to say that he had decided to come back to Russia. At first, I was astonished – and, I admit, disappointed. I was looking forward to having him as a friend in London, a delightful companion at the theatre, someone who knew everyone and might open up a new 'social' life for me. On reflection, I was not surprised. Russia and the extreme conditions of warfare seemed to have a strange hold over him: that intelligent, sensitive, rich Englishman was never happier than when consorting with uneducated, brutalized, impoverished Russians.

Maurice arrived in Petersburg in early August. I was summoned at once to his hotel and, over the next few hours, we talked our fill. In her six-week London season, Duse had offered no fewer than ten plays. It had been a truly international selection, all, save for Goldoni's *La Locandiera* and d'Annunzio's *La Gioconda*, in more or less inappropriate Italian: from England, Pinero's *The Second Mrs Tanqueray*; from Germany, *Magda* (Sudermann's *Heimat*); from Norway, *Hedda Gabler*; and, from France, plays that had been Bernhardt's preserve, *La Dame aux Camélias* and *La Femme de Claude* by Dumas *fils*, Sardou's *Fédora* and *Odette*, *Adrienne Lecouvreur* by Scribe and Legouvé. Maurice vowed as absolute a devotion to 'la Grande Sarah' as any man living. He also had more right than most to refer to her by her Christian name: he was a personal friend and had even stayed with her at her property on Belle-Isle, off the Breton coast. In view of Maurice's devotion, personal and aesthetic, to Bernhardt, I was all the more intrigued to hear his views on Duse.

'It is, I suppose, inevitable,' Maurice began, 'that everybody should compare her with Bernhardt. After all, she invites that comparison by taking on so many of Sarah's roles – not only the lady with the camellias, but also parts created for Sarah by Sardou. Mercifully, we have been spared Duse's Phèdre, in Italian. But' – and he held up an admonishing finger – 'Duse is a great artist, despite her limitations.'

My most vivid memory of Duse was as *'la signora dalle camelie'*. The contrast with Bernhardt was at its starkest here. Everyone went to see Duse with an image of Marguerite Gautier as played by Sarah Bernhardt. Bernhardt set the play at the time of Dumas *père* and wore a splendid series of costumes; Duse set it in 'modern dress', wore plain clothes and brought out the undercurrent of melancholy beneath Marguerite's gaiety. Maurice said how disappointed he had been when he saw her in the part: her simple dignity seemed to strike the wrong note. This was not one's idea of a Parisian *cocotte*. Yet, as the play progressed, her performance grew steadily in stature, so that the *fille de joie* found a certain nobility of her own. She conveyed the onset of her illness with a minimum of means: no dramatic gestures, no fits of coughing. Her death was horribly real, utterly untheatrical.

'Did you know she came here?' Maurice asked. I admitted that I did not. 'Oh, yes, it was quite early on. Twenty years ago. More importantly, she went to Moscow. Stanislavsky, who was just starting out, was very impressed. She had a great influence on him.'

Our conversation moved, inevitably, to the political situation in Russia. He had seen his old friend Cecil Spring Rice, when he was in London, and was having dinner with him and his wife that evening. Maurice was privy to some of the diplomatic moves afoot to bring the war to an end: during Cecil's visit to London in June, Maurice invited him to dinner at his rooms in Gray's Inn Place with his old friend Count Benckendorff, the Russian Ambassador.

'How's your Russian getting on?' Maurice asked.

'Much better since I had a young Russian friend.' I told him about Seriozha.

'It's always the best way to learn a language,' he said, with a searching smile. He seemed very interested in Seriozha and suggested that he join us for dinner the following evening. I agreed providing we went to somewhere not too smart and wore ordinary suits.

Maurice took us to a good Russian restaurant on the Moyka. We ate in the garden: it was a warm evening and the Petersburg days were still close to their longest. Most of the conversation was conducted in Russian, which put the rather intimidated Seriozha at ease. Afterwards, when Maurice had left us to return to his hotel, Seriozha said that he had found Maurice '*très, très gentil*', adding, not without some inkling of the truth, that he must be '*un très grand Monsieur*'.

Two days later, Maurice would be leaving for Moscow and, from there, for Manchuria and the hell of war. Once, during our last afternoon together, his face became grave and, looking straight into my eyes, he said:

'Sometimes, this summer, when I was sitting in the stalls, in my starched shirt, looking up at the stage, I had this over-whelming sense that it was all an illusion. I don't mean what was taking place on the stage, of course. That is *bona fide* illu-sion. I mean that I, the rest of the audience, the street outside, London in its entirety, was an illusion, a dream.'

He paused and stared into space. I should not have leapt in to fill the silence, but I could not help filling it with literature: 'We are such stuff as dreams are made on . . .'

'Yes,' said Maurice, kindly, 'of course. But the strange thing is that I feel reality is to be found in only one place, out there, where my beloved Russian soldiers are fighting those unspeak-able Japs . . .'

'If I were there,' I said, 'I'm afraid that would all seem an insubstantial pageant, a nightmare that I should yearn to wake up from.'

Maurice did not see very much more of 'reality'. On 5 September, a couple of weeks after his arrival in Manchuria, a peace treaty was finally signed at Portsmouth, New Hampshire. Success could be claimed by all the parties con-cerned: Witte managed to negotiate better terms for Russia than anyone thought possible, the British government, partly through our Petersburg embassy, succeeded in persuading its Japanese allies to accept less than they had justifiably expected and the tenacity of the American government, which had bro-kered the agreement, had paid off. Up to the last minute, Witte was still not sure whether the Tsar would accept the accord.

Meanwhile, in Russia itself, the Tsar was proving as obstinate in the face of domestic matters. In August the govern-ment issued plans for a consultative assembly to be elected by a complicated process of electoral colleges. Broadly speaking, this meant that the greater one's wealth, the greater one's electoral power; if, like the bulk of the population, one had no property at all, then one had no vote. Moreover, this new system would not apply to the non-Russian parts of the Empire, which, in any case, were now in the grip of various kinds and degrees of unrest. In Finland, the movement was purely political. The Tsar's response made matters worse: Finland's limited autonomy was withdrawn and Finns were subjected to Russian military service. In the Caucasus, Tartars and Armenians were killing each other by the thousand: Seriozha, a true Russian, had no time for either, as battles flared up without let in his native Baku. In Poland, martial law had been declared after strikes and nationalistic demonstrations had brought the country to a standstill.

We had known for some time that Grandmother Sheridan was not well and had intended spending Christmas with her. Then, one day, early in October, we received a telegram from Aunt Carrie, who had kept us informed of her mother's condition: cancer had been diagnosed and she could not be expected to live long. As it happened, the Ambassador was planning to go on leave at the end of the month, his task in Petersburg now accomplished. Nevertheless, he urged us to leave as soon as possible: as it was, few trains were running and the situation was getting worse with every day. The fastest of the trains, the Nord Express, would be leaving in two days; it would probably be its last run for some time.

I dashed down to the Nevsky and bought some books for Seriozha – volumes of Dickens, Balzac, Flaubert. That evening, I took him to Contant's, the restaurant where we had eaten with Maurice. He told me that he had no idea what to give me as a farewell present: I knew that he did not have very much money. Then he thought of a small icon of the Virgin that he had brought with him from Baku. It had been given to him by his grandmother, and must be very old. He knew that I was not a believer, any more than he was, but it was a very Russian thing and would help me to remember him in the years to come and, when my own *Babushka* died, it might comfort me. Under the onslaught of all this Russian emotion, I was almost in tears. I protested that I could not possibly accept so cherished a possession, but Seriozha insisted that he had decided that I should have it and nothing on earth would alter that decision. (Years later, knowing nothing about Russian icons, I took it along to Christie's. It was not, the expert told me, either very old – it was mid-nineteenth century – or very valuable. This knowledge made the gift all the more moving.) On that last evening, I walked with Seriozha to the Nicholas Bridge and stood there as he crossed over to the Island: every so often, we turned round and waved to one another. Happily, our hearts would not be broken by the parting. I knew that I had been an important event in his life. He had not played an equally important role in mine, but he had known this at the outset and knew, too, that before long I should be returning to London. This gave our relations a certain disengaged quality.

The day after I said '*Proshchaniye*' to Seriozha, I said '*Proshchaniye!*' to Piter[1] and my life in Russia. The city was looking suitably mournful as we drove to the Varshavsky Voksal: it was dark, raining and already the temperature was falling. One thing I should be glad to miss was the Petersburg winter, for all its sunny hours of skating on pond and canal.

The week after we left, a general strike was declared. Strikes were still illegal, but the workers were now organizing and

1 Goodbye. 'Piter' is the affectionate name by which Petersburgers refer to their city.

losing what remained of their respect for authority. Overnight, all the public services came to a standstill: posts and telegraphs, railways and all transport. Shops and offices failed to open, their employees being unable, or unwilling, to turn up for work. The strike spread rapidly to Moscow, then to the provinces. In desperation, the Tsar summoned Witte to Peterhof: he had put an end to the war, perhaps he could put an end to what looked like civil war. Witte informed his sovereign that he had a simple choice: make an immediate declaration that Russia was to become a constitutional democracy, like other European countries, or declare martial law throughout the empire, ruthlessly crushing all rebellion. He carefully refrained from expressing his own preference, but left for his master's perusal a report in which the reforms were described in detail. Still the Tsar temporized; days passed; Witte was summoned again and again to Peterhof, on one occasion being made a sort of prime minister. Finally, against all his instincts and prejudices, the Tsar opted for constitutional reform: on 17 October, what came to be known as the October Manifesto was published. But, Russia being Russia, that was not to be the end of the matter.

Through the night and early morning, the Nord Express sped through the endless wooded plain of the West Russian provinces. We reached Vilna at breakfast time and, a few hours later, we were at the frontier that separates the Russian and German Empires. The wretched little station, called Wirballen on the Russian side, Eydtkuhnen on the German, straddled a small river, the bridge marking the actual frontier. It was a sorry sight: on the Russian side, as far as the eye could see, was continuous barbed wire, with sentry-boxes at regular intervals. We were held up for a couple of hours, while passengers changed carriages and had their belongings searched by officials on both sides: the Russian officials were especially zealous, systematically fumbling their way through every item of every person's luggage. As I crossed the Russian–German frontier, my life, too, seemed to be in borderland territory, in no sounder state than the Russia I was leaving. I was twenty-five years old, yet I had no idea where I was going, other than back to London.

We arrived in Berlin after midnight. Late the following evening, I was standing on the pavement in Smith Square, looking up at the house. Mrs Ellis, my grandmother's house-keeper, was already at the door. Apologizing for being the bringer of bad news, she told my father that his mother had died the day before.

1890–92: London, Paris

I was carried back fifteen years, to the first time I stood there, beneath the towering mass of St John's Church. The two coachmen – a second carriage had followed us with our luggage – were unloading our trunks and boxes. A door opened and we were being ushered inside by a young woman in cap and apron. When the confusion of embracings and exclamations had subsided in the brightly lit hall, Grandmother led us upstairs to the drawing-room, while Grandfather took charge of the coachmen and luggage. After a few minutes I heard the gruff voices of the coachmen in the street and the receding clip-clop of the horses. Grandfather reappeared and soon began to dominate the scene, holding centre stage, with his back to the fire. And this is how it was always to be: he dominated every situation in which I ever saw him. To begin with, his appearance was imposing: taller than average with a substantial girth, highlighted by the glittering gold watch-chain draped across it, a full, reddish face, alert grey-green eyes, neatly trimmed grey-white beard and moustache, his hair quite long at the back. He had a voice that might have been considered loud by English standards, were it not so pleasing, so rich in tone, so well modulated – and were people not invariably delighted by what he said. He had an obvious good-naturedness, was lavish in attention and compliment to others, and possessed an extraordinary gift for words. At the time he was in his mid-sixties, nearing the end of a distinguished medical career. He and his family had moved into the house in Smith Square the year before my father entered Westminster School. About the same time building began at the present site of St Thomas' Hospital, where my grandfather was to be a consultant surgeon. He was undoubtedly a thwarted actor, one of the 'theatrical Sheridans', as he put it, but I wonder how much of this was inherited, how much the cultivation of a 'Sheridan style' and how much the result of years spent in the Garrick Club, rubbing shoulders with actors. How a man possessing his particular gifts ended up in medicine, which has so little need of them and offers them so little satisfaction, is even more of a puzzle. But it is also true that the most fluent speakers do not necessarily make the best writers, nor the most 'theatrical' people the best actors. So perhaps he had little choice in the matter: but it came as no surprise when I learnt, years later, that his performances with the scalpel at St Thomas' were accounted to be among the finest of his time. There, after all, he found his theatre.

Grandmother could not have provided a greater contrast. Her hair was of the same grey-white as his – she was only a year or two younger than he – but whereas he gave an impression of vigorous middle age, she could not have been described as anything other than 'a little old lady'. She always wore dark, full-length dresses of thick-looking material, with a high collar and a brooch at her throat. She wore gold-rimmed spectacles, one pair for reading, another for normal wear. The only time she ever drew attention to herself was when she had mislaid the pair she was not wearing. 'Mark, dear,' she would say, very quietly, waiting for what she hoped was the end of one of Grandfather's spoken paragraphs, 'have you seen my reading spectacles?' Grandfather, who missed nothing, would pause for a split second and say, 'they're on the table over there, my dear,' and take up where he had left off. Much of the time she would sit with a benign smile on her face, appearing not to react in any detail to what was going on around her; she was much given to what the French call *'absences'*, moments of day-dreaming, as if in reaction to her husband's sheer presence. When she did speak, what she said on any given subject was entirely predictable, which gave the impression that she spoke only out of politeness, never out of interest. As I later came to realize, Grandfather had long ceased to be the centre of her life, if he had ever been, that place now being occupied by religion. Though she lived in the shadow of one of London's most splendid baroque churches, she never set foot in it, preferring the studied 'medievalism' of architecture and ceremony at Butterfield's All Saints', Margaret Street. This church held as great a place in her affection as the Garrick Club did in my grandfather's.

The maid arrived with tea. I later discovered that this was Mary, the parlour maid, and that the household also consisted of cook, a middle-aged widow called Mrs Chapman, and a young chambermaid called Ethel, a relation of Mary's, who had been taken on for the duration of our stay. Knowing nothing of valets or coachmen, since Grandfather employed neither, I noted that in England all servants were female, whereas in China they were always male. Before the evening was up, it was also borne in on me that my grandparents' house consisted solely of that part of the building above and below the drawing-room and not the entire terrace, as I had assumed when we first arrived in that magnificent four-wheeler. Indeed, compared with what I had been used to in Peking, everything – hall, stairs, rooms, the street outside – seemed to be on a very small scale. However, I soon realized that London buildings make up in height what they lack in breadth. My grandparents' house, for example, consisted of four floors, in addition to a basement with its own entrance.

Meanwhile, the English Tea Ceremony which, quite exceptionally, had been postponed some two hours on our account, followed its predestined course. Under the distractions of its precise, ritualized questions and answers – 'Milk?' 'Yes, please.' 'Sugar?' 'Just one lump, please,' etc. – the underlying excitement ebbed away; before long the adults were behaving much as adults usually did. The serving of tea was the only occasion when I saw my grandmother take charge of anything. Even then, she did so with such gentleness, such sweetness that, unlike the formidable ladies of P & O ship *Peshawar*, who seemed to be performing some ceremony designed to enhance their own power, she managed to make it seem like an act of service.

After tea, we went up to our rooms and unpacked. My parents had a room on the second floor, while Matthew and I shared one of the front rooms on the top floor; the two maids shared the rooms next to ours and Mrs Chapman had a larger room at the back. Matthew thought it extremely odd that the servants were not housed in some outbuilding and even odder that we had been put on the same floor as them. 'Perhaps it's because they're English,' I suggested. 'I suppose so,' my brother conceded, not entirely convinced.

At some point in the evening, Father asked, more out of politeness, I imagine, than out of genuine interest, if there had been anything worth seeing in the theatre in recent months. Grandfather launched into exaggerated expressions of despair: if only we could have come earlier in the year! We had missed a splendid revival of 'The Scottish Play' at the Lyceum.

'Irving was much better than eleven years ago, though still not a patch on Macready – now there was a Macbeth! Miss Terry is, of course, always wonderful and her Lady Mac was most interesting, but she really cannot hide the fact that she is the sweetest, most delightful creature alive and quite the last person one would choose to play the "fiend-like Queen" . . . I cannot offer you any Terry this time, nor Irving in Shakespeare, but what I can offer is Irving in *The Bells!*' Here my grandfather froze into an imitation of Irving in the last scene of the play. Everyone laughed and clapped dutifully. 'A poor thing, the play,' Grandfather added, 'but very much his own.'

'You mean like Touchstone and Audrey,' I blurted out. I had listened enthralled to Grandfather's monologue and was anxious to show him that, although I had never seen any of Shakespeare's plays acted, I had read many of them. Grandfather feigned amazement at my precocity and turned to my father:

'There you are, Charlie. A true Sheridan! Ten years of age and he knows his Shakespeare by heart! Now why couldn't you have been like that at his age? In what oriental wilderness have you been hiding the child that he knows neither Irving nor Terry, neither Tree nor Alexander?'

'Well,' said my father, 'he may be sunk in histrionic ignorance, but he certainly knows his Shakespeare.'

'And I've been to the *Chinese* theatre,' I added lamely.

'The CHINEESE THEATAH! Well, well, well! And what did you see, pray? *Han-lee, Prince of Shanghai? The Merchant of Canton?* What on earth must Shakespeare sound like in Chinese, I wonder!'

'I don't think there was any Shakespeare, was there?' I asked, turning to Father.

'No,' he said, 'no Shakespeare. They have their own plays, some dating from the seventh century! I don't suppose we had much theatre in England then!'

'No,' Grandfather conceded, 'I don't suppose we did, or in Ireland either. I'm sure the Chinese theatre is very fine, very fine . . . Yes, I think we have a rich programme of entertainment laid on for you. Let me see, no Irving in Shakespeare, but the delectable Mrs Langtry as CLEOPAHTRA! Just imagine! "Give me my robes, put on my crown, I have immortal longings in me!"' The voice pitched itself into the right register, rising with every phrase, stretching the long vowels almost to breaking point. Realizing perhaps that he had gone on for rather too long, he fell silent and turned around to face the fire. Father took the opportunity of asking Grandmother something and the conversation took a different turn.

Next morning, on waking, I hurried over to the window, pulled the curtains and saw, almost opposite, the façade of St John's Church. Being at the top of the house, I was almost level with the base of the north-west tower, which rose up so high that I had to press my head against the window to see its topmost point. It was a view I never grew tired of, whether, as then, with the feeble sun highlighting the pinnacles, or, on a summer evening, with a red sky behind them, or at night, lit only by moonlight above and gaslight from below. Yet this church, designed by Thomas Archer, a pupil of Vanbrugh, has been the butt of critics ever since it was built in the 1720s. It was variously called 'Queen Anne's footstool', 'a parlour table upset, with its legs in the air', and so on. In the nineteenth century it fared no better. In *Our Mutual Friend* Dickens describes it as 'a very hideous church with four towers at the four corners generally resembling some petrified monster, frightful and gigantic, on its back with its legs in the air'. For me it will always remain a splendid piece of un-English exuberance, entirely at one with my grandfather's temperament.

Over the next few days, we visited our other London relations. Father's sister, Aunt Carrie (Caroline), Uncle Tom, who was a barrister, and their two daughters, lived in Lexham Gardens, Kensington. Matthew and I agreed that our female cousins made very poor company, were quite idiotically silly, and so on. Aunt Jacky was Mother's elder sister, Jacqueline: it had been through her that my parents had met. Her husband, John Payne (Uncle Jacky) worked in his family's wine and spirits business in St James's Street. They had two sons, Robert and Frederick, and lived in Redcliffe Square. My first impression of Aunt Jacky was that she was a more confident, more imperious, yet nevertheless more 'feminine' version of Mother. She was, in other words, more *'parisienne'*. Her self-confidence, which oozed out of her when she spoke in French, seemed in no way impaired when she spoke her by no means unflawed English. Despite her idiosyncratic syntax, her confused use of idioms and her accent, she seemed to imply that her version of the English language was at least the equal of that of us natives. Her presiding over the tea table struck me as an obscene parody of one of our most cherished traditions, combining a studied attempt to do the thing correctly with an irrepressible levity that seemed to rob the proceedings of all seriousness. She would pour the tea without paying the slightest attention to what she was doing, chattering in the most animated way, switching from English to French and back again, watched with a mixture of apprehension and benign tolerance by Grandmother Sheridan. 'Tea' she pronounced 'ty' as in 'beauty', 'cake' as 'kek' and 'sandwiches' as 'sonnvidge'. 'You want more kek,' she said to me, in the form of a statement rather than a question, 'all boys like kek.' She was, of course, quite right and had plenty of experience to prove it. Her two sons were at St Paul's preparatory school and, although they seemed to envy the fact that Matthew and I had never had to attend school, nevertheless painted a picture of life at St Paul's that seemed to consist of one hilarious episode after another. They were equally unrewarding about Paris, which they had visited several times. Our Dumollard grandparents were 'topping', most other things were 'all right' or 'quite good', while the only thing that really aroused their enthusiasm was the Great Universal Exposition, which had taken place the year before and which we would never see.

When it was time to leave, it was already dark and my aunt insisted that we go home in a cab, rather than by 'bus or train. We all walked to the corner, where my aunt summoned a 'four-wheeler' with two blasts on a special whistle that was kept in the hall of every house at that time, the rule being one blast for a hansom, two for the larger 'four-wheeler'. On our way home I became aware of how very comfortable travelling in a sprung carriage on a properly paved road was compared with Peking's combination of pitted mud roads and unsprung carts. At first Matthew and I talked a great deal about the differences between London and Peking. It was strange to see so many Europeans thronging the streets, with not a Chinaman in sight, and so many women, unaccompanied and in full view of everybody. We marvelled, too, at the small, paved roads, but regretted the clear light and clean air of Peking: for days I was aware of the all-pervading smell of coal smoke. We were always getting smut on our faces. To our great irritation, Mother would moisten her handkerchief with her tongue and wipe it away.

One afternoon, Grandfather announced that he would take Matthew and me to pay our respects to his 'illustrious great uncle'. I knew that we were distantly related to the great play-wright, but my father had never shown the slightest interest in the matter. I can only assume that it was because his own father was so 'Sheridanic', as Disraeli said of one of R. B. S.'s three granddaughters, that by way of reaction, my father had decided to pretend indifference to family history. Paying our respects to Grandfather's 'illustrious great uncle' consisted of walking down the road to Westminster Abbey to see his grave and the monument erected to his memory in Poets' Corner.

As we walked, Grandfather told us about the various members of the Sheridan family, most of whom seemed to be called Thomas (like himself) or Charles (like his son). A confusing story is difficult to repeat: what follows owes as much to published accounts as to my grandfather's impromptu anecdotes. The Sheridan clan was founded in the eleventh century by the second son of O'Connor, Prince of Sligo, who married the daughter of O'Reilly of County Cavan, taking the surname Ó Sirideáin, or O' Sheridan in its anglicized form. Their only son, Oster, marched into Cavan at the head of an army and established his rule at Castle Togher, where his descendants remained for the next six hundred years. In the reign of James I, they were dispossessed, as were the other noble families of Ulster, by English and Scottish settlers. The now landless Sheridans turned their talents elsewhere, principally to Church and Army. One of them, the Revd Denis Sheridan, collaborated on the translation of the Bible into Irish. Originally a Catholic priest, he conformed to the Established Church and married an Englishwoman: thereafter all his male descendants married Englishwomen. Two of his sons became generals and two bishops. A fifth, Thomas, became private secretary to James II, married one of his illegitimate daughters, and followed him into exile in France.

The nephew of this 'Jacobite' Sheridan was Dr Thomas Sheridan, the friend and mentor of Swift. Himself suspected of Jacobite tendencies, he lost his appointment as chaplain to the Lord Lieutenant of Ireland. He opened a school, which excelled at the performance of ancient Greek drama. He held a life-long correspondence in verse with Swift, who wrote most of *Gulliver's Travels* while staying at his house at Qualca, County Cavan. Thomas Sheridan's love of the theatrical was to be found in greater measure in his son, also called Thomas. At Westminster School and later, at Trinity College, Dublin, he was already noted for his acting talent. But it was a meeting with Garrick in Dublin in 1742 that finally decided him to go on the stage. He made his *début* in the title role of *Richard III*. The following year he was acting at Drury Lane with Garrick. Before long he was running his own theatre in Dublin, the Theatre Royal, Smock Alley. About this time, he married Frances Chamberlaine, an Anglo-Irish beauty of some literary talent. They had two sons – Charles, my great-great-grandfather, and Richard Brinsley Sheridan – and two daughters, Elizabeth, an author of successful novels, and Alicia. These two sisters married brothers, Henry and Joseph Le Fanu, descendants of French Huguenot refugees. The grandson of the latter was Joseph Sheridan Le Fanu, the writer of 'Gothic' novels and stories.

It has been said that Charles and Richard were as different in character as Joseph and Charles Surface in *The School for Scandal*. It has even been said that Charles had none of his father's intelligence, wit and charm, which Richard inherited in such abundance, together with his unreliability and inability to handle money. In mitigation it should be said that any brother would have looked dull in comparison with Richard. Charles was one of many lawyers in the family and its first diplomat. At the age of twenty he was appointed Secretary to the British Embassy in Stockholm. On his return, he studied at the Temple and, in 1779, was called to the Dublin Bar. He was then elected to the Irish parliament. When his younger brother entered a new Whig government, Charles became Secretary at War in Ireland and a member of the Privy Council. His oldest son, Charles, my great-grandfather, followed his father to Trinity College, Dublin and to the Middle Temple.

Richard Brinsley Sheridan was barely twenty-one when he

met and fell hopelessly in love with the beautiful young singer Eliza Linley. He outwitted half a dozen suitors, including his own brother. He then outmanoeuvred the girl's father, eloping to France after a breakneck coach journey from Bath to Dover. At twenty-five, with the profits from *The Rivals*, put on at Covent Garden the year before, Sheridan raised the £35,000 required to buy half the patent of Drury Lane Theatre from Garrick. Two years later, he bought the remaining share in the theatre. He became a confidential adviser of the Prince of Wales (afterwards Prince Regent and George IV) and an intimate of the Whig leaders. Fox persuaded him to enter Parliament: a seat was found for him at Stafford and he was duly elected, not without some of the financial inducements that were usual at the time. He was twenty-nine. Two years later, in 1782, with the fall of Lord North's Tory ministry, he joined the short-lived Rockingham government. The high point of his political career came in 1787, with his speech on the occasion of the impeachment of Warren Hastings. After this brilliant five-hour-long performance, one member remarked: 'Its effect upon its hearers has no parallel in ancient or modern times.' Pitt, a political opponent and himself a fine speaker, remarked of Sheridan's oratory: 'In most of his speeches, there was much fancy, in many shining wit, in all great eloquence, and in some few truth and justice.'

In 1809, he was brought to the brink of ruin by the destruction by fire of the new Drury Lane Theatre. He received news of the fire while in the middle of a speech in the House of Commons, but refused to allow the business of the House to be interrupted. When he reached the scene of the fire, he took a seat in the Piazza Coffee House opposite. From there, he watched his theatre burn. When someone remarked on his composure, he said: 'A man may surely take a glass of wine by his own fireside.' But the decline had set in. The theatre was heavily in debt and the building insured for one-tenth of its value. As a Member of Parliament he could not be arrested for debt (in similar circumstances, his father had fled to France). When Drury Lane Theatre was rebuilt he was not one of its shareholders. Eventually he lost his seat in Parliament. His last days were a characteristic blend of *misère* and *grandeur*. The bailiffs had already stripped the house in Savile Row of most of its furnishings and were stopped from removing Sheridan and his bed only by his physician, Dr Bain, who was also physician extraordinary to Sheridan's old friend and benefactor, the Prince of Wales. When the end was close no less a figure than the Bishop of London was considered fit to minister to the great man. The prelate arrived and Sheridan played the part of the dying man to perfection. It is said that a deep awe settled on his face. Perhaps the performance was too good, too memorable to be sincere. Certainly his wit did not desert him. To a message of goodwill from a former mistress, he replied: 'Tell Lady Bessborough that my eyes will look up to the coffin-lid with the same brilliancy as ever.' He died on 7 July 1816. It was decided that he should be buried in Westminster Abbey, with all the solemnity befitting a great political leader. He had wanted to be buried next to Charles Fox: he had to be content with a place in Poets' Corner, next to the grave of his friend Garrick (to be joined, later, on the other side, by Dickens) and a monument between those of Shakespeare and Addison.

R. B. S.'s son Tom inherited his mother's good looks and her consumptive tendencies. Believing that a warm climate might improve his health, the Prince Regent found a post for him in the Cape of Good Hope. But he did not survive for long, dying little more than a year after his father. His beautiful young widow returned to England and was given apartments in Hampton Court. This remarkable woman – she published several novels, the best known being *Carwell* – now devoted herself to launching her three beautiful daughters into Society. They all made 'brilliant' marriages. The youngest, Jane Georgina, married Edward Seymour, soon to become the Duke of Somerset. The second sister, Caroline, married the Hon. George Norton and went on to produce volume after volume of verse of a rather Byronic kind. Helen Selena, the eldest, married Captain Price Blackwood, whose family disapproved of the match: the Blackwoods were a rich landowning family in Ireland and Helen had no money at all. So, to avoid parental antagonism and to live as cheaply as possible, Price Blackwood took his young bride off to Italy. In 1839 he succeeded to the family title, becoming Baron Dufferin of Clandeboye. However, the couple did not take up residence in Ireland, but took a house overlooking the Bay of Naples. When a schoolboy of fifteen, their son and only child was told that his father had died on board ship between England and Belfast. He immediately joined his prostrate mother in Italy. In 1856, he set out on an expedition to the Arctic, the account of which he published with great success as *Letters from High Latitudes*. (Two years later he took his mother with him on a journey up the Nile and she amused herself writing a parody of her son's book, which she called *Lispings from Low Latitudes*.)

I first saw Lord Dufferin soon after his appointment as Ambassador to Paris. We were shown into one of the Embassy salons and were immediately joined by Lady Dufferin, a quite pleasant woman, as it turned out, despite her rather forbidding appearance. Suddenly the door opened and in came a very imposing old gentleman indeed – he was, in fact sixty-five at the time. He was very dark-skinned, not at all English-looking, with long, white hair and a full white beard. As he walked across the room, his eyeglass leapt from his face and dangled on the end of its cord. His voice was soft, mellifluous, seductive and he spoke with a slight lisp. He apologized profusely for keeping us waiting. The Marquis of Dufferin and Ava, former Governor-General of Canada and Viceroy of India, Her Majesty's sometime ambassador in St Petersburg, Constantinople, Rome and now Paris, then turned to Matthew and me and said: 'So you are the two young Sheridans. Of course, you belong to the rethpectable branch of the family.'

Grandfather had promised us a varied programme of theatrical treats for our first few weeks in London. I shall never forget my first visit to a London theatre. It had been a blustery, showery day. Matthew and I had not been out, but spent our time leafing through books and old copies of *Punch*, *Illustrated London News*, *Era*, *The Athenaeum* and *The Saturday Review*. Looking out over the square from one of the drawing-room windows, I watched the lamp lighter go round, lighting all the gas-lamps. Then Mary came in with tea, and drew the curtains. I felt that I was the only person there who seemed to be excited to what I regarded as the appropriate degree. Yes, the others were *looking forward* to the evening's entertainment, but my feelings were of an almost unbearable intensity. Only Grandfather, I knew, would have understood. He had seen hundreds of plays, but somehow he managed to maintain the same kind of excitement that I felt. About an hour later, I heard the maid letting him in. I rushed downstairs. He looked tired and despondent.

'Grandfather!' I shouted. 'You said that Charles Wyndham . . .' and I poured out a torrent of questions.

His face lit up: 'Why, of course! Our first night! My, what a treat!' For me, it was a first night twice over – my first night at a London theatre and the first night of Dion Boucicault's *London Assurance*, which Wyndham was reviving in memory of the Irish actor-dramatist, who had died in New York earlier in the year. I followed Grandfather up the stairs and, as he sipped his whiskey, he answered my questions, each of us feeding on the other's enthusiasm.

We stepped out of our carriage into Piccadilly Circus, the wet cobble-stones glistening in the light from the gas-lamps, and followed Grandfather into the Criterion Theatre. My first impression was one of disappointment: I found myself in a tall, but small room, covered entirely with green and yellow tiles. I had not been warned that this was the smallest theatre in London, the only one to be built entirely underground, the only one in which one has to go down to the dress circle. Before the play and during the intervals, we stood around while Grandfather, obviously enjoying himself as much as he had in his seat, moved about, speaking to this person and that. The play, that witty Victorian recreation of Restoration comedy, with Charles Wyndham in the role of Dazzle, fully came up to my expectations. I laughed and laughed, though not always understanding the jokes.

We could not have seen *The Bells*, with its eerie, wintry atmosphere, on a better night. That morning there had been more snow and, by evening, the temperature had fallen dramatically. In one scene, we actually saw snow falling outside the window of Matthias's inn. It was with this play that, at the age of thirty-three, Irving began his reign as manager at the Lyceum. It was a reworking of an earlier French play by an American playwright, substantially altered by Irving himself. As my grandfather had said, it was a poor thing, but very much Irving's own. Years later, in Paris, I realized what an ordinary piece of work the play was and what a spell Irving's performance threw over it, when I saw Coquelin, surely one of the greatest all-round actors of all time, in Irving's role. Coquelin's performance was a *tour de force* of sheer artistry, detail piled upon detail, yet it lacked what had been the heart of Irving's performance – that electrifying emotion, that profound psychological insight that marked Irving at his best. It is the story of an Alsatian inn-keeper, Matthias, who, long ago, murdered a traveller, a Polish Jew, and robbed him of a large sum of gold. Twenty years later, as the snow is falling, he is haunted by the hallucinatory sound of the sleigh-bells that he associates with the old Jew's arrival at his inn. No one who ever saw Irving in the part will forget his blood-curdling stare when the sleigh-bells are heard for the first time and come gradually closer – none of the other characters can hear them.

When the play was over, Grandfather took us round, as promised, through the stage-door to meet the great actor.

'Sherry, my dear, do come in!' said the great man, looking vulnerable, naked almost, without his wig and beard, his face shining with removal cream.

Grandfather presented my parents, reminding him that they had met once before, after such and such a play. Then, with a great flourish, he said, 'And these are my Chinese grandsons!'

Irving peered over at us and asked, with great concern, 'I do hope you were able to follow the play.'

'Oh, yes, Mr Irving,' I burst out excitedly. 'I thought it was wonderful!'

'Gudd, Gudd,' he murmured, with that way he had of pronouncing every vowel slightly differently from anyone else, his eyes fixed upon us with a sort of distracted fascination. Then, looking up at my grandfather, as if mildly perplexed, he said: 'Funny thing, they look as English as you or I.' Matthew and I giggled nervously. Irving may simply have been sustaining the joke as any adult might have done. If so, I know of no one who could have sounded more convincingly sincere. Grandfather, who knew Irving as well as most people, was not so sure: Irving lived in a world of his own, bounded by the walls of his theatre, and was quite capable of believing whatever he was told, providing it was said with enough conviction – if, that is, the acting was good enough. As Grandfather ushered us out, Irving looked up, obviously worried by our presence: 'Sherry, you will be coming to supper?' Grandfather reassured him that he would be back in five minutes, that he was just seeing his family to a carriage, and would walk round with him to the Club.

That night, Grandfather did not return home: in fact, he arrived back at the house about half an hour before luncheon the next morning and shortly after Grandmother got back from church. This, I later discovered, happened most weekends and the practice had been interrupted the week before only in our honour. That night, Irving was giving one of his Saturday night suppers at the Garrick, the last before Christmas, and, of course, Grandfather wanted to be there. Such gatherings would last until four or five in the morning, at which time some of the guests would go home and others, like Grandfather, would take a room at the Club and snatch a few hours' sleep.

That afternoon, accompanied by our parents, Matthew and I went off to skate in St James's Park. The ice, it seemed, was four inches thick and had been declared safe. In Paris, the situation was 'worse': ice-floes were floating down the Seine. The Bois de Boulogne would be thronging with skaters. Perhaps, after all, we would get several weeks of skating that winter, as in Peking. Indeed, the relative severity of the Peking winter, which had afforded us long months of uninterrupted practice on the Imperial Canal and on the lakes of the old Summer Palace, had made us much better skaters than most of the hesitant, stumbling crowd around us. Our duets were the envy of all.

Christmas – the first Christmas in England I remember –

arrived. On Christmas Eve, Grandfather made his only concession of the year to Grandmother's religious convictions and
joined us for Midnight Mass at All Saints', Margaret Street. I
had hardly ever attended a communion service before, so I had
nothing to compare it with. I warmed at once to the ceremo-
nial, the dignity of the robed priests, the punctilious
movements of the altar boys, the ringing of the bells, the glow
of the candles in the darkened church, the pungent, almost
sickening smell of incense, the haunting music. Thereafter, I
had greater respect for my grandmother's churchgoing – I now
had some inkling of what it meant to her.

Christmas Day was celebrated with a lavishness that had
not been possible in Peking. Those Christmases in Smith
Square were everything a Victorian Christmas should be, with
Grandfather as its presiding genius, utterly in his element.
On Boxing Day, we went over to Aunt and Uncle Jacky's,
where much the same sort of thing was repeated, with the
addition of lots of party games – for Aunt Carrie was also
there, with Uncle Tom, Vicky and Lisa. After a more than
usually substantial tea – we would get no dinner and we would
probably not be home until after midnight – we set off in
three carriages for Drury Lane.

The Christmas pantomime is the high point of the year for
many English children, whichever of the hundreds of productions up and down the country they are taken to.
Theatrical magic cannot be measured, especially where children are concerned: a panto in Bow or Bolton can work the
same magic on a child. But those lucky enough to see the great
Drury Lane creations in their heyday were witnessing something very special indeed: a spectacle of extravagance
unparalleled anywhere else, with the finest music-hall per-
formers of the time. 'Pantomimes' at Drury Lane go back at
least to Sheridan: he even wrote a *Robinson Crusoe* and played

the part of 'Harlequin Friday' himself at the first performance. But the modern pantomime was the creation of the then
licensee, Augustus Harris, universally known as 'Druriolanus'.
He was a good friend of Grandfather, which explains how we
always managed to get a couple of adjacent boxes for that
most sought-after first night. As a young man, Harris had
been an actor in Barry Sullivan's company. He was already
licensee of the Drury Lane Theatre when, in 1888, he took
over the Covent Garden Opera House, where his father had
worked as stage manager. Not content with his theatres, Harris
was also the owner of the *Sunday Times*. Yet his knighthood
came not as a reward for his services to stage or print, but
because he happened to be Sheriff of the City of London
during the visit, in 1891, of the German Emperor. In 1896, at
the age of forty-five, he died suddenly. Things would never be
quite the same again in either of the two great theatrical neighbours. 'Druriolanus' now stands, looking into Catherine
Street, from the water fountain erected in his memory against
the wall of the theatre that had seen his pantomimes
Christmas after Christmas.

For those privileged of the privileged who attended the first
performance of the Drury Lane 'panto' on Boxing Day, there
was a still greater sense of occasion. From the moment one's
carriage drew up outside the Theatre Royal, where real
guardsmen stood to attention outside and the door was cere-
moniously opened by liveried footmen with powdered wigs,
every child was momentarily a Cinderella at Prince
Charming's ball. Once inside, another footman saw you to
your box. The orchestra was already playing popular songs,
with the occupants of pit and gallery lustily adding the words.
They had probably joined the queue for seats by midday,
standing patiently until the doors were opened in the middle of
the afternoon. One can imagine their relief when the theatre

orchestra finally appeared to entertain them. Suddenly, the orchestra stopped playing; there was an expectant hush. The Princess of Wales appeared, followed by her party.

This year we were to be offered *Beauty and the Beast*. I already knew the 'story', but was surprised by the liberties taken with Perrault's *La Belle et la Bête*. In time, as each Christmas brought a new pantomime, I came to accept the conventions of the genre, the most obvious of which was the element of transvestism. The hero, known as the 'principal boy', was played by an attractive woman, 'his' mother, the 'Dame', by a male comedian. Each year Dan Leno, of the diminutive figure and the dry, husky voice, would desert the London Pavilion for the Drury Lane 'panto', joined by two other comedians, Harry Nicholls and Herbert Campbell. Another great star of the music hall, Marie Lloyd, often appeared, without change of sex, as the 'principal girl'. There were always spectacular set-pieces. I remember a 'procession of twenty-four nations', in which we were delighted to observe that the costumes of the Tartars and Chinese were the most splendid. Another such procession was of all the kings and queens of England from William the Conqueror to Victoria. Harris was often topical, too. One year, *Robinson Crusoe* opened with a dockers' strike at Hull. Another year, Cinderella went to the ball in a motor-car, a rare sight in the London streets at that time, her sisters being reduced to a rather shabby 'four-wheeler'. In *Dick Whittington*, in 1894, the year of the Sino-Japanese conflict, Harris depicted a spectacular sea battle between the two great oriental powers. To justify this particular scene, the future Lord Mayor of London and his cat found themselves, during their voyage round the world, unwilling guests in the court of the Chinese emperor. How strange it was to look out over the red plush edge of our box across the empty, darkened space to the animated, brightly-lit

stage, to that representation of a place where my brother and
I had spent much of our lives, where, even now, our parents
were held captive, not at the whim of an emperor, but in the
service of a queen. For almost everyone else in that theatre, the
designer's art had conjured up an exotic never-never land; for
me, it was a dream-like distorted image of what had once been
everyday reality. My delight was threatened once or twice by a
lump in the throat and a pricking behind the eyes.

Two days later, London and Christmas were over: Paris and
the New Year awaited us. Those six weeks in London had been
such a whirlwind of new experiences that Peking had faded
into the background. I had become very attached to our life in
Smith Square, and passionately loyal to London and England.
I had grown fond of my grandmother, with her quiet kindli-
ness, but, above all, I would miss my grandfather and I felt sure
that he reciprocated my feelings. However, any doubts I might
have had about our life in Paris were dispelled when I caught
sight of our Dumollard grandparents on the platform of the
Gare du Nord. They stood there, arms outstretched, smiling
broadly, brimming over with delight, he a thin, wiry man of
medium height, with blue-grey eyes and a goatee, she slim,
erect, well above the average height for a woman, wearing an
ankle-length, dove-grey coat, trimmed with black fur collar
and cuffs, and a matching Russian-style fur hat. She struck me
at once as being quite the most elegant *dame d'un certain âge* I
had ever seen: she had just turned sixty, but looked much
younger. Her elegance was not a matter of what she was wearing, though what she wore on that cold winter's evening was
quietly elegant. It was a more indefinable matter than clothes,
a quality that seemed to find expression in her bearing, in the
way she stooped down to pick something up, the way she
moved her hands, the combined grace of eyes and mouth.

Pépé and Mémé lived in an apartment on the rue de

Vaugirard. The drawing-room looked out, not at the Jardin du Luxembourg itself, but at the new museum devoted to the 'works of living artists'. What, in a less actively literary household might have been called the library, but was referred to as the *cabinet de travail*, was situated at the back of the apartment, overlooking the large, cobble-stoned courtyard. There my grandparents spent the best part of their days, sitting at each end of a long table spread with newspapers and books, writing, reading, talking and smoking – Mémé consuming endless black Russian cigarettes through an ivory holder, Pépé puffing away at one or other of his pipes. French windows, which provided very necessary ventilation, looked out on to a long roof-garden, in fact, the flat roof of a row of stables. This was only one of the peculiarities of the apartment, made all the odder in that Pépé was one of the few residents not to keep a carriage and horses of his own. Another was that it had its own entrance, reached from the courtyard by an external staircase. The kitchen and two of the bedrooms were situated on the ground floor.

Everything about Pépé was instinct with movement: his words, gestures, the expressions on his face followed in rapid succession. Everything seemed to be of the utmost importance to him. When he was sitting 'quietly' in a chair, reading, a ceaseless commentary seemed to be proceeding within him, erupting every now and then in a gesture of impatience, a sigh of despair, a grunt of approval or even, when the pressure inside him grew too intense, an appeal to anyone who happened to be in the room to vindicate his opinion. When this was not forthcoming or when, in the course of a conversation, a difference of opinion arose, he seemed positively perplexed, almost pained and would not rest until every effort had been made to bridge the gap; in practice, this meant trying to bring the other person over to his way of thinking. Yet there was not the slightest trace of overbearingness in this – he was the gentlest, least domineering of men. It was just that the matter at issue, as often as not an aesthetic judgement, seemed to him to be too important to be left unsettled. And in such matters he made no allowance for age or experience: he treated a demur from Matthew or me exactly as if it had come from some *cher confrère* of the republic of letters.

His father had made a modest fortune on the Paris Bourse, thus leaving his son free to indulge his literary ambitions. As a young man, Henri Dumollard wore his hair excessively long, in the manner of his heroes, Lamartine, Vigny, Musset, Hugo, the Romantic poets who had dominated the French literary scene of his youth. His other gods, which he later came to hold in higher esteem, were the second generation of English Romantic poets, Shelley and Keats in particular. His love of English literature, indeed his knowledge of the English language, he derived from his mother, an Englishwoman.

In his twenties, he published poems in the reviews and a couple of volumes of verse, at his own, or rather his father's expense. By the time he was thirty, however, his romantic muse had deserted him: the poet had dwindled, as is the way of the world, into a critic. It may be thought that this was the inevitable effect of a bourgeois domestic existence shared with a wife and two daughters. And so, I suppose, it was, except that it is difficult to imagine that this eminently sociable man had ever been capable of contemplating man's tragic isolation amid the awesome, but indifferent beauties of nature for more than half an hour at a time. One would have been justified in concluding that being a poet had been, at best, a natural extension of being in love with poetry or, at worst, a fashionable pose. Not surprisingly, this unappreciated poet settled for a life more in keeping with his gifts and inclinations. In the reviewing of plays and books he gained the respect and recognition that his youthful verses had denied him. In later life, he even became, with his *Les Poètes romantiques anglais* and *Shelley, vie et oeuvre*, something of an 'authority'.

Politically, he was still influenced by his Romantic idols: he was what Shelley would have called a radical and Hugo a *républicain*. For him, France was best represented neither by its divinely appointed kings, nor by its self-made emperor, but by the abstract principles of the Revolution, and he was quite content that the living embodiment of those principles should be a constantly changing committee of ordinary mortals like himself. As to those principles, it was liberty above all that held his allegiance: he would have been perturbed if equality had been taken beyond its narrow, legalistic confines and, like most Frenchmen, he had no clearer notion of fraternity than the average Christian has of the Holy Ghost. But, like most Frenchmen again, his statements of principle went well beyond anything that he would have countenanced in reality. His political thinking was entirely at one with that of France's third and probably ultimate Republic: radical in word, conservative in deed. Its radical rhetoric secures the allegiance of its intellectuals and its conservative reality that of the rest. It is generally uninspired and uninspiring, it can be maddeningly ineffectual, but it has the virtue of being constructed on a human scale. Its very humanity allows plenty of scope for grumbling, little for serious disaffection. For all its imperfections, it has produced a life that, for all classes, with the possible exception of the aristocracy, is as good as any to be found elsewhere. But, as the new century came nearer, those who rejected that present in favour of an idealized past or future were to swell in numbers.

But how did that *homme moyen intellectuel* come to meet the Countess Catherine Zichy? To answer this, we must go back to that fateful year 1848. Across Europe revolutions broke out and republics were set up: Hungary was no exception, nor, for that matter, was France, which became a republic for the second time. The Zichys, like many of Hungary's noble families, supported the rising of 1848 and the subsequent declaration of a republic, independent of the Austrian imperial crown. But the new *régime* was short-lived, the Austrian troops attacked and the more prominent leaders went into exile. Among them were Mémé's father and his family. Catherine Zichy was eighteen at the time. In normal circumstances, she might well have found herself married off to some eligible Hungarian count. Instead, she was transported from the restricted social life of a country estate and the closely regulated 'Season' in Budapest to the free, glittering world of Paris. In due course, she met and fell in love with a young French poet who, though untitled, had a fairly substantial private income. Given the harsh realities of exile and his daughter's declining value on the marriage market, the girl's father might still have given his approval if the aspirant son-in-law had held the right opinions – if, that is, he had been a good Catholic; after all, Count Zichy and Henri Dumollard were both sons of '48. But being a republican in Paris was a very different matter from being a republican in Budapest. For the Hungarians, it meant no more than a belief in the right of the Hungarian nobility to run their country without having to pay allegiance to the Habsburg Emperor. In France, a republican was a democrat, a liberal, above all, an anti-clerical. Count Zichy issued his ultimatum: his daughter was to give up any idea of marrying her commoner poet or be disowned. Catherine replied that she was already engaged. A few days later, the couple were married – with no member of the bride's family present. Five years later, when the amnesty of the 1848 rebels was declared, Count Zichy and his family returned to Hungary. Three years after that, the old count died. In time, something of a reconciliation was effected between Catherine and her mother, but my grandmother never forgave her younger brother, Reszö, for so firmly supporting their father's line. When we met her, Mémé Dumollard had still not revisited Hungary, though for the past twenty years, under an assumed name, she had written a fortnightly 'Letter from Paris' and book reviews for a Budapest newspaper. In recent years, she had also been visited by her married nephews and nieces and by an assortment of cousins, who usually stayed with a distant relation of ours, Ladislas Károlyi. Uncle Lázsló, as we called him, lived in a vast house on the quai d'Orsay that he had acquired in exchange for an island near Martinique inherited from French ancestors.

When strangers saw my grandparents together they tended to exclaim: 'What a wonderful old couple!' Indeed, without being in any sense embarrassing, they behaved towards one another like young lovers. It was as if this Parisian bourgeois and his Hungarian lady had long ago decided that the best possible life was that of young Latin Quarter bohemians, had adopted such a life and were determined to maintain it. In many respects they were living out a phantasy. Latter-day cynics – or socialists – might object, not without cause, that there was nothing bohemian about the realities that sustained this phantasy: the fine apartment overlooking the Luxembourg, the devoted housekeeper, assisted by a maid and, ultimately, the investments upon which everything depended. And it is true that what was actually produced during those long hours in their *cabinet de travail* would not have kept them alive, let alone supported them in their *train de vie*.[1] But would they have made themselves or anyone else happier if they had not remained young in heart and mind,

---

1 Way of life, or 'lifestyle', as we would say now.

but adopted a manner and outlook more in keeping with their age and station? The 'realities' on which their phantasy rested made it possible for them to act as hosts and mentors to successive waves of young writers, from the impoverished young Emile Zola and Alphonse Daudet, who were a mere ten years younger than Henri Dumollard, through the Parnassians, to the young Symbolist poets, thirty or forty years his juniors. They were in no way 'attached' to the things that made their lives comfortable: they never gave such things a thought. In no essential respect were their lives any different from those of many other, less 'fortunate' inhabitants of the Latin Quarter who actually did live in garrets.

I awoke the day after our arrival with two desires demanding immediate satisfaction: to go skating and to see Sarah Bernhardt. Indeed it had been the prospect of these two delights that had reconciled me to leaving London. We were assured that the first presented no problem: next morning, after breakfast, we would all go off to the Bois. As for the second, Madame Sarah would be in Paris for three more weeks prior to embarking on a world tour. She could be seen in Sardou's *Cléopâtre* and it had been announced that she would give a few performances as Phèdre, her greatest role, before leaving. Pépé promised to obtain tickets for both. He was as inveterate a playgoer as my other grandfather but, accompanying him to the theatre scores of times over the next few years, I realized that he seldom achieved the latter's childlike enthusiasm. He was no longer, if he had ever been, 'stagestruck', which, I suppose, was natural enough, since he did his theatre-going in the course of professional duty.

And so, the following morning, New Year's Eve, we set off in a cab for the Bois de Boulogne. As we crossed the Seine at the Pont de l'Alma, we got our first good view of the new Eiffel Tower, the centrepiece of the previous year's Great Exhibition.

The controversy that had accompanied its erection was now repeated *en plus petit* in our *fiacre*, Mother, representing the traditionalists, regarded it as a metallic monstrosity, out of scale and style with its surroundings, while Matthew, for the modernists, saw it as a symbol of the engineering skills of a new age. Father and I were unable to make up our minds.

We skated until sunset up and down the kilometre-long Lac Inférieur, breaking off only for a light luncheon in the island restaurant. How to convey the animal delight in prowess, the nerve-tingling combination of heat and cold, the joy of shared excitement of that day? Brueghel in certain of his winter scenes succeeds better than I can, as does Wordsworth in the *Prelude*, remembering his own Lakeland childhood:

> *I wheeled about*
> *Proud and exalted like an untired horse*
> *That cares not for his home. All shod with steel,*
> *We hissed along the polished ice in games*
> *Confederate, imitative of the chase*
> *And woodland pleasures – the resounding horn,*
> *The pack loud chiming, and the hunted hare.*
> *So through the darkness and the cold we flew,*
> *And not a voice was idle . . .*
> > *while the stars*
> *Eastward were sparkling clear and in the west*
> *The orange sky of evening died away.*

We returned to tea and special New Year cakes, and the long magical day ended with a splendid *Réveillon* dinner, with the traditional *dinde aux marrons*.[1] At midnight, all the lamps were extinguished and we kissed one another in the dark.

1 Eve – in this case, New Year's Eve. Turkey with chestnuts.

My first visit to the theatre in Paris took place two days later. At the Odéon, a few doors away, there was a revival of Alphonse Daudet's early play *L'Arlésienne*, with music by Bizet. This gentle, rather sentimental evocation of Daudet's native Provence had been a flop when first produced nearly twenty years before. Now everyone was wondering why such a charming piece had failed to please at its first reception. I must confess that the play itself made less impression on me than did the theatre itself. Indeed, I felt that there was something incongruous in depicting the inconsequential adventures of those simple provincials before that elegant Parisian audience, in that splendid theatre, the 'second house' of the Comédie-Française. But I would no doubt have taken the play more seriously if I had already met Alphonse Daudet and his family, as I was to do some weeks later.

My first visit to the Théâtre-Français was even more noted for a disparity between what took place in the auditorium and what was being presented on the stage. It was also my first introduction to the capacity of the French to see artistic endeavour as a matter of the utmost importance to the body politic. The first night of Sardou's *Thermidor* was to be one of those occasions when history is made immediately, obviously and noisily. Sardou, the most popular playwright of the day, was not one to stir up such fury, but, by treating certain heroes of the Revolution, Robespierre especially, with disrespect, he touched a raw nerve in the French body politic. Before long, the gallery grew restive. The stalls responded by expressing their displeasure at the interruptions. But not even Coquelin *cadet*, as Camille Desmoulins, or the beautiful Julia Bartet, as Fabienne Lecoulteux, could quell the audience. Fights broke out and the performance ended prematurely in uproar. As we left the theatre, the arguments, often conducted at the top of the speakers' voices, continued unabated. Yet the view of the

Revolution expressed in the play was broadly that of Michelet and of the majority of the French people at the time. It was the same, indeed, as that taught in the nation's schools – exalting '89 and even '92, while repudiating the bloody insanity of '93. Next day, however, the 'republican' newspapers were full of denunciations of Sardou's play, demanding that a theatre subsidized by the state should not be allowed to bring that state into disrepute. Performances were cancelled; a few days later, the play was banned by government order. The theatre management responded by substituting Molière's *Tartuffe*, the ultimate study in hypocrisy, for the banned performances. Jules Lemaître, in *Le Journal des Débats*, expressed the views of the play's defenders: 'It is not permitted, at the present time, for a dramatist to speak ill of the Terror, the Committee of Public Safety, the revolutionary courts and one gives offence to some state religion by protesting against the abuse that Robespierre and his accomplices made of the guillotine a hundred years ago.'

It was an exceptionally cold winter. The *bassins* and lakes of Paris remained stubbornly frozen for most of January. But our life in Paris was not to be all skating and theatre-going. The following Monday, Matthew and I turned up at the Cours Racine in the rue Racine, a small private school run by two unmarried sisters, the Mlles Augier. We would both be starting at Henri IV in October and the purpose of our two terms at the Cours Racine was not so much to bring us up to the required academic level, as to get us used to being with French boys of our own age. Skating and theatre-going would have continued with no other interruption than that required by school attendance had I not succumbed, a few days later, to the influenza epidemic. For over a week I was confined to my bed. But although I was able to return to my skating, my illness robbed me of seeing Sarah Bernhardt. On the day I was to accompany Matthew and my parents to *Cléopâtre* I was still feverish. According to the doctor, I would be on my feet in about a week; then Pépé would go with me to see Sarah Bernhardt. But it was not to be. No sooner had I recovered than it was announced that Mme Bernhardt herself was ill and her performances had been cancelled until further notice. I waited and waited, then, one morning, we read in the newspaper that Mme Bernhardt was still suffering from pharyngitis, brought on by cold and exhaustion: the run of *Cléopâtre* would not be resumed and the promised performances of *Phèdre* would not now take place. On 23 January, Sarah Bernhardt set sail for America. The one thing we shared, our illness, had kept us apart. She would not be returning to Paris until October 1893!

During our school years, Matthew and I were to see hundreds of plays and operas – in Paris during term time and at Easter, in London during the Season and at Christmas. In Paris, we would accompany Pépé and Mémé to most of the first nights; since each of them was accounted a member of the press corps, each had the right to take a guest. Pépé found nothing odd in this: if we were intelligent enough to enjoy the theatre, then it was quite natural that we should want to go as often as possible. There was no question of saying that we had had too many evenings out lately, or that we had to go to school next day. At all times we were treated, spoken to and listened to as equals. We would go to the Opéra (where everything was sung in Italian, unless the work was French) and to the Opéra-Comique (where the works were not necessarily comic, but always sung in French). We would go to see Sarah Bernhardt whenever she was in Paris, on her return from some world tour. Then there were the two theatres of the Comédie-Française, the incomparably beautiful old Théâtre-Français, also known as the Salle Richelieu and the 'Maison de Molière', and our dear neighbour, the Odéon, which had the excellent practice of giving performances at reduced prices on Thursday afternoons, when the schools were shut. There we saw many of the plays of the French classical repertoire, the great Mounet-Sully in Racine, perhaps, or the unsurpassable Coquelin *aîné* in Molière. Then there were the *avant-garde* groups, Antoine's Théâtre de l'Art and what was to become Lugné-Poe's Théâtre de l'Oeuvre.

My discovery of the theatre, at the age of ten, was more in the nature of a rediscovery; it was something that I felt I already knew instinctively. I had already read many of Shakespeare's plays and dreamt about how they might appear on the stage. The discovery of music, too, was like a rediscovery, as if something already inside me had been revealed to me. In China, of course, I had heard very little music and none that could be called great – no Bach and Handel, no Mozart or Beethoven, nothing, in fact, but a few sentimental salon pieces on the piano and a few songs equally sentimental or coyly comic. Soon after our arrival in Paris, we started going to concerts. For reasons that I have never been able to understand, all three Paris orchestras give their concerts at exactly the same time, on exactly the same day. The notion that only Sunday afternoon is a suitable time to go to an orchestral concert – mercifully, the same rule does not apply to opera, chamber music or recitals – brought some agonizing decisions for those whose loyalties were not entirely wedded to one or other of the three. Such single-minded devotees did exist however. There were those of an extremely fastidious – or snobbish – turn who acknowledged only the 'Société des Concerts du Conservatoire'. This orchestra was undoubtedly the best in France and the equal of many of the finest in Germany. Their programmes were heavily biased towards the German classics and more recent French works. At the opposite extreme were the Concerts Lamoureux at the Cirque d'été. In that huge, uncomfortable circus – actual circus shows took place there at other times – a mainly young, mainly 'modernist', that is, Wagnerite audience congregated. Charles Lamoureux was the pioneer of Wagner's music in France at that time and his concerts always contained at least some of Wagner's orchestral music and often whole scenes from the operas. Somewhere between the two, at the Théâtre du Châtelet, were the Concerts Colonne.

Later in the year, an event occurred at the Opéra that proved to be as big a *cause célèbre* as the Comédie-Française production of *Thermidor* earlier in the year. Charles Lamoureux had taken over the directorship of the Opéra and had decided, ardent Wagnerite that he was, to mark his new *régime* with the first full-length production of *Lohengrin* in Paris. Why should a city well used to a weekly diet of Wagner in the concert hall erupt in fury when one of the Master's earlier, more accessible works was produced at the Opéra? As in the case of *Thermidor*, the crux of the problem was that one of the national theatres, with its state subsidy, was involved. Charles Lamoureux could play what he liked in his concerts, but he should not use the stage of the Paris Opéra to insult the French nation. Just as *Thermidor* had been seen by the extreme republicans as an attack, subsidized by the republic, on the founding fathers of the republic, so, for the extreme nationalists, *Lohengrin* at the Opéra, was tantamount to the Paris City Council opening the gates of Paris to the Prussians, even though it contained no mention of France whatsoever and was sung in French by an all-French cast. For Charles Lamoureux himself the production was a personal act of revenge on the nationalists who had disrupted an earlier production of the opera that he had tried to mount at the Eden-Théâtre four years before.

On 16 September, a splendid late summer day, the great moment arrived. The government was taking no chances: police were posted in every part of the house and were lined up in formation outside. After such a build-up the actual performance must have come as an anticlimax to the anti-Wagnerites. For me, it opened a window on that very special world, tantalizingly brief and incomplete glimpses of which had been given me week after week at the Cirque d'été. From the first ethereal notes on the violins, the real drama outside in the streets was forgotten. I was in a world in which it was quite normal for a knight dressed in white to glide on to the stage on the back of a swan. I was brought back to the everyday world only when large sections of the audience greeted the knight's entry with tumultuous applause. Whatever opposition had found its way into the opera house was intimidated by the presence of the police in the side aisles. The curtain did not fall until after midnight. Next morning, we learnt in the papers that a crowd of two hundred singing the *Marseillaise* had been dispersed in the boulevard des Italiens and that, in the rue de Choiseul, another group surrounded hapless ladies and gentlemen on their way home from the opera and forced them to shout *'A bas Wagner!'*[1] If they refused, they were beaten up.

Our first week or so in Paris found us in a tiny theatre in Montparnasse. A new company, founded by actors at the very beginning of their careers, was to put on Shelley's *The Cenci*, a play so apparently ill suited to public performance that it had rarely been played in England. It was a first night that had eluded the notice of many of the critics, but one of those that, in retrospect, turn out to have had historical significance, even when there is nothing at the time to suggest as much. It

1 'Down with Wagner!'

marked the *début* as an independent theatre director of Aurélien Lugné-Poe, then only twenty-one. After studying acting at the Conservatoire, he joined first Antoine's Théâtre Libre, then Paul Fort's Théâtre d'Art. With the collapse of the latter, Lugné-Poe founded his own company, which became the Théâtre de l'Oeuvre. It was a reading of my grandfather's book on Shelley that first gave Lugné-Poe the idea of producing *The Cenci*. The two men met and Pépé continued to give advice during the preparation of the production. His unstuffy enthusiasm must have won the hearts of Lugné-Poe and his friends, forty years or more his juniors. We were honoured guests backstage after the play and, just as the auditorium of the Odéon had made more impression on me than Daudet's *L'Arlésienne*, so the sight of those young actors, sitting in various stages of *déshabille*, under the harsh lighting of a squalid dressing-room, fired my enthusiasm for the theatre far more than three hours of Shelley's verse in French had done. Why, when the business of theatre is illusion, did I find, on those two occasions, the realities behind and in front of the stage more interesting than what was on it?

Lugné-Poe was to become one of the most influential figures in the French theatre of the 1890s. His aim was to create a theatre that would be part of the literary movement of his generation, Symbolism. The essence of Symbolism was to deny the representative role of language, to set it free to play its own games. It had produced a theatre of the indefinite, indefinite in time and place, characters hardly distinguishable from one another, language that seemed to refer to nothing. Not surprisingly, there were few Symbolist plays. Lugné-Poe therefore broadened his aims to include plays that, by their very foreignness, seemed to speak of another world: very few of the plays presented by the Oeuvre were French. The favoured source was north European: English (Shelley's *The*

Cenci, Marlowe's *Dr Faustus),* German (Hauptmann), Russian (Gogol) and, above all, the great modern master from the fjords, Ibsen. Lugné-Poe's appropriation of Ibsen was founded on a misunderstanding: for him, Ibsen's world was exotic simply by virtue of its remoteness from anything that might be of concern to a Parisian audience. In England, on the other hand, Ibsen had been taken over by a group of social critics, led by Shaw, who saw him as the prophet of the new moral and political world that was coming to birth. The difference in approach was apparent in the acting styles adopted on stage. Whereas in London, the utmost naturalism was aimed at, in Paris the Oeuvre affected a sort of chant-like elocution that undermined any ambition that the play might have to 'represent' the world.

The Oeuvre productions were usually given two performances, only the second being open to the paying public. The first performance was strictly speaking the *répétition générale,* or dress rehearsal, and was attended by the theatre's friends and supporters. The performances were preceded by a lecture, which was often as controversial as the play itself. For *An Enemy of the People,* for example, the lecturer was Laurent Tailhade, one of the many young Symbolist poets who had espoused sympathy for the anarchists. For an hour, in the face of constant interruptions, Tailhade continued with his talk, which had less to do with Ibsen than with the iniquities of the close links being forged at that time between the French Republic and the Tsarist autocracy.

About this time, Paris was in the grip of a series of bomb attacks carried out by anarchists. In 1891 the May Day celebrations had led to a clash with the police in which nine people lost their lives. The following year three bombs exploded, two at the houses of judges, one in a barracks. In December 1893, the Chambre des Députés itself was the scene of a bomb attack, in which no one was killed, but several deputies wounded. Auguste Vaillant, the perpetrator of this crime, was twenty-three. Over-hasty readings of works of political theory had turned this mild-mannered young man into an anarchist zealot. When questioned about this attack, Laurent Tailhade's answer achieved a certain notoriety. Echoing Hedda Gabler, he said: '*Qu'importe la mort des vagues humanités, pourvu que le geste soit beau et si, par elle, s'affirme l'individu.*'[1] Vaillant's condemnation to death set in motion a campaign for clemency, but, on 5 February 1894, he went to the guillotine. Other bomb attacks were followed by more arrests of anarchists; each arrest by more bombs.

One evening we were having dinner when we heard an explosion: it sounded quite close. Pépé went down to see what had happened and found the concierge and a group of local residents standing inside the *porte cochère*. 'There's been a bomb at Foyot's,' he was told. Foyot's was a well-known restaurant about two hundred yards up the road. Next morning, we learnt that nobody had been killed, but that one diner had been seriously injured and was lying semi-conscious in the Charité Hospital. Later, we read in the papers that the victim was none other than Laurent Tailhade. It transpired that the bomb, disguised as a package, had been left on a windowsill – a few inches away from Tailhade's table – by one of the 'companions', as the anarchists were called. The original plan was to throw it into the Odéon, where the Prince of Wales was attending a performance of *Le Ruban* by Feydeau and Desvallières. The blast very nearly blew away one side of Tailhade's face and he lost his right eye. The public did not need to be reminded of Tailhade's endorsement of anarchists'

1 'What does the death of a vague number of human beings matter, if the gesture is beautiful and if, through it, the individual asserts himself.'

bombs. With understandable glee the press pounced on the poetic justice of a noted anarchist sympathizer being the victim of an anarchist bomb. 'Perhaps M. Laurent Tailhade will now tell us,' one newspaper wrote, 'whether he is happy to see the murderer's individuality affirmed at the expense of his, Tailhade's, vague humanity.'

Lugné-Poe did, occasionally, find a truly Symbolist play or one written in French, though the most famous of these came from Belgium, where, as far as most Parisians were concerned, the mists of the North began. In *Pelléas et Mélisande*, Maeterlinck's 'Symbolism' took the form of a drama that unfolds in a time and place no more defined than that of medieval Europe. Plot is motivated, not by personal decisions, but by a Destiny whose workings are beyond human intelligence. The characters scarcely exist or interact: they glide past one another without making contact, without hearing one another. What one character says often has no logical connection with what was said immediately before. A question ('Why do you look so surprised?') will be countered by another ('Are you a giant?'). Golaud stumbles on Mélisande when he has lost his way in the forest. Nobody knows where she comes from and she herself seems to be suffering from total amnesia. Her last words are: 'I don't understand everything I say either . . . I don't know what I am saying . . . I don't know what I know . . . I no longer say what I want . . .' A true disciple of Mallarmé, Maeterlinck operated on the boundary between poetry and silence. His pared-down, simple, fragmented prose aspires, not to the condition of music, but to that of silence. The central symbol of the play is a bottomless well. Pelléas says of it: 'There is always an extraordinary silence, as if one could hear the water sleeping.' All the characters seem to be drawn towards depths, abysses, mysteries and, ultimately, death.

Without Lugné-Poe it is doubtful whether *Pelléas et Mélisande* would ever have been performed at all. He raised the necessary financial backing, found a theatre, took on and rehearsed actors, had sets and costumes made, as well as playing the part of Golaud. Present at that single afternoon performance were artists like Whistler and Jacques-Emile Blanche, journalists like Georges Clemenceau and Léon Blum, writers like Barrès and Rachilde, patrons of the *avant-garde* like Robert de Rothschild and Comtesse Greffülhe – and, of course, Claude Debussy. Long before he had read or seen the play, Debussy had begun to dream of a kind of music-drama in which he could escape the dominating influence of Wagner and find his own voice. For him the relationship between music and text would not be one in which the former expressed the latter, but one in which music expressed what the text could not express. *Pelléas et Mélisande* did not mark the renaissance in the drama that advance publicity claimed: indeed, today, the play seems dated and has survived only as a libretto for Debussy's music.

On 9 December 1896 took place the Oeuvre's most famous – or infamous – production, *Ubu Roi* by Lugné-Poe's twenty-three-year-old assistant, Alfred Jarry. The written play was a deliberate emptying of dramatic convention and meaning, the resulting space being left to be filled by the actors, arousing and reacting to unprecedentedly vocal contributions from the audience. Indeed the Oeuvre audience was integral to the whole conception. What was happening in the auditorium was as theatrical as anything taking place on stage. The usual 'talk' was given by Jarry himself. What he said was inaudible, but the 'text' of his address had been handed round beforehand: it spoke, rather incoherently, of Don Juan and Plato, life and thought, scepticism and belief, medicine and alchemy, the army and duels. The audience may have rendered Jarry's talk inaudible, but the most famous exchange of the whole evening was also the work of a quick-witted member of the audience. After Ubu's first cry of *'Merdre!'* – the word *'merde'*, still unspeakable at this time on the Paris stage, was here thinly disguised by a redundant 'r' – some wag yelled back *'Mangre!'* In a sense, *Ubu Roi* was a parody by the Oeuvre of the Oeuvre. It was as if the audience were being presented with what the Oeuvre's enemies imagined one saw and heard at a typical Oeuvre production. The 'play' was set in a far-off country (not Norway or Germany, but Poland, the nearest possible allusion to the Tsarist tyranny, given the recent visit to Paris of Nicholas II) and at some indeterminate time. As if to insult the whole of European drama at its source and at its height, its title parodied that of Sophocles's *Oedipus Rex*. Indeed, next day, the *Figaro* spoke of *'terreur littéraire'*, seeing the production as the artistic equivalent of an anarchist's bomb.

Ever sensitive to the slightest shift in the thinking of his own generation, Lugné-Poe had left Symbolism behind and discovered the excitements of the 'real' world, politics and all. By 1898, there was only one matter of overriding importance to the young French intellectual: *'l'Affaire'*. This had the curious effect of bringing together the aesthetes and their arch-enemy, Zola, the most important living representative of 'naturalism'; indeed the Dreyfus Affair might be said to have been Zola's salvation. Where Ibsen was concerned, no *volte-face* was required. The Protean Norwegian was at least as fitting an ally of the now no-longer-Symbolist Lugné-Poe as he had been of the old Symbolist one. On 29 March, the Oeuvre gave an Ibsen gala to celebrate the great man's seventieth birthday. A performance of *An Enemy of the People* would be preceded by extracts from other plays. The choice of these extracts made it clear that Lugné-Poe had decided that the occasion would also be a Dreyfusard event. Indeed the text had even been tampered with, some speeches being altered, others added to bring out the parallel between Dr Stockman, played by Lugné-Poe himself, and Zola, both men of conscience standing up for their beliefs against the powers that be. Sarah Bernhardt, a Dreyfusard of the first hour, made her theatre available for the evening and, not surprisingly, the audience consisted almost entirely of Dreyfus supporters. We were quick to seize on any apparent allusion to the Affair and manifested our approval or disapproval vociferously. Every now and then a cry of '*Vive Zola!*' would go up and often it was impossible to make out what the actors were saying. After a while, they, too, abandoned any pretence to theatrical illusion and joined in the fun.

With the end of the school year, we would go to London, where we would be subjected to a concentrated dose of plays and operas. Pépé and Mémé, who stayed with their daughter in Redcliffe Square, came with us, writing up their reports for their newspapers. That astonishing phenomenon, the London Season, began in mid-May and continued unabated until the end of July. At Covent Garden, Augustus Harris presented some two dozen operas. Some of these seemed to appear summer after summer: *Aida, Carmen, Cavalleria Rusticana, Don Giovanni, Faust, Figaro, Lohengrin, Tannhäuser*. The greatest singers of the day appeared: a galaxy of sopranos, led by Melba, then in her thirties and at the height of her powers, but also Emma Eames, Margaret Macintyre, Emma Calvé; of tenors, the Belgian Ernest Van Dyck and that unique artist Jean de Reszké, Polish, but French by adoption; among the baritones and basses, Edouard de Reszké, Jean's brother, Pol Plançon, Victor Maurel. The full Season lasted ten weeks and we were there only for the last half of it. Yet, thanks to the repertory system, we were able to see about a dozen operas.

Then, to fill the remaining evenings, there were the plays. The theatre managers would put on their recent successes and revive earlier ones. Most years, Sarah Bernhardt would bring her company for a few weeks or there might be visits from the Comédie-Française.

In my memory, one London Season merges with another, but, for two reasons, Wagner and Sarah Bernhardt, that of 1892 stands out with particular clarity. That year, Harris had arranged for a complete Ring cycle (it was ten years since London had seen one), together with *Tristan and Isolde*, *Tannhäuser* and Beethoven's *Fidelio*. The German company would be led by the celebrated Max Alvary and Rosa Sucher, the bulk of the supporting cast coming from Hamburg, where its young conductor, Gustav Mahler, had repaired after being ignominiously removed from Budapest. One performance of each of the operas would be given. However, as the time came to book seats, excitement turned to anguish; the German season would be opening with *Tristan* on 15 June, while the school year did not end until the last day of the month. Here was a conflict of Racinian – or Sophoclean – proportions. For, as Pépé argued, what we were presented with was not a banal conflict between duty and pleasure, but a much more important one between duty as ordinarily understood, duty to the state (attendance at the Lycée) and a higher duty, a duty to the noblest aspirations and attainments of man (attendance at the opera house). He set about canvassing support for the second course: we missed the last two weeks of school.

After one Isolde and one Brünnhilde, Rosa Sucher left to be replaced by a young Hungarian singer who, for many people, was the great 'discovery' of the season. As well as replacing Sucher, Katharina Klafsky also sang Elisabeth in *Tannhäuser* and Leonora in *Fidelio*. I was allowed to go along to her hotel when Mémé interviewed her for the Budapest newspaper.

Since they spoke entirely in Hungarian, I understood not a word of what they were saying, which I found very irritating, all the more in that Mémé and Fräulein Klafsky seemed to find each other highly amusing. This, I remember, also shocked me; I was not at all prepared for this jolly, high-spirited, rather tomboyish woman in front of me. Not long ago, she had lost her (second) husband, the baritone Franz Greve, and one critic had even suggested that her recent bereavement had given Leonora's dialogue with her husband in the prison scene an unbearable intensity. Moreover, humour was a quality conspicuous by its absence in all the roles that she had sung. I could scarcely believe that this merry creature was the same as the bereaved tragedienne I had seen on stage. But, then, Katharina Klafsky's life and personality had little to do with those of the heroines she sang. What is more, she had just married again, this time to the conductor Otto Lohse. It is said that once Lohse was introducing her to a theatre manager. 'This,' he said, 'is my Leonora.' 'And this,' she retorted, jerking a thumb in her husband's direction, 'is No. 3.'

Mémé also interviewed Gustav Mahler, making her Budapest readers deeply regret, as so many of them already did, that their city had lost the services of such a musician. Only at the end of the interview did she confess – privately, for she wrote under a pseudonym – that her maiden name was Zichy, that she was distantly related to the man who had engineered his departure from Budapest.

I had missed seeing Sarah Bernhardt in Paris on account of illness, first mine, then hers, but, long before returning to Paris she visited London during that 1892 Season. Over eight weeks, she gave eight performances a week in six plays. 'The life of Mme Sarah Bernhardt,' Edmond de Goncourt declared, 'may prove the greatest marvel of the nineteenth century.' As a child, she saw little of either of her parents. Her father, Edouard

Bernhardt, was a Catholic from Normandy. Her mother, a *demi-mondaine* of Dutch–Jewish descent, gave birth to Sarah at the age of sixteen. The parents were not married. Before long, the child's father gave up his lawyer's practice and travelled the world, while her mother continued her life as the mistress of a series of rich, influential men. Sarah herself married only once: her husband, Ambroise Aristide Damala, a third-rate actor of Greek descent, became addicted to morphine and died a physical and mental wreck at the age of thirty-four. Her love affairs before, during and after her marriage were legendary. Her lovers included most of her leading men, one or two of her dramatists and a great many men too highly placed for suspicion ever to be confirmed. She had one child, Maurice, by Henri, Prince de Ligne, a Belgian. This son was to become the only real love and the only constant factor of her life.

It was her first visit to London, with the Comédie-Française, in 1879, that brought Sarah Bernhardt before a wider public. It began when she landed off the boat at Folkestone: the reception committee of admirers was headed by a strikingly handsome young actor, who, she said, 'looked like Hamlet', and who, indeed, was to become the finest Hamlet of his time, and a flamboyantly dressed young poet. The actor, Johnstone Forbes-Robertson, handed her a gardenia; the poet, Oscar Wilde, threw an armful of lilies at her feet. From then on the papers were full of her extravagant doings. A press conference was given, attended by some forty journalists, and her opinion sought on everything under the sun. Her menagerie of pets aroused enormous interest: the parrot Bizibouzon screamed, Darwin the monkey ground his teeth and rocked his cage; neighbours complained when her cheetah was let loose in the garden and set upon her dogs. Everyone wanted to entertain her, from the Prince of Wales and Gladstone downwards. The publicity was too much for the authoritarian Comédie-Française but, before she could be reprimanded, she handed in her resignation and embarked on the first of many world tours. Whatever vast sums she earned – and a few performances earned her the equivalent of a year's salary at the Comédie-Française – the more her debts accumulated, until yet another world tour paid them off. A single costume for *Phèdre* cost 4000 francs (£160 at a time when the best seats for one of her London performances cost half a guinea). She bought an island off the Brittany coast and proceeded to squander a fortune on it. In Paris, she kept innumerable servants, four carriages and six horses, and entertained ten to twenty guests at nearly every meal.

When I first saw her in that summer of 1892, she was nearing fifty, an age at which actresses give up many of their roles. Yet, when I saw her, she was embarking on what many regarded as her Indian summer. She went on to play a series of male roles: Musset's Lorenzaccio, Hamlet and Rostand's 'L'Aiglon' (Napoleon's young son, the Duc de Reichstadt). Many of Sardou's plays were written as vehicles for her genius, and when she no longer played them they were forgotten. *La Tosca* was rescued from oblivion by a great composer and it is in Puccini's version only that the play survives today. Shaw dubbed these perfectly made, if superficial, confections 'Sardoodledom', implying that they were all much the same sort of thing. They were a prime target for the Ibsenite, Wagnerite *avant-garde*, but, to my childish mind, a costume play by Sardou, with Sarah Bernhardt as the heroine, had more in common with my 'faerie' world of Isoldes and Brünnhildes than with the domestic problems of a Nora or a Hedda. In a few years, Sardoodledom began to wear thin with me, too, and I lamented with the highest of brows that Sarah did not confine her genius to objects worthier of it. But *La Tosca* was probably Sardou's best play and in it he had given Bernhardt a perfect vehicle. The moment she came on to the stage in the church scene of the first act, something extraordinary happened: for a fraction of a second, an electric charge seemed to shoot out into the audience, deadened only by the obligatory burst of applause. It was the moment at which the expectant, but hitherto disparate, listless, only half-attentive audience, still carrying with it the concerns of the day, was 'plugged in' to Sarah's electricity. From that moment on, she could manipulate the audience at will, varying the charge until the point in the last act when, as it were, a mass execution took place in the auditorium, upholstered stall and hard wooden bench becoming, alike, so many hundred electric chairs. This point usually, though not always, coincided with her own 'death' on the stage. I have had something of this experience at the hands of other actors – Irving, Mounet-Sully, Duse – but no one, by what seemed like sheer electrical force, so manipulated and overpowered an audience as Sarah Bernhardt did. Never was she expected to portray so wide a range of moods and emotions as in *La Tosca*. She began all grace and charm, an opera *diva* off-stage (played on stage by the greatest *diva* the theatre has ever seen). By the supper scene with Scarpia, all trace of feminine frivolity had gone and Bernhardt appeared in a long, almost entirely white dress, like some avenging angel. Her mental torture as she listened to the sound of Mario's physical torture rising from the cellar was almost unbearable. At this point the electric charge was about to blow a fuse. She saw a knife lying on the table, moved it nearer the edge while Scarpia's back was turned, then, a few minutes later, picked it up as she replaced her glass, turned round to face Scarpia's outstretched arms and plunged it into his heart. It was here, with her triumphant cry of '*Meurs! Meurs! Lâche*'[1] that the

1 'Die! Coward.'

fuse finally blew. Every time I saw her play Tosca, something between a gasp and a shudder ran through the audience at this point: the effect never failed. Sarah Bernhardt's death scenes are legendary, but this – a death scene in which she did not die, but killed – was even more moving or moving in an entirely different way. This, rather than her own 'death', when she throws herself off the walls of the Castel Sant'Angelo, was the true climax of the play.

A week later, I saw Sarah Bernhardt again, this time as Marguerite in *La Dame aux Camélias*. In many ways, no role could have formed a greater contrast with that of Floria Tosca, who lives, kills and dies with equal, unflinching determination. Dumas' heroine, on the other hand, is woman as passive self-abnegation, the social and sexual victim: what little will she has is being inexorably undermined by tuberculosis and can only be directed against her own interests. As a human being, Sarah Bernhardt had much of Tosca about her and nothing of Marguerite, yet, such was her art, she excelled equally in both, making both parts so exclusively her own that, when box office returns were flagging in some new venture, all she had to do was to revive *La Tosca* or *La Dame aux Camélias* and the receipts would come pouring in. Both plays died with her, though Dumas' play, like Sardou's, survived as an opera, Verdi's *La Traviata*. Neither play is a literary masterpiece: the older one is flawed by sentimentality, the later by melodrama. But when Bernhardt was acting, Tosca's killing of Scarpia was not melodramatic, nor Marguerite's death sentimental. Both seemed to be of an almost unbearable reality. It is as if both plays were really no more than *libretti* all along, in themselves lifeless until music was breathed into them, the evanescent music of Sarah Bernhardt or the more permanent music of Verdi and Puccini.

To see Sarah Bernhardt in *Phèdre* – since her departure

from the Comédie-Française she had played very few Racine heroines – was to witness a special kind of art. She abandoned the rich palette that Sardou and others had given her and returned to the severe, hieratic beauty of diction and gesture that she had learnt at the Conservatoire. Yet it was as if the years of expressive acting had so stretched her vocal and interpretative powers that when she returned to French classical tragedy she found within herself a strength of feeling and a vocal range that she had not possessed in her younger days. It was the opinion of both my grandfathers that the Phèdre that we witnessed on that July evening was the greatest thing she had ever done. For me it has remained the most potent theatrical experience of my life: that white-clad figure seemed incorporeal, as if consumed from within by a white heat, a medium in trance. As Phèdre's great speech near the end of Act II rose to its blood-curdling climax, I momentarily forgot the play I knew so well and would not have been surprised if Racine's five-act tragedy had ended there and then, in unclassical fashion, with a corpse on the stage.

It was during that summer of 1892 that I saw my first *Hamlet* – and saw Tree for the first time. How odd that, fourteen years after watching Tree die on the stage of the Haymarket, I should be standing on the stage of the new theatre opposite watching him die in the same customary suit of solemn black. Speaking of corpses, it never crossed my mind at the time that this was a very odd way for a twelve-year-old boy to spend his summer holidays, observing some of the greatest singers and actors of the age . . . dying. As well as seeing Tree die as Hamlet, I saw Irving die as two cardinal-statesmen (Wolsey and Richelieu). I saw Max Alvary die as Sigmund and Siegfried, Tristan and Tannhäuser, and Katharina Klafsky die as Isolde; I saw the immolation of Rosa Sucher's Brünnhilde and Maurel's Don Giovanni descend into the flames of Hell. I saw Melba and Eames die as an assortment of tragic heroines, and I saw Bernhardt die in everything I saw her in. Mozart's blest pair of servants apart, little of what we saw on stage that summer ended happily. But, such is the transmuting magic of art, I have seldom in my life felt less dejected or more stretched to the limits of excitement.

Yet, amid all that fictional tragedy, I did have my first real intimation of mortality. Sometimes, as we were sitting in the drawing-room, I would catch Grandfather looking at me in a thoughtful, scrutinizing way. One Sunday afternoon we happened to be alone in his study: he was sitting in an armchair reading and I was crouched on the floor looking at various books on the shelves. Suddenly, he said: 'You know, you're the spitten image of my Dickie.' A child's sense of treacherous adult depths told me not to ask who 'Dickie' was. 'The same grey-green eyes, the same reddish fair hair. He was like you in other ways, too – the same feeling for things. Got all excited about some book he was reading or the plays I used to take him to. Not like your father, always so cool, calm and collected. No, I had real hopes for my Dickie.' He smiled faintly and touched his left eye with a crooked finger. He didn't seem to want to say any more, so I just smiled back. Later, I asked my father who 'Dickie' was. It turned out that he had once had a brother, Richard, six years younger than himself, who had died of consumption at the age of twelve. I remember being astonished that no one had ever told me of the 'uncle' who died before I was born. Some years later, when I was staying with my grandparents, I went with them to visit the grave in Brompton Cemetery. On a simple upright stone was inscribed:

In loving memory of
Richard Thomas Sheridan
the second son of

Thomas and Esther Sheridan
who died 19 January 1872
aged 12 years.
'And youth grows pale and spectre-thin and dies.'

The quotation from Keats's 'Ode to a Nightingale' alludes, of course, to the consumption that killed so many of his contemporaries – and, incidentally, several of my ancestors and collaterals – and was soon to kill Keats himself.

On 15 August, at Prince Albert dock, Matthew and I saw our parents off on the P & O liner. It was, I noted in my diary, a particularly unpleasant day: the combination of cold, northerly wind and driving rain formed a fitting background for our dampened spirits. That most wonderful of summers had come to a premature end. Six weeks later, our parents would be back in Peking. We were not to see Father for four years, when he next came to Europe on furlough, though Mother promised to come and spend the summer of 1894 with us. Meanwhile, Father had been promoted to Assistant Chinese Secretary. A few months after my parents' arrival in Peking, John Jordan, the Chinese Secretary, was transferred to the Korean capital, Seoul, as Consul-General, thus providing my father with his second promotion in twelve months: he was now Chinese Secretary.

1905–06: London

So, on that morning in October 1905, standing on the pavement in Smith Square, I learnt that the last of my grandparents had died. Grandparents die when one is still young: they are usually the first harbingers of death. I should imagine this is the case even when one does not feel close to them. Matthew and I were devoted to ours; for much of our childhood and youth they also served us in the office of parents. The fell sergeant had been swift in his arrest. Those four repeated blows had marked so many stages in the demolition of the stable structures of my childhood and youth.

The first of those blows occurred on the morning of 1 December 1901, a Sunday. I was awoken by the College porter hammering on my 'oak'. 'A telegram, sir.' It was from Matthew: Grandfather Sheridan had died the night before. Matthew had gone down in June and was now living at Smith Square, having entered the Foreign Office in September. Trying to concentrate on what I was doing, I packed all the things that I should normally have packed in five days' time at the end of Full Term. I went to see my Moral Tutor, obtained my Exeat[1] and took leave of my friends. I was back in London that evening. Grandfather Sheridan had died of a heart attack

1 Literally, 'let him go out'. Permission to leave the City of Cambridge during term time.

243

at the Garrick. Two days later, Pépé and Mémé arrived from Paris. The funeral took place, with fitting theatrical splendour, at All Saints', Margaret Street, the 'theatrical' members of his club outnumbering by far our poor contingent of relations. The house in Smith Square seemed like a shell, its very life and soul departed. Pépé and Mémé returned to Paris. In a way, I wished that I could have gone with them. Christmas, spent at our aunts', was like a grim mockery of Christmases past. There were, of course, no visits to the theatre, though, in the New Year, I did go to the theatre once. With great courage, given the prevailing atmosphere, George Alexander had decided to revive his production of *The Importance of Being Earnest*. It had been a great success, seven years earlier, before being summarily taken off when the Wilde scandal broke in April 1895. As a sop to 'public opinion', the author's name appeared nowhere on theatre wall or programme: the play was attributed to 'the Author of *Lady Windermere's Fan*'.

So I went off to the St James's Theatre,[1] alone and in secret, as if to some den of iniquity. It might seem odd, so soon after Grandfather's death, to be sitting in a theatre chuckling at such irreverent witticisms as 'The truth is rarely pure, and never simple', 'All women become like their mothers. That is their tragedy. No man does. That's his', 'The good ended happily, and the bad unhappily. That is what fiction means', but I knew that Wilde's fellow Anglo-Irishman would have approved.

It would be hyperbolic to say of Grandfather Sheridan that 'nothing in his life became him like the leaving it', but he could not have gone in a more appropriate manner, sitting over a brandy with his friends after a convivial supper in his

1 The St James's Theatre, King Street, St James's, was closed in 1957 and later demolished.

beloved club. My other grandparents were less fortunate. The second and third hammer blows occurred, five months apart, in 1903. I went down from university in June 1902 and, by September, was back in Paris. I had last seen my Paris grandparents at Grandfather Sheridan's funeral almost a year before: that summer they had not come to London, not only because Grandfather Sheridan was no longer there to organize our outings, but also because Mémé had been ill and did not feel well enough to travel. I was shocked by how much she had changed in nine months. I had never noticed her grow old over the twelve years that I had known her. She was now an old lady, enfeebled, wasting away, coughing constantly. Pépé, too, was looking older, drawn, anxious; he had lost all his mirth. For all three of us there was something deeply moving about our reunion: as we embraced, they clung to me, almost desperately, as if to life itself. Mémé stared up at me, her smile failing to conceal the sadness in the eyes. As in London that summer, visits to the theatre had largely ceased. Not once during that period did Mémé go to the theatre: she was afraid, she said, of inconveniencing other people with her coughing. She no longer wrote for her Budapest newspaper. Pépé, too, had given up his reviews: he did not like to leave his wife alone at home. Occasionally, at her insistence, he went along to a play with me. Next day, Mémé made a great show of interest in what we had seen, enough to show that she was glad that Pépé had decided to go, not enough to show that she regretted that she had not gone herself. Behind all this carefully calibrated piece of acting I sensed that she was already elsewhere: she no longer cared that she had not been there or even whether Pépé had gone or not. The conversation invariably led on to her remembering some other play, some other performance that she had seen long ago.

Throughout those long months, I did my best to distract

myself. The past was slipping away, the future a blank, the present a repetitive compulsion to fill a space that emptied as fast as it was replenished. I read a great deal. I went to concerts, operas and plays. I saw Lucien Daudet when he was in Paris and, once or twice, I saw old friends from the Lycée. The rest of my time was given up to escaping from my mental anguish by going through all the time-consuming business of satisfying my physical needs: visits to *bains vapeurs* – those in the rue Rochechouart and rue Oberkampf, more usually the Hammam near the Opéra – or, if I did not want to go so far afield, or if it was too late, the *tasses* of the Latin Quarter, followed, if fortune smiled, by a visit to my room in the rue Cujas.

Mémé's condition worsened soon after Christmas and she was taken to the Hôpital Laënnec. She died in February. I organized the funeral: Pépé was too distraught and, by this time, too ill himself to do anything more than stand in the wings. In July, he, too, was coughing more or less constantly: I took him into hospital, where he was to have various tests. Half an hour after I left him, he had a heart attack and died: another funeral to organize, another mournful family reunion. I later learnt that he, like Mémé, had had cancer of the lung. Matthew returned to Morocco shortly after Pépé's funeral. Some weeks later, I turned the key in the door for the last time, paying my last respects to what had been the nearest thing that I had ever had to a home, walking from room to room, communing with my life's ghosts. I moved into my hotel in the rue Cujas. Last to go was the old familiar furniture, which found a temporary shelter *chez* Drouot.

One September morning in 1903, in a notary's office near the Bourse, the lease on the rue de Vaugirard apartment was transferred from my grandparents' estate to its new owner. He was not himself present in the notary's office, which was a pity: he was a man who had given me much pleasure at the Opéra-Comique. Nor was he a stranger to the apartment or to my grandparents; indeed I had seen him on a few occasions at receptions given by them. He was one of those men who are really only happy in the company of women and are constantly falling in love with youth and beauty. Yet, in many ways, he was a very feminine man. The overwhelming impression one had of him was of a certain softness, an almost cloying sweetness – the very fault that his music is sometimes criticized for today. Craving affection and admiration, he lavished both on others. His flattery was often so excessive, so obviously undeserved, that in the mouth of anyone else it would have had the opposite effect from the one intended. Yet so winsome was his manner that one could not but, for the moment, believe him, because perhaps he believed it himself. I have watched him pouring forth a stream of seductive flattery to some aged patroness of music, then, suddenly catching sight of some delectable young creature in another part of the room, extricate himself from the first and, without trace of a *diminuendo*, move purposefully, but with apparent nonchalance, in the direction of the second, hit precisely the right note of a new aria, without appearing to have finished the first, then, finding some such insuperable obstacle as a husband, retreat from the field to the fortified safety of the piano and, snatching victory from the jaws of defeat, pour forth a stream of notes, apparently addressed to both women at once, that hinted at the untold delights of romantic longing. With his soft, bright eyes and his drooping moustache, turning grey as his long hair thinned on top, there was a touch of comic pathos in his appearance.

My first introduction to Massenet's music was at the first revival of *Manon*. It had first been produced, to immense success, in 1884. However, the untimely death of Marie Heilbron, who had created the title role, had persuaded Massenet to postpone a revival. Now, however, he had discovered a new Manon, the young American soprano Sybil Sanderson, who promised to be even more beautiful in voice and certainly in person.

The following winter we attended the first night of *Werther* at the Châtelet, to which the Opéra-Comique had repaired after the fire at its own Salle Favard. The germ of the work had been sown seven years before, when, in the summer of 1886, Massenet visited Bayreuth for the first time. He was accompanied by a large contingent from the Parisian musical and literary worlds, including Vincent d'Indy, André Messager, Paul Bourget, Georges Clemenceau – and my grandparents. Before returning to Paris, Massenet's publisher, Hartmann, took him to Wetzlar, to the house in which Goethe had written *The Sorrows of Young Werther*. Hartmann put a French translation of the novel into Massenet's hands. The composer reacted enthusiastically, a *libretto* was written and in under two years the work was finished. The night of the *première* turned out to be the coldest of the year. The temperature fell to ten degrees below freezing, the snow-storms reduced visibility to a few feet and the roads were already covered with ice. The omnibuses had ceased to operate and there were few cabs in the street. The brave souls who set out in their own carriages could be seen slithering from one side of the road to the other. Fortunately for us, the theatre was well within walking distance of home but, when we arrived, we found a lot of the seats unfilled. As the curtain rose on the tableau at the beginning of the last act – the scene of snow falling over Wetzlar, which accompanies the sound of the orchestral interlude – a titter spread through the audience. Pépé, who was sitting next to me, muttered: 'Ah! Good to see some snow again!' It had been snowing on and off all day, but we had last seen it all of a quarter of an hour before, during the interval, falling on the place du Châtelet. At the end of the evening it was announced that members of the audience who so chose would be allowed to spend the night in their seats. We made our way across the bridges and up the Boul' Mich'. The few score people in the icy streets were in holiday mood. Matthew and I slid on the ice, throwing snowballs and singing endlessly the rousing '*Noel! Noel!*' of the children's Christmas carol with which the opera begins and ends, as if, we, too, like the children of the opera, were quite unaware of the tragedy that had enveloped the doomed lovers.

Had Massenet not felt the need to devote himself to composition, he would have become one of the great pianists of his time. At the age of ten he was supplementing the family income by giving piano lessons in a poor school and playing in a Belleville café. Later he played the timpani in various orchestras. He entered the Conservatoire and, at the age of fifteen, was awarded the Prix de Rome. While at the Villa Medici, he was introduced to his future wife by Liszt, who passed her on to him as a pupil. She, too, could have made a career as a professional pianist, but chose instead to devote herself to her more talented husband. All his life Massenet worked ferociously hard, often up to sixteen hours a day. He would get up at four in the morning and compose on a 'piano' that had a keyboard, but produced no sound – in this way, he did not disturb his neighbours. He took the simple, sentimental tradition of French *opéra comique* and raised it to the level of serious music drama. His music seems to grow quite naturally out of the gentle, caressing, susurrating quality of everyday French. In his day, he won universal acclaim, from the Wagnerite intellectuals to the *midinettes*[1] and their *beaux* in the gallery. He

---

1 Seamstresses.

probably earned more money from his music than any serious composer in history. By the time that he bought our apartment, this thirteenth child of an impoverished family was already the proud owner of a beautiful Renaissance *château* set in over two hundred acres at Egreville, south of Fontainebleau.

My last sight of Massenet was a few years later and, again, inextricably associated with the rue de Vaugirard. Very early one morning I left the room of a young man whom I had picked up a few hours earlier in the *tasse* outside the Lycée Saint-Louis. Usually I would have proposed going to my hotel in the rue Cujas – I was still faithful to my old establishment on my visits to Paris – but, since he offered, I agreed to go to his, which was situated a little further away, near Saint-Sulpice. It was one of those occasions when one has no particular wish, once proceedings are over, to outstay one's welcome. I kissed my companion good-night and walked out into the chill morning air: it was about four o'clock. I cut up to the rue de Vaugirard, through the rue Férou. As always, my heart missed a beat as I reached my old home. I looked up to the first-floor terrace and there, leaning over the railing, smoking a cigarette, was Massenet. I waved; he waved back. *'Bonjour, Monsieur!'* I called up. *'Bonjour, jeune homme!'* he responded. *'Vieillesse se lève quand jeunesse se couche!'*[1] I was not sure whether he had recognized me or not.

Grandmother Sheridan had outlasted the first of my grandparents to die, her husband, by less than four years. On a suitably lugubrious autumn day in 1905, we entered the old house in Smith Square. Next day, Matthew arrived, after an exhausting three days' journey by boat and train from Tangiers. I had not seen him for two years, since my visit to Morocco.

1 'Good morning, young man . . . Age rises when youth retires!'

He had become more of a diplomat, more self-effacingly self-confident, more quietly efficient in dealing with the minor practicalities of life, more than ever unconcerned about what others might call its major questions. In this respect, he seemed at times older than I by more than his fourteen months of seniority. Yet I also felt protective towards him, as towards a younger, more innocent brother. How much more had I seen of life than he in his ordered, conventional existence! How much more must I have let my body have its way! I felt certain that he was still a virgin, unless, in that Muslim outpost, so attentive to female virginity, so prodigal in its offering of young male bodies, he had found some neglected diplomatic wife who had taken a fancy to him. Yet my suspicion was that he would have rejected such an advance as being as unseemly as the others to be found all along the sea-front, in every public garden, at every street corner. It was, of course, as much out of the question that I should enquire too closely into such matters as that I should proffer revelations about my secret life. We found it difficult enough to speak of the deaths of our grandparents. The nearest he got to a personal question came just before he left to return to Morocco. 'Are you any nearer to deciding what you're going to do with your life?' he asked. With what must have seemed like lordly disdain, I replied that I was not. 'I want to write . . .' I added, lamely. He gave a half-embarrassed grin and let the subject drop: we were skirting dangerously close to intimacy.

I may have come to man's estate, yet, outwardly, nothing had changed: I still had no idea what I was going to do with my life. There had never been much doubt as to what Matthew would do with his: he had fulfilled his own and others' expectations and embarked on a career in diplomacy. Edward Werner once pointed out to me that the word 'diplomacy' shared the same Greek root, *diploos*, 'double', as 'duplicity', which, he claimed, was why he was a better scholar than a diplomat. My own chosen vocation would have been one that also practised duplicity, with its *diploi*, its counterfeit presentments. But, unlike Werner, who believed that there was a truth, out there in the real world, that could be uncovered by patient, honest labour, and unlike Maurice, who, troubled by the 'unreality' of London, on stage and off, sought reality among the poor, bare, forked animals of the battlefield, I believed that it was only in the 'show' of art that some truth could be glimpsed. Were not Werner and Maurice, in their different ways, manifesting a latter-day version of puritanism? It was an earlier form of puritanism that had closed London's theatres, not so much because they were places of 'vice', that was mere pretext, but because, through illusion, through words that could not be confined by commentary, they conveyed truths of the same order as were to be found in 'holy scripture'. All art conveys truth through illusion. Of all the arts, this is most evident in the theatre, of all theatre in Shakespeare, and of all Shakespeare in *Hamlet*: it is by means of the players' art, the 'play-within-the-play', where Claudius's secret is 'imitated', that Hamlet obtains corroboration of the 'truth' told him by the Ghost. It was to that sacred art, which, they say, emerged from esoteric cults to become a ritual performed in the open before the entire citizenry, in which the acting out of familiar stories produced an effect of *catharsis*, of cleansing, of purification, that I should like to have devoted myself. It was not to be because I bore the stamp of one defect, my stammer. No one, the afflicted any more than anyone else, understands why some people stammer. Stammering causes embarrassment in imperfect speaker and listener alike. When those not regularly affected stammer, it is presumed that embarrassment is the cause, even embarrassment about the lies they may be telling. What verisimilitude would remain if an actor, one who lives by show, began to stammer? By that time, I had almost lost my stammer, but it could return at any moment. Without it, I might have made a good actor. I could deliver a long Shakespeare speech without mishap – and often did when no one was within earshot. The problem would have occurred in short pieces of dialogue. When I was expected to say something and had no control over what I was to say, my throat might tighten up and nothing but a strangulated sound come forth.

By this time, I had long since ceased to be simply 'stage-struck'. When Grandfather Sheridan died, our Christmas and summer holidays in London were no longer packed, night after night, with visits to theatre and opera house, for he, 'stage-struck' to the end, had organized everything. And, after Mémé and Pépé died, I no longer went to Paris *générales*.[1] I now read more, thought more, saw less. My mind played less on individual performances, more on the overall production. I imagined what I should do if I were what was coming to be called a 'producer'. Yet I knew that I could never become one of these new artists of the theatre, a Lugné-Poe, Granville Barker, Max Reinhardt, Stanislavsky or Gordon Craig, for they were all actors – and good ones, too. No one was going to employ me as a theatre reviewer either. As a child of ten and eleven I dreamt that when I grew up I should become a playwright: I even sketched out ideas for plays, complete with Italianate names of characters and plots reminiscent of *Two Gentlemen of Verona* or *As You Like It*. They never got any further. Now I could not imagine how I could set about writing a play: I knew of no play that might serve as a model for anything I might be capable of.

1 *Répétitions générales*, dress rehearsals – in reality, the first nights, to which the press was admitted.

For most of the past ten years or so I had thought of myself as a poet: I now had to admit that I was no longer even that. As with most sensitive, literate youths, the penning of verses coincided with the onset of puberty. It was, in my case, a perfect coincidence, for at that age one feels great waves of emotion for which there is no specific object. The absence in Symbolist poetry of any specific idea, but its suppused presence behind the mask of the symbol, accessible only to intuition, accorded perfectly with my state at that time. I have kept none of those early efforts, but do remember that they all seemed to inhabit a kind of mythical Arcadia, a Hellenic springtime of the world, filled with the imagery of nymphs and satyrs, hills and streams, moon and water.

I was an ardent reader of the 'Symbolist' reviews: the *Revue Indépendante*, the *Revue Blanche* and, above all, the *Mercure de France*. What provided me with the best possible guide to the theories and personalities at work in the French literary world of the day was Jules Huret's *Enquête sur l'évolution littéraire*. In the course of conversations with my grandparents, in which I tried relentlessly to satisfy my curiosity and clarify my confusion about the great intellectual questions of the day, Mémé suddenly said: 'He should read Huret.' Pépé agreed enthusiastically and thrust the book into my hands. It was, indeed, just what I needed at the time. While writing this, I went back and skimmed through Huret's book. What a colossal achievement it was! How, on the basis of no fewer than sixty-four interviews with writers, did he produce such a clear, yet detailed account of the state of French literature at that time? The secret lay, I think, in his training as a court reporter. With a few brilliantly chosen words he would bring to life the appearance and vocal mannerisms of each writer and the setting in which he worked. He asked his subjects two main questions: Is Naturalism Dead? What is this Symbolist movement that claims to have replaced it? Reading through these interviews, I am struck by how permanent certain features of the French mind seem. How easily the much-vaunted clarity and rationality of the French veer into blind, quite unwarranted dogmatism; how seriously the French intellectual views his mission and how different he is from his English counterpart – or, rather, how odd that he has no such counterpart. One thinks of the French intellectual signing manifestos and joining demonstrations, while the most an English writer might do by way of public activity is sit on a committee devoted to some minor, practical reform. Here is Edmond de Goncourt, that gentle, most private of aesthetes, declaring the novel dead and taking some pride in his part in the killing of it: 'Despite the ever greater sales of novels, I believe that the novel as a form is worn out, down-at-heel. It has said all that it has had to say and I have done my best to destroy its fictionality by turning it into something like auto-biographies, memoirs of people who have no history.' That is the authentic voice of the French intellectual: 'It' – the novel itself, not novels or novelists – 'has said all that it has had to say.' Edmond de Goncourt was classified, rather uneasily, among the 'Naturalists', but the true Naturalists, the followers of Zola, were not so willing to see the end of their chosen medium. Joseph Caraguel saw the Naturalist novel leading the way in man's 'civilizing ascent by and towards truth, as a kind of imperfect advance-guard for science itself. But, as such, it should shake off its fictional elements and strive to be as documentary as possible.' There were more visionary souls. When asked what direction he expected the novel to take, Octave Mirbeau declared: 'A socialist one, it will become socialist, obviously; the evolution of ideas wills it, it's inevitable . . . Yes, everything will change at the same time, literature, art, education, everything, after the general upheaval, which I expect this year, next year, in five years, but which will come, of that I am sure!' For Charles Henry much of our lit-- erature, all those love stories, for example, will become incomprehensible, 'when society is organized differently, the children brought up by the state and women taking full pos- session of themselves, becoming free to choose and love in whatever way and with as many men as they please'. Much, in all conscience, has changed since 1891, but that socialist utopia, expected by many as inevitable and imminent, even by some who feared it, seems as far-off as ever.

The beauty and splendour of the requiem mass at Grandmother Sheridan's beloved All Saints provided a strangely unfitting end to her quiet, unprepossessing life – less fitting for that faithful member of the congregation than the same ceremony had seemed, four years before, for her 'theatrical' husband of few or no religious beliefs. It seemed to speak of a Christian belief in the redeemed human soul as par- taking of the celestial, democratically similar state of the angels, with all earthly, unequal individuality sloughed off. By contrast, the burial, in Brompton Cemetery, beside her husband, spoke of our all too human state. Yet, even here, beneath the stonemason's attempt to retain something of the social differences that had existed in life, was another demo- cratically similar state, that of our earthy reality.

Matthew and I accompanied Father to the solicitors'. Grandmother's will revealed that her estate amounted to rather more than any of us suspected. It consisted entirely of investments inherited from her own parents. We were all – her two children and her four grandchildren – named as benefici- aries. My own share was considerably more than I had inherited from my Dumollard grandparents. I could now live very comfortably without working at all. I found this financial 'compensation' for the loss of much loved human beings almost obscene. I was immensely grateful for my good fortune, but should have been much 'happier' had I not cared so much for my benefactors. It was as if we were devouring our ancestors' very substance, like some primitive tribe might eat their parents immediately after death, believing that they were thus magically preserving them and their attributes within themselves. Had I not read of some such practice in Frazer?[1]

Matthew left for Tangiers a week after the funeral. My parents were on short leave and would not be going back to St Petersburg until early November. It was agreed that I should stay on at the house for the time being. The lease had a couple of years to run, though I might, at some point, decide to take a flat of my own. Mrs Ellis, the housekeeper, had been left a pension and a sum of money: she would stay on after my parents left until I made other arrangements. Father called at the Foreign Office, where it was confirmed that he would be transferred back to Peking: my parents would stay at St Petersburg only long enough to collect their belongings.

On 14 October, I read in *The Times* of the death, the previous night, in Bradford, of Sir Henry Irving. In previous weeks, Irving had often been faint and scant of breath. During the performance of Tennyson's *Becket*, on Friday 13 October – thespians are exceedingly superstitious – it looked as though Irving would not stay the course. He 'fluffed' one or two lines, but managed to get to his last words, 'Into Thy hands, O Lord! into Thy hands!' and 'died'. They were the last words he spoke as an actor: the rest was silence. This tragedian, who 'died' almost with every performance, had

1 Sir James Frazer's highly influential *The Golden Bough: A study in comparative religion* (12 vols. 1890–1915). Frazer (1854–1941), born and educated in Glasgow, went on to Trinity College, Cambridge, where he read Classics and became a Fellow. He was Professor of Social Anthropology at Cambridge from 1908.

nearly died, like that greatest master of comedy, Molière, on stage. The curtain fell. A dazed and bewildered Irving had to be helped to his feet. 'What now . . .?' he asked. In front of the curtain, he began a halting speech, paying tribute to Shakespeare instead of to Tennyson. A cab took him to his hotel, where he collapsed in the hall. He died in the arms of Walter Collinson, his devoted, diminutive dresser-valet, a former wig-maker, who had been with him for twenty-seven years. Irving was sixty-seven – and penniless. Next day, it seemed as if the whole of Bradford had turned up, to stand silently, hats in hand, as the carriage took the body to the railway station. Tree learnt the news as he sat with his friends over supper at the Garrick, as Irving had done so often. The message was handed round and everyone left the club in silence. The pillars of the abandoned Lyceum Theatre were hung with black and every London cab-driver tied a black bow on his whip. George Alexander and a group of fellow-actors approached the Dean and Chapter of Westminster with a view to a funeral and burial in the Abbey. There was some opposition – the old prejudice against the stage was still active among some churchmen. No further burials were permitted in the building, but it was agreed that the actor's cremated remains could be placed in Poets' Corner.

In the past three years, I had had an excess of death, yet I was determined, on my own and Grandfather Sheridan's behalf, to attend the funeral. I went along to see Bram Stoker, Irving's manager, who arranged to get me an invitation. (A few years before, that most genial of Dubliners had astonished everyone by publishing a gruesome tale of horror, *Dracula*, surely the result of watching Irving chill the blood of audiences night after night.) The day before the funeral, I queued for an hour to spend a few moments before the coffin. Irving's friend, Lady Burdett-Coutts, knowing that the flat at 17

Grafton Street would be too small to accommodate all those who wanted 'to pay their respects', had converted the dining-room of her house on the corner of Stratton Street and Piccadilly into a *chapelle ardente*. The room was filled to over-flowing with wreaths and flowers. On the coffin itself was a floral cross from Queen Alexandra; on a ribbon attached to it, she had written Irving's last stage words: 'Into Thy hands, O Lord! into Thy hands!' On a small table was the wreath sent by Ellen Terry, a cushion of rosemary, dotted with carnations. On the wall behind the coffin was an enormous pall, consist-ing of thousands of fresh laurel leaves woven together: on it, a card proclaimed 'sent anonymously'.

Next morning, I made my way through the crowd that began almost as soon as I was outside Smith Square. Everywhere were flags at half-mast. Inside the Abbey, I was shown to my seat by one of the ushers, all fellow-actors of the dead man: the house was full on that first and last 'night'. The fourteen pall-bearers were headed by two gentlemen I did not recognize: I later learnt that they were the Duke of Devonshire and Earl Spencer. Of the others, many were fellow-actors – Bancroft, Wyndham, Tree, Alexander, Forbes-Robertson – or other artists associated with the theatre, such as Pinero and Alma-Tadema. The austere, gloomily beautiful Service for the Burial of the Dead came to an end with Handel's Dead March from *Saul*. The procession moved round to Poets' Corner, where two members of the Comédie-Française, the Maison de Molière, knelt before the coffin. I later learnt that the coffin was a 'stage prop'. The day before, Laurence Irving had taken his father's body to Golder's Green to be cremated. The ashes would occupy the place next to Garrick – and our 'illustrious ancestor'. Nothing could have pleased my grandfather more, save being there himself. And so England gave the first of her 'rogues and vagabonds' to be knighted a funeral of a kind that she rarely accords any of her artists.

When I first saw Irving he was in his early fifties and two-thirds of the way through his residence at the Lyceum. For ten years or so, whenever we were in London, we managed to catch his latest production, together with the odd revival of an earlier one. And those that I was too young to have seen Grandfather would evoke for me, accompanied by a stream of anecdote and reminiscence. John Henry Brodribb came from a strict Nonconformist family in the West Country, beginnings as inauspicious as his name. At the age of eleven, he moved to London with his parents, his father having found work in the City. They lived on the top floor of a house in Old Broad Street, near the Stock Exchange, their son attending the City Commercial School. John was already an avid reader of Shakespeare; he soon became the school's best actor. The headmaster persuaded the boy's father, against his mother's puritanical protests, to take him to see Samuel Phelps in *Hamlet* at Sadler's Wells. The following year, young Brodribb left school and became a junior clerk in a city export firm. Though he could not leave the office before seven, as often as he could he went straight off to the theatre. He joined a certain 'City Elocution Class' and took part in their theatrical efforts. Hearing that an amateur production of *Romeo and Juliet* was to be put on at the Royal Soho Theatre in Dean Street, he put his name down for the part of Romeo – and paid the three guineas required. Before the programmes were printed he changed his name to 'Henry Irving', after one of his favourite authors, Washington Irving. His Romeo led to an offer to join a company at the propitiously named Lyceum Theatre, Sunderland: to the horror of his parents, he gave in his notice at the office. He was eighteen.

Three years later, he returned to London. By 1871, he was

leading a company at the Lyceum. In 1874, now thirty-six, he put on his first London *Hamlet*. Word got about that history was going to be made. During the afternoon of the first night, a large crowd had gathered at the pit and gallery entrances. When the doors opened, the theatre was quickly filled to overflowing. The production was a complete break with the slapdash amalgam of half-remembered customs that passed for tradition on the English stage at this time. He restored most of the text, with the result that, with the intervals necessitated by scene changes, the performance lasted over five hours. Irving's interpretation of the title role was also a break with tradition. Gone was the generalized gloom in delivery and the bombastic declamation of the soliloquies. This was a subtle, minutely calculated psychological study, one that delineated Hamlet's relationships with the other characters. At first the audience was puzzled by this new Hamlet but, as the evening wore on, he won it over, forcing it to listen more attentively.

Four years later, Irving took over the Lyceum as actor-manager, persuaded Ellen Terry to join him and the legendary partnership began. At enormous expense, the theatre was refurbished and the auditorium redecorated in its unforgettable sage green and turquoise blue. The old gimcrack, all-purpose sets were thrown out and artists commissioned to design scenery for each new production. It may seem strange now, but this way of presenting Shakespeare, with sumptuously realistic sets and costumes, was revolutionary in its day, the scenic counterpart of the detailed realism of Irving's acting style. With each year, the splendour of the Lyceum's productions seemed to break new bounds. There were many stories of Irving's wanton extravagance. A costumier was dispatched to Rome to find the precise shade of red silk required for Cardinal Wolsey's robes. Real armour was ordered for a dozen or so soldiers in one play, which, when delivered, was so heavy that the actors could barely stand up in it; it was replaced by fish-net painted silver and the audience was none the wiser. He would order a costume for Ellen Terry, reject it on arrival, successively order two more, only to revert in the end to the first. For one play, several hundred copies of a foreign bank-note were printed, in case, said Irving, one should happen to be blown into the stalls and thus destroy the theatrical illusion if too obviously fake.

For me, the pinnacle of Irving's art was his *King Lear*, which I saw at Christmas 1892. Grandfather Sheridan had attended the first night in November and had been back again. It was quite possible, he said, that nobody in the audience had ever seen the play before – certainly none of the cast had. Earlier in the century, Macready had been a great Lear – as a young man of twenty-five my grandfather had seen Macready's last and greatest role, Macbeth, but not his Lear. Indeed, for over a century, between Betterton and Kean, the only version to be seen was Nahum Tate's, which gave the play a happy ending, with Lear recovering his wits and Cordelia marrying Edgar – and the part of the Fool, in some mysterious sense the heart of the play, being cut altogether. Irving's performance was, I suppose, what we should now call naturalistic. Indeed so anxious had Irving been to establish the decrepitude of the old king that he was at times inaudible to those in the cheaper seats. At the end, he reappeared as usual before the curtain and made his usual gracious little speech of thanks for 'the patience, kindness and sympathetic en-couragement of the distinguished audience'. He was, he concluded, 'the public's most humble, obedient servant' and was about to bow himself off when a young cockney lad in the gallery shouted, more in sorrow than in anger, 'Oh, guv'nor, if you'd only spoke like that orl night!' By the time of our visit

Irving had found that golden mean necessary in all good acting, between holding the mirror up to nature and employing all the resources of the actor's art to move the audience. In his advice to the players, Hamlet shifts the balance towards truth to nature, presumably because the actors of his day, like most of those between Burbage and Irving, erred on the side of effect; but the pendulum can swing too far in the opposite direction, as Irving found on that first night.

A few years later, we attended the first night of *Richard III*, Grandfather having performed the almost impossible task of obtaining seats for us all. Irving had first produced the play at the Lyceum nineteen years before, when he surprised everybody by using Shakespeare's version, rather than Colley Cibber's, which, while cutting much of the original, incorporated not only scenes from *Henry V* and *Henry VI*, part 3, but also verses of his own. This did not please all: what, they said, had been good enough for Garrick and Kean should be good enough for young Irving. He had not revived the play since, so expectations were high. Like Shylock or Mathias in *The Bells*, the title role appealed to his dark alter ego, though my grandfather once told me that there was no trace of this alter ego when the great actor was not acting. Then he was the mildest, sweetest of men. The trouble was that he did not cease acting when he left the stage; he could assume his histrionic mode at any moment, for no apparent reason; with strangers he acted the whole time.

After the performance, Grandfather took us all backstage to congratulate Sir Henry. We followed in his wake through the host of admirers, Grandfather seeming to know half of them and, exuding such delight, exchanging a few urbane words with each, that one would have been forgiven for thinking that the evening was his triumph. We eventually reached the great man, whom we found seated once again on the throne that should now be Henry VII's and which had been brought back from the wings and placed incongruously in the middle of 'another part of the field', surrounded by a crowd far larger than any that could have been artistically arranged on the Lyceum stage. This time, matters were too hectic for us all to be presented: we stood meekly to one side, grateful for a leer of acknowledgement, if not recognition, from the now crownless, but still hunchbacked 'King'. Seeing him, slumped there inelegantly on his throne, I saw on his face something that I have often seen on the faces of actors after their performances, but never carried to such a degree of intensity: an expression at once of exhaustion and manic excitement.

'You will stay with us, Sherry, won't you? Or do you have to accompany your honoured consort and multitudinous descendants?'

Grandfather reassured him. And so, having paid our homage, we went on our way. It was after midnight before the last of the visitors had left the Lyceum stage and Irving, Grandfather, Professor Dewar, another medical man, and a few close friends then went on to the Garrick for the usual Saturday-night supper. Grandfather spent what was left of the night at the Club, but Dewar walked with Irving back to his house in Grafton Street, finally leaving as dawn was breaking. On his way up to bed, Irving struck his knee against a chest on the landing. His manservant found him later that morning in considerable pain and sent for the doctor. Apparently, he had ligatures of the knee-cap: he would not be able to work for some weeks. *Richard III* was cancelled and not resumed until the end of February. The effect on Irving, who had never failed to appear on stage in his life before, who had no life whatever except his work, was devastating. *Cymbeline* was revived as a stop-gap, but without success. By the time of Irving's return, the accounts showed a loss of £10,000 on the

season. It was a demonstration of the knife-edge on which the
fortunes of even the greatest actor-manager rest: it was merely
the first of a series of misfortunes that were to end with the
closing of the Lyceum and Irving reduced to a wandering
player, compelled to embark on exhausting tours of the
provinces and North America to raise enough money to keep
going. The second disaster occurred in 1898. On 18 February,
two hundred and sixty sets from forty-two plays, the work of
the greatest scenic artists of the day, were destroyed by fire in
the Southwark warehouse where they were stored. They had
been insured for £6000, a fraction of what they would have
cost to replace. The final blow came four years later when the
London County Council decided to impose on all theatres
under its jurisdiction repairs necessary to conform with its
safety and fire regulations. The cost of the work was to fall,
not on the owners, but on the licensees. In the case of the
Lyceum, this would amount to £20,000. Irving had no savings
of his own and could never raise such a sum. In any case, his
lease on the theatre would shortly run out. The public authorities had always refused any help to theatres; they were now
closing them.

Though undoubtedly the greatest English actor of his generation, Irving was curiously lacking in many of the attributes
of a good actor. His diction was poor, his gait ungainly. There
was a rough, untrained character about his speech. His vowels,
in particular, were eccentric by the standards of polite society.
He refused to use the long 'a', making 'pass', for example,
rhyme with 'lass'. His 'o's were broad, as in northern English
accents. He would say 'gudd' for 'good', 'sate' for 'sight',
'hond' for 'hand', 'waarr' for 'war', 'ye' for 'you', 'me' for
'my'. He was not an all-round actor and, despite his early
stage experience, had little aptitude for comedy. He would
never have played Falstaff, though, when the comedy was at

the character's expense, when the character had a tragic dimension, as in Malvolio, he was incomparable. With Benedick, he pushed his comic limitations to the limit – fortunately, for it gave us Ellen Terry's finest role, Beatrice. What he did possess was a sort of demonic power, an irresistible magnetism, an instinctive intelligence. An actor's art is a transient thing; in the absence of any real tradition or standards, any English counterpart to the Conservatoire or Comédie-Française, Irving's lasting achievement was the reformation of the English stage, which he carried out single-handedly and single-mindedly. His first nights became as much an occasion for Society to meet as those at Covent Garden. In 1883, soundings were made as to whether Irving would accept a knighthood. The prime minister's emissary reported back: 'Mr Irving thinks that it would be very ill taken by his profession and, like the gentleman and true artist he is, he wishes to stand well with his profession and not seem to be put over them.' In 1895, the then prime minister, Lord Rosebery, did not risk a second refusal: he wrote to the actor informing him that the Queen had conferred the honour of knighthood on him in personal recognition of his services to his art.

On 19 July 1902, I attended Irving's last performance in the theatre that he had run for thirty-one years. That night, he played Shylock. He was the first English actor to make audiences sympathize with the Jewish money-lender. Never had he been closer to his character, a man, like him, ruined by the mysterious workings of money and the law. It was also the last time I saw Irving. His career as an actor survived a little longer. The following year brought an expensive production of *Dante*, a sort of dramatization of the *Divine Comedy*, commissioned from the elderly Sardou. It played for ten weeks at Drury Lane, but I was in Paris at the time: Mémé had just died and I was keeping Pépé company. The summer of 1905

saw a 'farewell season' of revivals at Drury Lane: I was in St
Petersburg.

On an inclement November morning, I saw my parents off
to a no doubt even more inclement St Petersburg and walked
back to Smith Square. Over the past fourteen years or so, I had
said goodbye to my parents many times and it had always
been a dreary, heart-rending occasion. This time, for the first
time, if I were to be entirely honest, I felt no sadness. After all,
I had been living with them for the past eighteen months – the
longest period I had done so since they left us in Paris fourteen
years before. As I put my key into the lock of the front-door,
I felt a certain exhilaration at the prospect before me. I was
now master of the old house, living alone, free, in London. I
could not wait to say goodbye to Mrs Ellis and live entirely
alone. When she had gone, I should get a char-woman who
had no allegiance to my grandmother's *ancien régime*, who did
not live in, but would come at certain hours, on certain days,
and perhaps do a little cooking. I thought enviously of Nikolai
and Nikita, and their household of attractive young male servants. Could I not find one, tempt some young Frenchman
from the Carlton, say, to move in and become a sort of general
factotum, a charming servant-companion, a Leporello who
could not only recite my all too numerable conquests, but
would not be averse to a little cleaning, a little washing and
ironing, a little cooking, a little conversation or even, were I so
inclined, to joining me in my bed? Of course, the idea was the
merest phantasy: no such person existed. Servants exist in a
strict system of boundaries and hierarchies. No male servant
would do the cleaning and washing. A valet would do valet's
work, and only in a properly run household with the right
number of staff to perform all the other duties required.
Similarly, a male cook would require a few underlings of his
own, in addition to the other servants. No, there was nothing

for it but to get a char-woman; Leporello would remain a creature of the stage, a probably corpulent bass-baritone of a
certain age.

What I had missed more than anything else during the
three years that I had spent away, in Paris, Peking, Petersburg,
was hearing my own language, the tongue that Shakespeare
spake, spoken from the stage. Within hours of seeing my parents off at Charing Cross, I was in His Majesty's Theatre for
a single matinée performance of *Twelfth Night*. The Christian
'twelfth day of Christmas' is a transmogrification of the
Roman Saturnalia. With its wintry undercurrent of death and
mourning, but its stronger pull towards festivity, towards the
celebration of love and pleasure, *Twelfth Night* was the play
that most closely fitted my mood at that moment. In some
mysterious way, it is a sister play to *Hamlet* and was written at
about the same time. In each, it occurred to me, the values of
the other are reversed: Claudius, indulging in 'heavy-handed
revel', draining 'draughts of Rhenish down', turns into Sir
Toby, making 'an ale-house of my lady's house', and the
black-suited, mourning Hamlet into a disapproving Malvolio.

Tragedy ends with the death of the hero and heroine,
comedy with their marriage, but the two words were not originally antithetical. Tragedy and comedy were both associated
with worship of Dionysus, the god of wine and fertility. It is
said that the Dionysiac rite began with the sacrifice of a goat
(*tragos*) to the god and that the celebrants wore goat-skins to
make them look like satyrs. In time, the priests became actors,
the sacrifice of the goat the death of the hero. A comedy was
a short piece, entailing much play with phallic symbols, and
followed the tragedy. In time, like tragedy, it became less literal, the phallic horse-play turning into the pairing off of
characters. The notion that tragedy and comedy are part of the
same whole, rather than distinct opposites, survives in the

Latin languages: in French, for example, *comédien* is synonymous with *acteur* and the national theatre company is known
as the Comédie-Française. Though, curiously, it is above all in
classical French drama that the two forms become most distinct, each purified of any element belonging to the other.

Shakespeare moves in the opposite direction: in *Hamlet*, the
Prince himself indulges in witty repartee and the wise-
cracking gravediggers are referred to in the text as 'Clowns'.
A particular actor specialized in the playing of 'Fools' or
'Clowns': Feste in *Twelfth Night* would be played by the same
actor who played the First Gravedigger, the very same who
philosophizes on death, the skull of Yorick, the old king's
jester, in his hand. *Twelfth Night* begins with music, 'the food
of love', but throughout the play it has a 'dying fall'; Feste's
songs speak readily of death. 'Come away, come away death,'
he sings and his invitation to 'mistress mine' is made all the
more urgent because 'youth's a stuff will not endure'. Olivia is
in mourning for the deaths of her father and brother; each of
the twins, Viola and Sebastian, believes the other to be dead.
In tragedy, as in life, death triumphs in the end; in comedy, the
inevitable end is suspended, replaced by the new beginning of
marriage, with its promise of new life. Love may seem to triumph, but, not only do we know that it may not survive, will
not survive unchanged, in the future beyond the play, the play
itself has shown that love is based on illusion. Orsino is not
really in love with Olivia, whom he has scarcely ever seen,
has not seen at all for at least a year and who cares not at all for
him: he is in love with love. He comes to love Viola, while
believing her to be a boy – and, as soon as he realizes that his
'dear lad' Cesario is a girl, drops his 'love' of Olivia. At the
end of the play, he is still calling Viola Cesario and seems in no
hurry to see his 'fancy's queen' in female attire. (Did the term
'queen' have the same sense in the inevitably homo-erotic

world of the Elizabethan theatre, I wonder, as it has come to
have in Uranian circles today? If so, these words would have
'brought the house down'.) The figure of the beautiful boy
Sebastian/Cesario is the principal source of eroticism in the
play. The sailor Antonio is infatuated with Sebastian and urges
him to go away with him: 'If you will not murder me for love,
let me be your servant.' When Sebastian insists on staying in
a country where Antonio is wanted as a criminal, Antonio
declares that he will not leave his young friend: 'I do adore
thee so That danger shall seem sport . . .' Later Antonio
speaks of his 'desire', his 'willing love', 'jealousy' even. This is
the most explicit example of homophilia to be found in the
plays, one rivalling the love of the 'lovely boy', the 'master-
mistress of my passion' of the Sonnets. And what is so
astonishing to the modern reader – and such a source of pride
and delight to me – was how admirable and normal the great
Shakespeare makes it seem. Sadly Sebastian does not reciprocate Antonio's love, only his friendship. Antonio is not alone in
his choice of love-object. Orsino falls for 'Cesario' on sight,
his 'love' of Olivia continuing as a pretext to talk to 'Cesario'
about love. Olivia, who has rejected the rich, handsome Count
out of hand, on the pretext that she is in mourning, a mourning that will last, she has sworn, seven years, also falls instantly
in love with 'Cesario' and – off-stage – marries 'him' (in fact,
a Sebastian she does not know, such is the capacity of love to
delude) in no time at all.

This sexual uncertainty is at the heart of the play, play at
the heart of the sexual uncertainty and the Elizabethan practice of boy actors playing women at the heart of both. Love is
seen, not as access to some immutable Platonic essence of
identity, but as a shifting, treacherous play of show and decep-
tion, in other words, theatre. Orsino instructs 'Cesario' 'to act
my woes' to Olivia as audience; in fact, Orsino is 'playing the

lover', convincing himself that he is in love with Olivia. When Viola-playing-Cesario plays Orsino, Olivia is taken by the first, but not by the second. 'Are you a comedian?' she asks. 'I am not that I play', Viola admits: she is playing a phantom twin brother and bewitches both Orsino and Olivia into believing that they are in love with 'him'. Sir Toby and his friends trick Malvolio into thinking that Olivia loves him, persuading that inveterate Puritan (and therefore enemy of the stage) to play the part of the lover, cast aside his customary suit of solemn black for a 'costume' of yellow stockings and fashionable crossed garters. When the unfortunate is then 'confined' as mad, Feste acts the role of a priest who has come to visit him. At the play's still centre is the aptly named Feste, that strangely empty character, empty because we never see him not playing his professional role, that of jester. The play ends with Feste's curiously disjointed, yet haunting song, a parody of the 'ages of man', with its relentlessly depressing refrain: 'For the rain it raineth every day.'

Mysteriously, words that suggest the illusion of representation – play, player; act, actor – are also words that refer to reality. 'Play' comes from the Latin *pläga*, originally a blow, stroke or wound. Is it that the first plays were representations of combat? 'To act' comes from the Latin *agere*; *actum* is the thing done, *actus* the doer. In Latin and the modern languages, these words refer to actual deeds and their perpetrators, but they also refer to the art of the theatre, to the representation of actions: to act a part is to pretend, an actor is someone who pretends to be someone else, an act a section of a play. Why is this? Is there something, not only buried in our languages, our civilization, but deep down within our human nature, that makes it difficult for us to distinguish between that which is done and its representation? Is this the secret power of the theatre? Does this explain its perennial fascination? Are we just children at play?

I had seen *Twelfth Night* only once, during the first run of Tree's production, in 1901. Tree had been a splendid Falstaff, but in *Twelfth Night*, he rejected that minor Falstaff-figure, Sir Toby Belch, in favour of the more interesting Malvolio. It was one of Tree's most fascinating tragi-comic interpretations; the production, too, was one of his most successful. The scenery looked as exquisite as ever: Orsino's palace, its walls a blaze of colour from its Byzantine mosaics, a suffocating, over-heated enclosure, Olivia's garden, by contrast, a cool, airy arrangement of grassy terraces and box-hedges, a bridge over water and a real fountain playing, statuary and a flight of steps leading up to a clear blue sky. Some of the actors had been in the original production, notably the curiously named Courtice Pounds as Feste. That excellent actor was also a trained singer and had spent many years in D'Oyly Carte productions of Gilbert and Sullivan. We had a new Viola, no longer the beautiful Lily Brayton, but Tree's young, suitably tom-boyish daughter, Viola. There was, too, a new Orsino – Basil Gill, whom I had not seen before, so dazzlingly handsome I could hardly take my eyes off him.

Over the past year I had read with growing excitement of the 'Vedrenne-Barker' venture at the Court Theatre in Sloane Square. For most of my theatre-going life, I had scarcely been aware of the existence of this little theatre, well outside the West End, that had been more often closed than open. Now a new owner had invited an enterprising theatre manager, J. E. Vedrenne, and a twenty-seven-year-old actor, Harley Granville Barker, to put on a season of new plays. Barker was a devoted Shavian and, like Shaw, a member of the Fabian Society: he was determined that Shaw's plays would find a proper audience. Though nearly fifty, Shaw was still better known as a political activist and thinker, even as a theatre and music critic, than as a playwright – and as the author of plays published in book form, rather than performed on a stage. Apart from *Arms and the Man*, which had run for some weeks in 1894, the half-dozen plays of his that had been performed so far had been given only one or two performances, often matinées, on days when actors who were otherwise employed were free to perform. Barker had gathered together a group of dedicated actors who were prepared to work for very little money. So far the Vedrenne-Barker management had put on a dozen plays, five of them by Shaw, the latest being *Man and Superman*.

On the November evening when I went along to Sloane Square, not only had I never set foot in the Court Theatre before, I had never seen any of Shaw's plays. Barker was in charge of the overall artistic direction of the company, acted in most of the plays and served as the 'producer'. Would he, I wondered, turn out to be an English Stanislavsky? Would London, in its own modest way, now have something resembling the Moscow Art Theatre? So it was with excited anticipation, but with little idea of what to expect, that I mounted the few steps up into the small foyer. My first impression was that I had arrived at a reception wearing the wrong clothes. Calculating that this little theatre, in its 'bohemian' Chelsea outpost, with its reputation for 'socialistic' ideas, would not be the place to arrive in formal evening dress, I had donned an inconspicuous 'lounge suit' – only to find myself surrounded by boiled shirts and tail-coats. What I had not realized was that the Court had suddenly become a 'fashionable' venue for the residents of Kensington and Knightsbridge, even of Belgravia and Mayfair, and that Bernard Shaw had been turned from a proponent of revolution and immorality into a licensed fool, the jester at the Court.

Man and Superman began conventionally enough. Behind a

desk in his study in Portland Place sits a middle-aged man, a 'captain of industry' perhaps. The walls of the room are decorated with busts of Herbert Spencer and John Bright, and various photographs, including ones of Huxley and George Eliot. Mr Ramsden is a 'Manchester Radical' and regards his opinions as 'advanced' – except where morality is concerned. At first, the dialogue, too, between Ramsden and the *jeune premier* (Lewis Casson), seems conventional enough, except that the young man is curiously called Octavius. It seems that Ramsden's dear friend Robinson, stepfather to Octavius and his sister Violet, has recently died. Ramsden presumes that the role of guardian to the two young people will fall to him. The conversation turns to a certain John Tanner, a friend of Octavius's, but someone whom Ramsden seems to regard as the devil incarnate, an advocate of 'Anarchism and Free Love and that sort of thing'. He is the author of *The Revolutionist's Handbook*, 'the most infamous, the most scandalous, the most mischievous, the most blackguardly book that ever escaped burning at the hands of the common hangman'. (Later, when I read the published version of the play, I saw that Shaw had included the sixty-page pamphlet at the end of the book.) When John Tanner, the handsome Granville Barker, disguised to look like a younger Shaw, complete with red beard, entered, there were hoots of laughter from the audience: he is Shaw's spokesman, the 'Superman', a sort of Nietzschean *Übermensch* with socialistic views. Ramsden then learns to his horror that, according to his old friend's will, he is to share the guardianship with Tanner. As if that were not bad enough, it then transpires that Violet is pregnant and refuses to reveal the name of the future father. Another character enters, Ann Whitefield, very much the 'New Woman', a person who delights in speaking her mind: Octavius is besotted with her, but she does not reciprocate his feelings. A great many shocking new ideas are bandied about: women's emancipation, the abolition of private property, the immorality of religion, the 'Life Force', which Tanner sees as gloriously at work in Violet's pregnancy. (This last, very Shavian concept did not come from Karl Marx or Friedrich Nietzsche, but was a translation of *élan vital*, an invention of my old philosophy teacher, Henri Bergson.) I gasped with disbelief – and delight – at what was being said on the stage. How could all those respectable ladies and gentlemen around me in the stalls bear to listen to such things? The reason was, I concluded, that Shaw was able to make them laugh at the same time as he shocked them. Moreover, none of the things being said was spoken with any degree of seriousness or developed with any consistency. The 'ideas' were discussed as if they were the most normal things for respectable people, people like those in the audience, to talk about in Society. John Tanner posed no threat: he was clearly a man of means who sported his Shavian ideas rather as he sported his Shavian beard. The first, one felt, could be dropped as readily as the second. Similarly, Ann Whitefield was an attractive young woman who would soon marry and be taken over by the 'Life Force'. What this play reminded me of most was not so much Shaw's revered master Ibsen as his fellow Dubliner, Oscar Wilde: Ibsen, perhaps, rewritten by Wilde. Shaw even lapses into Wildean epigrams: 'There are two tragedies in life. One is not to get your heart's desire. The other is to get it.' But what of the young woman who, cheered on by Tanner, shamelessly boasts of her coming motherhood, while refusing to reveal the child's father? Surely the audience could not listen to that with the same equanimity with which it had listened to the 'advanced ideas' of Tanner and Ann: for the English, if not for the French or the Irish, deeds were an altogether more serious matter than words. Here Shaw plays a wonderfully comic, but face-saving trick on both the Shavian 'superman' and the audience. It turns out that, although Violet is indeed pregnant, she is in fact secretly married – to the son of an Irish–American billionaire. Act II opens in the avenue to Mrs Whitefield's house in Richmond. Tanner is talking to a man underneath a motor-car, Tanner's chauffeur, a 'stage Cockney', complete with dropped aitches, who is nevertheless a graduate in engineering: a discussion ensues as to the advantages of the chauffeur's education (board school and London Polytechnic) over that of Octavius (Eton and Oxford). The last act brings the younger members of the cast to Granada, Spain. Tanner launches into an attack on marriage as 'violation of my manhood, sale of my birthright, shameful surrender, ignominious capitulation, acceptance of defeat. I shall decay like a thing that has served its purpose and is done with; I shall change from a man with a future to a man with a past . . .'

What I did not realize until I read the play was that it was conceived as a meditation on the Don Juan legend and, more specifically, on the *Don Giovanni* of da Ponte and Mozart. John Tanner was an Englished Don Juan Tenorio; Octavius derives his unusual name from Don Ottavio; Ann 'is' Donna Anna; 'Enery Straker, the quick-witted chauffeur, Leporello; Roebuck Ramsden the Commendatore. The 'Superman' theme is developed at length in a detachable 'dream sequence' – it was not included in the production of the play that I saw – in which Shaw's characters take on the identity of their Mozartian ancestors. Without it, one could be forgiven for not realizing the play's connection with *Don Giovanni*: Shaw's characters bear little resemblance to their operatic counterparts and what relation they have is only by ironic antiphrasis. Thus John Tanner is no Don Juan (any more than he is a 'superman'); in fact, he is tracked down by the 'New Woman' and securely captured in the marriage net. Of course, this may well be Shaw's light-hearted version of the descent into hell. The play ends, not with tragedy's death, but with comedy's proposal of marriage, with words, rather than deeds – deeds being postponed beyond the confines of the play.

For me, at this stage in my life, London was a city that I knew well, as a constant visitor can know a city well. In certain respects, I hardly knew it at all: I had never lived there. On one, rather pressing matter, I had little idea how it worked. I discovered, to my astonishment, that, after nightfall, Piccadilly Circus and its adjoining streets were a seething mass of debauchery. Countless women and only slightly fewer young men were soliciting the attention of clients quite openly. In those first few evenings of excitement and urgent need, I was often on the point of choosing the likeliest candidate and going off with him. Only fear of unknown dangers (robbery, violence, disease) and a sense of my own value on the 'market' (I should not have to pay for it) held me back.

I moved on, along Coventry Street, to Leicester Square. By day, this large open space, with its trees, flower-beds and benches, provides a retreat from the surrounding warren of crowded, traffic-filled streets and alleyways. By nightfall, it becomes all that the words 'West End' conjure up. Yet here were none of the theatres that I frequented. In their stead were those twin palaces of 'pleasure', the Alhambra and Empire music halls which, thanks to the marvels of modern electrical illumination, dominate the square at night. Here, too, were women – and young men – plying their trade. In dress, deportment and general behaviour, they seemed a better (more expensive) class of prostitute than those in and around Piccadilly Circus; many of the more *soignée* women frequented the large 'promenade' at the back of the Circle at the Empire. Around the square were dotted hotels, restaurants, cafés, public houses. All the stranger, then, that, at its centre, should be a statue of Shakespeare. There he stands, towering above a fountain, with four dolphins spouting water at the corners, looking serenely in the direction of the Empire, his right elbow resting nonchalantly on a pillar. Below is the optimistic inscription, 'There is no darkness but ignorance'. What, I wondered, did the worthy burghers who erected the monument thirty years before have in mind? Perhaps Leicester Square did not yet have its present rather disreputable character or perhaps it was hoped that the presence of the Bard would illuminate the surrounding moral darkness with the light of Knowledge. Not that Shakespeare, caught in mortuary marble at its still centre, would have regarded with disapprobation the pleasure-seeking turmoil swirling about him. The same could not be said of all his companions in the square. Of the four former residents whose busts sat at each of the four corners – my fellow Trinitarian Isaac Newton; Reynolds, wearing a splendid hat; John Hunter, Scottish anatomist and surgeon, and Hogarth – only the last would have taken merciless delight in the progress of the rakes around him. This had once been a very French quarter: after the revocation of the Edict of Nantes, many of the better-off Huguenots who had taken refuge in England lived on Leicester Square or in nearby streets. Those sober Protestants would have been even more shocked by the moral depths to which their square had now sunk. Quite incongruously, this French connection survived in the name of a public house, the Provence, so called after the Huguenot heartland in the South of France. It was, to all appearances, an ordinary English 'pub', though, unusually for a pub, there was also a basement. Hearing a great deal of noise, raucous shouting and singing, I ventured down the steps and was met by a cloud of cigarette smoke and cheap scent coming from a *clientèle* that was as much female as male. I beat a hasty retreat.

Across the road, under the ensign 'Café de l'Europe' and down more steps, I discovered a *Bierkeller*. Sitting at a table, with a pint of excellent German beer before me, real German waiters waltzing around me, bearing aloft on their trays an unlikely number of foaming glasses, I was taken back to Petersburg, to Leinner's on the Nevsky. Then, next to the Alhambra, I noticed a sign: 'Bartholomew's Turkish Baths'. So, in Leicester Square alone, there were *banya*, *kloseti* and *Bierkeller*: I was beginning to feel at home in this strange new city of mine. I did not know at the time that Peter the Great himself had once dined on the square – not, of course, in one of the modest establishments that it now boasted, but as a guest of the Marquis of Carmarthen at Savile House, which stood on the very site now occupied by the Empire Theatre.

Over the next couple of weeks, I made a more systematic study of the West End's 'conveniences', which I named to myself according to their location ('St James's Park', 'Leicester Square', 'Charing Cross Road', 'Embankment Gardens', and so on). It was important not to 'loiter with intent' in any of these places after going to the theatre: wearing formal evening dress, I was sure to stand out and attract the attentions of 'professionals'. Better to make an expedition into the West End specifically for that purpose. There were certain other rules I had worked out for myself: for example, I left my wallet at home and carried no more than a few pounds on me.

Late one afternoon, I had reached 'Charing Cross Road' and was about to leave in desperation and go and look at some pictures in the National Gallery, when a youngish man came and stood next-but-one to me. As far as I was concerned, he was very much a 'borderline case', a few years older than I, slightly receding hair, rather too plain-looking. As he buttoned himself up, he smiled, a rare extravagance, and motioned his head, ever so slightly sideways, as who should say: 'I'll see you outside.' He left and I followed.

'I'm Bill,' he said, offering his hand. He then gave a great guffaw: 'I don't feel at all like a Bill, but there you are, that's what my friends call me.'

No, he was not for me, but he seemed a pleasant enough individual. I invited him to have a drink with me. He took me to a 'pub' round the corner in St Martin's Lane: the Salisbury, whose interior seemed to be entirely covered by mirrored glass, turned out to be an establishment particularly frequented by the 'fraternity'. Looking around, I could see some evidence of this. Bill was a mine of information. He warned me of how 'extremely careful' one had to be in the 'conveniences'. He told me of cases where a young good-looking plain-clothes policeman might stand there 'playing with himself', invite his 'neighbour' to look, then, when 'the poor sod' had an erection, if he hadn't got one already, the 'copper' would make a sign to a colleague, who would then come up and make his arrest. 'Leicester Square' was best avoided. He told me of others, further afield.

'But,' he said, 'don't you know Dansey Place?'

My confession that I did not elicited exclamations of astonishment.

'Why? Where is it?' I asked excitedly.

'Ah, that's a closely guarded secret,' he said, with an exaggerated air of mystery. 'Well, no. It's just round the corner, actually. It's a little alleyway, so small it isn't on most maps. When we leave, I'll take you. You'd never find it unaided. Even the boys-in-blue seem to forget about it most of the time. It's really just a tin box, just a urinal, none of the usual works and, of course, no attendant.' It was not much good, it seemed, during the day, when it was used by the staff of the shops that backed on to it, but, later in the evening, it was 'extremely busy'. 'You never know who you might see there. Lots of stage people, even certain rather well-known ones . . . but there are all sorts hanging around.'

He kept me entertained for the best part of an hour. He worked in the costume department at the Empire and was an unending flow of back-stage gossip. He had, he said, 'a little place in Kennington' and would like to invite me back. Unfortunately, he would have to be at the theatre before long. 'I'll just show you Dansey Place before I go in.' We walked round to Leicester Square and turned up Wardour Street. Then suddenly, to the right, there it was, a narrow entrance that widened out to form an alleyway between the backs of the buildings in Gerrard Street and Shaftesbury Avenue. Half-way up was a rectangular metal construction which, on closer inspection, turned out to have three places along each of the two sides, with an opening at each end. I saw at once that they were very like the Petersburg open-air *kloseti*, though shorter.

I was back at Dansey Place the following evening at around ten o'clock. There were three others there when I arrived, two on one side, one in the middle position on the other. However, as soon as they saw my erection, they all turned round and faced the others, exposing theirs. Each in turn got down on his knees in front of me, while the others kept a look-out. Over the next half-hour, each of them came – and went. With some effort, I managed not to come – and stayed. I did not really care for any of them but, by now, I was desperate and, in any case, there is something about the loose, non-committal character of the 'orgy' that allows one to lower one's standards. Towards the end, we were joined by two newcomers. I had moved into one of the middle places – an old Parisian trick – and had one on either side of me. I had noticed a young man wandering around outside, so I discouraged their attentions.

After a while, one of them gave up and 'crossed the floor' to the other side. As I hoped he would, the young man came and took his place. He gave a little smile of satisfaction. He was even better-looking – and younger – than I had thought. He had dark hair and blue eyes, was slim to the point of thin, almost as tall as I – and, as I soon saw, was 'well endowed'. After a while, he gave my coat a pull and left.

Outside, he introduced himself as 'Jamie'. He was from Glasgow, seventeen and had only been in London for six weeks. I asked him if he'd like to go for a drink 'or anything'. He offered to take me back to his rooms in Seven Dials, a few minutes' walk away. As we were turning off Shaftesbury Avenue, he suddenly stopped in his tracks and, looking very serious, said, 'You know I'm on the game, don't you?'

'Well,' I said, untruthfully, 'I thought you might be. I've made it a rule never to go with rent boys, but I've taken a fancy to you. I don't mind giving you money – things must be difficult.'

He looked me straight in the eyes and said with charming seriousness: 'I've taken a fancy to you, too. I'm no fool. I dare say you could get anyone you wanted. I liked the look of you as soon as I saw you. That's why I hung around outside. Rent boys don't often get clients like you. I try to be choosy, but sometimes . . . Anyway, I'm still learning . . . Oh, Gawd,' he giggled, 'I've a lot to learn . . . I'm warning you!'

'How much do you usually get?'

'Never less than five shillings, sometimes more. Will that be all right? I wouldn't charge you more than five bob.'

'Don't worry about it,' I said.

He had a friend from Glasgow called Andy. When he came to London, Andy had put him up in his room until he could 'get started himself'. Andy was his best, his only friend, in London: he owed him everything.

'Andy dinned it into my head that I must never get soft on a client and, whatever I do, I must never go with a man for nothing – in fact, for anything less than five bob. That's Andy's golden rule. He told me: "If you start doing that, you'll never get anywhere in this game. You've got to look after yourself," he says, "No one else will." So it's more than my life's worth . . .'

'But you live alone now, don't you?' I asked anxiously. I didn't want to find myself cornered by two or three Glaswegians.

'Oh, yes,' he said. 'Andy lives round the corner. I've got just the two rooms. It's quite small, but Andy helped me to make it nice.'

I wasn't afraid of Andy any more and decided to risk it: in any case, I couldn't wait to get my hands on young Jamie. At Seven Dials, we turned into Great St Andrew's Street: still slightly apprehensive, I noted the name. He unlocked a door at the side of an ironmonger's shop and we climbed three flights of dilapidated, dingy stairs, lit, on each landing, by a small, solitary gas-lamp. We were no sooner in the door than Jamie began to kiss me passionately. Was I so special, I wondered, or was this the unspoilt enthusiasm of the *débutant* or, my suspicions were not entirely allayed, an attempt to lull me into a false sense of security? His hand went to my flies, mine to his. We began tearing off each other's clothes. He sank to his knees and began furiously kissing, licking, biting my cock, before plunging it into his mouth, my fingers playing over the soft, smooth skin of his neck. He took my hand and led me into the bedroom. On the bed, he pushed me on to my back and knelt up in front of me. As I caressed his cock, I was astonished again by the softness and smoothness of his skin, the skin of the cock itself and, above all, of an area around the middle of the inside of his thighs. He came down on top of me, kissing me. I sensed that he was reaching for the petroleum jelly, then, to my surprise, I felt his finger entering me.

'No,' I said, 'give me the jelly.'

'Sorry, dearie. It's what most of them want. Even when you least expect it. You don't wait to ask.' Then, with a broad smile, he added: 'Suits me!'

I took the jelly, inserted one, then two fingers, threw him on his back, raised his legs on to my shoulders and entered him. As I expected, there was no let or hindrance. I went right in, then stayed still, hardly daring to move, lest I explode at once. He was staring at me ravenously – no doubt, I was doing the same back. I slipped my left hand behind his neck and raised his head to kiss him. I then let him fall back, my left hand beside the base of his neck, my right on his cock. I moved out of him, then thrust it in again: after a few movements, we both came. I fell back on to the bed, took that thin, smooth, delicious creature in my arms and pulled the bedclothes over us. I gave him a few pecks on the neck, then began, imperceptibly, to doze off.

At no point did I really fall asleep. After what must have been about half-an-hour, I felt Jamie's hand on my cock. I fell to kissing him again, then turned him over on to his belly. I entered him in one forceful thrust. He moaned, with pleasure rather than pain. I went on thrusting at him till I came. Shrinking, but still inside him, I moved him over on to his side and made him come again. We smothered each other with kisses.

We went over to the remains of the fire and chatted for a while. I told him nothing about myself, nothing that was true, that is: I was called Matthew and was setting out as a journalist. Jamie told me how his mother had died the year before, how he had nothing in common with his father, who worked in the docks, and how Andy had befriended him.

'Oh, I've a confession to make,' he said. 'You know I told you that Andy lived round the corner? Well, he doesn't. He lives on the floor below. I knew what you were thinking. You were scared of being led into a trap, weren't you? Well, I didn't want to lose you. But you don't have to be scared of him – he's a real dearie, wouldn't hurt a fly. But you were right. You have to be careful. Most of the lads are all right, but there are one or two funny customers.' He laughed. 'Well, not customers . . . but you know what I mean. Oh, there's something else, too. I said I was seventeen. I'm nearly seventeen, but not quite. My birthday's next week. I didn't want to scare you off . . .'

I said that I should have to be leaving. I got dressed – he had slipped into a dressing-gown. I held him in my arms and kissed him.

At the door, I gave him a sovereign: 'Here, this is for your birthday.'

Astonishment, delight and embarrassment passed across his face in rapid succession. It was four times his minimum fee but, for me, it was not quite the price of a stall at Covent Garden or supper for two at the Savoy.

'I'd like to see you again,' he said, unsurprisingly. 'I think you're lovely!'

'Yes, I think you're lovely, too. I expect I'll see you in Dansey Place or somewhere around there. If I don't see you before long, I'll leave you a note in your letter-box downstairs.' A final kiss and I was gone.

A letter arrived from Maurice Baring. He was in London for two weeks: could I have luncheon with him at the Cecil next Tuesday? In that huge palatial dining-room, on the way back to Gray's Inn Place and sitting in his flat, he brought me up to date with his life. He had spent a fortnight in Petersburg on his way back. He had heard from his friend Cecil Spring Rice about my grandmother's death and our rapid departure.

Cecil was now acting *chargé d'affaires*. This I knew: Sir Charles Hardinge had returned to London on leave a couple of weeks after we left. What I did not know was that Sir Charles would not be going back: apparently, he would be succeeding Lord Sanderson as head – Permanent Under-Secretary – of the Foreign Office in the New Year. Did that mean that Cecil would be made Ambassador? I asked. Alas, no, the Embassy would be going to Sir Arthur Nicolson. I reminded Maurice that Sir Arthur was a distant cousin of mine and had been Matthew's boss in Tangiers until the beginning of the year. Maurice protested that he had intended no disrespect, but shouldn't I agree that no one could be better qualified than Cecil? I agreed: he would surely have his Embassy before long. Maurice would have written to me from Petersburg but, as I had probably read in the papers, Russia was in the middle of a revolution and the posts, like everything else, were hardly working.

'In fact, hardly anybody is working – and that goes for the government, too. Meanwhile, His Imperial Majesty sits around in Peterhof playing with his children. He hasn't been seen in Petersburg for months – he daren't set foot in the place. His ministers have to go back and forth the whole time – nothing can be decided without his say-so. A divided, incompetent opposition faces a divided, incompetent government. Result: nothing happens. The eternal Russia, the same old story. Meanwhile, of course, everyone talks, endlessly talks.'

The Tsar had finally been persuaded to accept freedom of the press, assembly and association; elections on a wide franchise would take place and a Duma, or parliament, with legislative powers would be set up. Maurice only hoped that these measures would not be blocked by the reactionaries – or rejected by the revolutionaries as not going far enough.

Maurice had been travelling for fourteen days, when the

train came to a stop at Kuznetsk, about eight hundred miles
from Moscow. An attendant informed them that they could
not get any further on account of the '*niepriatnosti*', literally,
the 'unpleasantnesses', his euphemism for the strikes.
Everyone imagined that they would be held up for a few
hours – such incidents had become quite frequent. By evening,
passengers were sending telegrams to the Transport Minister
complaining of their treatment. They spent four days at
Kuznetsk, until one of the passengers said that he could probably drive the train. Two days later, and after innumerable
stops and starts, they finally reached Moscow. There Maurice
moved into the Hôtel Dresden, only to find that there was no
lighting and that the lifts were not working. At the end of
dinner at the Métropole the following evening, the band,
hedging its bets, preceded the National Anthem with the
Marseillaise. Next day, he found all the shops shut. A few
days later, he joined the funeral procession for a veterinary
surgeon who had been shot by Cossacks during a protest: a
hundred thousand men walked in orderly fashion, wearing
their best suits, along the streets of the city to the cemetery.
Throughout the strike, the theatres remained open: Maurice
returned to the Art Theatre and saw Chekhov's *Chaika*
(*Seagull*), Ibsen's *Ghosts* and a new play by Maxim Gorky,
The Children of the Sun. I asked him if he had seen
Stanislavsky.

'Oh, yes. I shouldn't have got in otherwise.'

'And Baliev and Tarasov?' I asked, as lightly as I could.

'I saw Nikita briefly. Nikolai is ill again, poor fellow. Ah, of
course, you went to one of their *réceptions*, didn't you?'

'Yes,' I said as neutrally as I could, shifting the emphasis
slightly, 'have you been to their house?'

'Yes,' said Maurice, rather coldly, 'but not to one of their
réceptions. By the way, I'm going to be based in Moscow for

the next few months. I'm taking over as correspondent for the *Morning Post*.'

After a week in Moscow, Maurice went to Petersburg, where he stayed for a couple of weeks. Things were no better than in Moscow, but there, too, the theatres were still open: he saw *Fidelio* at the Marie. On the train from Petersburg to Berlin, he travelled with the Japanese Military Attaché and a Russian student, who declared that he loved English literature – and that his two favourite authors were Jerome K. Jerome and Oscar Wilde. Also with him was Constantine Benckendorff, the son of the Russian Ambassador in London. Maurice had known him since his days in Copenhagen. They were, said Maurice, with as much candour as he could ever muster, 'very, very good friends'; he was 'very, very fond of Constantine'. But how was I to understand that? Were they just 'very good friends' or was he hinting at more, saying, in effect, 'I am like you, too.' I veered in the direction of the second but, with Maurice, one could never be sure. Hector Munro, otherwise known as the writer Saki, would shortly be retiring as *Morning Post* correspondent in Petersburg and Maurice would replace him. Constantine and he would probably take a flat together.

We talked a lot about the theatre, the plays that I had seen over the past few weeks and his time as reviewer of foreign plays during the summer.

As I was leaving, he said: 'Oh, by the way, a good friend of mine is coming to London in the New Year – a German called Harry Kessler. I say "German" and German he certainly is; in fact, he's a *Graf*, a count, but he was actually born in Paris and went to school for a time in England. So you won't have to speak German – his French and English are perfect. I'll get him to look you up. Anyway, I think you ought to meet him.'

Since going down in June 1902, I had lost touch with all my

university friends. The truth was that I had lost patience with their parochial, enclosed, immature world and yearned after other, to me, more exciting things. Of course, retreating to Paris and then going off to Petersburg had not helped, but had I stayed in London I doubt if I should have gone back to Cambridge or spent much time chasing up my contemporaries. Now I was in London, and enjoying my freedom enormously. But one cannot spend all one's time chasing after adventure and going to the theatre. Indeed it was going, alone, to the theatre that began to give me a yearning for the less dramatic pleasures of social life. For me, going to the theatre had always been a social activity: it was a quite new experience to find myself in the bar at the interval with no one to discuss what I had just seen. My aunts and their families apart, I knew no one in London as yet. Clearly, by this time, a few of my university acquaintances must also be living in London. I decided to chase up Strachey: if anyone knew who was where, he would. He was also the most entertaining of the bunch. I wrote to him at College, suggesting that, on his arrival back in London at the end of term, he have lunch or dinner with me. A week later, I received a letter from Lancaster Gate saying that he was no longer at the University – but had already been back twice.

We met *chez* Roche, a modest French establishment in Old Compton Street. Strachey looked no older than I remembered him, the same thin, gangly figure, ill at ease in his clothes, as if cosseting his body against some inhospitable draught, the same unkempt moustache, the same anachronistic pince-nez, the same prematurely middle-aged look. Over dinner, he unburdened himself of some of his Cantabrigian concerns. A few weeks before, he had been informed that the dissertation on Warren Hastings, on which he had been working for two years, had failed to win him the College Fellowship that he had coveted. He was now banished from Conversations in Heaven's Courts and doomed to spend his days in a miserable little room in the family mausoleum in Lancaster Gate, with no conversation over the lugubrious dinner-table other than with the remnants of his family. His life was at an end (like me, he was twenty-five). He needed little encouragement to talk about his dissertation. He had been drawn to the subject of Warren Hastings's administration in India by his family's Indian connections over three generations, from his great-grandfather, who had been secretary to Clive in India and supported Hastings at the time of his impeachment.

'Ah!' I said, 'Sheridan, Burke and Fox. I suppose that makes us ancestral enemies.'

'Yes, I'm afraid it does,' said Strachey, with a wan smile. 'What's more, I have to say that R. B. S. was by far the worst of the three. The trouble was, like most people who have anything to do with the theatre, he was incapable of distinguishing between illusion and reality. For him, the Front bench in the Commons was just another stage to perform on. That five-hour-long speech was pure theatre, splendidly written, by all accounts splendidly performed, but actually based on nothing but malicious rumour. By the way, we have a Frenchman in the family now. You won't know, but one of my many siblings is an older sister called Dorothy, who, at the advanced age of forty, has taken it into her head to marry an impoverished French painter, Bussy by name, her junior by some few years. Mother, whose views have usually managed to keep abreast of the times, balked at this. The man could certainly paint pretty pictures but, my dear, he actually uses pieces of bread to clean up his plate! I explained that, in France, this did not necessarily mean that one was a person of low social standing or disreputable morals. She said that she had seen plenty of French people in her time and had never seen such a thing. Father, in many ways a more conventional person than Mother, looked upon the hapless French bohemian more kindly and has bought them a charming little house overlooking the sea near Mentone. I went down to see it – and them – the April before last. I found their connubial bliss rather disgusting, but there were plenty of visual compensations down by the beach.'

So, Strachey's six-year Cambridge career was at an end. To the astonishment of all who had witnessed the brilliance of his mind in operation, the College had supported the judgement of the University, which had awarded him a second in both parts of the History Tripos. He seemed in the depths of despair, yet he had embarked on a literary career that I could not even dream of. Over the past two years, he had been doing book reviews for the *Spectator*, of which a cousin, St Loe Strachey, was editor, and for a new periodical, the *Independent Review*, run largely by members of the Society – Lowes Dickinson, Trevelyan and Wedd, 'that don at King's, all Wagner, socialism and red ties'. The editor was another (former) King's Fellow, Edward Jenks. 'It's all very advanced, anti-imperialist, anti-protectionist, anti-Joe Chamberlain but, of course, they pay a pittance – I do an article every six weeks for three guineas a time.'

In response to a half-hearted question as to 'what I had been up to' since going down, I gave a much-condensed, highly selective account of my life over the past three and a half years. The conversation then moved smoothly on to the fate of our Cambridge contemporaries. Woolf stayed up another two years but, despite his First in Classics, Part I, only got a second in Part II. He and Sydney-Turner then took the Civil Service exam, but Woolf can't have done that well because he has ended up in the wilds of northern Ceylon, 'absolute lord of a million blacks'.

'And S. S. T.?'

'Oh, he's ended up in the Estate Duty Office, with an attic flat in Somerset House. Not surprisingly, the job suits him down to the ground, all very Dickensian. If anything, he's even less scintillating than ever but, underneath that dull exterior, he's a dear fellow. I'm really rather fond of him.'

'And Moore? I read the *Principia Ethica* in Petersburg and . . .'

'Ah, you must belong to a very select band! And?'

'And I must confess I found it rather irritating . . .'

'Ah, we can't have a word said against the *Principia* . . . Moore's *inamorato*, Ainsworth, left Manchester for Edinburgh, where he got a job teaching Greek at the university. The Yen promptly upped and went to join him. They've been there ever since. Mind you –' he came closer and lowered his voice '– I can't imagine what they do together, if anything.'

'And Stephen? The Goth?'

'He's in London, reading for the Bar. When Sir Leslie died last year, Thoby, Adrian and their two sisters left Hyde Park Gate and took a house in Bloomsbury, Gordon Square. The Goth has started what he calls "Thursday evenings". Funnily enough, they've got much better since the two Wise, but anything but silent Virgins joined us – they have the Goth's brains and beauty, I mean both have both. In fact, it's beginning to look as if they have more of both than he has. I'm afraid the Courtly Inns are rather blunting the Goth's brains and fattening him up, still he's as sweet a soul as ever. Vanessa is the perfect hostess, *le charme même*, while Virginia often abandons charm to display her own extraordinary mind. She now talks to working men and women about books at something called Morley College and writes learned reviews for the *Times Literary Supplement*. She's a very strange, very mysterious young lady. I must take you along one of these Thursdays. It will be a painless way of catching up with everyone. Who? Well, Bell . . . On going down, he took himself off to shoot at animals in British Columbia. He then spent a couple of years in Paris, you know. Well, no, I don't suppose you do. Despite his Second, the College gave him a Studentship to go off to Paris to research in the French archives on "British Foreign Policy at the Congress of Vienna". He then moved to Montparnasse and spent his time drinking with Irish artists and fornicating with French models. Bell never ceases to astonish me. At Cambridge, he always managed to hide his intellectual light under a hunting cap. Having failed to become "one of us", in the "Apostolic" sense, indeed in a number of others, too, he's now trying to be an artist, while living in some style in chambers in the Temple. He probably never realized that, like everyone else, he was in love with the Goth . . .'

'I wasn't . . .'

'Ah, but you, my dear, if I'm not mistaken, were actually *doing* things. Anyway, I think he now imagines that he's in love with Vanessa. But I think Vanessa is too much in tune with herself to believe him. Of course, they have their paintings to talk about. Who else now? There's dear, dear, clever, clever Hawtrey. He was in the Admiralty for a year and is now in the Treasury. He's usually at Gordon Square on Thursdays.'

I went through the names of more contemporary Trinitarians. Richards? ('The first First in Classics, Part I, Chancellor's Medal, College Fellowship, future professor.') Robertson? ('First in Classics, Part I, now working for some steamship company.') Anderson? ('Gone off to teach Latin in Manchester.') Salter? (?) Boughy? (?) Rothschild? ('Probably in the Bank. The family are still in Lancaster Gate – in an even bigger mausoleum than ours.')

'Did you hear about Llewellyn Davies, Theodore?'

'No, what about him?'

'He died in August. Drowned while bathing. I really can't tell you any more than that. Such a beauty, too. Remarkable family, one way and another. The father's still alive, over eighty, a clergyman, one of the first Christian Socialists. When very young, he coached Leslie Stephen for his Cambridge Entrance exams. Imagine! An older sister, a Girton girl, runs the Women's Co-operative Guild and organizes all the Suffragette things. Theodore's brother, Crompton, is a solicitor now. Someone told me that another of the brothers is the father of the boys that Barrie first told the Peter Pan stories to. You won't have seen the play last Christmas, but Boucicault and du Maurier are doing it again this year. You must see it. Barrie's a sentimental old bugger, but I'm sure he's one of us. But let's leave the realm of the divinely One and Undivided for the secular realm . . .'

I frowned in puzzlement.

'*Collegium Regale.*'

'Ah!'

'In my last year, I spent more time in King's than in Trinity. My spies there tell me that you raided the royal treasury once or twice. Sheppard, for example?'

'Yes, I knew Sheppard quite well.'

'I was rather besotted with him for a year or two – after you'd gone down. But I'm afraid I'm not his type: he became rather besotted with the Goth.'

'Like everyone else except me.'

'The trouble is that he likes everyone: he has, to a supreme degree, that King's man's charm, that ability to oil the social cogs with honey. The trouble is, you never know where you are with such people. It's all too easy to imagine that they reciprocate your feelings because they don't want to spoil the pleasant atmosphere by disabusing you. It probably all comes from the Eton connection – not that Sheppard is an Etonian, of

course, but he might just as well have been. It's the antipodes
to the Trinity spirit. We hardly like anyone, because we spend
so much time being honest to one another. It's all there in a
paper Sheppard gave to the Society: "King's or Trinity?"
Meanwhile, he quietly continues his brilliant career. President
of the Union, Firsts, College Fellowship next. He worked
harder than anyone else I knew and has been at King's ever
since, where, no doubt, he will live out his days. Last winter, I
saw quite a lot of him in the British Museum library: he,
Lowes Dickinson and I used to meet for tea.'

'Is he looking any older . . . or younger?'

Strachey laughed. 'No, just as cherubically young in the
face, still white-haired, still doddering around on a stick . . .
Have you read *Where Angels Fear to Tread* yet?'

'Yes.'

'Really quite surprisingly good, isn't it? Quite a dark horse,
that *Taupe*.'

'*Taupe?*'

'Sorry. My nickname for him. I always thought Forster was
like a mole.'

'Well said, old . . . But why in French? What's mole in
Italian?'

'I've really no idea – or why it's in French.'

'I met him once at the end of my second year. I was taken
along to one of Oscar Browning's tea-parties. He was there.
Yes, mole is quite good. I thought he was a bit like a mouse.'

'And what a wonderful old baggage Oscar Browning is!
Like some wicked old auntie who likes to spoil her nephews,
but might suddenly gobble one of them up. Yes, at that time,
Forster was always coming back to Cambridge, to King's
anyway – for him, the two are synonymous. It was the time the
little *Taupe* was mooning after the tall, handsome Hom –
Hugh Owen Meredith. He got a lectureship at Manchester

and the *Taupe* was always going up to see him. Hom then got engaged to some schoolmistress, which brought on what is nowadays called a "nervous breakdown", for Hom, I mean, not the *Taupe*. The *Taupe* then came into money and he and his mother went off to Italy for a year. This year he spent several months in Germany. A year ago he bought a house in the suburbs, somewhere called Weybridge, where he lives with mother, cook and parlour-maid. He comes up to town every week to take a Latin class at a Working Men's College in Great Ormond Street. I wonder what the Working Men make of our *Taupe*? Have you been back to Cambridge recently?'

'I haven't been back since I went down. I never really had any desire to.'

Strachey looked at me with blank incomprehension, for once bereft of words. Our coffee arrived, together with brandy, which I had persuaded him to join me in.

'Then, my dear, you must allow me to take you back. A new spirit is abroad – all sex and socialism. Well, talk of sex and socialism. My brother James is up at the moment – I usually stay with him. He has my old rooms, which he has painted all green and white, very *art nouveau*. But my real spy – and hardly a day passes but letters fly between us – is an Old Etonian King's man called Keynes. I got him into the Society in his first year – he's now in his third. He's a perfect scoundrel, very mature for his age, sleeps with everybody. It makes me feel quite old, a sort of transitional figure between Moore and him. It's quite awful. Freshmen regard me as a sort of mythological figure from the distant past. When one of them is presented to me, I can tell, he can hardly believe his eyes. If Moore really knew what the tone of the Society is these days, he would have a fit. You see, Keynes is a sensual Mathematician, not a Platonic Classicist or Moral Scientist. He doesn't waste time with soul-searching, just calculates. He has spent all his life in Cambridge. Imagine! His father's a don at Pembroke and lectures in Moral Science. His mother's a Newnham girl. I call him "Pozzo", by the way, which he hates.'

'And is he your current *inamorato?*'

'Oh, no! The master-mistress of my passion is not an Apostle, or even a Cambridge man. He's twenty years old, an artist, my cousin and is called Duncan Grant. Unfortunately, the beautiful, charming creature is far too good for me and therefore can be very cruel. He's particularly bad at answering letters. In fact, he's not very good with words at all, so I never know what he's thinking. He sees, notices everything, lives entirely through his body and has the most lascivious lips. Quite extraordinary! He has a studio in Upper Baker Street. The day before yesterday, he invited me there for the first time. I saw all his paintings. I think he's a genius. He made an omelette on the fire and we ate it on a bare table, with bread, cheese and beer. All deliciously bohemian! *Et tu, carus meus,* have you an *amitié particulière,* or are you content to break hearts all around you?'

'Neither, really. I haven't been back in London long. *Faute de mieux,* I've had to make do with quantity, rather than quality.'

'It sounds all very wicked and exciting. I'm afraid I'm not very good at that. Ah, some people have all the fun!'

Strachey said that he would get the 'Central tube' home to Lancaster Gate and I left him walking up to the Tottenham Court Road station. A few minutes later, I was in Dansey Place. I hung around for twenty minutes or so, but nothing of interest turned up.

Over the next few weeks, I began to investigate London's 'Turkish baths'. There seemed to be about a dozen within two miles of Piccadilly Circus. I soon realized that some of these

were mainly bathing establishments that also had a small
steam-room as an added facility. Though cheaper, and therefore more open to the young, I found, on the evidence of a
single visit, that the *clientèle* was there almost entirely for legit-
imately hygienic purposes: indeed such places were so laid
out and so supervised that they offered little opportunity for
any other. There were no fewer than four in the City alone.
One of these, in New Broad Street, seemed more propitious
than the others. I noticed a few, quite attractive young men,
but it soon became apparent that they were interested, not in
me, but in the older, more corpulent gentlemen from the City
financial houses: indeed, one or two of them seemed to resent
my presence, as if I were in competition with them. The West
End itself had at least three: the Charing Cross Baths, in
Northumberland Avenue, Bartholomew's, which I had already
noticed in Leicester Square, and the 'London and Provincial',
also known as 'The Hammam', in Jermyn Street. One
evening, after spending an hour or two in the London Library,
I called in at 'Jermyn Street'. With the slight quickening of the
heart-beat that always accompanies such visits, especially if
one is venturing somewhere for the first time, I pushed open a
door between two shops. At the end of a passage, I paid an old
crone sitting behind a counter. She took my wallet and other
valuables, put them into a metal box, which she locked, and
handed me the key, with a rubber band attached, which I was
to wear round my wrist. The 'undressing-room' consisted of
rows of doorless cubicles, where one left one's clothes.
Wearing my 'loin cloth', I went down the stairs, as instructed.
At one end of the room an ugly-looking, over-muscular individual was pummelling a customer lying on a marble slab: the
house *masseur* was about his work. I ventured into the dry-
heat room. There half a dozen men were sitting on slatted
benches, sweating profusely, wearing on their faces the same

expression of preoccupation, of isolation from their surroundings as I knew so well from men standing at the stalls of
public lavatories. After, I suppose, ten minutes, I moved on to
the first of the steam-rooms. In the dry room, my arrival had
passed apparently unremarked; here, under cover of relative
obscurity, some of the inmates seemed more willing to
acknowledge those around them. As I made my way through
the billowing steam, through the ever increasing heat of the
three chambers, several pairs of eyes were turned enquiringly
upon me. So far I had seen no one who particularly attracted
me. Here, too, the corpulent and middle-aged were disproportionately represented. Here, too, were a few 'rent' boys
plying their trade. I took a shower, returned for a couple of
minutes to the dry-heat room, then went upstairs to investigate the 'sleeping' area. This consisted of hard beds made of
wooden slats, separated off from one another by shoulder-
high partitions. A few men were lying down, a few others
standing around, chatting *sotto voce*, or wandering about rest-
lessly. I took up position against a wall, not too far from the
group of chatterers. By this time, my erection had returned,
not that I found anyone I had so far seen attractive. I untied
my towel and held it loosely against my body, in a semi-
concealing, semi-revealing manner. I knew from experience
that unless someone took the initiative nothing would happen.
The least unattractive of them left the group, walked slowly
towards me, fixing my gaze as he passed, returned, stood next
to me, beckoned to me with his head to accompany him to one
of the cubicles in the farthest corner. He would be, I guessed,
a few years older than I, of medium height and build, with
brown hair and eyes. I sat down on the bed and he sat down
beside me. Meanwhile, his friends had taken up position in the
doorway to the cubicle, ostensibly to keep guard, but, of
course, also to behold the swelling scene. I drew away my

towel and exhibited my glory to the gathered throng. My companion took hold of it, squeezed it hard, staring at it the while, moved the foreskin backwards and forwards, then suddenly plunged his mouth upon it. Before long, other mouths were feeding there. I had decided that I should be leaving shortly, so I let myself come. In this way, I could decently leave without causing offence.

My second visit to 'Jermyn Street' took on a rather different character. Late one evening, my eye alighted on a small, slim young man, about my age, with dark hair and eyes, not exactly good-looking, but with a certain, rather 'decadent' attraction. I stood next to him and he began to feel me. What I noticed most of all were the eyes: they had a sullen, rather haunted look about them. Having ascertained, after a few minutes' conversation, that I should be unlikely to murder or rob him, he invited me back to his house in South Kensington. In the cab, he seemed nervous, distracted, unwilling to make conversation. On arrival, he said that he wanted a scotch. Would I join him? I did. He swallowed his drink at speed and said: 'Follow me!' We climbed two flights of stairs to a room, dimly lit by gas, at the top of the house. The only furniture was a mattress on the floor, covered in a sort of rubber material, a chair and a table on which lay a rather pathetic collection of canes, whips and other implements of 'torture'. He started to undress; I did the same.

'Put these on!' he commanded, handing me what turned out to be a pair of tight black leather shorts, with an oval removed at the front, where the fly would normally have been. I found this garment strangely exciting as I stood there, my *membrum* erect before me. Meanwhile, my host had put on a dog collar and, as it were, the 'sister' garment to the one I was wearing: his had a bare oval at the back. He fell to his knees before me, smothering my cock with kisses, rubbing its length against his cheeks and neck, thrusting its head into his mouth, moaning with pleasure. After several minutes of such attentions, he looked up and said: 'Oh, it will hurt me so much, so much. But first, you must punish me! I've been such a bad, bad boy! Perhaps one of the canes to start with, though you must decide what you want to do with me.' His voice had lost all the authority that came from giving orders to servants: it was now quiet, wheedling, that of a contrite schoolboy. He got up and bent over the back of the chair, *cul en l'air*. I picked up one of the canes and administered a few strokes, firm, but not too hard, suggesting that harsher measures were to come. After a while, I tried a leather belt. This I found more exciting than the cane – it even sounded more exciting to my ear. Perhaps having been spared an English public-school education, being punished for misdemeanours by handsome older boys one secretly lusted after, then graduating to the role of the punishing prefect, I had never acquired a taste for the cane. In fact, I had never acquired a taste for these practices at all but, providing I was in the 'active' role, I was quite prepared, on occasion, to oblige the right young man, if he asked me nicely. My host fell to his knees before me again.

After a while, I said, 'I'm now going to fuck you!' I had no wish to stay there any longer than necessary.

'Oh!' he moaned. 'Yes, you must, of course! Oh, but it will hurt!'

'Yes,' I said, getting into the spirit of the thing, 'of course it'll fucking hurt!'

He reached out for the lubricant and put a little of it up his bum. 'I won't put any on you,' he said. 'I mustn't make it too easy. You want to hurt me, I know!'

'Get over the chair!' I commanded.

Holding him down with my left hand, I positioned my cock just inside his hole and teased him by moving it ever so slightly. He began to moan in expectation. Then, suddenly, I thrust it in, to its full length. He gave a little cry: as I guessed, the hole was quite capacious enough to take it without much pain. I went on fucking him, with strong, long strokes, slapping his bum with my right hand. Once it was over, he showed no inclination to engage in polite conversation and I left at once.

I arrived, as arranged, outside Tottenham Court Road 'tube' station at nine o'clock. Strachey had warned me that no supper would be provided and that no one would 'dress', so I took the precaution of putting on a lounge suit and having an early dinner in a cheap Italian restaurant in Soho. When I arrived at our *rendez-vous*, Strachey was already there, with what I took, correctly, to be two Cambridge undergraduates. Neither was remotely attractive, so neither could be Strachey's beloved cousin. The younger, thinner one of the two turned out to be Strachey's brother James, the other Keynes, who was staying with the Stracheys for a few days. Keynes was about my height, with dark hair, blue eyes, full, sensuous lips, yet, taken as a whole, his appearance was unprepossessing. He was already a little too plump for his age, had a rather large, awkwardly shaped, slightly retroussé nose, bad teeth and a moustache that, for me, put years on him. But his face had only to light up with that bright, intelligent smile of his for it to become almost attractive.

James Strachey had very little to say for himself as we made our zig-zag way through Bloomsbury streets and squares – for that matter, he said very little all evening. He mumbled some brief answer to my enquiries about Cambridge, but failed to reciprocate with any questions of his own. Keynes could not have been more different. By the time we had reached Gordon Square, I felt that I already knew a great deal about him – about his parents, about his activities in the

Union and Liberal Club (he had been President of both), how he was staying up for a fourth year, had decided not to read Economics after all, but to study for the Civil Service exam. All this, in a quarter of an hour's walk, and without the slightest trace of self-importance. Moreover, with the greatest skill, as if I were quite the most interesting possible subject of conversation, he had extracted an amazingly large volume of information about me and, I felt sure, stored it away for possible future use. In the course of the evening, I began to understand what Strachey had meant when he told me that his own period of dominance over the Cambridge undergraduate *élite* (by which he meant the Apostles and their friends) now seemed like an interregnum between Moore's reign and Keynes's. There were still pregnant (or sterile) silences, with their Quaker-like awaiting of revelation. Lytton had introduced a dose of well-needed levity into their solemn, high-minded proceedings, but the easy-flowing talk about the world, the flesh and politics did not come about until Keynes's reign. Lytton's description of him as a 'sensual mathematician' was brilliantly accurate. He had had the same classical education as the rest of us, but did not waste his time contemplating Platonic archetypes or dreaming of male lovers in the morning of the world. He was all mind, which was razor-sharp, and body, which was no doubt already clamouring for attention, and he was ready to place the one at the service of the other. He seemed to lack what we call 'soul', the Germans, with greater enthusiasm and conviction, '*Seele*' and the French, who have no notion of what it is, '*âme*'. In fact, he reminded me very much of a certain type of Parisian intellectual, a graduate of the Ecole Polytechnique perhaps.

It was peculiarly heart-warming to be received from the cold, damp London streets by Thoby Stephen's shining face, his twinkling blue eyes and charming smile. We had been exact contemporaries at Trinity and become quite good friends, in an unintimate, unemotional, relaxed kind of way. He was the only one of our Trinity circle whose not being invited to join the 'Society' was intended as a compliment. The Goth's sheer physical splendour, combined with a complete absence of emotional complication, with all its obscure, unrealized desires, set him apart, an object of veneration, rather than a companion. He was still as handsome as ever, if a little fuller in the face, a little more massive of build.

I had not yet met his brother and two sisters. I had just missed Adrian at Trinity. He was clearly a Stephen, though less good-looking than the others: thin, gaunt and even taller than Thoby. Like James Strachey, he seemed in awe of his older brother, and was indeed following in his footsteps in Lincoln's Inn. He said very little throughout the whole evening. Sir Leslie Stephen's two daughters, the 'Visigoths', as Strachey called them, were exceptionally beautiful. With their fair hair, their blue-grey eyes, their tall figures, their rather long, serious faces, they were possessed of a classical beauty, rather than mere prettiness.

While the men with moustaches and pipes discussed the new minority Liberal government and its prospects in January's General Election, with much talk of Campbell-Bannerman and Grey, Asquith and Lloyd-George, and the clean-shaven and pipeless said nothing, I spent a most agreeable half-hour talking to the Misses Stephen. Each, in her own way, was a 'Modern Woman', concerned that she should be listened to for what she said, on an equal footing with any man. Virginia talked with great seriousness about her work at Morley College. She was, I discovered, immensely well read and talked with intelligence, with controlled passion, of authors and books. Indeed, I felt that there was an air of controlled passion, of concealed intensities, about her altogether.

She made me feel that she was under no obligation to charm me, as woman or hostess, but that she could weave spells if she so wished. I sensed a certain distance within her, as if a large part of her were not entirely present but, even as she was speaking to me, somewhere else. I felt that I had aroused her curiosity; she was trying to reach out to me, but I seemed almost too far away from that distant, absent part of her. Vanessa, the elder by three years, was altogether more at ease, perfectly at one with her body and her surroundings. She, one felt, was the one in charge, the one who ran the household, her sister being, for such matters, to be accounted one of the men. Her passion in life was her painting. She had studied under Sargent at the Royal Academy Painting School and later at the Slade.

From the outside, the house in Gordon Square looked like thousands of other London terrace houses built in the first decades of the nineteenth century. Inside it looked like nothing I had ever seen before. The walls had been stripped of paper and the woodwork of dark brown varnish, and painted in dazzling white. As if that were not enough, the old, gentle glow of gas and oil had been replaced by the new, harsh light of electricity. All of this, I discovered, was Vanessa's work. Relief and colour came only from the paintings, many of them her own, that lined the walls: they looked very 'modern', in the latest French manner. Presumably, the pictures in the old house had been sold off or banished to store. The furniture, on the other hand, looked as though it had come from Hyde Park Gate, though the wicker *chaise longue* and chairs in the drawing-room had no doubt been in the conservatory. This all added, I thought, to the contrived air of simplicity and informality: this was how the rebellious well-to-do pretended that they were poor. This impression was reinforced by the sight of our hosts and hostesses sitting on the bare floor. Goodness knows what their three or four servants must have thought! One modern innovation that might have improved matters on that cold December night was central heating, which was sweeping bourgeois, if not aristocratic, Paris, but which, in London, had scarcely extended beyond the best hotels, such is our inveterate belief in the moral virtue of discomfort. Here, as in Smith Square, we had to be content with the old coal fire, a cheerful, but less efficient mode of heating than the tiled Russian stove, let alone modern cast iron radiators.

It never occurred to me that I was seeing, not only the interior decoration, but also the morals, of the future, for there was many a good soul in London that would have been profoundly shocked at the idea of two young ladies sitting around until the early hours of the morning, unchaperoned, among a throng of pipe-smoking young men. In fact, of the young men who had attended the 'Thursday evenings', few would have shown the least sexual interest in them at that time in their lives. Of those who might have done, Desmond MacCarthy had just become engaged to the daughter of his former house-master at Eton, while that other notorious heterosexual, Clive Bell, had been banished, after proposing marriage to Vanessa a few months before. After flirting with one another for years, Vanessa decided that she did not, after all, love Bell and turned him down, adding that it would be better if he did not visit the house any more. All this I learnt from Strachey; I later learnt that Bell was readmitted some months later.

Also there was Saxon Sydney-Turner. He had been my exact contemporary at Trinity and had read Classics, so I knew him well, much as one knows a building that one walks past every day, but never enters. He promised much: academically brilliant, he also painted pictures, wrote poems and composed music. Friends who were much closer to him than

I believed in his future greatness. For me, he was one of those
double-First workhorses who never produce an original or
amusing idea. He had, however, a colossal memory for facts,
the more useless the better. When I had to speak to him, I took
refuge in the subject of music, more particularly of opera,
even more particularly of Wagner. Most summers, he went to
Bayreuth, though, even here, he had nothing of interest to
say. He was happiest when reeling off the name and roles of
every singer who had sung at Bayreuth since the Festival
began. He seemed much the same as I remembered him: same
moustache, same spectacles, same fussy, old-maidish manner.

Desmond MacCarthy was next to arrive. He was three years
my senior and had gone down before I went up, but I had met
him two or three times in Strachey's rooms, on his visits to
Cambridge. Like mine, his mother was half-French, the other
half being German; on his father's side, he was Anglo-Irish
with, like me, a small proportion of native Irish blood. He was
handsome, usually the best-dressed man in the room, so over-
whelmingly charming that there were those who whispered
that he was nothing else. He never dominated a conversation,
never seemed to come out with any very definite ideas of his
own, yet he gave any conversation in which he participated an
emollient quality that was entirely his own. He had a passion
for the theatre and already reviewed plays for the *Spectator*
and *The Speaker*. To the surprise of some, perhaps – he had
never been noted for advanced views – he had become a champion of Ibsen, Shaw and the Court Theatre. He talked about
Man and Superman, Major Barbara, The Voysey Inheritance; I
told him about Isadora Duncan and my visit to the Moscow
Art Theatre. He was the first of that evening's guests to show
any interest in what I had been doing and seeing in Russia.

Soon afterwards, Jack Sheppard turned up. I remembered
that his parents lived in London, so he was probably spending

the Christmas Vacation with them. His father, quite improbably, or perhaps not, given Jack's aspirations to higher things socially and culturally, and his enthusiastically espoused atheism, was a Baptist minister in Dulwich, or Balham or some such outpost of Empire. As Strachey had warned me, he had not changed: the same clear, fresh-skinned baby face, the same white hair, the same good spirits and infectious giggle. If he seemed older, it was only in the sense of greater self-confidence. He caught my eye from across the room, waved and beamed at me. After greeting his hostesses, he came over. He grasped my left hand in both of his:

'How wonderful to see you, my dear! What a lovely surprise.' From time to time, he gave me complicit looks that suggested that we had once had a passionate relationship, rather than the brief, rather unsatisfactory one that it had been for both of us. I could only conclude that he was now a good deal more experienced in such matters, as indeed I was, and might like to take up where we had left off. It would not be a good idea, I decided. Had we been in Timbuctoo – or Tomsk – things might have been otherwise, but, outside, in the London streets, the new and unknown always beckon.

As Strachey had forewarned me, little in the way of physical sustenance materialized during the evening. Cups of weak, milky coffee had been passed round soon after our arrival. At one point, we were being threatened with cocoa. Was this a hint that we should shortly all retire to our beds? Or encouragement to participate in a further few hours of talk? In any case, I decided to refuse the cocoa and leave. MacCarthy had already left – and people seemed to be forming themselves into a circle. I had a good idea what would happen next: idle talk, pleasantries, gossip would be banished, some abstract problem would arise, attempts would be made to pluck out the heart of its mystery, silences would ensue, as the spirit of Moore hovered over the gathering like some metaphysical paraclete. Sheppard gave me an appealing look and said that he ought to be leaving too. Strachey raised an eyebrow and smiled to himself.

Outside, I asked Jack how he would get home. He would get a train at Victoria. I said that I should be getting a cab and could drop him off there. We chatted pleasantly enough. I asked him if he had been to many 'Thursday evenings': he had been four times before, during the Easter Vac and just before the beginning of the Michaelmas Term. Yes, I was right in thinking that this evening had passed off rather differently from usual: on other occasions, the social pleasantries had been got over quite quickly and the chairs arranged in a circle much earlier on. The 'refreshments' were usually the same, though, in the course of one warm September evening, Thoby had offered the men a bottle of beer each. Jack insisted that, before the vacation was out, we should meet again.

'And don't leave it too long! I'll be going up after the New Year – I've promised Maynard to help out at the Liberal committee-rooms.' At Victoria station, he thrust into my hand a piece of paper on which he had written his father's address. 'And don't let it go the way of all the others you no doubt collect, you wicked man!'

My evening at the Stephens', and that earlier evening with Strachey alone, had left me with mixed feelings, the same that I had had about my fellow-undergraduates at Cambridge. I enjoyed the gossip, the rapid cut and thrust of intellectual exchange, once it stirred itself into life, but was also repelled by the physical unawareness, the schoolboy immaturity of those indulging in it. Some of those 'brilliant minds' had already sunk into the recesses of the Civil Service or the Inns of Court; two of them, MacCarthy and Strachey, were already launched as minor *littérateurs*, reviewing books and plays. Only Forster, conspicuous by his absence that evening, had actually created anything. I exempted from these criticisms the two Stephen sisters, who, it seemed to me, only tolerated the 'talk' of their brothers' friends. Vanessa had already found herself in the physicality of her paintings: was it significant, I wondered, that so many of her portraits, hanging on the walls and stacked against the wall, were faceless, almost headless bodies, without mouths to speak? Virginia, too, I felt, had withdrawn, not into her body, but into a higher, or deeper, level of consciousness.

When Matthew left London, shortly after Grandmother's funeral, he had intended to come back to Smith Square for a few weeks' leave at Christmas. Christmas Day would be spent at Aunt Carrie's; New Year's Eve at Uncle and Aunt Jacky's. To keep us entertained between the two, I booked a couple of stalls for Tree's production of *The Tempest* and for James Barrie's *Peter Pan*. Matthew then wrote that he would not, after all, be coming back to London, because he had been invited by his former boss, Sir Arthur Nicolson, to spend Christmas with his family in Madrid. I returned one of the tickets for *Peter Pan*, but asked Jack Sheppard to join me for *The Tempest*.

It was my third visit to His Majesty's since my return: already I was beginning to have the proprietary feelings about it that, as a boy, I had had for Irving's Lyceum. I had seen Tree several times during his management of the Theatre Royal, Haymarket, from our side of the footlights one of London's most beautiful playhouses. From the other side, however, it did rather cramp Tree's style as a producer. It was his yearning for ever greater spectacle, for all the latest in stage machinery, that led him to acquire the decrepit old opera house opposite, pull it down and build a new theatre in its place. There a system of sliding stages made it possible to construct one complicated set, ready to be slid on behind the curtain as soon as the preceding scene had ended.

In *The Tempest*, supposed by some to be his final work, Shakespeare/Prospero abjures his 'rough magic'. In this production, the 'magic' of modern stage-craft was there from the moment the curtain went up. It was as if Shakespeare had finally listened to Tree's entreaties and given him a proper beginning. This time there would be no courtiers entering stage right on to a curtained forestage, muttering such inconsequentialities as 'I thought the King had more affected the Duke of Albany than Cornwall'. 'On a ship at sea. A storm with thunder and lightning' declares the first stage direction. Tree did not need to be told twice: the curtain rose to reveal a ship's deck lurching up and down, and from side to side, wind tearing at the sails, gallons of water sloshing around. The mast and fo'castle, or whatever it is called, then proceeded to break up before our eyes, to the accompaniment of shouts from the terrified crew and the most convincing thunder and lightning any theatre had ever seen. Tree, the theatrical magician *par excellence*, chose to play not Prospero, but the poor, less than noble savage Caliban. This was a wise choice: the old duke has little to do but look dignified and speak his fine speeches well; Caliban offered Tree the character-actor full scope for his quirky, eccentric insights. Prospero may have the last word on the page, but it was Tree, the actor-manager, who brought the curtain down. Prospero breaks his staff: the thunder and lightning from the first scene return, the stage darkens. As the lights go slowly up, we hear the nymphs singing 'Come unto these yellow sands' and the yellow sands duly appear out of the purple haze. In the distance, the ship, carrying its human load, grows ever smaller. Caliban creeps out of his cave, master again of all he surveys. He stares at the departing ship, then, overcome with mute despair, stretches out his hands towards the master who taught him language.

Over supper at the Criterion, Jack – he needed no

persuasion to drop the anachronistic use of surnames – bubbled over with enthusiasm. He had not got round to seeing the play when it was first put on the year before. He didn't go to the theatre nearly enough, yet he, too, was 'stage-struck'.

'You played once i' th'university.' I wondered if he would take the cue. He did:

'I did not enact Julius Caesar, nor did Brutus kill me in the Capitol. But, like Cicero, I spoke Greek. I was Peisthetaerus in *The Birds*. I was accounted a good actor.'

Three years before, in my second year, the Triennial Greek play had been the occasion of my one and only entrance upon a stage. Hiding behind a grey beard, I had been one of twelve Elders of Argos in the *Agamemnon*. At Cambridge, I should dearly have liked to join the Amateur Dramatic Club, but the most I ever dared to do was speak Greek in unison as a member of the chorus. Then, as I sat in my stall in His Majesty's, the thought came to me in a flash: why don't I offer my services as a supernumerary? Not only might I find distraction among those carefree creatures that live by show, but I knew, too, that it was among actors that I was most likely to find the 'brave' creatures that I was seeking.

With Irving gone, the mantle of London's premier actor-manager had fallen on Tree's shoulders. Only he regularly put on the kind of productions, usually Shakespeare, that required large crowds, and therefore a supply of 'supers' to walk on. In April, he had put on his first Shakespeare Festival: half a dozen Shakespeare revivals in the week of the Bard's birthday, 23 April. I knew that the Festival was going to be repeated this year. If extra 'supers' were ever to be needed, it would be then. My grandfather was my only link with Tree. They had not been close friends, but had known each other well enough to exchange a few words at the Garrick. I wrote to Tree. I was, I unashamedly declared, the grandson of Tom Sheridan whom, I believed, he had known quite well. Could I see him with a view to my 'walking on' at His Majesty's Theatre?

Beside me in the Duke of York's Theatre was an elderly gentleman, who informed me that he had been extremely fortunate in obtaining a cancellation for *Peter Pan*: tickets were unobtainable weeks ahead. I admitted that the ticket had been mine: he was all confusion. He hoped that nothing too terrible had befallen my companion, that I should not find the company of an old man too boring. Throughout the play, he was clearly in a state bordering on ecstasy, chuckling and ah-ing to himself.

At the interval, he leaned over to me and said, 'Last year, I saw Miss Boucicault in the role of Peter Pan: she was very good. Miss Loftus is also very good . . .' He paused, then as if confessing to some secret vice, he whispered: 'I don't know what you think . . . I expect I am alone in thinking this but, in my opinion, I think it would be so much better if Peter were played by a boy.' His pronunciation of 'boy' – the diphthong being almost endless – managed to infuse the word with untold sensuality. I put my hand on his arm and said that I quite agreed with him and that, as far as I was concerned, the same went for Puck and Ariel. He could hardly believe his good fortune: his eyes shone with delight. It was indeed an extraordinary play, admirably produced and acted – even by the unhappily female Cecilia Loftus. Gerald du Maurier turned in a superbly contrasted rendering of Mr Darling and Captain Hook; as the latter, he brought the house down with a splendid imitation of Irving.

A card arrived from 'Harry, Graf Kessler': he apologized for the short notice, but he would not be in London for long. Would I, by any chance, be free to have lunch with him at the Hôtel Cecil on Wednesday, 10 January?

Three days later, I was about to leave the house when the postman arrived with a letter. The envelope bore the imprint of

His Majesty's Theatre. I tore it open. It was from Mr Tree himself. Would I care to call on him at the theatre about six o'clock on the following Wednesday? Wednesday, I reasoned, was a matinée day: Tree obviously wanted to see me during the gap between the two performances. I put the letter into my pocket and, with light heart, set off along the Embankment to the Cecil.

I enquired after Count Kessler at the reception desk and was conducted to a table in the lounge. Harry Kessler turned out to be a good-looking man in his late thirties, with fair hair and blue eyes. He clearly possessed immense charm, a charm, I soon felt, that sprang from genuine kindness, rather than serving as a mask to conceal its absence. As Maurice had said, he spoke English and, as I later discovered, French, with great fluency and without accent. We moved, almost at once, to the vast, palatial dining-room. While in no way diminishing the attention that he paid me, I noticed that he did not conceal his interest in the young waiters that buzzed around us.

'I think I ought to warn you,' he began, pausing slightly for dramatic effect, 'that my good friend Maurice Baring has told me a great deal about you.'

'But,' I protested, 'my good friend Maurice Baring knows practically nothing about me – nothing of any importance at least.'

'Ah, that sounds most intriguing.' A slight giggle broke through his serious mien. 'It is true that Maurice does nothing to encourage revelation – his English reserve, I suppose, though he is more than a little German. I know precisely what you mean. Nevertheless, he reveals more than he realizes – about himself and others.'

Ever so subtly, he had revealed that Maurice and he were to be accounted members of the fraternity, and that Maurice, and now he, regarded me as one too. It was a fleeting moment and he soon changed the subject:

'So you are one of *the* Sheridans.'

'It depends what you mean by *the*.' I explained that I was a descendent, not of *the* Sheridan, but of his much less interesting brother.

'My beloved mother is Irish, a Blosse-Lynch. She was barely seventeen when she gave birth to me. She never went on the stage, but she is a very good amateur actress and singer. Your mother's French, isn't she?'

'Yes . . . and half-Hungarian.'

'Ah, French, Hungarian, Irish, an explosive mixture! I hope you have enough English *restraint* and *common sense* to keep all that under control! But enough of this nonsense: fortunately, we are not horses, though one of our Irish brothers thought that it would be better if we were! I was born in Paris, you know, and went to school there, so I suppose I'm French, too. But I then went to school in England, to a prep school in Ascot run by a certain *Reverend Herbert Sneyd-Kynnersley* . . .' (The words were pronounced slowly, with great care, his face betraying not the slightest amusement.) 'He tried to turn me into an English gentleman. If I learnt nothing else I acquired a sense of "fair play" . . . Maurice tells me you are *fou du théâtre*. I too was – "stage-struck". My youthful infatuation has now been replaced by what can only be called true love, a much more serious matter. In the new century, the arts in general, but the theatre in particular, must save civilization from the barbarism of armies and factories; we must try to recapture something of what the theatre meant in Ancient Greece. I have persuaded our Archduke to let me help him make Weimar once again the cultural heart of Germany, as it was in Goethe's day. I have got my friend Henry van de Velde – do you know of him? – he's a Belgian disciple of William Morris, but now lives in Germany. He started something he calls the Deutscher Werkbund, the German Work League. I've had him put in charge of the School of Arts and Crafts at Weimar – I'm responsible for the theatre, the museums and goodness knows what else in Saxe-Weimar-Eisenach – and he's now working on my house there. He has already transformed my Berlin apartment. It is now a modern work of art. Do you know –' he giggled self-deprecatingly '– I hardly dare to set foot in it. Before long, I shall have nowhere to live at all. I shall live abroad in hotels like this!'

'Saxe . . . Isn't that where the famous theatre company is?'

'I'd like to say "Yes, of course", but I suspect you mean our good neighbours Saxe-Meiningen. Their duchy is even smaller than our grand duchy which, I suppose, is how it should be. It must be very difficult for an Englishman – or Frenchman – to understand the German political system, if something so chaotic can be called a system. Saxe-Weimar-Eisenach practically runs itself. We have our Emperor in Berlin, of course, but, as far as our few hundred thousand inhabitants are concerned, he's the King of Prussia, Berlin its capital and we don't care for either. They have the soldiers and the money; we have the culture – or, at least, a quite disproportionate amount of it. I like to think that, in my own humble way, I will do for Wilhelm Ernst what Goethe did for Karl August. As for the theatre, yes, Saxe-Meiningen is better known. It has had a tremendous influence. Your Beerbohm Tree, who, of course, is half German, was much influenced by Saxe-Meiningen; Stanislavsky, too . . . I understand you saw *La Cerisaie* in Moscow . . . Unfortunately, the Saxe-Meiningen company is still the best *nineteenth-century* theatre. In Berlin, Max Reinhardt has already broken away from its influence. He's a genius. Last year, he did a wonderful *A Midsummer Night's Dream*. I'd like him to do something for us. At the moment, I'm trying to get Hugo von Hofmannsthal to come and manage our theatre. I want to make Weimar a temple to *twentieth-century* theatre, *twentieth-century* art, *twentieth-century* thought. We already have the Nietzsche Archive in Weimar! God may be dead, but Nietzsche lives – in Weimar! The great man's sister, Frau Förster-Nietzsche, is a tower of strength at Court, one of my stoutest allies! . . . Do you know Edward Gordon Craig? Now he is a genius – he is the theatre of the future. A theatre of the mind, the imagination: for that we have no need of architectural historians. Electric light! That is the key to it! Did you see his *Vikings*? I met him about that time – two or three years ago. I went to see him in his studio in Manresa Road, in Chelsea. But he's living in Berlin now, you know. I helped him find a dealer to sell his prints. I always see him when I'm in Berlin and he often comes down to Weimar. I tried to get him to work with Reinhardt on a production of Shaw's *Caesar and Cleopatra*, but, after months of discussion, the whole thing broke down. He isn't an easy man to work with . . . You saw Isadora Duncan in St Petersburg? She and Craig are living together, you know. What an extraordinary pair! What kind of child could that produce? . . . Do you ever go to Germany? If ever you do, you must come and see me. Weimar is a charming place, but, of course, there is much more to do in Berlin – I am sure you would love Berlin. Things are getting very *free* there – a great change. It used to be so stuffy! Now everyone's a sun-worshipping naturist. You see, the twentieth century is doing its work there too. Even if I'm not there, you can always stay at my beautiful apartment in the Köthener-Strasse. I'm sure you would like it – it's all very *modern style*, as the French say. You call it *art nouveau*, I think. Curious, isn't it? In German, we give it a German name, *Jugendstil*, youth style, which is more attractive, don't you think?'

The above, of course, is not a stenographic record of a conversation, merely a recreation of some of the things that Harry

Kessler said. I too said things, though they were not worth the recording, during the three hours we spent over our splendid luncheon.

On my way back to Smith Square, I called in at His Majesty's. The two-week revival of *The Tempest* was now over and *Twelfth Night* was being given again. On Wednesday of the following week, they were doing *Oliver Twist*. This I had not seen: it had first been put on the previous summer. I bought a ticket for the matinée.

At the house, I found another letter awaiting me: it was from Matthew, now back in Tangiers.. Sir Arthur Nicolson had asked him to join him at St Petersburg as his private secretary. He was, of course, delighted to accept: he had got on extremely well with his distant kinsman and, although his formal rank would still be that of third attaché, it would be at an embassy, not at a mere Legation. He would be back in London on 2 February and be leaving with Sir Arthur on the 7th. How strange to think that Matthew would be living on the Dvortzovaya Naberezhnaya, perhaps in my rooms overlooking the Marsovo Pole. His Petersburg would end up being different from mine, of course. He would no doubt have a wonderful time, dancing his feet off in ball after ball, falling in and out of love, perhaps even meeting his future wife.

The following Wednesday afternoon, I entered His Majesty's with a quite special excitement. I watched that performance as I had never watched a play before: I now knew what it was like to be a critic, to have copy ready within an hour of leaving the theatre. I had less time than that, of course, but I needn't have worried. Afterwards I was met inside the stage-door by a slight, balding man in his late thirties. I knew at once that he was not an actor: he had the blend of amenability and stiffness, attentiveness and distance of a

good waiter. He was, I later learnt, Tree's dresser, Alfred
Trebell. I was conducted upstairs to Tree's dressing-room and
there, staring back at me was Fagin – or, rather, it was and it
was not Fagin. The grubby clothes, the long, pointed, straggly
beard were Fagin's but, on closer inspection, I noticed that
Fagin's bright red 'hair' had been removed and was lying on
the dressing-table. Tree got up and took my hand: 'How do
you do? Take a seat.' Now he was even less Fagin. Tree was
tall, taller than me, a couple of inches over six feet; as Fagin,
he had never once stood up straight. I now saw his pale blue
eyes, disguised by a lot of black paint around them. But, above
all, the voice was not Fagin's, of course, and provided a ludi-
crous contrast with the filthy clothes and beard.

He stared at me for several seconds without uttering a word.
Then: 'I had red hair once. Redder than yours. When I was
young, I worked in the City. On Sundays, I used to take a
Sunday School class at a church in Bayswater. The local kids
used to call me "Ha'p'orth o' carrots".'

Another pause, then: 'So you're Tom Sheridan's grandson.
Splendid fellow. Always at the Garrick. Do you speak French?'

'Fluently,' I replied, with relief. 'My mother's French and I
was educated in Paris.' I felt I had jumped the first hurdle.

'Perhaps you should apply to the Comédie-Française. My
father was German and I was educated in Thuringia. Do you
speak German?'

'Hardly at all, I'm afraid.'

'Pity. I might have offered you the role of Octavius.
Unfortunately, I've already given it to Basil Gill . . .'

I grinned. I was yet to learn that no conversation with Tree
ever followed a logical course. At twenty-eight, Basil Gill was
already an actor of some standing: the role of Octavius Caesar
in the forthcoming production of *Antony and Cleopatra* was
the third most important in the play. And I had asked to 'walk

on'. Quite apart from my stammer, which I had not confessed to or, so far, revealed, I could not conceivably have done anything else. I was untrained and quite without experience.

'Did you see much of old Irving?'

'Yes, I must have seen him . . . getting on for twenty times. My grandfather—'

'A strange personality, but hard . . . hard . . . I couldn't get on with him at all. Quite unlike his two boys, Harry and Larry. Such nice lads. I like 'em both. D'you know them?'

'No, but I have a Russian connection with Laurence. We've both lived in St Petersburg. In fact, I only got back some weeks ago.'

'Excellent, so you speak Russian as well as French and German.'

'Well . . .'

'Good! Well, you're a handsome young fellow, look good on the stage, soldier, courtier, that sort of thing. I've nothing to offer you at the moment but, who knows, something might crop up. I'll let you know if it does. Of course, you do realize that I shan't be able to pay you anything, but it'll be wonderful experience, an education. Don't worry, I don't charge fees either. By the way, will you be free later this evening? Good, because I'm giving a little supper party after the show. It's the last night, you know. Do come along. You'll be able to meet the company. It'll be up on stage – nothing formal. Come round to the stage-door at eleven thirty.'

I walked back through the chill January evening, my mind in a state of delicious anticipation. Sometimes, when in *flâneur* mood, I would go into the Park, on reconnaissance; this time, I kept to the roadway, trying to look neither to left nor to right, lest distraction waylay me. I did catch the eye of a boy standing rather provocatively against a tree on the park side, but I pressed on. Back in Smith Square, I ate a little of the food left me by Mrs Wrigglesworth, who came over from Lambeth every morning to 'do' the house. I read for a while, changed, then set out, retracing my earlier steps.

At His Majesty's stage-door, I was directed up some steps and along a corridor to the stage. I stood in the half-light of the wings, preparing to enter downstage left. I did not, of course, 'make my entrance', but edged tentatively forward, as yet unnoticed. I looked out across the footlights to the darkened auditorium, the broad gilt sweeps of dress circle, upper circle and balcony glowing in the light from the stage. I stared back at where I imagined I had sat, near the end of row J, that afternoon. On stage, otherwise denuded of scenery and 'props', was a long trestle table. Busying themselves over it were a middle-aged man and three young underlings. At a side table, a very attractive young waiter stood behind champagne bottles and glasses. I went over, smiled and looked straight into his eyes, eliciting, I fancied, a slight blush, and took a glass. Some thirty or forty guests were standing around in groups. I saw Tree's tall figure from behind. With him was his daughter Viola and two couples. I recognized one of the women as Constance Collier, the Nancy in *Oliver Twist*. Then, right across the stage, downstage right, my eye alighted upon a group of four young men; they could not have been more than eighteen or nineteen. One of the two facing in my direction must have said something, because the other two turned round and looked straight at me.

Just then, Mr Tree turned round and saw me: he gestured me over. The man with Constance Collier turned out to be her husband, Julian L'Estrange. The other man was Laurence Irving. I had not seen him on the stage for some years; close up, I was struck by his astonishing resemblance to his father, still further accentuated by the pince-nez. I turned to him: 'I'm afraid I've been outside London rather a lot in the last few years, but I was at your father's last appearance at the Lyceum, in *Merchant*. You were Antonio, weren't you?'

Before he could reply, Tree said: 'He's the grandson of Tom Sheridan, a great friend of your father's.'

'Ah . . . yes . . .' said Laurence Irving, with a sad smile.

'I was at the funeral,' I said. 'I felt I had to represent my grandfather.'

'Yes . . . of course,' he said, with another sad smile. He introduced me to his wife, a dark-haired woman, who, I later learnt, was the actress, Mabel Hackney.

'He's just come back from St Petersburg and speaks fluent Russian,' Tree went on.

I tried to protest.

'Yes, I was there myself for a time,' said Laurence Irving. 'What were you doing there?'

'Nothing, really. My father's at the Embassy.'

'Ah, I see . . . Yes, I had a go at the Diplomatic Service myself, but nothing came of it. The theatre, you know, the theatre . . .'

'Ah,' said Tree, oiling the social cogs into motion, 'I must present you to young Esmé Percy. He studied with Sarah Bernhardt, you know, and speaks perfect French.'

He took my right arm and steered me across the stage to the group of young men I had seen earlier. Two of the group looked familiar from the afternoon performance. The other two looked more interesting: one tallish, very slim, with dark, wavy hair; the other shortish, with a round, chubby face – *potelé*, I said to myself, like a baby – and very black wavy hair.

'Allow me to present Mark Sheridan.' Then, turning to the short one, said: 'Esmé, you two must talk about Paris and Sarah Bernhardt.'

'Well,' said Esmé, without a moment's hesitation, 'the Chief must be obeyed and I don't think these gentlemen want to hear any more about Sarah.' He pronounced the name 'Sahrah', *à la française*. I had just enough time to stare into the pale blue eyes of the taller, prettier one, before Esmé seized my arm firmly and projected me to the opposite side of the stage. On the way, we got our glasses refilled by the attractive young waiter.

There was an incongruous discrepancy between, on the one hand, Esmé's imperious manner, the knowing twinkle in those dark eyes as of a man twice his age, who has lived life to the full and, on the other, that round, plumpish baby face.

'Are you a friend of Sarah's?' he asked.

'No, no . . . not a friend. I've met her a few times. And you?'

'I was taught by her or, to be more precise, she supervised my studies. My actual teacher was Monsieur Leloir at the Conservatoire.' The last word was pronounced not only with a perfect French accent, but also with the intonation of a *comtesse*.

'I miss Paris,' I said.

'Ah, yes . . . When were you there?'

'From the age of eleven until I went up to university. My mother's French . . .'

'*Veinard! Vous avez sûrment vu la grande Sarah beaucoup plus que moi! Il faut que nous en parlions plus tard . . . Cela ne vous gêne pas de parler français? Cela me donnerait grand plaisir.*' The prospect of our speaking French together was made to sound quite lascivious.

'*Le plaisir sera entièrement le mien,*'[1] I responded, with mock

---

1 'Lucky fellow! You must have seen much more of the great Sarah than I! We must talk about her later . . . It doesn't embarrass you to speak French? It would give me great pleasure if you did so.' 'The pleasure would be entirely mine.'

gallantry, 'but I don't think we ought to speak French here. It might look too conspiratorial.'

Esmé giggled delightedly. 'Oh, yes! Who can we stab in the back?'

'What about your three friends over there?'

'Oh, I shouldn't say they were my *friends*, not *particularly*.'

'Who are they?'

'They're students from Mr Tree's Academy.'

'Oh, yes, I think I read something about it in the papers. What is it exactly? A sort of English Conservatoire?'

Esmé's face took on a pitying look. 'Yes, I suppose that is what it is, a *sort* of English Conservatoire – *toutes proportions gardées!*'[1]

'How did you learn to speak French so well? Not, I take it, on Sarah's knee.'

Esmé threw back his head in delight. 'Oh, no, no, no, no, no! It's all rather complicated. My mother, like *Madame votre mère*, is French, though largely of Italian descent. My father is a North Briton, vaguely Scottish and a distant scion of the Northumberland Percys. So you see, in my own small way, I am a veritable Hotspur!' More giggles. 'As a child I went to France quite a lot, but actually I was brought up in Windsor.'

'Now,' I persisted, 'the three *académiciens* . . . I think I recognized one or two of them from the play.'

'Ah, still harping on my *friends* . . .' and he gently poked a finger at my belly. 'Yes, the one with the dark straight hair is Reginald Owen, though his friends call him John. He was Tom Chitling in *Oliver Twist*. He's a *good* actor.' He made 'good' sound more like a limitation on the young man's talent than an affirmation of it. '*Quite frankly*, he's the only one of them who's any good, the only *real* actor among them. He

1 'Relatively speaking.'

won the Academy gold medal last year, the one they've named after Bancroft. The one with mousy-coloured hair is known as "S. Yates Southgate" – S for Sidney – and the other one calls himself "E. Egerton Hine" – E for Esmond. You know, it's really quite *extraordinary* –' all six syllables clearly enunciated, with little trills on the 'r's '– Tree cannot abide hyphenated surnames, won't have any appear in the programmes – one of his little *manies*.[1] But the company is full of people with double names and no hyphens – like so many would-be Beerbohm Trees. In addition to the two aforementioned, we have J. Fisher White, Mary Price Owen, Winifred Arthur Jones. Even that estimable actor Lyn Harding started life as David Llewellyn Harding.' His face cracked open into a broad, malevolent smile, emitting a long, beautifully modulated giggle. He did not mention, as I later learnt, that, in his earliest stage appearance, he had been billed as 'Saville Esmé Percy'.

Three or four waiters appeared bearing trays. People were already sitting down. Esmé steered me towards the table and, quickly calculating what he imagined to be his maximum status, left three places between himself and Mr Tree, who was already seated at its head, and pulled me down beside him. His three young friends were hovering around the far end, waiting for the others to be seated before them.

'I suppose you're in *Nero*,' I said, referring to the new Stephen Phillips play that was opening the following Thursday.

'Yes, I am.'

'As . . .?'

'Britannicus.'

I looked impressed. 'Why, that's wonderful.'

1 'Eccentricities.'

'Not so wonderful! You can't have read the play – of course it isn't published yet. Ah, I know what you're thinking! No, *Nero* is not *Britannicus*. Racine gives far more lines to Néron than to his title role. Phillips, I'm afraid, doesn't repay the compliment – in fact, I have only eighteen lines. Nero, the Chief –' and his eyes darted up to the head of the table '– bumps me off in the second act. As you'll remember from your Racine, they're half-brothers. Now, neither Racine nor Phillips is specific about the young men's ages, though I'm the younger by a few years . . .'

'How old are you by the way?'

'Eighteen,' he whispered, with almost tragic solemnity, as who should say 'eighty-one'. 'But –' he held his right index-finger aloft '– the historical Claudius Tiberius Britannicus, *surnommé* in honour of his father's exploits on this island, was a mere fourteen at the time of his death, poisoned by Nero, then eighteen. Now, historically, I'm perhaps a trifle old for the part, but . . .' His voice dropped to the merest *sotto voce*, though no one could have heard him in the surrounding hubbub. '*Qu'en dire du patron?*' I nearly choked at the thought of Tree, then in his fifties, playing a youth of eighteen. His face assumed the expression of a Frenchman recounting one of Nature's evident absurdities. '*En plus, la femme du patron joue sa mère!*[1] Speaking of youth and age, I don't suppose you saw my Romeo?'

'No, I'm afraid I didn't. I haven't been back in London for long. When was it?'

'Last April. Oh, just a handful of performances at the Royalty. It was one of Poel's productions, you know.'

'Ah, yes, the Elizabethan Ssstage Society. I saw an *Everyman* . . . and a *Twelfth Night* a few years ago. No sets, full texts and rapid ssspeech.'

---

1 'Nicknamed . . . What about the Chief? . . . What's more, the Chief's wife plays his mother!'

Esmé put his left hand on my right knee. 'Ah, but you have the slightest of stammers! I find it quite charming. Anyway, Poel's idea was that Romeo should be played by an actor of roughly Romeo's age. Oh, there be players that I have seen play Romeo . . . Most of them should be playing his father.'

I laughed, not so much at Esmé's barbs as at the idea of *his* playing Romeo, with that figure and that voice.

I had hardly noticed the smoked salmon and the *hachis parmentier*[1] come and go. We were now on bread-and-butter pudding and our glasses had been filled with sauternes. I noticed that Laurence Irving, in a break in his own conversation, had been observing Esmé, who was sitting immediately opposite him, with some amusement. He then turned to me:

'Did you ever get to the Art Theatre in Moscow when you were over there?'

'Yes, only once, I'm afraid. I saw a revival of *The Cherry Orchard*.'

'Another world, isn't it?'

I agreed, but confessed that I didn't know Russian very well.

'So that's where you've been!' said Esmé, with an inexplicable, and possibly unintended, glint in his eye. 'I assumed you were in Paris!'

'I remember very well being at the first night of your *Peter the Great*,' I said, adding hastily, 'I was very impressed.'

'Very kind of you to say so . . .'

Suddenly Mr Tree rose to his feet and the assembly fell silent. He thanked everyone involved for the success of *Oliver Twist*.

'Mr Dana informs me that we have given no fewer than a hundred and twenty-two performances of the play. Most of

1 A French version of cottage pie.

them between these sacred, but apparently not entirely secure, walls.' Laughter. 'I don't have to remind most of you assembled here of the rather disturbingly large crack that appeared in the proscenium arch last year and required our safe remove to the Waldorf Theatre.[1] For that relief much thanks to Messrs Shubert and their estimable Mr McLellan. However, the crack appeared to be more of a decorative than of a structural order and we were back within these familiar and, as it turned out, perfectly safe, walls before three weeks were up.' Applause. 'Next Thursday, God willing, we shall open in Mr Phillips's new play, *Nero*. It is one of the sadder facts of our profession that we must needs take leave of friends: there is not always a part for everyone. In this theatre, fortunately, there are usually plenty of parts to go round, so many of you will be joining us next week. As for the others, our sincerest thanks and best wishes. In April, we shall again be celebrating the Bard's birthday with half a dozen of his plays. No doubt those of you who will not be joining us next week will be able to do so then. To one and all, our heartiest thanks. However, I would remind those of you who *will* be joining us next week that rehearsals will start tomorrow as usual at ten o'clock sharp.' Groans. 'Well, perhaps in view of this morning's festivities, rehearsals will begin at midday . . . with no break for luncheon.' Laughter and cheers. That, apparently, was the Chief's little joke: there never was a 'break for luncheon'; people snatched what refreshment they could when not required on stage.

People began to get down from the table and form into small groups. I felt elated, and a little tired. It would not be a very good idea to invite Esmé back tonight, I decided, even if he agreed; he would have to be at rehearsals next day.

1 Now the Strand Theatre.

'Look,' I said, 'we must continue this conversation some time soon. Would you be free this weekend?'

'*Avec le plus grand plaisir!*'[1]

We agreed that he would come round to Smith Square around six o'clock on Sunday. The food, I warned him, would not be up to Parisian, or even tonight's standards, but the wine would be good – Grandmother Sheridan had made few inroads into her husband's excellent cellar. Esmé's parents, it seemed, still lived in Windsor, but he had a *pied-à-terre* in Kennington. Perfect, I concluded, we'll get a cab and I'll drop him off at his lodgings.

Throughout the hour or two that I had spent with Esmé, his playing of the cynical, *désabusé* man of the world had been so accomplished, his self-assurance so assured, that I had completely forgotten that he was a boy of eighteen. I was in very little doubt as to what would happen on Sunday. I was strangely excited at the thought that, for the first time, I would go to bed with someone who not only excited me physically, but with whom I felt perfectly at ease, with whom I could talk, for hours on end, about things that were of passionate interest to both of us. It was not love: I knew that. I knew that love was yet to come. Esmé, I instinctively felt, was not *disponible* for love. His emotions were probably too weak, or too much under control, to risk exposure to the dangerously invasive power of love. His only love was the theatre or, rather, himself as actor. This was just as well, since I was in no mood to give so much of myself either. Esmé, I concluded, was someone to enjoy, physically and socially – and someone to give pleasure to, physically and socially. No hearts would leap up – or be broken.

On Sunday, Esmé arrived precisely on time. Once we were

1 'With the greatest pleasure!'

installed in the drawing-room with a bottle of champagne, I asked how rehearsals were going.

'Oh, I think everything is going according to plan. I don't foresee any disasters. The scenery, as always, will keep the audience in its thrall. Tell it not in Gath, publish it not in the streets of Askelon, lest the uncircumcised Philistines rejoice, but in my not very humble opinion, the problem lies with the play, which should be the thing, but here isn't.'

'That's extraordinary. I didn't expect . . . That's exactly my feeling about Phillips nowadays. I used to be besotted with him, like everyone else. He came to Cambridge while I was up and read extracts from *Paolo and Francesca*. Nowadays, I think all that talk of his being the new Marlowe or Webster quite preposterous. His verse is more a parody of Marlowe's mighty line – regular iambic pentameters, usually with the full ssstops and commas at the end of the lines.'

'My dear, I must teach you to say "prreposterrous". On second thoughts, no . . . Your "pwepostewous" is more *attendrissant*.'[1]

'The trouble is I can rrroll my "r"'s like an Italian and the French "r" poses no problem, but I simply can't do the normal English "r". My "r" isn't a "w", either, by the way. But, to return to Phillips, like everyone else, I was besotted a few years ago when all those plays of his were put on. Did you see any of them?'

'Alas, no. In those days my theatrical outings were severely limited. My mother did her best to indulge me – and herself. But, apart from the annual pantomime at Drury Lane, my father would only allow a few very safe, very educational plays. That usually meant Shakespeare.'

'So you missed the divinely beautiful Henry Ainley in *Paolo*

1 'Touching.'

and Francesca. Apparently, at the first night, when he first came on, wearing his gold armour, a gasp of admiration came from the audience, men as well as women.'

'So have I heard, and do in part believe it.'

'Anyway, Alexander had his Francesca, that pre-Raphaelite beauty Evelyn Millard, though she must have been well past thirty, but no Paolo. So, like every London manager in search of talent he went off . . .'

'To Benson.'

'To Benson. It was a toss-up between Ainley and Matheson Lang – same age, twenty-one or two, both playing small parts. Quite rightly, he chose the prettier.'

'No, I didn't see *Paolo* or either of the Tree productions – *Herod* and *Ulysses* – but I've read them all and agree with you entirely. I'm afraid my mind has been going in a quite different direction lately – Ibsen, of course, and Shaw – I much prefer Shaw, he's rather more fun than the lugubrious Norseman. But I digress . . . Let's just finish Phillips off. Though, to be quite honest, I don't think he needs any help from us. You know he's a terrible drunk? Pretty far gone, too. I feel sorry for Tree – he's been so good to him, so loyal. He's even agreed to doll himself up as a pretty youth of eighteen . . .' Guffaw. 'I know he's a master of make-up, but there are limits. Mind you, he does a terribly good job, with curly wig, rouged cheeks and pouting cherry-red lips. Close up, it all looks ridiculous, of course, but, a few yards away, in the right lighting, one is taken in – and that's what matters. Phillips has given him no help whatever. He turned up once, early on in rehearsals, and hasn't been seen since. Quite the *enfant gâté, n'est-ce pas?*[1] Stories about Phillips still circulate in the Benson company. When I was with them last year . . .'

---

1 'Quite the spoilt child, isn't he?'

'I didn't know you had been with Benson . . . And there was
I telling you all about . . . Why didn't you stop me?'

'Because I like to hear the sound of your voice, *cher* . . . It
makes a change from my own.' Guffaw. 'Anyway, you know
that Benson and Phillips are cousins?'

'Yes.'

'Same churchy background. Benson's the nephew of that
Archbishop of Canterbury and Phillips's father was a Canon
of . . . Lichfield, Peterborough or some such place. They even
look similar – same immense height, same auburn hair. Of
course, Phillips has lost his looks now, got rather bloated,
though I believe he was very handsome once. All the women
in the company fell for him, he ended up marrying May
Lyddard, poor girl. He was an excellent cricketer. That counts
for a lot with Benson, though it doesn't explain *my* presence
among them. On the cricket field, I'm usually banished to
silly mid-off or something and try to keep out of the way of
the ball.'

'How long were you with Benson, then?'

'I was out with them two years and away I shall again.'

'But how could . . .? You're still only eighteen.'

'Ah, I started *very young*.' Giggles. 'And I don't mean as a
child actor, either. No "Peasblossom . . . Master Esmé Percy".
I first trod the professional stage – and I had trodden no
other – when I was fifteen, with Benson, at the Theatre Royal,
Nottingham.'

'But how did you get into the Benson company so young?'

'It's a long story. Can you bear to hear it? It does concern
Sarah.'

'That I do long to hear.'

At some point in this dialogue, Mrs Wrigglesworth came
up and asked if I should like her to serve dinner; we went
down to the dining-room; over the soup, we finished off the

bottle of champagne. With the simple, but excellent roast chicken, I served one of my grandfather's better wines – a Château Latour of a little more than Esmé's years. I did this not with any desire to impress, but simply because I had a guest to dinner, a rare enough event, and was rather averse to indulging myself to this extent when alone. Esmé did not know precisely what he was drinking, but a combination of palate and eye – the latter surreptitiously examining the label – made him declare it good.

'Do you remember when you first went to the theatre?' I asked.

'Yes, of course. It was *Robinson Crusoe.*'

'At Drury Lane . . .?'

'At Drury Lane. I was only six. I remember a lot of ladies dancing around dressed as fish and a long procession of the kings and queens of England . . .'

'That must have been one of the first Druriolanus pantos I saw when we came back from China . . .'

'China now, is it? First Russia . . . How ever are we to find the time to recount the stories of our lives?'

'Indeed. My father was in the Consular Service there . . . And then . . . apart from pantos?'

'Apart from pantos, my first visit to the theatre came a few years later when my mother thought I was ready to appreciate opera. She is very musical – sings well and plays the piano. In fact, she taught me both. My parents took me to *Faust –*' perfectly pronounced *à la française* '– at Covent Garden – Melba and the de Reszké brothers. My father probably thought that Faust's ultimate fate put the work on the right moral side, and that the little business of Marguerite's moral lapse would not be understood when sung. He was quite right, of course. But my first real experience of theatre came, funnily enough, with Tree. I was twelve and my mother took me to *A Midsummer*

Night's Dream at His Majesty's – I suppose it was still Her
Majesty's then. You can imagine the effect it had on me. I
imagined I had grown out of pantomime and ascended into
some infinitely superior sphere. Even the scenery seemed more
splendid than at Drury Lane – and altogether more tasteful,
more real. Everyone remembers the live rabbits in a wood near
Athens, but they were the least of it. You saw it, of course?'

'Oh, yes. Tree was terribly good as Bottom, wasn't he?
Actor-manager playing the impenetrably vain Bottom the
Weaver, playing the impenetrably vain actor-manager.'

'When did *you* see a Shakespeare play for the first time?'

'Ah, Lillie Langtry's Cleopatra, days after our arrival from
China – I was ten.'

'And Tree?'

'Shakespeare again, I think. Yes, *Hamlet*, no less.'

'Did you see Irving's Hamlet?'

I laughed. 'No, no, I'm not that old! Tree's was my first
Hamlet.'

'I saw it when he revived it last spring. Not a natural
Hamlet, but very interesting, well thought out, as always. Now
that's a part I want to play!' A smile must have escaped my
lips, for Esmé pounced:

'Smile on! I shall probably be playing Hamlet this year . . .'
I attended to my lips as best I could. '. . . in one of Benson's
companies – he now has three touring provinces and Empire.'

'Who is the best Hamlet you've seen?'

Esmé looked thoughtful. 'Oh, I suppose I should have
to say Sarah. And that means in French, so not really
Shakespeare, I suppose. The first Hamlet I saw was Benson's.
He'd taken over the Lyceum for ten weeks and put on half a
dozen Shakespeare plays . . . The best Hamlet I've seen? Sarah
apart, I suppose I have to agree with everyone else and say
Forbes-Robertson. Not that I think he has everything, but

then who does? He still has more than anyone else. And, for
me, diction like his goes a long way. I saw you nodding when
I said that I didn't think he had everything. What do you
think he lacks?'

It felt like a *viva*. 'Ideally, he would be a little less statuesque, less cool, calm and collected at all times, less of the
noble mind and a bit more o'erthrown, not mad, of course,
he's only putting on an antic disposition . . .'

Esmé had assumed the face of an appraising, but sympathetic supervisor. 'Excellent, excellent, exactly my feeling.
And that mercurial quality is precisely what Sarah gets, every
shifting mood, responding to every twist and turn in the dialogue, responding to the other characters far more than anyone
else I've seen, all that plus the best diction in the world. But,
yes, it's not Shakespeare's English.'

'Well, now, how did you come to study with Sarah?'

'Well, you'll have gathered that my father and I don't get
on. About the age of fourteen, things came to a head. Benson
came back to London again in half a dozen plays – we saw
them all. Then, during the summer, there were endless arguments over our theatre outings. Mother and I became real
conspirators. Before the school year was up we went to a lot of
matinées, even on Wednesdays, which meant inventing some
indisposition for school. That July, we must have gone to the
theatre two or three times a week. We went to Covent Garden
and to Irving's last season at the Lyceum. But! . . . What
meant more to me than everything else put together was seeing
Sarah for the first time. But this was easier said than done. It
had to be done in secret. My father totally disapproved of her.
"A tart playing tarts . . ." As for parading herself before the
public dressed as a man! She had taken over His Majesty's for
six weeks and we saw her in Rostand's *L'Aiglon*. I must confess
that it was not the *coup de foudre* – that came later. I found

some difficulty in accepting this dumpy creature in her tight
white trousers, possessing so obviously the hips and thighs of
a woman, as the Duc de Reichstadt, the Eaglet to Napoleon's
Eagle. Quite frankly, I was disappointed. Then, over the next
fortnight, she gave a few performances of *Dame aux Camélias*,
La Tosca and . . . *Phèdre*.'

Esmé stood up, eyes blazing, transformed. He began to
speak, his voice more highly pitched:

> *J'aime. Ne pense pas qu'au moment que je t'aime,*
> *Innocente à mes yeux, je m'approuve moi-même,*
> *Ni que du fol amour qui trouble ma raison*
> *Ma lâche complaisance ait nourri le poison.*
> *Objet infortuné des vengeances célestes,*
> *Je m'abhorre encor plus que tu me détestes.*
> *Les dieux m'en sont témoins, ces dieux qui dans mon flanc*
> *Ont allumé le feu fatal à tout mon sang;*
> *Ces dieux qui se sont fait une gloire cruelle*
> *De séduire le coeur d'une faible mortelle.*

He had begun quietly, pleadingly, almost seductively, the voice
growing quieter, the pace slightly slower. After the briefest of
pauses, there was now a shift of key, pace and volume going
into reverse:

> *Que dis-je? Cet aveu que je te viens de faire,*
> *Cet aveu si honteux, le crois-tu volontaire? . . .*
> *Venge-toi, punis-moi d'un odieux amour.*
> *Digne fils du héros qui t'a donné le jour,*
> *Délivre l'univers d'un monstre qui t'irrite.*
> *La veuve du Thésée ose aimer Hippolyte!*
> *Crois-moi, ce monstre affreux ne doit point t'échapper.*
> *Voilà mon coeur. C'est là que ta main doit frapper.*

> *Impatient déjà d'expier son offense,*
> *Au-devant de ton bras je le sens qui s'avance.*
> *Frappe.*

As he uttered the single word *'Frappe'*, the invitation to strike was itself transformed into a whiplash. The voice rose and accelerated further:

> *Ou si tu le crois indigne de tes coups,*
> *Si ta haine m'envie un supplice si doux,*
> *Ou si d'un sang trop vil ta main ferait trempée,*
> *Au défaut de ton bras prête-moi ton épée.*

The crescendo was reached in another single-word, single-syllable imperative, *'Donne'*,[1] the short vowel being extended into a bloodcurdling scream.

It was a mesmerizing performance. He did not, could not embody Sarah Bernhardt; it remained an imitation, but I could

---

1 Yes, I am in love, but do not imagine that, in loving you,/ I see myself as innocent or approve of myself,/ Or that my cowardly compliance has fed the poison/ Of the insensate love that has disturbed my reason./ A hapless object of the gods' vengeance,/ I abhor myself even more than you hate me./ The gods will bear me witness, it is those self-same gods/ Who lit the fire that is poisoning my blood,/ The very gods who have taken cruel delight/ In seducing the heart of a weak, mortal woman . . ./ What am I saying? Do you believe that this avowal,/ This shameful avowal, is freely given? . . ./ Take your revenge, punish me for such an odious love./ Hippolytus, be worthy of the hero who gave you life,/ Rid the world of a monster who offends you./ Does Theseus' widow dare to love his son?/ Believe me, this frightful monster must not escape you./ Here is my heart. This is where your hand must strike./ Already impatient to expiate its guilt,/ I feel it leap up towards your hand./ Strike! . . . Or if your arm would be defiled by blood so vile,/ If you refuse me your hand, then give me your sword . . ./ Give it to me.

not imagine a better one, even by a Frenchwoman. I knew now that he was a very good actor. To clap or to shout 'Bravo!' would have demeaned the performance, I felt. I paused, then said simply:

'*Superbe!*' Then, taking liberties with Phèdre's first lines, invited him to continue with his story: '*Allons plus avant, cher Esmé. Je ne me soutiens plus: ma force m'abandonne.*'[1]

Esmé's face broke into a delighted grin. 'Do you really want me to go on?'

'Yes, of course. You haven't even met Sarah yet.'

'Very well. Where was I? Oh, yes . . . My father had come to the conclusion, quite correctly, that I was out of control – at least out of his. What's more, I was having a bad influence on my mother. What I needed was discipline! But he, of course, was quite incapable of applying it himself. I must be sent away to school. Now, my dear mother is a Catholic, but a *French* Catholic, which means that she has only the haziest notions about matters of faith and morals. In other words, she's really rather broad-minded, civilized. She was entirely on my side, but realized that there was no opposing my father, so she pretended to go along with his silly idea and accommodate me as best she could. She had convinced herself that an English public school would be quite unsuitable for her sensitive darling son and applied her mind to the problem. Now, since the recent *loi des congrégations*,[2] there were, *hélas!*, no Catholic

1 Let's go no further. Stop here, dear Oenone./ I can no longer stand: my strength is failing me.
2 The Law of the Congregations (1904) served as an act of revenge on the part of the anti-clerical left against the Church's role in the Dreyfus Case. All religious orders were obliged to apply for recognition, which was usually refused. This led to the closure of most of the religious houses, their properties being put up for sale. A number of religious orders emigrated, many to Great Britain.

schools in Paris. However, she has some friends in Brussels and they recommended the Jesuit school there. Knowing nothing about Jesuit schools and wishing, above all, not to do what my father wanted, I agreed. My French was very good and the idea of lessons being conducted in French amused me. In discussions with my father, Mother stressed how disciplined the Jesuits were, how important it was that I should make the best of my French – it might be the opening to a career in diplomacy.' Guffaws. 'And then she played her ace, reminding him that I had been baptized a Catholic and that she alone had responsibility for my moral upbringing. To our surprise, he gave in. The truth is, he probably had some idea what the Jesuits were like and, in any case, his main concern was probably to get me out of the house – and as far removed from the West End of London as possible. Well, this idea certainly returned to plague the inventor! Now, wait . . . this is worthy of Sophocles. So I went to the *pères jésuites* in Brussels. It was true that they did pride themselves on their discipline. But, somehow, I accepted it, even came to like it – unlike my father's notions of discipline, it had a certain intellectual coherence. Anyhow, one of the advantages of the Brussels school was that I was allowed to spend the occasional weekend with my mother's friends, who turned out to be quite delightful and spoiled me quite shamelessly. Well, at the beginning of my second term I learnt that Sarah Bernhardt would shortly be coming to the Théâtre de la Monnaie. My Belgian friends agreed to take me to see her in *L'Aiglon*. And, do you know, her performance was quite different from the one I had seen in London: I couldn't understand why she had not overwhelmed me the first time. I later learnt that this did happen sometimes. If a performance goes well, Sarah says: *"Le dieu était là."*[1]

1 'The god was there.'

Occasionally, the god withdraws his favours. Anyway, I went back to the theatre and booked seats for other performances. I became completely obsessed with her. After the plays, I would stand outside the stage-door waiting for my goddess to appear. Suddenly, there she was, swathed in chinchilla. She then disappeared into her carriage and was gone. I began romancing about her to my school friends. I recounted how I had spoken to her, how she had fallen madly in love with me. "Have you heard from Madame Sarah this morning?" they would ask. "No, not this morning," I had to admit. They went on, each day, tormenting me with questions. I decided I should have to run away from school. I wrote to some cousins of my mother's in Paris, announcing my arrival. At the Gare du Nord I caught the *métropolitain* and went straight down to Châtelet, to the Théâtre Sarah-Bernhardt, and purchased a, for me, very expensive *fauteuil*[1] for that evening's performance. I then went round to the stage-door and left a note for Madame Sarah. I should be in the theatre that evening, I declared, and gave my seat number. I must see you. If I do not, I shall throw myself into the Seine. You can imagine my feelings as I entered that splendid theatre – first the foyer, with its ten enormous murals of her in her most famous roles, then that auditorium with its buttercup-yellow velvet seats. I waited – no message came. The play began. Then, just before the curtain went up on the last act, an attendant came and told me that Madame Bernhardt would see me at the end of the play. When I was finally admitted into the presence, her physical appearance, close up, came as something of a disappointment. She was, after all, a rather plump lady nearing sixty playing a very young man. But that was the least of it! What she then said infuriated me. "It would have been a great pity," she said, "for such a nice

1 Seat in the stalls.

child to have thrown himself into the water. Now, you must promise to be good – and here is a photograph to remember me by. Go back to school and, after the summer holidays, if you still want to go on the stage, and your parents allow you to, come to Paris and I'll see what can be done." And that was what happened. Of course, my father knew nothing of Sarah's role in all this. He was told that I had excelled in the school play and, as a result, had been offered a place at the Paris Conservatoire. So I attended classes given by Georges Berr and Maurice Leloir and, every Saturday, between her performances, I would go along and report to Sarah on my work and go over the scenes I had been studying.'

'So you started studying in Paris in October 1902. Funny, that's when I went back to Paris after university. How long were you there for?'

'Only two terms, I'm afraid. Near the end of the second term, the connection with Sarah came out and my father decided that my Paris days must end; he gave the impression, without actually saying so, that he thought Sarah had seduced me and we were having a *liaison*. I think that was really an excuse. He didn't like the idea of his fifteen-year-old son being alone in Paris, even if I was living with cousins of my mother's. He had probably got tired of paying my fees and my allowance, too. Anyway, when Sarah heard that I would have to return home at the end of term, she wrote wonderful letters of recommendation to Tree and Benson. Given my age and inexperience, Tree was obviously out of the question, but Benson, bless the man, replied that he had no vacancy at the moment but, with a recommendation like that, he would have to make one. And that is how I came to study with Sarah Bernhardt and act with Benson.'

'And Duse?' I asked. 'I take it you disapprove.' In those days, Bernhardt versus Duse was a common subject of drawing-room conversation and, by now, we were back in the drawing-room. Few seemed able to accord the two great actresses equal admiration. The more traditional-minded declared that there was no comparison possible, Duse could not hold a candle to the great Sarah; some, Shaw *en tête*, saw Duse as the theatre of the future, Bernhardt as a rather splendid old anachronism.

'Disapprove? Not in the least. I think the whole business of setting up one against the other is quite tiresome. G. B. S. is being very naughty but, of course, one never knows when he's being serious. After all, he says he's greater than Shakespeare. I don't think that helps his cause either – and I am a great admirer of Shaw. As for Sarah and Duse, they act in different languages and one is old enough to be the other's mother. In fact, Sarah has been something of a mother to Duse. She even lent her the Théâtre de la Renaissance for her first Paris appearances. I think there can be no doubt that Sarah is the greater artist: her technique is more varied, more assured and she can reach greater heights. But Duse has a quite extraordinary quality, an intense sincerity that hits you between the eyes when she comes on to the stage. Last May, after my *Romeo*, I stayed on in London to see her at the Waldorf. It was the first time I'd seen her. I didn't see everything: she was here for six weeks and was in about ten plays – and, anyway, they were all in Italian. But I saw her *Seconda Moglie*, which, being interpreted, is *The Second Mrs Tanqueray*, her *Magda*, her *Signora dalle Camelie*, her *Hedda* . . . You must have seen her in all these and more . . .'

It was true – and I agreed entirely with his comments on the two women. I confess that what he had said came as a surprise: with his precious, rather old-fashioned diction, he did not seem a natural admirer of Duse.

'I first saw her during her first season in London. I'd be

about thirteen. We'd just arrived from Paris. It was *Antonio e Cleopatra*. As usual, she looked as inconspicuous as possible. If it hadn't been for those staring eyes, she'd have been indistinguishable from one of her serving-women. I can't imagine why she took on the role. A few days later, my Paris grandparents went to the Savoy to interview her – Mémé wrote for a Budapest paper. My brother and I went along with them. After about ten minutes, an attendant came and told us that Signora Duse had asked to see us and took us up to her rooms. It's a funny thing: great stage artists can act quite differently on stage and off. Bernhardt and Duse are just the same on stage and off. Of course, they couldn't have been more different. Bernhardt always wears the most stylish clothes, Duse looks almost dowdy. Duse never wears make-up, on or off stage; Bernhardt would never be seen without it. When I met Madame Sarah, she made a great fuss of me, in that effusive, rather formal way the French have with children. Duse received us quietly, without fuss, saying little, conveying her pleasure at seeing us through her eyes and a slight, gentle smile. Towards the end of the interview, she said something quite extraordinary: '*Pour sauver le théâtre, il faut le détruire*.'[1] It sounded oddly extreme, coming from that gentle, nun-like creature.'

Esmé and I discussed what Duse could possibly have meant. Again he proved to be surprisingly sympathetic to various attempts to 'renew' the theatre. Over the past six months, he had seen many of the productions at the Court Theatre. He talked about Poel and his work. He was fascinated by what I told him about the Art Theatre in Moscow, Gordon Craig and Isadora Duncan.

Suddenly, he mentioned the time. 'I suppose I ought really

1 'If the theatre is to be saved, we must destroy it.'

to be getting along.' This was said, I thought, *pour la forme*, with deliberate lack of conviction.

'Oh, there's really no need,' I countered, as lightly as I could manage it. 'There's a room with a bed already made up.'

'Then that settles it,' he said, with an equivocal grin. 'Good, I'm enjoying myself far too much to drag myself away to Kennington. I don't have to be at rehearsals till eleven.'

I offered a brandy. He thought he had probably drunk enough. Given my plans, I had too. All evening, I had been looking at his face. It was, I decided, pretty enough, if a little rounded. The lips were thick and voluptuous, the smile daz-zlingly bright, the eyes mercurial in the speed of their reactions, witty, intelligent, often *méchant*.[1] We were getting on famously. We could have talked, not only all night, but right through the next day. I wanted him as a friend. I was sure he felt the same about me. I also wanted to get him into bed. There are people one may want to get to bed that one would not want as friends and the vast majority of those one may want as friends one would not want to be in bed with. There are many men who cannot bring the two things together in the same person. I am not one of them: I always yearn to do just that. Yet, with Esmé, the two things did not really hang together. I liked him, or rather I didn't know whether I did like him. I certainly liked being with him. What I liked was the head, the head talking to me. For all his bril-liant powers of speech, employed very largely in recounting his own life, he had revealed very little of himself. Excellent performer that he was, he used speech to present, not to expose himself. I then realized that the lack of connection between wanting him as a friend and wanting to get him into bed lay not in me but in him. Esmé seemed to stop at the

1 Malicious.

neck. The head was not native to the rest: I did not expect to meet Esmé there.

At this point I claimed to be tired and suggested we went to bed. I showed him the bathroom and 'his' bedroom, the one with the double bed, my grandparents' old room, and retired to mine. Minutes after I heard that he had 'retired', I knocked on his door, carrying a couple of glasses of Grand Marnier. I was wearing nothing but a dressing-gown.

'What about a night-cap?'

'*Ah, quelle bonne idée!*'

I turned off the light and opened the curtains. There was enough light from the street and from the dying fire.

'*Qu'est-ce que tu fais maintenant?*' he giggled. Even now, his body did not speak through his eyes. Why was he speaking French? Was it embarrassment or was French for him a necessary accompaniment? I lay down on the bed beside him and started to kiss him. I slipped out of the dressing-gown and got into bed beside him, pushing back the bedclothes. His hand went straight to my erect cock.

'*Eh bien, dis donc!*' This silly chatter, in French, irritated me, aroused my aggression. I'd shut him up, but because he seemed to want it, I would speak French. I knelt up astride him, slapping his face with my cock.

'*Ouvre ta bouche!*'[1] I commanded. He obeyed and I inserted it, nearly choking him. I then let him move his lips and tongue around it; he even held it in his mouth sideways and exerted gentle pressure on it with his teeth. Meanwhile, I played with his little thing. As I expected, his body did not excite me, in the sense of drawing my whole body towards it, to be explored and delighted in by lips and hands. It was a young, soft object

---

1 'What a good idea! . . . What are you doing now? . . . I say!' 'Open your mouth!'

on which I wanted to pleasure myself – and which, I liked to think, wanted to be pleasured upon, too, if only it could stir itself into consciousness. I was not prepared to spend a lot of time trying to awaken it. After a little more kissing, which he didn't seem to take to, I slipped into the *soixante-neuf* position and got to work lubricating his *cul*. I then turned him over, rather roughly, knelt over him, between his legs and lubricated myself. I had to stop myself thrusting it in there and then. But I had no wish to hurt him and I knew from experience that such lack of control usually put an end to proceedings. I gently inserted the head a little, then lay down on top of him.

'*Relâche toi!*' I whispered.

'*Oui, oui,*' he murmured resignedly.

'*Je ne te ferai pas mal.*'

'*Oh, non! Elle est grosse, tu sais . . . et je suis quasi-vierge!*'[1]

I almost laughed out loud at the absurdity of the words. I went in further, moving in an inch and back out half an inch, holding my hands on his shoulders. Other than clenching his hands, he was showing no reaction. I gave the final thrust and he let out a cry, which he stifled in the pillow. I then gave it to him, with long, firm thrusts. I was no longer I, nor he he. It was all over soon enough.

'*Monstre cruel!*' he said, for all the world as if it were a term of affection. '*Tu m'as presque tué!*'[2] The '*tué*' was pronounced as Sarah might have said it in a Racine tragedy.

I held him for a while, kissing him on the neck every now and then, without, I felt, much conviction. He got up and went to the bathroom. When he came back, I went. There was

1 'Relax! . . . I won't hurt you.' 'It's big you know . . . I'm practically a virgin.'
2 'Cruel monster! . . . You nearly killed me!'

shit on my cock. Back in bed, I held him in my arms, in case
that was what he wanted – the first time, it is often difficult to
know what the other one wants – and gave him one or two
quick kisses. We then separated and went to sleep, each on his
own side of the bed.

I woke, noticing that he was not there. I also detected a
smell of shit. I investigated and saw that there were large shit
stains over his side of the bed. After a while, I got up and went
to the bathroom. The door was locked. I knocked gently and
called out: '*Ça va?*'

'*Oui, oui, ça va, ça va. J'arrive.*'

He appeared at the door. I put my hands on his shoulders.
'*Pauvre chéri!*' I said and, taking his hand, led him to my bedroom. '*Ne t'en fait pas. Ce n'est rien.*'[1]

We went back to sleep for a while.

We got up an hour or so later. I made some coffee and
improvised a light breakfast. It was as if we had never been to
bed and done there what we had done. Yet it was not, of
course, a total resumption of the *status quo ante*. We talked,
but without the sense of urgent exploration that we had had.
I left him at the door, ready to walk to the theatre for
rehearsals. We made no arrangements to meet again. Our
physical congress was not resumed. We remained friends. The
next time I saw him was on the stage of His Majesty's four
days later.

It was some years since I had been to a 'first night' in the
West End, certainly not since Grandfather Sheridan died.
Tree's first nights were now the most fashionable in London,
but I managed to get hold of a seat. I walked out of the square
into Millbank and hailed a cab. As we entered Pall Mall, we
were met by an impenetrable mass of cabs and four-wheelers,

1 'Don't worry. It's of no importance.'

horse-driven carriages and motor-cars. I got the cabby to drop me off and I walked the rest of the way to the theatre.

When Herr Schmid had finished conducting Coleridge Taylor's overture, the curtain went up to reveal the splendid 'Great Hall in the Palace of the Caesars', with a spectacular view of Rome in the background. A 'meteor', intended to presage gloom to the emperor and his family, began its course across the sky, then, stage centre, got stuck, swivelled on its wire and sank like a damp squib. Notwithstanding, the Emperor Claudius duly died, poisoned by his wife Agrippina (the usually gentle Mrs Tree). By the end of the act, she had excluded their son and rightful heir, Britannicus, from the succession, in favour of her son by another man, Nero (Tree, a full ten years older than his 'mother' and some thirty-four years older than his slightly younger half-brother). Act II, surprisingly for a Tree production, was 'the same', though now a scene of riot and excess, with a dozen 'maidens' disporting themselves around the stage. Esmé delivered Britannicus' 'poem' with great beauty of tone and modulation – and died from poison. Act III, Nero's chamber at Baiae, provided a splendid view of the bay, its villas and temples, water lapping the marble quayside, stage left, with the prows of moored galleys bobbing up and down. The last act was set in a tower overlooking Rome. Suddenly a handsome, bare-limbed youth entered and announced to Poppaea (Constance Collier):

> Mistress, below
> The lady Acte stands and asks to see you.

Ah, my Slave – or rather Nero's. He is sent off and returns with Dorothea Baird. He had waited all evening to say his few meagre words, said no more and was never seen again. In the last scene, Poppaea lies dead: after murdering his half-brother, his mother, his wife, Nero has dispatched his mistress. A messenger arrives announcing that Rome is on fire: soon the entire city is under his pyrotechnic sway. Herod stands, a tyrant who once had ambitions as poet and actor, observing the conflagration, as if it were one of Mr Tree's stage effects. I had been told of the *coup de théâtre* at the end, how 'flames' gradually 'consume' the view of Rome.

> See, see
> How Beautiful!
> Like a rose magnificently burning!

Tree intoned. Unfortunately, nothing happened: not even so much as a reddening of the horizon.

> Blaze! Blaze!
> How it eats and eats!

Still nothing.

> Mother!
> See what a fire I have given thee,
> Rome for a funeral couch!
> Had Achilles a pyre like this or had Patroclus? . . .
> Blaze! Rage! Blaze! . . .
> Thy blood is no more on my head;
> I am purged, I am cleansed;
> I have given thee flaming Rome for the bed of thy death!
> O Agrippina!

Still nothing, save for a few pops and sparks, and the play, textually speaking, was over, without its visual climax. Tree went on strumming his lyre, staring despairingly at his disobedient scenery. Constance Collier, long since dead, wondering what was amiss, opened her eyes. People noticed and a titter went round the audience. Suddenly there was a loud explosion and a mass of soot fell on them both. The curtain was brought down, then raised at once to reveal a couple of nigger minstrels grinning nervously at the audience. In his curtain speech, Tree apologized for 'the little electrical difficulty'. There were, he said, 'limits to an actor-manager's omnipotence, if not to that of a Roman emperor'. He apologized, too, for the absence of the author: 'I promise to crown him with Nero's laurel wreath, which I find too big for myself.'

Rather than go straight up to the 'dome' afterwards, with everyone else, I spent twenty minutes at the Carlton over a glass of champagne. I knew that the actors would take some time to get there and I had noticed no one in the audience that I knew personally. I then walked round to the stage-door and was taken charge of by a rather short youth with a slight cockney accent.

'Ah, a lift!' I said. 'There can't be many theatres in London with a lift – and backstage, too.'

The boy smiled. I had spoken to him, so he risked a reply. 'There aren't many actors in London who sleep on the premises.' With a rather obvious look and a slight snigger, he added: 'We're now going up to the bedroom.'

I laughed. There was indeed a bed, I was told later, a modern contraption that went up into the wall and disappeared behind cupboard doors. It was there simply because Tree could hardly be parted from his theatre and often rehearsed late. Many a night only two people remained in His Majesty's, the boss aloft and the night watchman below.

The lift opened and the boy led me along a short corridor to a door.

'Your room, sir.'

I put my hand on his arm and asked: 'What's your name?'

'Claude Rains.'[1]

'Thank you, Claude.' He did not, of course, ask me my name and I did not take liberty, equality and fraternity as far as to proffer it. I gave him a tip about four times what it should have been. He smiled again, thanked me and returned to his lift. I later learnt that he was the prompt boy. (After some years spent as, successively, assistant stage manager and stage manager, he attained his ambition and became an actor.)

The 'dome' was oddly out of keeping with the style of the theatre itself. I had imagined some light, elegant, pavilion-like room, all Louis-Seize pale blue and gold, but the heavy, dark beams inside the dome itself, the primitive-looking iron-work chandelier, the oak panelling around the walls, the Tudor-style stone fireplace and doorways gave it the air of a Jacobean country house. The guests were all standing around in a smaller room beyond open double doors. As I went in, Esmé glimpsed me at once and hailed me over.

'Mark,' he said, 'allow me to present my posthumous half-sister-in-law and very dear friend, Poppaea-Mrs L'Estrange-Constance Collier.'

The lady dropped into broad cockney: 'Oh, don't mind 'im, dearie, just call me Connie.'

'Congratulations!' I said, smiling at the dark-haired beauty before me. 'I think you gave a splendid performance – and don't look so jealous, Esmé, that goes for you, too.'

'And this is my *terrrible* friend Mark Sheridan,' said Esmé, raising an eyebrow. Miss Collier did likewise.

A young waiter appeared with a tray of champagne glasses.

---

1 Claude Rains (1889–1967) became an actor, moving to the United States in 1926. He went on to play leading roles in several Hollywood films.

'What on earth happened at the end?' I asked. 'Tree ssstrumming while Rome refused to burn!'

'Oh, poor Mr Tree!' said Constance Collier. 'He just stood there and nothing happened. And everything went so well at the dress-rehearsal, too. Cecil, the stage manager, said it was a short circuit, whatever that is.'

After a while, I looked around and, over by a small table where the champagne was being served, standing in a group of young men and women, obviously the supernumerary 'revellers' and handmaidens from the 'Palace of the Caesars', I saw him. I excused myself and made my way through the throng.

'Ah, Nero's slave,' I said. 'I saw you here last week. What does the "E." stand for?' Esmé had told me, but I had forgotten. This time, I was careful to memorize the name in the programme.

'Esmond.'

I introduced myself. He had a nice smile, broad, but very natural, spontaneous, almost nervous. Esmé, too, had a nice, broad smile, but I sensed that it was under control at all times, the effect calculated. In other words, Esmé, off-stage, was still acting; Esmond was not. Unlike Esmé, too, he did not take hold of me and move me away from his companions – apart from anything else, judging by the speed with which he was consuming glass after glass of champagne, but to no evident effect, he would have been reluctant to move away from the table. We went through the usual page-filling question-and-answer dialogue: How long have you been in the company? This is my first play with them. Were you at Mr Tree's Academy? Yes, I've just finished my year there. What do *you* do? . . . Esmond did not seem interested in anything either of us was saying. He seemed in abeyance.

We moved back to the large room, Tree taking charge of his

more eminent guests and distributing them around himself and Mrs Tree. I followed Esmond to the far end of the other table. We ended up opposite one another, with handmaidens on either side of us.

As course followed course and the conversation moved across between us, and sideways to our 'ladies', I could not but pursue the comparison between the two young actors. Mentally, Esmé was totally there: for him, conversation was an immensely pleasurable art and, like all arts, skilfully performed, required conscious decisions only intermittently. This left his mind free to play over the wider situation, noting every nuance in what the other was saying, constantly adjusting his response accordingly, to extract as much as possible of the truth about the other and to project the desired image of himself. It is 'social accomplishment' carried to the highest degree. Yet, *physically*, he did not seem to be there at all. No, this requires qualification. He did not, like many Englishmen, seem uncomfortable in his body, as if operating it from a distance, with a certain inevitable clumsiness, inexpressiveness. Esmé was very comfortable in his little body, had it perfectly under control; no one could be less clumsy or more expressive with it. It was a perfect instrument for his mind to play upon. Nevertheless, it had no presence of its own. It was just that – an instrument. Esmé had no physicality.

With Esmond, the reverse was the case. I had a very strong sense that *mentally* he was not there at all. It was not, I hazarded, that he had 'inner depths', a distrust of the glib performance, or simply an inability to express complex thoughts in that situation, at that time of night. It was rather, as I later discovered, that mentally he hardly existed: he was happiest when gossiping, preferably with the female members of the company, about the company and its works. He seemed to have very little knowledge of, or interest in, anything beyond that. He was talking to me there, in the 'dome', because that is what one did when one found oneself in that situation: he would not have taken any initiative himself. His pale blue eyes – those windows of the soul – were curiously sad, vacant. But if he seemed mentally absent, he was intensely present physically. I don't think he was aware of this, aware that, in this respect, he was different from anybody else, but, for me, his physical presence acted like a powerful magnet. I wanted to take him, to run my hands over him, there and then. I gulped when I looked at his long thin neck, with that special quality of the skin to be found only on the necks of youths and young men, with their slightly off-parallel pairs of lines, brought about perhaps by the sudden growing of the body. He was quite tall, perhaps an inch off my six feet, and very slim; his face fresh and pink, given to quick flushes at the slightest provocation, high cheek-boned, fairly full, beautifully shaped lips, a mass of dark, slightly wavy hair.

He seemed impressed when I pointed out a few titled ladies and gentlemen, and a couple of members of the new government – Asquith, the Chancellor of the Exchequer, and the President of the Board of Trade, Lloyd George – but I don't think he had heard of any of them: he was impressed because they had titles or were members of the government. As the guests began to leave, I decided on my course of action. A few hours of entertainment would not be required to get this one to bed. I asked Esmond if he would like to come back with me for 'a brandy or something'.

Staring into space, he said: 'Yes, I would. The brandy or something would be very welcome.' He then turned his eyes full upon mine and added, with the utmost seriousness: 'But I must warn you of one thing. I shall fall asleep the moment my head touches the pillow.'

I could not help but smile. I had not even asked him to spend the night with me.

'That's perfectly all right,' I grinned. 'The morning is yet young.'

'And we are yet young in deed,' he countered, with a serious, non-committed look.

'Ah, *Macbeth*.'

'My first big part.'

'Macbeth?'

'Of course not. The butcher's fiend-like queen. At school.' Evil darted from eyes and mouth, evil that turned at once into a sarcastic giggle. 'Right! Let's go. We lack the season of all natures, sleep. Let's go before we get on to the ravelled sleeves of care . . . and balm of hurt minds . . . and nature's second course. I don't suppose you have a carriage and pair waiting for us in the Haymarket?'

'No, we'll have to get a cab.'

In the cab, somewhere along Whitehall, he took my hand and held it.

'So that was my first night on the professional stage. "Mistress, below the lady Acte stands and asks to see you." Not even a very good line, is it? More butler than slave, no?'

I gave his hand a squeeze.

In the house, I took his coat and we went up to the drawing-room.

'Would you like to retire at once, or would you like . . .'

'A little of that brandy would be nice.'

We chatted for a while over our brandies. He then drained his glass and said: 'Let's have a little top up and take it to bed with us.'

Upstairs, I showed him the bedroom and bathroom, and went into my own bedroom to undress. When I finally reappeared, in my dressing-gown, Esmond was in bed, apparently asleep, his brandy drunk. I got into bed and lay outstretched on my side against him and put my right hand over his body. I could hardly contain myself. My hand went down to his cock. It was erect: good size, I thought to myself. His head disappeared under the bedclothes, emerging a few seconds later:

'Mm! As you said earlier, the morning is yet young. I'm now going to go to sleep.' He gave me a kiss, turned over and was asleep in a few seconds.

How could I do the same? How could I contain myself? I was glad of the glass of brandy beside me: it would help me on my way. I turned off the oil lamp and lay down beside him, my arm over him. Gradually, the passion subsided, to be replaced by an enveloping feeling of warmth and well-being. Sleep was not too long in coming.

Next morning, I woke to find Esmond with his head back under the bedclothes. I put my hand down and stroked his hair.

He emerged: 'Good morning!'

We kissed passionately and long, our hands roaming voraciously over each other's body. I knelt up, my knees on either side of his chest. I felt like a conquering hero who owed his allegiance to Venus, not to Mars. His lips parted in anticipation. With my right hand I masturbated him. We shifted to the *soixante-neuf* position, sharing our like pleasures. I reached out for the jelly, which I had left expectantly beside the bed. I put one finger up, then two, then three. It felt delicious: yielding, yet firmly encompassing. I took his hand away from my cock: if it had stayed there any longer, I should have come. I sat up, turned him over on to his belly and knelt up between his legs. His face was turned to one side: young, beautiful, submissive. I came down on his back and kissed his lips, his closed eyes, his neck. I moved back on to my knees and stroked his delicious, smooth buttocks with my left hand.

When would this cloud of pleasure burst? I pushed my knees
further apart, thus parting his thighs. I inserted my cock about
an inch, then came down on his back, my left hand around his
neck, my right on his cock. I went in further, moving backwards and forwards. I could wait no longer: I thrust it in as far
as it would go and, with a great cry, exploded. Holding myself
inside him, I rolled our bodies on to our left sides. He came in
a few seconds.

We stayed like that for a long time, until my diminishing
cock found its way out.

'My love! My love!' I said. 'Sorry it was all so quick. I just
couldn't wait.'

'Well, we'll just have to do it again later, won't we?'

We dozed off for half-an-hour or so. We had the rest of the
day to ourselves. Esmond would have to be at the theatre for
six thirty: not on account of his own part – Nero's Slave did
not appear until the last act – but because he was understudying Basil Gill as Otho, who appeared in the second.

'What are his first lines?' I asked.

Esmond laughed: 'Nothing is left but to eat and drink.'

I laughed. 'And the last?'

He paused, for a split second, then, with a tone of exasper-
ation that he would never have used to speak the words on
stage, yelled: 'What! You will come?'

We both fell about laughing. Over breakfast and then
throughout the day, we told each other the stories of our lives.
He was eighteen: how odd, I thought, that in little more than
a week I had slept with two actors in the same company, of the
same age, both with names beginning with the same three letters. The family was originally from Cheshire. The 'Egerton',
it seemed, referred to a distant relationship to the Duke of
Bridgewater. His father was a specialist at a hospital in
Sheffield, where his parents had lived for the past eight years.

He had gone to a minor public school in the North of England. He was beloved of his English master, who also taught elocution. It was this master who recognized Esmond's talent, spent whole evenings teaching him all he knew about Shakespeare and acting. He was mad about the theatre and produced the school's annual play.

'Did you and he . . .?'

'Most evenings ended with him going down on me. I had no objection. I didn't find him attractive, but I let him get on with it. It was the least I could do. I quite enjoyed it anyway. I kept in touch with him when I left school. Then, the following December, during his Christmas holidays, I met him in London and he took me to *The Tempest* at His Majesty's. It was a revelation. There was the acting, of course, but what I found most astonishing was the spectacle. I had never seen anything like it. I never imagined that such things were possible in a theatre.'

More than ever he was determined to become an actor. Since leaving school, he had done nothing but sit at home, pouring scorn on any ideas for a possible occupation that his father proposed. 'How,' he asked his schoolmaster friend, 'does one become an actor?' His friend had an idea: the previous April, Tree had started acting classes at his theatre. Perhaps Esmond could attend them. Enquiries were made; parental approval was obtained. Esmond was interviewed, not by Mr Tree, as he had expected, but by a small gentleman with black wavy hair, large black eyebrows and small black beady eyes.

'So you want to be an actor?' The usual dire warnings ensued: the poor pay, the uncertainty of employment, the disappearance of many of the provincial stock companies, in which actors used to learn their art. However, he sympathized with the optimism of theatrical aspirants – he was himself the

son of actors. Yes, he was the son of Sir Squire and Lady
Bancroft, and had been something of an actor himself – he
had been in Alexander's company at the St James's. He had now
retired from the stage to concentrate on writing plays, and to
assist Mr Tree in the work of his Academy. He asked Esmond
if there was anything that he could recite from memory:
Esmond did Lady Macbeth's letter speech. He was then asked
to read from a modern play. Good, he could start in January.
For that first term classes took place in the 'Dome', then, after
Easter, they moved into new premises in Gower Street, in
Bloomsbury. By now there were almost a hundred students,
each paying six guineas a term. Classes, too, had expanded: as
well as speech and deportment lessons, and mock rehearsals,
there were lessons in mime by an Italian, and in fencing and
dancing by a Frenchman. Mr Tree himself rarely put in an
appearance, but some of the most celebrated actors of the day –
Alexander, Du Maurier, Hare, as well as the Bancrofts – were
persuaded to share their experience with the students. Members
of the Company also gave lessons, notably J. Fisher White,
who taught the Emil Behnke system of voice production; if he
had had a few inches more in height, he would have had a more
successful career as an actor. Students were used as 'supers' in
productions, and paid half a crown per performance. Towards
the end of their time at the Academy, the more promising were
given small parts. Thus, in his last term, Esmond had been
given just such a part in *Nero* – at a salary of £3 a week.

I reminded Esmond of our first meeting. 'I wanted you
then,' I told him. 'But you suddenly disappeared at the end.'

'Ah, yes, but Esmeralda got her claws into you, didn't she?'

I spluttered with mischievous delight. 'Esmeralda? Is that
what you call him behind his back?'

'Behind his back. I wouldn't fancy my chances in face-to-
face combat.'

'Have you got a behind-your-back name?'

'Well, if there'd been no Esmé Percy in the company, I expect I'd have been landed with Esmeralda. You see, she's even taken my name. At the moment, I seem to be stuck with Rosamund. But wait for further developments. Before long, it will be Rose, even Rosie.'

There was something incongruous about hearing him talk like this. There was nothing of the quick-witted, quick-tongued 'theatrical lady' about him, nothing girlish. His face was boyish, young-manly even, his body almost athletic. His voice was on the deep side; when he spoke it was usually with slow deliberation, seldom smiling, never moving his hands.

'Who else has a secret name?'

'Well, we have Glendower – Reginald Owen, who everyone calls John. Roberta Too-far – Robert Farquarson – whose real name is Robert Coutart de la Condamine; his father's French, as you may have guessed. Warming-pan – Stan Warmington. Fish or Fishy – Fisher White. Basil the Great . . .'

'Monk, bishop, saint. What a waste!'

Esmond looked blank.

'Never mind. Basil the Great. I don't suppose for one moment he's one of us?'

'Alas and alack, no!'

'Who is?'

'Sidney Southgate, of course, otherwise known as "Come in!".'

'Come in? How . . .'

'Oh, "I hear a knocking at the south entry" – *Macbeth*. Quite appropriate. I suspect Jimmy Hearn, though he probably doesn't know himself. Reggie Owen definitely not. Nor David Powell and Robert Atkins, though at the Academy they're known as David and Jonathan. Alec Begbie definitely yes.' I raised an eyebrow. 'We had a little thing last year.

Unfortunately, I had to do all the work. I don't believe it's better to give than to receive.'

Unlike me or Esmé Percy – we had both been to the theatre constantly since we were children – Esmond had not seen a lot of plays. At one point the conversation got on to Irving. I told him how I had first seen him when I was ten in *The Bells*, how my grandfather had been a good friend of his, how I had seen all his productions almost until the end, how I had attended his funeral.

'I only saw him at the end,' said Esmond.

'How, not . . .'

'Last spring, everyone from the Academy went to his farewell season at Drury Lane – *Becket, Merchant, Waterloo, Louis* . . . wotsit . . .'

'*The Eleventh. Louis XI.*'

'I've never seen anything like it, the most extraordinary lesson in acting. Tree's all very well, but he doesn't have the power. Then, last October, I went home for the weekend. I knew Irving would be at the Lyceum – the Sheffield Lyceum – the following week and got my mother to book seats. I knew this would probably be my last chance to see him. We went every night. *Merchant, Becket, Waterloo, Louis* wotsit again – and . . . *The Bells*. Extraordinary. The man was obviously ill. Sometimes I think he forgot where he was, even what play he was in. But the power was still there – sometimes like a distant echo, sometimes in full force. It was the week before he died at Bradford.'

As we talked about Irving, Esmond's eyes lit up, his speech quickened in a way I had not seen before.

'You took over from me. I saw everything from 1891 to his last performance at the Lyceum, Shylock again. Then you saw everything I missed. Extraordinary! To think you saw him in Sheffield, the week before he died.'

Esmond picked up on what must have sounded like a note of contempt in the way I said 'Sheffield' – and reproached me in a broad Yorkshire accent: 'We Sheffielders 'ave our Lyc-ee-oom, too, yeh knor!' Then, adopting an accent at the opposite extreme, almost a parody of Esmé Percy, added: 'I even saw Saaraah there, and as a maaan!'

'What?' I exclaimed. 'Not as Hamlet?'

'Pelléas. With Mrs P. as Mélisande. There the old dears were, all of sixty and forty, playing young lovers. We really shouldn't mock. Neither looked remotely her age and they were both rather splendid. Unfortunately, it was in French.'

'When was that?'

'Last summer. They only came for the one performance.'

I had forgotten about that latest version of Mrs Patrick Cambell's *Pelléas et Mélisande* – it had always been in English before. For Esmond, the play had come out of the blue; he had never heard of Maeterlinck and knew nothing of Symbolism. I gave him a little lecture on these matters: on Lugné-Poe and the Oeuvre, the first night of the play, twelve years before, when I was a mere thirteen.

'Did you know,' I said, in an attempt to end on a lighter note, 'that the dress that Burne-Jones designed for Mrs P. came to be known as the "the gold umbrella case"?'

Throughout my peroration, Esmond's face had worn an expression of amiable candour, ranging only from bemusement to inattentiveness. He now came alive and laughed, 'You are an old clever clogs, aren't you?'

About four o'clock, we went back to bed, our recovered lust enlivened by memories of the morning. This time, we took our time, each luxuriating in the other's body. It all ended an hour later, when I took him as he lay on his back, each staring into the other's eyes until we let forth our cries one after the other.

We went downstairs, made some tea and gorged on toast and fruit-cake in front of the drawing-room fire. I then walked him back to the theatre. I arranged to pick him up afterwards and take him to supper at Romano's.

He more or less moved in with me at Smith Square. Almost every day we found ourselves in the house by the end of the afternoon and, when we did, we always went to bed, though our exertions grew shorter and our post-coital sleep longer. I was never at my best first thing in the morning – nor he, as he had warned me, last thing at night. Sometimes I met him at the theatre after the play and we would go off somewhere for supper. More usually, he arrived back around midnight, already a little drunk, have a bite to eat and more to drink, and tumble into bed. My mind and body were in bonds, but I also felt free, free of not being taken on long, often fruitless walks by my cock.

I had explained to Mrs Wrigglesworth that an actor friend would be staying for some time and that he would be occupying the double bedroom. When Matthew arrived, he moved into his old room, which, fortunately, was on the floor above. On the few occasions they were together, he and Esmond got on well.

A few weeks after Matthew had left for Petersburg, a letter arrived from Tree, inviting me to take part in the productions for the Shakespeare Birthday Week – rehearsals would begin at the end of March.

Tree's sheer energy, organizational genius, blind faith that whatever he undertook, however much he undertook, everything would be right on the night were boundless. While playing the exhausting role of Nero eight times a week, he was directing the rehearsals for no fewer than six Shakespeare productions, in all of which he would play leading roles. Of course, it could not have happened if the plays had not all been revivals. Nevertheless, I could hardly take in the immensity of what had been achieved until it was all over.

My admiration for Tree grew with each day. Unlike the other half-dozen actor-managers who dominated the London theatre, he was not the licensee, but the owner of his theatre. It was on him alone that the whole enterprise, financial as well as artistic, rested. Though even he, with all his boundless energy and determination, could not have succeeded without the assistance of two men, both failed actors. On the other side of the curtain from us was the sphere of the theatre manager, Henry Dana. He was no ordinary theatre manager. From King's College School, he had gone to Queen's College, Cambridge. Then, after four years of cattle rearing in the American Wild West, he returned to London and became an actor. He had been with Tree since the opening of the new theatre. It was he who handled the often delicate balance between incomings and outgoings, providing the necessary ballast to the Chief's mercurial flights of fancy. On our side of the curtain, the stage manager ruled. Cecil King, a genial Irishman, now in his early thirties, had been with Tree since first walking on in 1900. It was he who made sure that whatever the Chief decided during rehearsals was implemented and maintained. His role was especially important in the smooth restoration of the many revivals that Tree put on. He had a prodigious memory and seldom referred to the prompt book, lighting plot or stage plan. Before the first rehearsal he assembled all the 'supers' and read us the riot act. We were to be punctual at all times, not to smoke, not to hang around in the wings during rehearsals, to obey the call boy and not to go wandering along the ladies' corridor. We then joined the rest of the company on stage – they knew to be there five minutes before rehearsals were due to start. King then moved to the swing doors that led on to the stage, opened them and, exactly on time, Tree entered, immaculately dressed, bowed to the assembled company, then, adopting his usual stance, hand on hip and one leg bent, he began: 'Good morning, ladies and gentlemen!'

Under these two men, Tree had a superbly disciplined team at his disposal. It was also a happy team. The Chief demanded perfection from everybody, but everybody knew that Tree drove himself far more than he drove anyone else: at certain times he hardly left his theatre, working long into the night, snatching a few hours' sleep in the Dome before the company and staff turned up next morning. He was respected – and loved – by all. He never threw tantrums and did not expect anyone else to: he had a wonderful ability to entertain, to break tension, when required. His Majesty's Theatre was certainly an autocracy, but, if unrelenting, it was also selfless. Tree was entirely without personal vanity: all that mattered was the successful embodiment of his dream. We knew that we were privileged to be there at all, in the greatest theatre in the land, the theatre that our Chief already saw as the nucleus of a future National Theatre.

Two of the plays in that Shakespeare Week required less work by Tree than the others: *The Tempest* was a new production, put on at Christmas, and *Twelfth Night* had been revived in January, though even in these cases there were changes in the cast. The Week opened on Monday 23 April, Shakespeare's birthday, with *The Tempest*, the first play that Esmond saw at His Majesty's. This time, he was on stage, four times at least, as Francisco, 'a lord' from Alonso's court. Since I, too, was a lord attending the same king, we were always on at the same time. In the first scene, like everybody else on stage, we got soaked by the 'wild waters' conjured up by Prospero's (and the Chief's) art. Off-stage, we all changed into fresh clothes, identical with the ones we were taking off, ready for our next appearance, when Gonzalo remarks that 'our garments being, as they were, drenched in the sea, hold notwithstanding their freshness'. Esmond spoke only twice in the play, but he did have a good speech of some nine lines. Alonso fears that his son, Ferdinand, is drowned. Esmond begs to differ:

> Sir, he may live. I saw him beat the surges under him
> And ride upon their backs; he trod the water,
> Whose enmity he flung aside, and breasted
> The surge, most swoll'n, that met him. His bold head
> 'Bove the contentious waves he kept, and oared
> Himself with his good arms in lusty stroke
> To th' shore, that o'er his wave-worn basis bowed,
> As stooping to relieve him. I not doubt
> He came alive to land.

Each morning, before we left for the theatre, we went over the plays, attending with special observance to his lines. He had a pleasing, very open voice that carried well, an instinctive sense of how to shape a speech, yet stumbled occasionally over Shakespeare's knottier, late-period language. He had particular difficulty with 'The surge, most swoll'n, that met him.' One morning, the more he tried, the worse it got, ruining his delivery of the rest of the speech. How, he roared in fury, could Shakespeare of all people write a line like that? He then asked me if the word 'basis' in this speech meant what he thought it did. We laughed at the idea of Basil Gill's bum being 'wave-worn', but I explained that, in Greek, *basis* primarily means a step taken and, by extension, foot, or, in the case of a statue, for example, base or pediment. Shakespeare probably meant therefore the legs or the entire lower half of the body. This broke the tension and, thereafter, he moved from 'swoll'n' to 'that' without mishap. He did it, too, without eliding Shakespeare's elision further, which would have made it incomprehensible, but by slowing it down, stressing it, with big open 'o's on 'most' and 'swoll'n'. The help did not go all in one direction: Esmond taught me how to make up, how best to move on the stage, how to stand and do nothing.

Tuesday evening, my twenty-sixth birthday, and Wednesday afternoon, brought *Henry IV*, part 1. It had been Tree's last production at the Haymarket and I saw it in the summer of 1896. I had seen him play Falstaff the year before in *Merry Wives*, but Prince Hal's companion, though he may look exactly the same, is a richer, more complex character than 'Sir John in love'. Both Falstaffs were among Tree's finest interpretations, the actor being quite unrecognizable to eye or ear: it is a simple enough matter to take on the girth required, but Tree also managed to 'fatten' his voice. Apart from Tree himself as Falstaff, only three of the original cast were still in place. Ten years on, it might as well have been a new production. As Hotspur, Basil Gill showed that as well as looking handsome and delivering perfectly the mellifluous speeches that were usually his lot (this week as Ferdinand, Orsino, Horatio, Brutus), he could also turn in a powerful, very human performance when given the motive and the cue for passion. One of Esmé's two performances of the week was as Mortimer, curiously brother-in-law to Hotspur, a Percy. The choice of Esmé in a small part that appears only in one scene showed that Tree saw through his slight figure and eighteen years to the special gifts of voice. For the duration of the scene, which he shares with Hotspur and Glendower (beautifully spoken in English and Welsh by Lyn Harding), one would have been forgiven for thinking him the star of the show, for he had some excellent lines, as when he describes his father-in-law, Owen Glendower, as 'valiant as a lion, And wondrous affable, and as bountiful As mines of India'. Esmond played John of Lancaster, the king's second son. He appeared only three times and had only six lines. What is more, after walking on in the first scene, he does not reappear until the last act. His best line is his response to Falstaff's boastings of how he had just killed Hotspur: 'This is the strangest tale that e'er I heard.' I appeared twice as a lord, then twice, in the last act, as a soldier.

In *Twelfth Night*, on Wednesday evening, I was an anonymous attendant on Orsino, Esmond a named one, Valentine, not that he had more than a dozen lines in all. In *Hamlet*, on Thursday and the Saturday matinée, only the Trees remained from the original 1892 production – and Mrs Tree was no longer Ophelia, but the Queen. This time, the Ophelia was the pretty Beatrice Forbes-Robertson. *Hamlet* brought Esmond his largest part of the week (Rosencrantz) and a slight precedence over his rival from ADA, Reggie Owen (Guildenstern), who had generally done better than Esmond. Again, he had some good lines (many of the less good ones had been cut). We pondered long and hard as to how he should say 'As the indifferent children of the earth.' Had it been one of Mr Tree's lines, it would have been given a certain poetico-philosophical 'depth' by slowing the pace, drawing out every syllable of 'in-diff-er-ent', with a slight pause to facilitate the move from the final 't' of the word to the initial 'ch' of the next. Esmond could not have gone so far, but he could not help relishing the beauty of the phrase, only to be slapped down at rehearsal by the Chief, who told him not to make such a meal of it, all that Rosencrantz meant, in reply to Hamlet's 'How do ye both?' was 'Not too bad, so, so.' Again, when Rosencrantz says to Hamlet, 'Even those you were wont to take delight in, the tragedians of the city', Esmond's face lit up with his usual broad, good-natured smile. Tree interrupted: 'You don't have to look quite so delighted, young man. Our characters can't be expected to feel the same degree of enthusiasm that we feel for the tragedians of the city.' Dutiful laughter all round; an even wider grin from Esmond. I was a courtier throughout, appearing in some half-dozen scenes. Once, after he had said to Hamlet, 'My lord, you once did love me . . .', he looked straight at me. I felt a shiver down my spine: would he ever have tongue to charge me thus?

Merry Wives of Windsor was the oldest production to be revived that week, only Tree himself remaining from the 1890 company. It was the only one of the plays in which neither Esmond nor I appeared. This was a pity, for the very good reason that Tree had persuaded Ellen Terry to play Mistress Page: it would have been a boast worth making to say that we had shared the stage with Ellen Terry. It was rumoured that some special event was planned to take place the following evening after the performance. So, on our only free evening, we turned up at the Theatre in time for the last act. At the final curtain, Tree recited an address in verse, in honour of Ellen Terry's fifty years on the stage. (She was not quite as old as this might make her seem: she made her *début* at the age of eight as Mamillius in *Winter's Tale*.) Tree's address ended: 'We praise you; we admire you; we love you!' The poor woman just stood there, bewildered and confused, caught between laughter and tears. This most eloquent of advocates when Shakespeare wrote her brief was always struck dumb when called upon to speak on her own behalf. Tree knew this and had made provision. After allowing everyone to enjoy the spectacle of her discomfort for a few seconds, Tree gave a signal and a dove descended from the flies, bearing in its beak a paper. With a great cry of delight, she seized it and, mastering her emotion, read out its contents, thanks mingled with allusions to her past triumphs. As the audience rose to its feet and broke into a storm of clapping and cheering, those of us who had been standing in the wings joined our colleagues on stage.

The Shakespeare Week ended on Saturday evening with *Julius Caesar*. I had seen the original production in 1898, when it was recognized as the most splendid of any so far, in terms of scenic spectacle, though, such is theatrical illusion, what seemed like Alma-Tadema's impossibly truthful depiction of, say, the Forum, looked very different at a couple of feet's distance. Mark Antony was not one of Tree's better roles and this master of verisimilitude had some difficulty removing the decades in his portrayal of the part. The more appropriately aged Basil Gill as Brutus and Lyn Harding as Cassius turned in superb performances. Esmond was Caesar's unnamed servant, with few, but important, fatefully unheeded words. Asked for the prognostications of the augurers, he reports to his master: 'They would not have you set forth today. Plucking the entrails of an offering forth, They could not find a heart within the beast.' But Esmond also joined me in other scenes as citizen or soldier.

At the end of that exhausting day – the morning had been taken up with the dress rehearsal for the evening's *Julius Caesar*, separated, in the afternoon, by a second performance of *Hamlet* – supper was served on the stage, which we had hardly left all week, on two long trestle tables, one headed by Tree, the other by Mrs Tree. As I looked at the faces around me, I was conscious of the spirit of cameraderie that had sustained us all week. I was reminded, too, of how young the company was: well over half was under thirty, no more than ten could have been over fifty. Only two, I think, were older than Tree himself: Henry Neville (Claudius and Julius Caesar) and Lionel Brough (Trinculo, Bardolph, Belch, First Gravedigger). At the other end of the scale, there were the latest recruits from Mr Tree's Academy, Maud Cressall (a much promoted, but admired Miranda) and the promising, very assured Robert Atkins (Marcellus in *Hamlet* and, more unexpectedly, Basil Gill's father in *Henry IV*, at twenty-two, six years younger than his 'son').

We emerged into Charles Street in the early hours of Sunday morning. I should have enjoyed the fresh air on the walk home, but Esmond would have been incapable of reaching the Duke of York's steps without stumbling. We took a cab in the Haymarket and held hands all the way. By the time we reached Smith Square, Esmond had recovered enough to require a good glass of whisky before collapsing into bed. We awoke late and rose even later, after making love more passionately than we had . . . for a week or two. Next day, Esmond did not have to be at the Theatre until six thirty, but on Tuesday morning rehearsals began for a new play, an adaptation of Thackeray's *The Newcomes*.

Throughout May and June, I found myself recreating, for myself alone, what Grandfather Sheridan had created year after year for us all. That Season, the incomparable Hans Richter was conducting the Wagner operas: a complete Ring, *Tristan, Tannhäuser, Mastersingers, Flying Dutchman*. During my first London Season, aged twelve, I had been thrown into the deep end with just such a programme, conducted on that occasion by the young Gustav Mahler. Being so inexperienced in such things, I had not realized at the time how courageous Augustus Harris had been in bringing such an event to the Covent Garden stage. It was the first time that the entire Ring cycle had been performed in London – and the first time that Wagner had been sung in German. In earlier years *Lohengrins*, *Tannhäusers* and *Flying Dutchmen* had been sung in Italian by the likes of Melba, Eames and the de Reszké brothers. In deference to his German guests, Harris installed electricity in his theatre (turning the house lights off during the performance, as in Germany) and dropped the 'Italian' from its title (Covent Garden now became officially known for the first time as simply 'The Royal Opera House'). Hearing the music dramas sung in their original language made the Italian and French versions of Wagner seem like theatrical artifice. The French might claim that the use of the vernacular in Paris renders opera intelligible – a claim that I would dispute on the grounds that one understands only a small part of what is sung. The use of Italian in a London *Tannhäuser* had no such justification, its adoption being solely for the convenience of the singers, who preferred to sing in the language in which they had been trained and who would no doubt have regarded German as inherently ugly and unsingable in any case. No one at the time suggested that, in London, all opera should be sung in English, though this would have been Wagner's own preference. In this, he was the last person to judge. Firstly, as the author of the text, he knew it better than anyone, and therefore imagined that he could follow what the singers were singing. Secondly, as a German, he was in no position to judge what would be lost by the work's not being sung in German. The real objection to 'translated' opera is that Italian, French, German and English inhabit entirely different sound-worlds. What is important is not their shared ancestry, but their extraordinary divergence. Take French and Italian, for instance: they have much in common, similar grammar and vocabulary, but what makes their sound-world so different is what they do not have in common. Italian is highly stressed (like German); French is not. Italian has what we call 'pure' vowels (again like German); French (like English) vowels are notoriously eccentric. What makes French so distinctive is its nasality, a strange effect produced by the consonant 'n' on certain vocalic sounds. The Italian sound-world is particularly marked by the elision of awkward consonants in favour of vocalic smoothness; German operates in the opposite direction, using vowels almost to separate clusters of consonants.

Wagner exploits this consonantal quality of German to the full in The Ring, reinventing an alliterative verse form used in medieval German and English. In other words, what Wagner's libretto does is create an archaic-sounding German that more than usually stresses its hard, consonantal character, thereby increasing its Germanness. In this way, he turns German back to its Teutonic roots, to the kind of world portrayed in the Icelandic sagas. It is a German that sounded very odd indeed to Wagner's contemporaries and still more so to later generations of Germans. Wagner's aim, therefore, is not primarily communication, but the recreation of a primitive world, the attempt to forge a language suited to giants and gods. Not the least surprising thing about Wagner is that, whereas his language is deliberately backward-looking, his music makes one of the greatest leaps forward in the history of the West – and both seem so inseparably welded together as to seem to spring from the same source. What is being rejected in each case is the present as Wagner knew it.

Since that 1892 Season, Wagner in German has never been absent from the Covent Garden stage. In 1906, Richter had managed to persuade the theatre management to follow Wagner's wishes and perform the entire cycle in seven days. Seen in this way, one can take the accumulated experience with one from one day to the next; one has a greater sense of the aeons of time spent by Wotan as the 'Wanderer' from his disappearance at the end of *Walküre* to his reappearance in the second act of *Siegfried*, or by Brünnhilde from her 'dormition' at the end of *Walküre* to her reappearance at the end of *Siegfried*, or of the span of generations between the lives of Sigmund and Siegfried. I know of no other experience in the theatre that so has the effect of dissolving the world of friends and city streets into which one finally re-emerges, as if at the end of one's life.

With the end of the Wagner operas, I turned my attention elsewhere. Caruso, short, unprepossessing, rather plump, now considered, at thirty-three, the finest tenor in this *répertoire*, seemed to be in all the Italian operas. With Melba, who, at forty-five, one assumed, quite wrongly as it turned out, to be near the end of her career, he sang in *Rigoletto*, *Traviata* and *La Bohème*. He sang Cavaradossi to Rina Giachetti's Tosca and Pinkerton to Emmy Destinn's Madame Butterfly. In *Don Giovanni* Caruso again partnered Destinn in the smaller roles of the lovers. Neither soprano had ever been matched by such a tenor voice.

I saw several plays, including two by Shakespeare that I had never seen before. *Measure for Measure* was a courageous, if perverse choice on Oscar Asche's part: this amiable Australian giant of Norwegian descent seemed particularly unsuited to the role of the ascetic, tortured Angelo. *Othello* had some fine performances from Evelyn Millard as Desdemona, H. B. Irving as Iago and the still beautiful Henry Ainley as Cassio, but the stalwart Lewis Waller was woefully underpowered in the title role. I saw the latest Shaw at the Court, *Captain Brassbound's Conversion*. Ellen Terry played the irresistibly bossy Lady Cecily Wayneflete who, in no time at all, had Arab brigands and English soldiers alike obedient to her slightest whim.

At the beginning of June, I received a letter from Tree asking me if I should care to join the company, in the same capacity as before, in a production of *Winter's Tale*: rehearsals would begin shortly, but my services would not be required until 21 August. I was mildly surprised that the Chief himself had taken the trouble to write to me, a mere walk-on, rather than leaving it to Mr Dana, the manager. But, then, I was an unpaid gentleman, not, like Esmond, an ill-paid player. He had already been informed by Dana that there would be no speaking part for him in *Winter's Tale*, but that he would be walking on and understudying.

I attended the dress rehearsal of *Colonel Newcome*. As it happened, I had not read Thackeray's *The Newcomes*. As soon as I knew that Esmond would be in the play, I set about reading the novel. To my delight, Esmond's part, the oddly named Nadab, appeared in the first chapter, the scene in the 'Cave of Harmony', the drinking den to which young Newcome and his Cambridge pals – King of Corpus, Jones of Trinity, Martin of Trinity Hall – repair after the theatre. My name, too, cropped up: 'all the wits used to come here,' says the Colonel, 'Mr Sheridan . . .' Nadab is referred to as an *improvisatore*, poet and professional storyteller who, judging by his dropped and misplaced aitches is a Cockney. Alas 'young Nadab' never appears again, even in the novel, let alone in the play, which, of course, was a fraction of the length.

The run of *Colonel Newcome* lasted for six weeks, after which the theatre was locked up and the company set off on a three-week tour of the provinces, beginning with a week in Dublin. Three plays were taken – *Nero*, *Oliver Twist* and *Trilby* – so there was no call on the services of extras. Esmond went with them: it was our first separation. We had been together for almost six months, during which time hardly a day had gone by but we made love. I had grown used to feeling him fall asleep with my left arm around him, then waking and putting my arm around him again, and falling back into sleep; to our chats over breakfast; to our suppers after the theatre. The first week of his absence was like being in a dream in which nothing happened. By the second, I had begun to wake up, to feel Esmond's absence less acutely, even to have thoughts of benefiting from it. I spent more time in the West End, less in Smith Square: I returned to *bani* and *kloseti*. But I had become more particular. My heart was not really in it, even if another of my organs was. So, once or twice, after undue provocation, I allowed the latter to have its way, satisfy itself in the quickest, easiest manner, without word spoken, thus leaving the heart inviolate.

It was mid-July, the Season was over, many of the theatres shut. At the Court, I saw a revival of *You Never Can Tell*. This charming play opens, in original, perverse Shavian mode, with a girl sitting in a dentist's chair. But this is the pleasantest of 'plays pleasant', set on a sunny August day in a resort on the Devon coast, ending happily with a masked ball. Dionysus is not far away, though, with Shaw in charge, very much under verbal control, with the elderly waiter acting as a sort of Chorus and his barrister son as *deus ex machina*.[1] The dentist's patient and her twin brother have been brought up in Madeira without benefit of a proper English education. They don't know how to behave in polite Society: they say the first thing that comes into their heads. Their mother, 'a veteran of the Old Guard of the Women's Rights movement', is the author of a best-selling series of books known as the Twentieth-Century Treatises, bearing such titles as *Twentieth-Century Children*, *Twentieth-Century Parents*, *Twentieth-Century Conduct*. She is a woman clearly ahead of her time, since the play is not only set in 1896, but was written in 1897 and first performed in 1898. Though forty-four at the end of the nineteenth century, Shaw had always belonged to the twentieth. Five or six years into that same twentieth century, Shaw's time had come.

Esmond arrived back on a Sunday afternoon at the end of July, his face shining with happiness. After the merest

---

1 God from the machine – a device in Greek classical theatre by which at the end of a play a god descended from Olympus to solve problems in the plot. The 'machine' (*mechane*) was the crane that could raise or lower an actor.

exchange of words, he took my hand and led me upstairs. We hugged one another and kissed and kissed and kissed. Soon we were tearing the clothes off one another, our hands all over each other. When the end came, we were both howling like wolves. It was like our first day together, but with familiarity added unto it.

We had three weeks of idleness before we were required for the later rehearsals of *Winter's Tale*. The Theatre was still closed and Tree had gone off to Baden-Baden. We opted for the other side of the Rhine, joining thousands of other visitors in a Paris deserted by those of its inhabitants who were free to do so. We spent ten days at my old hotel in the rue Cujas, warmly welcomed, with much ogling of us both, by the old owner. I showed Esmond Paris, the 'sights' that everyone visiting Paris has to see and my Paris. I showed him Versailles and Fontainebleau. It was our first holiday, almost our 'honeymoon'. Our love-making was more energetic than ever, with the further stimulation of seeing all day long the young of another country, dressed for hot summer days, with the uninhibited gaze, the flirtatious curiosity of Parisians.

That autumn, Tree divided his company, taking the smaller part on a provincial tour in a number of modern revivals, leaving the greater part of it in London in *Winter's Tale*, a play that had scarcely been staged in living memory. Reading it again, I began to understand why. As in many of the tragi-comedies, Shakespeare o'erflows the measure of our credulity. One minute, Leontes is urging his wife to persuade his friend to stay longer; the next, when the friend finally gives in, he is thinking: 'Too hot, too hot: To mingle friendship far is mingling bloods.' (By contrast, it takes a few scenes and all Iago's diabolical skill to make Othello doubt his wife's honour.) Before long, Hermione is being publicly accused of infidelity. So great is the shock that she collapses and dies – before the message from the

Delphic oracle arrives, confounding Leontes' accusations. This apparent unconcern for plausibility is as nothing to what we are expected to believe at the end: a statue of Hermione comes to life, to be reunited with her repentant husband. At which point, that ingrate Shakespeare, not content with leaving his leading lady off-stage for over half of the play, now gives her a mere seven, rather perfunctory, lines.

Apart from the play's intrinsic shortcomings, there was another reason why it had been ignored for so long: few actor-managers would see themselves as Leontes. Tree certainly did not; indeed it was the first of his productions that I could remember in which he did not himself perform. What, then, made Tree bring this play back to the stage? A clue lies in his curtain speech to *Merry Wives* in April. In that tribute to Ellen Terry on her fiftieth year on the London stage, Tree reminded us that her first role had been that of Mamillius. What finer compliment than to offer her the part of Mamillius's mother, Hermione, especially as, in terms of verisimilitude, it was one that she should have played when she was half her present age? Age aside and, in any case, Ellen Terry looked fifteen years younger than her sixty years, no woman on the English stage could better convey that playful, innocent seductiveness, turning to dignified, incredulous out-rage when her innocence is impugned, all delivered with the kind of elocution that sends shivers down one's spine and makes one gulp with emotion. As long as I had been going to the London theatre, she had been its undisputed queen. I had been privileged to see almost every part that she had played over the past fifteen years. She had played in plays that were not by Shakespeare, but only Shakespeare released her gifts to the full. I first saw her as Katherine of Aragon in *Henry VIII*; I saw her Cordelia, her Portia, her Beatrice (her finest part of all), her Lady Macbeth, her Imogen (in *Cymbeline*) and her

Volumnia (in *Coriolanus*). I never dreamt that we should ever stand on the same side of the footlights but, for eight weeks, we did. In my usual role of an attendant lord – by way of a change, I was also transmogrified into a shepherd for the sheep-shearing scene – I was in every scene in which she appeared and on stage almost the whole time that she was. We sensed that she was coming to the end of her career. What gradually dawned upon us during those weeks was that she had embarked on an affair with a young man almost half her age. He was the American actor James Carew, who had played the American naval officer in *Captain Brassbound's Conversion*. A year later, he became her third husband. Two years after that, the marriage came to an end.

That production of *Winter's Tale* was less blessed in its Leontes. Charles Warner had been a pillar of the West End as long as I could remember, specializing in the kind of plays that occupy most of the West End theatres at any time and are usually forgotten. As a result, I could not remember ever having seen him. Like Ellen Terry, Charles Warner was also at the end of his career: they were the same age but, unlike her, he looked his sixty years. One sympathized with the old fellow trying to make what sense he could of his part, but the result was so much sound and fury, delivered with much rolling of eyes. He also had the irritating habit of 'improving' on Shakespeare's lines, to the detriment of scansion. For example, in the line 'My heart dances, but not for joy, not joy', he interpolated 'no, no' before 'not joy'. This became something of a joke among the younger members of the company. X might ask: 'You haven't seen Y, by any chance?' Z would reply: 'No, I'm afraid I haven't', then, eyes rolling and voice assuming sonorous tones, add: 'No, no!' Half-way through the run, Charles Warner fell ill and had to be replaced by Lyn Harding, the Camillo, who did as well as any man could in the part. (Charles Warner did not act again; he died three years later.) The young, spring-time lovers, Basil Gill and Viola Tree, were enchanting, as was, said everyone who saw it from the other side of the footlights, the set in which they gambolled and in which we danced our shepherds' hey. For this the stage was largely covered in turf and backed by trees, behind which a back-drop depicted a valley. Stage-right was an old hut; stage-left, a cascading brook (of real water, of course), leading to a pond, which we crossed on stepping-stones. *Winter's Tale* played for the whole of September and October, when it was replaced by a further three-week run of *Colonel Newcome*, during which Tree was rehearsing *Antony and Cleopatra*, the major new production of the year, and a revival of *Richard II*.

Esmond was my latest friend, but he was also in a sense my first. There was nothing in my past to compare with what I felt for him, with the experience of our daily, almost hourly contact – a contact that seemed electrical. We had only to look at one another across a room for the charge to shoot between us. When our eyes met as we stood on the stage of His Majesty's, looking even more seductive than usual in our scanty costumes, the tension could be unbearable. There we could not rush across and run our hands over each other's body. We had to be content with blank looks, rapidly averted. Esmond had been living with me at Smith Square for several months and we were at the height of our happiness, living from moment to moment, plunged in the present. In the first week in November, a letter arrived from my first friend, Lucien Daudet: I had managed to keep up a correspondence of about one letter a year, usually exchanged around the New Year. This one was devoid of news: would I be free to meet him in London the following week?

1891–97: Paris

Lucien's father, Alphonse Daudet, was, after Zola, France's best-known – and best-selling – living novelist. I first met Lucien a few weeks after our arrival in Paris, at the wedding of his brother Léon to Jeanne Hugo, the poet's grand-daughter. At this time, Léon Daudet was as fervent a republican and atheist as his wife's stepfather, the politician Edouard Lockroy. His mother, though a devout Catholic of royalist sympathies, was pleased by the marriage. She was anxious about her son's restless, truculent character. Marriage to the sensible Jeanne Hugo, she believed, would have the same beneficial effect that marriage had had on her own wayward husband. Alphonse Daudet, however, did not welcome the marriage. He had an intense dislike of Lockroy, in particular, and of the world of anti-clerical Jews and Freemasons in general. Though an unbeliever, he was a reluctant one: he not only tolerated his wife's Catholicism, he envied it.

My Paris grandparents were old friends of the Daudets. On arrival at the reception, Matthew and I were put in the charge of Lucien, then nearly thirteen. He had inherited his father's Southern looks, the soft, dark eyes, the black, wavy hair, the olive skin. But, if he resembled his father physically, he was, in all other respects, his mother's child. He had adopted all her mannerisms – her gestures, her facial expressions, even her way of ending each sentence on a trailing, lingering note. His manners were already exquisite, his charm perfected almost to excess. Matthew did not take to him at all; I was already intrigued.

Lucien was a shy, withdrawn, rather melancholy boy. Though he could be very droll, in a purely verbal way, he did not possess my own good spirits. He would call in after school and take his *goûtée*[1] with me in the kitchen. Sometimes I would call on him. The Daudets lived in the top two floors of an *hôtel particulier*[2] situated beyond the courtyard at 31 rue de Bellechasse. It had a round tower that rose through four or five storeys from the square, first-floor balcony, which gave it a 'Château de la Loire' look. In Alphonse Daudet's study hung two pictures by Renoir – a portrait of Mme Daudet and a smaller portrait, in pastel, of Lucien, holding a biscuit in one hand.

On Thursday afternoons, Lucien and I might go to a matinée at the Odéon or visit an art gallery. He had a prodigious knowledge of painting and was himself a good draughtsman. I still have two sketches he did of me, one in that first year of our friendship, another when I was eighteen and he was attending the Académie Jullian. On Sundays, he would often join us for the concert. All the Daudets were very musical and ardent 'Wagnerites'. Mme Daudet had a good singing voice: I heard her sing on several occasions, accompanied variously by Massenet, Reynaldo Hahn, Pierre Loti – and Mémé.

One September morning, I received an invitation from Lucien to spend a week or so with his family at Champrosay, a village about twenty miles south of Paris. So one bright morning Mother took me to the Gare d'Austerlitz, bought my ticket and put me on the train, impressing upon me the

1 The French equivalent of afternoon tea.
2 Town house.

extreme importance of getting off at Ris-Orangis. It was the
first 'journey' I had ever undertaken on my own. As it happened, it was quite uneventful: Lucien was waiting for me on
the platform at Ris-Orangis and a carriage took us across the
Seine to Champrosay. Mme Daudet met us at the door:

'Zézé, take Mark to his room, then come out on to the terrace and have some lemonade.' ('Zézé' was Lucien's pet name
in the family.) So that I should not be isolated in the guest-
wing, Lucien was to share a double room with me. It looked
out, across the garden, to the Forêt de Sénart. At the other side
of the house, the garden ran down to the Seine. The grounds,
which, as Lucien nonchalantly informed me, covered some five
or six hectares (about thirteen acres), were dotted here and
there with pavilions. One of these, I discovered, was the 'billard', which was not, in any practical sense, a billiard-room –
the rather worn-looking billiard table had been pushed into a
corner – but a play-room, full of toys. I particularly remember
a splendid rocking-horse and a model theatre. I could see that
Lucien was very glad of my company, since, mealtimes apart,
he saw nobody all day except his young sister, Edmée, so
named after Edmond de Goncourt, her godfather, her
'*Anglaise*' (English nanny) and the servants. If the weather was
fine, we spent our time walking through the woods or canoeing
on the river; two days of wind and rain we spent sitting around
in the *billard*, trying to entertain a bored Edmée.

On the last day of my stay, a Sunday, there were to be
guests at luncheon, including my grandparents, parents and
Matthew, who were to accompany me home in the evening.
Léon arrived in a carriage with his young wife and Edmond de
Goncourt. And, from his house in the nearby village of
Soissy-sous-Etiolles, came Édouard Drumont, the author of
La France juive, a symptom and an exacerbation of a certain
climate in French society that was to erupt in a few years'

time in the Dreyfus affair, though to listen to this quiet, scholarly man, one would never have thought him to be so totally in the grip of such virulent views. He was devoted to Alphonse Daudet. Indeed, he owed a great deal to the novelist, who had persuaded Morpon to publish Drumont's 1200-page anti-semitic tract in the first place – a debt he repaid by the nefarious influence he was later to exercise over Léon.

Léon, I noticed, ate, drank and talked twice as much as anyone else. At twenty-four, he already had the exuberance, the self-assertiveness, the arrogance that were to become more marked as he grew older, but he still had the boyish charm that made such traits more palatable. It was the first time I had seen him since his wedding, the first time I had been able to see him at close quarters. Without any trace of condescension he talked to Matthew and me about London, which, he said, he had recognized from the pages of de Quincey, Dickens and Stevenson. Not content with finding de Quincey's Oxford Street, 'that stepmother with a heart of stone', he marked in every face he met the familiar marks of fictional characters, there the expression of the young prostitute Anne, there the touching smile of Florence Dombey or the pitiful features of Nancy, murdered by the terrible Sikes. He then waxed eloquent about Shakespeare, how Macbeth's castle, with 'its temple-haunting martlet', or the battlements of Elsinore were as real to him as Versailles or Notre Dame de Paris.

Edmond de Goncourt, then nearing seventy, made less impression on me. With his shock of white hair, his full white moustache and dark, almost black eyes, he had the air of a distinguished, if rather eccentric retired general. His manners and mode of speaking had something old-fashioned about them: he was elaborately, almost laboriously polite to the Daudets, his most intimate friends, with whom, in Paris, he dined twice a week. He spent most of the afternoon talking about the Far East with Father and Mother. He was deeply interested in everything they had to say, for he was one of the foremost European collectors of Japanese art and artefacts. At this point in his career, Father had not yet been to Japan, but, for Edmond de Goncourt, who had probably never been further east than Strasbourg, a Sinologist like my father would be accounted both receptive to the beauties of his treasures and a well-stored mind to plunder. He accordingly invited us to visit him in Auteuil.

The Goncourt brothers had acquired their house in the avenue de Montmorency soon after their mother's death and proceeded to fill it with their possessions. Though both brothers had had relations with women, it may be said that they had love only for one another. Once, wishing to express his admiration for what he imagined to be their perfect marriage, Edmond told the Daudets that theirs was 'a *ménage* like the one I had with my brother'! They had identical views on all matters. They worked together at the same table, collaborated on the same works, ate together, went out for walks together, even slept in the same room. From the day they moved into the house until the day of Jules's death, they had not been apart for longer than twenty-four hours. Jules died in 1870, at the age of forty, from the syphilis that he had contracted twenty years before. Edmond remained in mourning for the rest of his life; alone, he continued the work of writing the journal, novels and plays, and collected the books and *objets d'art* that he had once shared with his brother.

We arrived at about three o' clock on a fine spring afternoon. I sensed that M. de Goncourt was somewhat apprehensive at first about the presence of two boys, aged twelve and thirteen. We began in the garden which, as one might expect, had been subjected to the Goncourt aesthetic quite as much as any of the rooms in the house though no gardener is invested with the absolute power enjoyed by the collector of human artefacts. He may bring rare plants from Chinese mountain side or Japanese woodlands, but he cannot command them to bloom in April.

The house was quite the most remarkable, for its size, of any I have ever seen. Every available space seemed to be occupied by some beautiful object, yet the overall impression was not that of an antique shop or sale room, for each object had been chosen specifically in relation to its space and surroundings. The objects came almost exclusively from two sources: the French eighteenth century and the Japan of the late eighteenth and early nineteenth centuries. It was a curious conjunction, given not only our greater familiarity with the former, but also the intrinsically bolder, more dramatic quality of much of the latter: inevitably the Japanese exotica turned the quiet furniture and faded tapestries of the *ancien régime* into a setting, a foil, which, after all, is probably what they had been in the first place.

The Goncourts were not mere decorators: they were collectors. It is inconceivable that they would have done for anyone else what they had done for themselves. But, unlike most collectors, they paid little heed to rarity – and therefore commercial value. Their choices were dictated solely by aesthetic considerations and their aesthetic crossed all such barriers. Indeed most of the Japanese objects were not, at the time, considered to be the best of their kind. The earlier, finer examples were still jealously guarded in Japanese houses and monasteries. To obtain his treasures Edmond de Goncourt went no further than a few Paris antique shops: Madame Desoye's in the rue de Rivoli, Sichet's in the rue Pigalle, Bing's in the rue de Chauchat – or to the Japanese dealer Hayashi, who did not have a shop and with whom Goncourt worked on translating Hokusai's preface for an edition of his prints.

To appreciate the astonishment one felt on entering the Goncourt house one must remember how similar to one another houses and apartments of the same social standing were in those days – and how unchanging. It was quite normal for a couple to die with precisely the same furniture that they had acquired at their marriage. Fashion in such matters changed slowly and hardly affected anyone except those setting out in life. The Paris interiors of my youth were almost all filled with Second Empire *commodes*, tables and chairs. Such interiors were intended not to be noticed. By contrast, the Goncourt house screamed at you as soon as you were inside the front door. The floor of the entrance hall was paved in red and white marble; the walls and ceilings were covered in leather, decorated with brightly coloured parrots. The dining-room was hung with a series of eighteenth-century French tapestries and two great coats-of-arms in gilt bronze. There was a pair of Sèvres vases on Boulle stands, but my attention was particularly caught by a large piece of furniture carved with fables from La Fontaine. On the first-floor landing was a red lacquer chest-of-drawers containing albums of Japanese prints. On entering the study I was struck at once by a pair of fierce-looking beasts, staring out at me with blood-shot eyes, against a ceiling covered with black velvet. They were, M. de Goncourt explained, lions and came from Korea. A Boulle bookcase, which M. de Goncourt had inherited from his mother, contained some of his most prized possessions: books illustrated by Boucher, Gravelot and Eisen. Doors, hung with heavy oriental rugs, led to a *cabinet d'Extrême Orient*, crammed with *netsuke* depicting gods, holy men, heroes, monkeys. The next flight of stairs, lined with French drawings and Japanese *kakemonos*, led to the celebrated *grenier* or attic, in which Jules de Goncourt had died – the dead brother's revered rocking-chair was still in place. Here, in 1885, Edmond de Goncourt had inaugurated the Sunday afternoon meetings of writers that were to outshine any of the literary salons of the period.

Over tea, my father told our host a Chinese story about the origins of the beverage. In the Goncourt *Journal*, readers will find it in the entry for 18 April 1892:

> Once, long ago, Dharma, a greatly esteemed ascetic, had decided to give up sleep, on the grounds that it was an all too human weakness. One night, however, he fell asleep and did not awake until the following morning. Indignant with himself for such weakness, he cut off his eyelids and threw them away, as pieces of base flesh that prevented him from attaining the superhuman perfection to which he aspired. But the bleeding eyelids took root where they had fallen. The local people picked the leaves of the bush that grew there and made a scented infusion of them that dispelled sleep.

One day, in July, 1896, we read in the newspapers of the death of Edmond de Goncourt at Champrosay. Two days after the death, the lawyer read the Goncourt will to Daudet and Léon Hennique, its executors. The house at Auteuil and its contents were to be sold and the sum invested to provide capital for an Academy, whose task would be to award a prize each year to a new work of literature. The will was contested by Edmond de Goncourt's surviving cousins, none of whom Alphonse Daudet had ever heard of. Raymond Poincaré, former Minister of Public Instruction and future President of the Republic, was secured to fight the Academy's case through the courts. Most people, unaware of the value of a collection on which Goncourt had spent up to 130,000 francs a year, were surprised that he had left enough money to finance a literary foundation. The books alone fetched 3 million francs and the

sale of the objets d'art realized a further one and a half million
francs. The Académie Goncourt finally won its case in March
1900 and the prize was awarded for the first time later that year.

One summer, Pépé had arranged to borrow a villa in
Trouville for the last three weeks of August. In those days,
Trouville in August was a fixture of the social calendar. The
rule was inflexible: Parisians went north in the summer, south
in the winter. It was to be some years before they followed the
intrepid English and exposed themselves to the Riviera
summer. In those far-off days prolonged exposure to sun and
sea, nowadays considered essential to a summer holiday, was
shunned: clothes were kept on and the sea was dipped into,
preferably with the help of a bathing-machine, not because it
was enjoyable, but because the best medical authorities had
declared it to be invigorating to the organism. But Paris
'Society' did not tire of its rituals and ceremonies, or yearn for
something 'different' from what it experienced every day in
the Faubourg Saint-Germain, the Champs-Elysées and the
Bois; no sooner had it transported itself to the sea, than it set
about recreating its daily round of visits, dinners, receptions
and dances. The race track in neighbouring Deauville made up
for the loss of Longchamps and excursions by carriage into the
forest of Touques were an acceptable substitute for rides in the
Bois. There was gaming in the Casino; concerts were given
almost daily and the latest theatrical successes of the Paris
boulevards could be seen. The ladies, sporting their finest of
finery, paraded up and down the *planches*, the wooden promenade, *entre quatre et six*.[1] It was difficult to believe that fifty
years before Trouville had been a small fishing village, a scattered collection of cottages on the hillside surrounded by apple
orchards and that its adjoining township of Deauville did not

1 Between four and six o'clock.

even exist. Deauville was the creation of two men: a Dr Oliffe, physician to the British Embassy in Paris, and the Duc de Morny, minister, confidant and half-brother to Napoleon III. The railway arrived and fashionable Paris followed.

Our *'rapide'* from Saint-Lazare pulled into the little station of 'Trouville–Deauville', situated on a narrow tongue of land in the river separating the twin towns. It was early afternoon. The sky was not the unremitting blue we had left in Paris, but varied in intensity, opalescent with light cloud. But what first struck one was the air: the dry, dusty air of the city, savourless were it not for the faint smell of horse dung, had given way to air that was moist, salty, heavily scented by the innards of mackerel left that morning on the fish dock. A hired carriage took us across the bridge, along the quay, where yachts were moored, and up the hill to our villa. From there we commanded magnificent views. Before us the hillside sloped gently down, dotted with villas and gardens, to the white mass of the Hôtel des Roches Noires, so named after the black rock that littered this part of the coast; the Jetée des Anglais, the pier, completed the year before by an English company, pointed out into the sea. To the right, across the gaping mouth of the Seine, stood the great port of Le Havre (literally, 'the harbour').

Leaving our grandparents to settle into the house and make the acquaintance of the servants who came with it, Matthew and I ran down the hill to the sea. We found a secluded spot on the other side of the pier, well away from the Établissement des Bains, the cabins and bathing-machines. There we spent a blissful hour or two swimming and sitting on rocks, dangling our feet in pools. We walked back over the damp sand, which the receding tide had so lately yielded up, leaving behind it, like a retreating army, bedraggled clumps of seaweed and the odd jellyfish, ready to risk all in a last rearguard action. We went back to where we had left our clothes, secured by large pebbles, dressed and walked off towards the town centre. We soon met the impeccably turned out ladies and gentlemen, who gave amused glances at our dishevelled hair, grubby white flannels and crumpled blazers. We bought ice-creams from one of the Italian *glaciers* near the Casino, inspected the yachts, watched the fishermen unloading their catches on the quay opposite and climbed the hill back to our villa. We found our grandparents in the garden talking to Thérèse, the house-keeper, who quite evidently disapproved of our appearance. When she heard where we had been, disapproval turned to disgust that we had dared, in such a state, to show our faces in polite society. Mémé spoke a few words of remonstrance, but Pépé failed to hide his delight. We were told to change at once and Thérèse would see that our clothes were sent to the cleaner's first thing in the morning.

We soon learnt to fall in with the ways of Trouville society. We bathed occasionally in the proper manner at the Établissement des Bains – and, when we bathed among the mussel-encrusted black rocks beyond the pier, we wore second-best clothes and went straight back to the villa, trying not to be noticed. We had tea at the Salon or *chez* Planta, the *pâtissier-glacier* in the rue de Paris, where we gorged ourselves on *choux à la crème, financières aux amandes, tartes aux framboises, millefeuilles,* not to mention an endless variety of ice-creams. There, in the rue de Paris, the town's most fashionable shops were to be found and there the morning promenade took place. There were some obligatory visits, since, inevitably, my grandparents knew some of the people staying in the villas nearby. We attended a few concerts in the afternoon and a few plays in the evening. On Sundays, we lunched at the Hôtel des Roches Noires.

For the last ten days of our stay at Trouville, we were joined by Lucien. Matthew, never one of his most ardent admirers, was not looking forward to his arrival. He wreaked his vengeance by doing extremely funny imitations of Lucien's manner and way of speaking. However, he was not too put out, since he had made friends with a boy staying nearby and could happily leave Lucien and me to our own devices. Matthew complained that I became a different person when I was with Lucien from the one I was with him: it was true. Each appealed to quite different sides of me. Lucien would never have bathed in the 'wild' territory beyond the Hôtel des Roches Noires. On the other hand, there were things I could discuss with him that would have been met with blank incomprehension or embarrassment from Matthew. Some days Lucien and I would set out, armed with nothing but packed lunches prepared for us by the cook, a sketchbook and a couple of books, along the Corniche road that led eventually, along the cliff tops, to Honfleur. We might get as far as Criqueboeuf, where we would eat our picnic overlooking the extraordinary twelfth-century church. Arm-in-arm and slightly drunk on cider, we would then cut inland for a mile or more and make for the shade of the forest, where we would spend the rest of the day sketching, reading and talking, endlessly talking.

There was another side to Lucien. Though only fourteen, he was an avid observer of the Trouville social scene. Once, with an excitement verging on veneration, he informed me that the gentleman with the full, grey beard some ten yards away was none other than King Leopold of the Belgians. Another time, he took me off to Mme Doucet's antique shop: there, in the late morning, the *crème de la crème* of Trouville society was to be found. While appearing to examine a pair of *bergères* in the window, he soon apprised himself of who was in the shop. The handsome, fair-haired young man who seemed to be the centre of attention was Comte Boni de Castellane, who would be staying at the Château de l'Abbaye, near Blonville, a few miles away. The nephew and heir of the Prince de Sagan, he had already spent his way through one fortune and was about to embark on another by marrying an American heiress, Anna Gould. The beautiful lady who had passed just now in her landau was Comtesse Greffülhe, while the middle-aged lady followed by a little Negro page dressed in red satin was the Princesse de Sagan, who lived at the Villa Persane. It even took Lucien to inform us that the Prince of Wales was in town – yes, Pépé added, he would be visiting the Manoir des Roches. Mémé gestured to him to say no more, but this intelligence astounded even Lucien. What he did not know, but Pépé clearly did, was that Mme de Gallifet, the separated wife of General the Marquis de Gallifet, was the Prince of Wales's current mistress. I soon learnt that Lucien had neither preternatural vision nor personal acquaintance with any of these exalted personages. He just spent hours studying the illustrated magazines in which the doings of its members were constantly recorded.

That winter was to be one of the longest and coldest in living memory. Skating in the Bois began on the Saturday after we went back to the Lycée after the Christmas break, with the Princesse de Sagan, Edouard de Rothschild and Lord Dufferin leading Society on to the ice. It continued, with little interruption, it seemed, till the end of February. For days on end Paris looked like a stage set for St Petersburg in winter: in the Luxembourg, the Mediterranean divinities of the Fontaine Médicis, Polyphemus and Leda, Acis and Galatea, Pan and Diana, seemed, with their fantastic excrescences of icicles and snow, to have emerged from some Nordic saga. Influenza, too, hit London and Paris with unusual ferocity, sparing few and killing many elderly and weak. We all succumbed in turn. Pépé and Mémé fell ill in rapid succession, then, as I was recovering, Matthew took to his bed.

I was off school for two weeks. It was the first time since early childhood that I had had an illness involving fever and therefore a change in consciousness. It is not an enjoyable experience, especially when your head and every bone in your body ache, but, for him who seeks experience rather than comfort, for the mental traveller rather than the mental stay-at-home, there are gains to be had. These come in that no-man's-land into which one emerges as the fever subsides and normal consciousness slowly returns. During the last few days of my convalescence, the weather suddenly became springlike. I strolled round the Luxembourg in the afternoon, deserting the comfort of a coal-fire for the amorous touch of fresh, but mild air on my pampered cheek. It is a special moment, that first venture out of doors after a prolonged illness, feeling the strength slowly return to weakened, unpractised limbs. I wrote some poems in which I tried to recapture in a sort of sensuous abstraction the journey that I had returned from: they would no doubt have been incoherent to anybody else but, for a time, they had a more powerful effect on me than any other poetry.

The evening of the day that I went back to the Lycée I insisted on going with Pépé and Mémé – Matthew was now in the prostrate state that I had been a week before – to the latest Oeuvre production. The spectacle of Scandinavians chanting oracular statements about moral problems that had never occurred to the average Frenchman still possessed a certain exoticism, but by now it was a familiar exoticism. Lugné-Poe had not deserted Ibsen (later that year he was to give us *Little Eyolf* and *Brand*), but his search for the arcane was taking him further afield. The latest Oeuvre offering, *Le Chariot de terre cuite* (The Terracotta Chariot), came from India and had been written (in Sanskrit) some three thousand years before. As we entered the Nouveau-Théâtre, I caught sight of Lucien

Daudet, whom I had not seen since before Christmas. At the interval I went over to him and he introduced his companion, Albert Flament, 'a painter', he said, with a gravity that soon subsided in a giggle, 'of immense talent'.

Lucien had been my best and closest friend. He was only fifteen months older than I, but at that moment I felt and must have seemed what I was, a schoolboy who was not yet fifteen. Lucien, now sixteen, but looking at least two years older, and behaving like a young man in his twenties, seemed suddenly to have risen into a higher, unattainable sphere. He was friendliness itself, but a certain formality had crept into his manner. It was plain that the intimacy that had been ours had been superseded by another, more mature intimacy between him and Albert Flament.

'Let's meet up afterwards,' he said. 'We'll go back-stage. Albert knows all the cast.' It was my first introduction to jealousy: it was no more bearable for being beyond the reach of my understanding. I found it hard to concentrate on the second half of the play, so much so that I almost missed what must have been the first and probably sole instance of male nudity on the Parisian stage. For most of the evening the huge crowd of 'Indian' walk-ons had sported a motley collection of Algerian bedspreads, Japanese dresses, Turkish kelims, Spanish skirts, Liberty scarves, bits of stuff picked up at the flea market. For reasons that I cannot recall, these twenty or so 'Indians' suddenly abandoned their heteroclite apparel for nothing more than a uniformly dusky make-up. Afterwards, backstage, we stumbled across several *Hindous* in a huge bathtub busy washing themselves back to their original identity as Parisian art students. Some of them were at the Académie Jullian, where Lucien's painter friend was a student. Lucien told me more of his 'grown-up' plans. He would be leaving school in June. In October, he too would be going to the

Académie Jullian. Albert had his own studio, in the rue du Cherche-Midi. I must go round one Thursday afternoon and see his work. There were one or two Americans who also had studios in the same building: I could talk to them in English. In the event, neither Albert Flament nor Lucien pursued careers as painters: both became writers.

By this time, Léon Daudet's marriage was at an end. He had moved back into his parents' apartment in the rue de Bellechasse and was having an affair with Lucienne Bréval, a rising star of the Paris Opéra. To everyone's surprise, Georges Hugo, Jeanne's brother, sided with his best friend, against his sister. Indeed the trio of Léon, Lucien and Georges Hugo was becoming ever more inseparable. Léon suddenly took it into his head to go off to Amsterdam and from there into Sweden. Of course, he had no wish to go alone – Léon was lost without an audience – and Georges and Lucien would accompany him. After spending a few days in Holland, the trio travelled on to Copenhagen and Elsinore. They then forged northwards. Léon was in ecstasy at the sight of the snow-covered land-scapes of northern Europe. What we did not know at the time was that Léon was gathering material for a historical novel, which appeared in due course as *Le Voyage de Shakespeare*. An admirable example of the genre, full of fascinating, well-researched detail, it was nonetheless based on a fallacious premise: that if Shakespeare sets a play in Denmark (or Venice, Verona or, for that matter, Scotland), he must, in the manner of a nineteenth-century novelist, have visited the place. The novel describes the journey of the twenty-year-old Shakespeare and two companions through the Spanish-occupied Netherlands, to Copenhagen and Elsinore. In the novel Léon did not stop short of attacking the Spanish occupiers and their clergy: he went on to heap abuse on the pope himself. As a result, *Le Voyage de Shakespeare* was placed on the Index: an ironical fate for an author who, within a few years, was to become an ardent Catholic (and still more ardent royalist).

I next saw Lucien at the first of Colonne's concerts of the autumn Season. The programme included Beethoven's First Symphony (the series was to present all nine symphonies), Sarasate playing Lalo's *Symphonie espagnole* and Saint-Saëns playing his own brilliant Piano Concerto in C minor. But that concert was remembered by most people as the one in which, for the first time, they heard a work by a former student of Massenet, Claude Debussy. *L'Après-midi d'un faune* was not the first work by the young composer to be played in public, but it was the first to gain public recognition. That afternoon, in an overheated Théâtre du Châtelet, the strange harmonies, the elusive development, the flagrantly erotic charge of Debussy's musical interpretation of Mallarmé's poem caused a sensation among the Sunday afternoon Parisian public. There were those who found it incomprehensible, or indecent. But, in the noisy reception that Debussy received at the end of the piece, approval won the day. For me, *L'Après-midi d'un faune* seemed like the swan-song of that long, hot summer, but it also unnerved me, haunted me. I longed to hear it again, but it was to be months before I heard it or anything else by Debussy.

I saw Lucien during the interval: he was in the company not only of Albert Flament, but also of a sickly-looking young man with jet-black hair, a drooping moustache and enormous dark eyes. His politeness was excessive to the point of unction, especially towards Mémé. The new friend was, Lucien had informed us, 'Monsieur Marcel Proust, son of Professor Proust.' Pépé and Mémé knew who Professor Proust was: he occupied the Chair of Hygiene at the Faculty of Medicine, best known for his work on cholera. Marcel Proust had not yet published anything, though *Les Plaisirs et les Jours* was to appear the following summer. Lucien had first seen him at one of his parents' Thursday evenings, when he had been brought along by a young Venezuelan-born musician, Reynaldo Hahn, already a firm favourite of Mme Daudet's. I took an instant dislike to Marcel Proust, but so did most people, with the exception of certain elderly ladies and effeminate young men. I, too, succumbed to his persistent flattery, his constant solicitude, his requests for my 'expert opinion' (on one or two points in his reading of Ruskin). But, once won over, I came to see a very different Marcel Proust. Behind the polite flourishes and syntactical convolutions that mark his conversation as much as his writings lies an individual of great kindness. His sallies are directed only at those capable of defending themselves. To social inferiors he consistently breaks the prevailing code. Albert Flament told me of the time when they went together to visit an elderly couple who had once been servants in the Proust household and who were now living, at Professor Proust's expense, in a retirement home in the suburb of Vaugirard. Flament told me how Proust's face lit up at the sight of his old friends. He chatted to them about members of the family, questioned them about their health, begged them to tell him if there was anything they would like him to bring next time. One could imagine how important Monsieur Marcel's visits were to those two old people. Similarly, Lucien told me how he once asked the Daudets' old maid-servant to accompany him to the theatre and how he refused to allow their old Italian valet to carry his suitcase, always shook hands with him and talked to him of Dante.

As my friendship with Lucien Daudet became less intense, less constantly nurtured, my relationships with one or two of my school friends became less 'trivial'. In the *'classe de seconde classique'*, I had become very friendly with two boys in particular, Jean Boutroux and Pierre Champion. Jean's father, Emile Boutroux, was a professor of philosophy at the Sorbonne. His work represented the 'spiritualist' reaction against the dominant materialist, scientific outlook of French academic philosophy. Even more untypically in that milieu, he was a practising and believing Catholic and had brought his children up to be so. It was with Jean Boutroux that I attended the Holy Week services at Saint-Gervais and sometimes, while strolling through the streets of the *quartier*, browsing in bookshops, discussing, in the way of intelligent *lycéens*, the most abstruse philosophical problems, we might pop into Saint-Sulpice and sit close together, in some deserted corner of the cavernous church, as the Sulpician fathers chanted their way through one of their monastic hours. He was a quiet, withdrawn boy, who must have been in the grip of an ever-present conflict between religious aspirations and the assaults of oncoming sexuality. I suffered no such conflict: I had had no contact with Christianity as a strict moral code that concerned itself with sexuality. Our friendship did not long survive our school-days. I looked him up once or twice when in Paris during university vacations, but gradually we lost touch with one another. He became, like his father, a *prof' de philo'*.

I was in many ways even closer to Pierre Champion, with whom I have kept up contact over the years. His father ran a bookshop and publishing business on the quai Voltaire, actually inside the Thibault bookshop founded by Anatole France's father. ('France' was the writer's *nom-de-guerre*, his real surname being Thibault.) With Pierre Champion, the talk was not of religion, but almost exclusively of literature. After the Lycée he went on to study at the Ecole de Chartes, that seedbed of archivists and palaeographers. It was with Pierre that, on Saturday 11 January 1896, I joined the enormous crowd that followed Paul Verlaine's coffin across Paris.

For the previous few months the man that many regarded as France's greatest living poet had been living in sordid rooms in the rue Descartes, just behind our Lycée, with an ex-prostitute who now earned a meagre living sewing. It was the last of many temporary lodgings in which the sick, prematurely aged poet – he was actually only fifty-one when he died – lived out the last years of his life. Finally, on doctors' orders, he had given up his addiction to absinthe. But it was too late: cirrhosis of the liver was already well advanced.

Paul Verlaine reversed what has become a cliché of the artist's life: bohemian youth ending in recognition and respectability. Before the arrival of the seventeen-year-old schoolboy Arthur Rimbaud, Verlaine, ten years his senior, was a respectable married man, his wife expecting a child. From that point on, the lives of the two poets embarked on a course first of mutual, then of self-destruction. Verlaine, the once respectable bourgeois, ended his days as a *clochard*.[1] Four years before, after a 'silence' covering the whole of his officially adult life, Arthur Rimbaud, merchant and ex-poet, arrived back from Africa, only to die at Marseille. He was thirty-seven.

Verlaine may have looked like a man abandoned by all his friends. The truth is that, while he lived, he was beyond their help. But they all visited him as he lay dying and, together with the Minister of Education, organized and paid for the funeral. Our Saturday morning classes were cut short to coincide with the end of the requiem mass taking place across the road at the church of Saint-Etienne du Mont. By the time Pierre and I emerged into the place du Panthéon on that bright winter's morning, a crowd of students, artists, writers, well-wishers and the merely curious had already assembled. The predominantly young Latin Quarter crowd swelled still fur-

1 Down-and-out, tramp.

ther as it made its way to the Cimetière des Batignolles, at the northernmost edge of Paris. On arrival at the cemetery – the walk had taken over two hours – François Coppée took out a piece of paper and read, with perfect Conservatoire elocution, his 'Adieu Verlaine'. He was followed by Mallarmé who, in a quiet, hesitant voice, seemed to express what we all felt. There were more speeches, listened to in absolute silence by a crowd standing around wherever there was room, or sitting on neighbouring tombs. Finally, with the sun going down, those who had stayed until the very end besieged the Batignolles–Odéon omnibuses, grabbed *fiacres* or simply wandered off, as Verlaine would have done, for an early *apéritif* in a nearby café. It had been the greatest 'literary' funeral in Paris since Victor Hugo's some ten years before and, as we sat on our homebound omnibus, Pierre and I were aware that we had taken part in an historical event. I felt proud, as a young Frenchman, of the way France, both government and people, had honoured a poet, even one whom, in the street, one would have taken to be a drunken tramp – and ashamed, as a young Englishman, of how my own country had treated Oscar Wilde.

One afternoon, Lucien turned up at the rue de Vaugirard. A new seriousness seemed to have come over him. He had, he told me, a big secret to tell me. Was he in love? We went out into the Luxembourg. He first saw her, he said, some months ago, one Thursday afternoon, in the rue Cambon. She was pointing to some object in a shop window. Lucien recognized her at once, saluted her discreetly and was rewarded with an equally discreet smile. That summer, Lucien discovered that the lady had a house a mere five minutes' walk from their hotel at Cap Martin, near Menton. By a letter of introduction from the Marquise de Casa-Fuerte, the mother of a school friend of Lucien's, a visit was arranged. A card arrived summoning Lucien to the Villa Cyrnos. Lucien paused, obviously expecting disbelief at his good fortune at being allowed to meet so exalted a personage. I looked blank. The Villa Cyrnos meant nothing to me.

'Well, who is she?' I asked.

'You really don't know?' Lucien gasped in disbelief. 'I thought you, as an Englishman would understand. The Empress Eugénie, of course!' True, her Imperial Majesty lived most of the year in England, but that, I discovered, was not it at all. What Lucien meant was that, as an Englishman, and therefore a monarchist, I would understand his feelings of pride. Apparently, Lucien had long been obsessed by her, reading up all about her in old volumes of the magazine *Illustration*. At the Villa Cyrnos, a conversation with the Empress alone was followed by tea, where they were joined by a few French and English guests. Two days later, he was invited to luncheon on board the Imperial boat, the *Thistle*, which was moored at Menton. As they parted, the Empress said to Lucien: 'You must come and see us this summer in England.' He was to become one of her most assiduous courtiers, spending summer after summer there.

The first letter from 'Farnborough Hill, Farnboro', Hants' arrived in Smith Square in July 1897. Lucien, it seems, had spent one of the most wonderful weeks of his life. Indeed he had got on so well with the Empress and her 'court' that he had been asked to spend two more days than anticipated. In view of the change of plan, he felt sure that it would be too much to ask us if he could spend the following Monday, rather than the promised Saturday, at Smith Square. In fact, Lucien's change of plan did present a problem. On the Saturday, we had intended taking him to the first night of *The Silver Key*, Sydney Grundy's adaptation of Dumas *père's*, *Mademoiselle de Belle-Isle*, at Tree's new Her Majesty's Theatre. It would not have been an unforgettable theatrical experience, but Lucien would have enjoyed being at a London first night, hearing characters from French history speaking impeccable English. It was also a play that he knew and therefore would find easier to follow than many. The problem raised by the change of date was that on the Monday we were going to *Siegfried* at Covent Garden. Our tickets had been booked weeks before and none would be available for what was one of the Season's most sought-after productions. Could a ticket be found? If not, what would we do with Lucien during the long hours of *Siegfried* – I not being at all inclined to forego the experience in order to keep him entertained. This was just the kind of challenge that Grandfather Sheridan excelled in. By Monday evening, between the Opera House offices, the Garrick Club and, for all I knew, the homes of members of the Grand Opera Syndicate, the extra ticket for *Siegfried* was obtained.

During the afternoon and in bed after a post-*Siegfried* supper, Lucien told me of his week at the 'Imperial Court'. When speaking of the Empress, his voice would grow quieter, as if it would be irreverent to say anything about her other than in a whisper: he referred to her simply as *'Sa Majesté'*. Also there were *'les* Eugène Murat', he being a descendant of Joachim Murat, Napoleon's brother-in-law, general and one-time King of Naples. There were outings to Aldershot and to Sandhurst, where the Prince Imperial had trained. When he had nothing better to do, Lucien got on his bicycle and rode far into Hampshire, Surrey and Berkshire, finding nothing but good to say of all he saw. Certainly his stay at the Empress Eugénie's seemed to have wrought a subtle change in him. Far from giving him an irresistible desire to dazzle others with his new connections, it seemed to have given him a quieter, more inward confidence. Lucien's new-found gravity may also have owed something to a sudden realization of the full implications of his father's illness. Alphonse Daudet was suffering from *locomotor ataxia*, a form of creeping paralysis, diagnosed by his friend Charcot some fifteen years before. He had long known that the origin of his illness was *spirochaeta pallida*. It had already carried off many of Daudet's generation of Paris bohemians. His greatest fear had long been that the tertiary stage of syphilis would take the form of a 'softening of the brain', as in the case of Guy de Maupassant and Jules de Goncourt. There were times when, his pain assuaged by morphine, his eyes illuminated with intellectual excitement, that handsome face of his did not show his age. But one had only to see him making the effort to walk across a room to see a man twenty years older. He now found it almost impossible to go out: the three or four flights of stairs were proving a terrible burden. As a result it had been decided that, on Lucien's return, he and his mother would look for a new, preferably first-floor apartment. So they left 'Bellechasse', where they had lived for twelve years, for a new apartment in the rue de l'Université. Alphonse Daudet did not remain there long. The morning after our arrival in London the following Christmas, we learnt in *The Times* of his sudden death, at the age of fifty-seven. He could not have wished for a better end: instantaneously, at the family dinner-table.

1906–07: London, Berlin

It was nine years since that first letter from 'Farnborough Hill, Farnboro', Hants' and Lucien's first visit to Smith Square. I responded at once to this latest one, inviting Lucien to spend a few days with me the following week. We would be rehearsing *Richard II* during the day, but my evenings would be free. Esmond would not be free in the evenings, since *Colonel Newcome* was still running. This suited me perfectly: it was important to me that Lucien should meet Esmond, while leaving Lucien and me time to be alone together.

Lucien arrived on a Sunday afternoon in the middle of November. I had not seen him for three years, the last time being in Paris, before I left for Peking and Petersburg. His life had already taken on the unchanging pattern that it was to pursue for years to come. The autumn was spent at Farnborough Hill. This would be followed by some eight weeks in Paris, at the Hôtel Continental. (Lucien professed to detest Paris, as opposed to London, which he claimed to adore.) He would then join his mother at the Château de la Roche, in the Touraine, the property that Mme Daudet had bought after leaving Paris and selling Champrosay. In the spring, he would join the Empress at Cap Martin, then return to the Touraine for the summer. In other words, his entire year was divided between two elderly women, his mother and an eighty-year-old honorary 'grandmother'. As one might expect, his personality had taken on something of the inflexible regularity of his calendar. It was as if what he feared above all was the unexpected and the unfamiliar, and had arranged his life to avoid them as far as possible. The once charming young man, alternately shy and frivolous, seemed already middle-aged. When he giggled, it was no longer the girlish boy that I remembered, but a slightly embarrassed old spinster. With spectacles on nose and hair rapidly thinning, he was looking much older than his twenty-eight years. Judging by the frequency with which his name cropped up, Lucien's 'best friend' was now Joachim, Comte Clary, who was 'some years older' than he, had 'the most beautiful blue eyes' and was known to his familiars as 'Siegfried'. His father had been a faithful companion of Napoleon III. Like many of the regular courtiers, Clary was unmarried but, I wondered, did anything actually take place between him and Lucien or, indeed, between any of the courtiers? I concluded that it probably did not, that there would be a good deal of malicious gossip, full of hints and *doubles entendres*, and that, if anything took place at all, it was probably with servants. Certainly, Clary, who had lived in Japan and written a book called *L'Ile du Soleil couchant*, had a young Japanese manservant to whom he was devoted.

What, I asked in some wonderment, did they do all day? The day had as pre-ordained a pattern as the year. Luncheon was served precisely at twelve-thirty, dinner at seven-thirty, after which the gentlemen would retire to the billiard room, rejoining the ladies at nine forty-five. Weather permitting, they would go for walks or bicycle rides. They would go into Aldershot or, more rarely, to London for the day, for a little shopping. Clary and Lucien were both good amateur painters, and Clary had a good, if untrained voice. Then there were the amateur dramatics: that year they had put on Mürger's *Le*

Serment de Horace and the last act of Hugo's *Hernani*, in which Clary had played the title role and Lucien Dom Ruy Gomez.

I enquired after Lucien's mother, sister and brother. Edmée, it seemed, had recently married André Germain, the immensely rich son of the founder of the Crédit Lyonnais. I stared at Lucien in disbelief, before we both collapsed into laughter. André Germain was an old friend of Lucien's, a member of the same circle of Society waterflies as Montesquiou and Marcel Proust, and definitely shared their sexual tastes. Mention of Léon brought on a stream of commentary, more in sorrow than in anger. Léon had long since abandoned his youthful radicalism, together with his first wife, Victor Hugo's grand-daughter. Three years ago, he had remarried: his new wife, his cousin Marthe Allard, was of an extremely conservative disposition. Lucien had no time for the new Radical government in France which, not content with putting the final touches to the Dreyfus affair, was now bent on destroying Church and Army, but Léon had now gone to the opposite extreme and taken up with those dreadful Royalists. Not content with coming to London to meet the Duc d'Orléans (the chief Pretender to the French throne), he had thrown in his lot with Maurras, Drumont and the violently anti-semitic Action Française. And if there was one thing Sa Majesté could not abide it was any anti-semitic talk.

Talk of relations led to talk of friends, of Albert Flament . . . and of Marcel Proust. With horror in his eyes, trying, but failing, to appreciate the immensity of what the loss of his own mother would mean to him, he told me of the death of Mme Proust the previous year. The apartment in the rue de Courcelles had now been vacated and, prior to moving in to his apartment in the boulevard Haussmann, Marcel was living in Versailles, at the Hôtel des Réservoirs. A few months before, he had finally published his translation of

Ruskin's *Sesame and Lilies*. He had thought of taking up the novel that he had been writing before that, but nothing had come of it: he could now see that it was no more than a collection of brilliant fragments. In Lucien's view, Proust lacked the assiduity, the single-mindedness, the ruthless self-control, the unifying idea even, to produce a single work of fiction of respectable length. How different from Léon, who, despite all his multifarious activities, had managed to produce seven novels in the past ten years! Even I, Lucien added, have embarked on a novel! It was to be called, he said, giving me a lugubrious stare, *Le Chemin mort*.

One of the two nights available for theatre-going would have to be spent in His Majesty's, the same theatre that Lucien should have gone to on that first visit, nine years before. It was a pity that *Richard II* was not yet playing: it was a splendid production, provided Tree with one of his best roles, and had the added advantage of displaying the talents of both Esmond and me. On the other hand, I felt sure that Lucien would enjoy *Colonel Newcome*. For the other night, I thought the revival of *Man and Superman* would be good for his education. Lucien was duly impressed by both evenings and, over supper afterwards, showed signs that he was moving away from his own preoccupations sufficiently to consider mine, if only from some considerable distance. Lucien left for Paris, leaving me happy to be brought up to date about various matters of common interest, but feeling that there was little point in his remaining part of my life: I had as little understanding of him as he had of me.

One morning, the week after *Richard II* had opened, I found a letter from Lytton Strachey, whom I had not seen for almost a year. Had I heard that Thoby Stephen had died on 20 November? An infrequent reader of *The Times* 'Births, Marriages and Deaths' column, I had not. Lytton had just got back from seeing Thoby's sisters at Gordon Square.

Perhaps we could meet and he would tell me all he knew. Over lunch in the West End, I learnt that Thoby and Adrian had set out for Greece in August, travelling from Trieste, through Montenegro and Albania, on horseback. They had then met up at Olympia with Virginia, Vanessa and Violet Dickinson, who had travelled there by boat and train. By the end of September, they were all ill. Thoby decided to return to London. The others went on to Constantinople, but were back in London a few days later, to find Thoby in bed with a temperature. Vanessa and Violet also took to their beds. The doctors decided that Thoby had malaria. Later, typhoid fever was diagnosed, as it also was for Violet. The reaction of everybody was the same: could 'The Goth' die? He had always seemed stronger, healthier, more normal than any of us, the least susceptible to such Jacobean or nineteenth-century notions as illness and death.

After a decent interval, conversation shifted to other matters. Lytton's *inamorato* of a year ago, Duncan Grant, was now back from Paris and studying at the Slade. He, in turn, was now unrequitedly in love – with Hobhouse, a Natural Scientific Trinitarian with whom both Strachey and Keynes had been besotted. I told him about Esmond and His Majesty's which, he agreed, were sufficient explanation of my failure to stay in touch with any of our Cambridge friends.

Richard II was not a new production, but it was the first time I had seen it. First put on in 1903, it was as spectacular as any of Tree's productions, a series of magnificent stage pictures: the scene of the tournament lists on Gosford Green, Coventry, complete with colourful banners, splendid armour and several live horses, which, though well trained, had to accustom themselves to the strange, noisy world of the stage; the scene before Flint Castle, on the Welsh coast; a London street, with the Tower of London in the distance; Westminster

Hall. I was in all these – and more – for I was by turns
courtier and soldier in a play that seemed to take place for the
most part at court or on field of battle. I was also called on to
make up the numbers of the London crowd in two scenes not
to be found in the published versions of the play. Taking the
Duke of York's description of the deposed Richard entering
London on a white horse behind the triumphant Bolingbroke,
Tree created a masterpiece of stage-management. The vast
stage was filled with a seething mass of some three score
'supers', cheering on the new king and hurling 'dust and rubbish on King Richard's head'. The second such interpolation
was the coronation of Bolingbroke as Henry IV, also performed in dumb-show, save for music and the cheering
crowd, which replaced Shakespeare's own rather lack-lustre
ending.

Richard II was, by general consent, one of Tree's finest
performances. This surprised many and it surprised me. He
was not particularly noted for perfection of elocution, yet this
role, so full of rich, mellifluous speeches, seemed to call for it.
Again, Tree was a 'manly' actor, one who excelled in portraying the comically quirky. His king was 'noble' and sensitive to
the point of effeminacy; not so much as a smile was to be
raised by any of his lines. Yet, such is the true actor's art, that
he was able, beginning with mimicry, but not ending there, to
summon up unsuspected qualities within himself, to convince
himself and so convince others that he was Richard.

Esmond played Sir Henry Greene, one of Richard's vil-
lainous 'creatures'. As usual, we went over his thirty-odd
lines together, but most of them were of the most perfunctory. When he was not saying things like 'The Lord
Northumberland, his son young Henry Percy, The lords of
Ross, Beaumont, and Willoughby, With all their friends,
are fled to him', he was spouting clichés like 'My comfort is,

that Heaven will take our souls, And plague injustice with the pains of hell' or 'Alas, poor duke! the task he undertakes Is numbering sands, and drinking oceans dry', though the last phrase was one that I would quote at him from time to time.

Tree had been planning his *Antony and Cleopatra* for the best part of a year. For weeks he had been working with his principal actors, not to mention his scenery makers and costumiers. None of Tree's productions had had so much time – or money – lavished on them. Full rehearsals began in the second week of the run of *Richard II*. Two weeks later, the theatre was shut down (as far as the public was concerned) and we embarked on a further two or three weeks of rehearsals. We began at ten o'clock in the morning and continued for most of the day, sometimes late into the evening. For those with large parts, above all for Tree himself, it must have been an exhausting time. For us menials, it meant a great deal of sitting around, though we never knew when the summons might come. There were far more of us than usual. It was not only the Theatre that was now closed: Mr Tree's Academy was, too, its students turned into Cleopatra's attendants, citizens of Alexandria or Roman soldiers.

The choice of play had little to do with Tree's own acting ambitions: Antony is *un rôle ingrat*; a long, tiring, unrewarding part. Shakespeare's other great couples – Romeo and Juliet, Petruchio and Katharina, Beatrice and Benedick, Othello and Desdemona, Macbeth and his fiend-like queen – are well balanced in terms of what they offer the two players. This play is Cleopatra's. Often the actor playing Antony is himself blamed for the role's shortcomings. After his *Julius Caesar*, Tree's mind may have toyed with the scenic possibilities of Rome and Alexandria, but it was surely not until he had seen Constance Collier in *Nero* that he realized that, with coaching, he had a

Cleopatra. The coaching began while *Nero* was still playing, continued on tour and was taken up whenever Tree found time between acting, rehearsing other things and the sundry cares of theatrical management. Tree knew that Constance Collier looked the part: she was a young woman of great beauty, of a Southern type, with large, very dark, widely spaced eyes, a large sensuous mouth, a mass of jet-black hair. His problem would be getting her to sound the part. Her experience of 'serious' acting was limited; what she did know she had taught herself. But she was a born, instinctive actress and learnt quickly. Tree was also more than half in love with her, as were many other men. When I first turned up for rehearsals with the other 'supers', I was astonished by how word-perfect she was already and how little Tree had to guide her: the hours of coaching had paid off. She was Tree's latest discovery, the 'star of the show', but she never behaved as if she were. She was a strange combination of shyness and exuberance: once she had overcome her natural reserve, she could give full vent to her zest for life. For her, life was the theatre, and the theatre was not the glamorous world that was now hers, but the harsh world that she had known all her life, that of a besieged community whose members had to sustain one another against all the adversities that beset them. As the run continued and routine brought its own relaxation, she told us something of her life.

Connie, as we all called her, got her dark, exotic looks from her mother: her maternal grandmother was a Portuguese dancer. Connie's mother, too, became a dancer, touring the provinces for a pittance. Her father was an actor, though Connie and her mother did not see much of him – he was usually touring in another company. Later, a religious crisis led him to abandon the theatre, which he now saw as a den of iniquity. As a small child Connie was taken everywhere by her mother; there were no other children of the marriage. She

even spent her evenings in the theatre, wrapped in a blanket
and left in the dressing-room. Sunday was travelling day: they
had to be up at four or five in the morning to catch the first
train. Each week brought a new town, new dreary lodgings
and, later, a new school. When a little girl, Connie's mother
had played child parts in Phelps's company at Sadler's Wells –
one of them had been Fleance, Macduff's son, in *Macbeth*.
Not to be outdone by her mother's tales of early triumphs on
the London stage, Connie was determined to win her own
audiences. At the age of eleven, she got hold of an old
Shakespeare and began to learn whole scenes by heart. While
her mother was in some provincial theatre playing in the
Saturday matinée, Connie would find a piece of ground near
the theatre and start declaiming there and then. Before long,
she would have assembled a motley audience around her.

When in London, they stayed in Kennington. If Connie's
mother was out of work, the two of them would set out to see
the agents in the West End. Her mother was often tired and
dispirited but, for Connie, it was a great adventure – an adventure that began as soon as they crossed Waterloo Bridge. The
Strand was the beginning of fairy land. Saddened by her
mother's failure to get work, she tried to get work herself. She
was now barely fourteen, but looked a few years older. Her
first London engagement was in the chorus of a musical
comedy at the Criterion. The job lasted for only six weeks, but
it was a beginning. Connie told us how, after the show, she
would wait for the omnibus in Piccadilly Circus to take her
back to Kennington and would be solicited by men assuming
she was a prostitute and abused by women who imagined that
she was encroaching on their territory. Weeks later, she was
about to embark on her round of agents' offices when, passing
the Gaiety, she entered the stage-door on impulse. A man who
happened to be passing asked what she wanted. She said that

she had come to see Mr Edwardes and wanted an engagement in the company. The man turned out to be George Edwardes himself, the proprietor. He took her into his office, gave her a cup of tea and listened to her plea: he offered her a job, beginning in a few weeks' time, providing he could see her mother and get her permission. And so Constance Collier became one of the legendary Gaiety Girls.

At sixteen, Connie was engaged to a millionaire admirer thirty-five years her senior. He was a kindly man and lavished presents on her, but marriage would have meant that she would have to give up her career in the theatre. She broke off her engagement. At nineteen, she joined Charles Hawtrey's company at the Comedy, then George Alexander's at the St James's, then Cyril Maude's at the Haymarket, where I first saw her, as Lady Sneerwell in *The School for Scandal*. The following year, she joined Tree's company in Stephen Phillips's *Ulysses*. While playing Pallas Athene she met a young man of her own age, Julian L'Estrange, who was playing Mercury. Three years later, after his return from the United States, they married, though, in the meantime, she had been engaged again, this time to Mr Tree's half-brother, Max Beerbohm.

I had first seen Basil Gill as a delicious Ferdinand in *The Tempest*. As Octavius, he was almost as delicious, *en plus masculin*, his legs bare between boot and military skirt, hoisted well above the knees, his gleaming scallop-shell helmet adding a further foot to his height. Off-stage, without make-up, without the wig of curls to conceal his already receding hair and with his thick spectacles (he was very short-sighted), he looked his twenty-nine years, less dashing, more studious, but even more lovable. He had spent his early childhood in Cambridge, where his father was a clergyman. The family then moved to London and Basil attended St Paul's choir school. He was twenty-two when he made his London *début* at the Lyceum, not under Irving, but with Wilson Barrett, before moving up the road to Drury Lane and *Ben Hur*. The show ran for four months, then went on tour to Australia and the United States for the best part of a year. While on tour, he married a junior member of the cast, Margery Cavania. On their return to London, he joined Tree, as Aumerle in *Richard II*, and had been with him ever since.

One much-loved member of the company – and one of the most versatile – was Lyn Harding, known to everyone as David. This tall, well-built Welshman of about forty, with a face that could only be described as ordinary, was quiet, reserved in manner, but had a genial smile and a kind word for everyone. After an apprenticeship travelling the country in stock companies, he joined a tour of *The School for Scandal* that took him to India, Burma, China and Japan. He did not make his first West End appearance until 1903; then, a few months later, he joined Tree. I had first seen him as a superbly spoken Prospero and, in *Antony and Cleopatra*, his rendering of Enobarbus's celebrated speech in praise of the 'enchanting queen' was an elocution lesson to all. He was also a superb comic actor: his Ague-Cheek was unmatchable. He was one of those 'neutral' actors who seem unrecognizable whatever part he plays; all his characterizations were minutely detailed, subtle, understated, the result of observation and long-practised invention. As a young man, Lyn Harding had been a policeman in Cardiff, before going on the stage. But he preferred the country to the town and had a farm that he loved as much as the theatre. He had a great love of dogs: the bull-terrier that I had seen him with in *Oliver Twist* was his own pet. The two had only known each other for a year, but were already devoted to one another. The dog had been found at very short notice to replace another. Connie told me the story of the two bull-terriers. The first had been a great favourite

with the company. He was also, in his way, as good an actor as
his master. In *Oliver Twist*, when Bill Sikes shouted at him, he
crouched down, his tail between his legs and slunk off, looking
very disconsolate. Once off-stage, he would wag his tail furiously, delighted at his act. When the scene in which he
appeared was over, he would rush out of the stage-door, cross
the road to the 'pub', push open the swing-door, jump on a
stool and partake of the beer and biscuit that awaited him.
When they were both off-stage, he followed his master wherever he went: it was his undoing. One day, they were out
walking, when David paused at the kerb, as if to cross the
road. The dog began to cross then, realizing that his master
had not followed him, turned tail and rushed back. He was
run over by a motor-car and killed. His successor soon won his
master's heart and he his, but he was less good an actor. When
he was shouted at on stage, he refused to believe that his
master was angry with him and came bounding up, wagging
his tail. He was a great success with the audiences, however, if
not for the right reasons.

But, naturally, it was with the younger members of the
company that I spent most of my time. Of Esmond's fellow
students from the Academy, only Sidney Yates Southgate
remained: Reggie Owen had gone off to play larger parts with
Benson. But, from the next intake from the Academy, there
were three who had joined the company earlier in the year.
Sidney and Esmond had discovered that two of them – Ted
Ouston and Cyril Sworder – were 'queer'. They were pretty
young things, hardly turned twenty. Neither had Esmond's
sultry physical magnetism but, I had to admit, they were more
amusing company: off-stage, they were more obviously feminine, quicker witted. I flirted with both and they with me,
but we all knew that I was spoken for. If Esmond was present,
he never seemed to react: his reaction to anything seldom went

beyond a wan smile. Robert Atkins, the other Academician, was not, it had been decided, a member of the fraternity. He was clearly a much better actor than any of his contemporaries in the company. He specialized in playing older men – the Bishop of Carlisle in *Richard II*, the Sea Captain in *Twelfth Night* – a considerable asset in so young a company.

Though Esmond never got round to formulating his feelings in sentences, I knew that he felt that he was being overtaken by some of the other Academicians. His biggest part so far had been Rosencrantz; since then he seemed to have declined in favour. His Greene, in *Richard II*, had been a shorter, less interesting part; in *Winter's Tale*, he had even been expected to walk on; and, now, apart from the second messenger's two lines, he was walking on again. It rankled with him that someone like Alfred Goddard should be given the part of Agrippa on his first appearance at the theatre. Of course, in our tight little circle, the name of the character, with its feminine-sounding ending, was too good to miss. Poor Alfred, who must have felt for much of his life that his name, with its association of greatness, stolidity and beardedness, was singularly inappropriate, was now nicknamed 'Grip 'im'. There was another inaptly named Alfred, the rest of whose name, Corney Grain, earned him the pet-name 'Seedy'.

As the Day of Judgement, 27 December, approached, excitement and anxiety mounted. Despite the months of preparation, the unusually long rehearsal period, time seemed to be running out as Tree strove to protect his vision of perfection against the ravages of human and material shortcomings. We went in batches to the costumiers, B. J. Simmons, to be fitted for our costumes and to Willie Clarkson, in Wardour Street, for our wigs. There was not one dress-rehearsal, but a week of them: what the audience saw on the stage was so important to Tree that he dared not leave the final

417

effect to chance. They might go on until dawn, everybody breaking off for supper around midnight, the actors proper eating up in the Dome with Tree, the 'supers' in our under-stage dressing space. More and more, we were becoming like the Chief himself, residents of the Theatre. We got what sleep we could, dotted over stalls and dress circle or in some corner back-stage, until prompted into action. Scene hands and lime-light men were nodding off at their posts. The only person to keep awake the whole time was Tree himself: throughout the night, his voice could be heard, giving directions, when he was not speaking Antony's lines. The less fortunate spent the night in the Theatre; Esmond and I would go out into the Hay-market at the earliest opportunity and hail a cab. As often as not, we had only to scent the morning air for our bodies to be momentarily tricked into thinking that, for them, too, a new day had dawned, as it had for the sun and most of London's population. But, having eaten what Mrs Wrigglesworth had left us, assisted by a bottle of wine, we would retire to bed, I with a brandy, Esmond with a glass and the whisky bottle. As soon as we were in a horizontal position we fell asleep, Esmond, as always, preceding me. By two o'clock we were back in the Theatre – morning rehearsals had now been abandoned. The announcement that there would be no rehearsals on Christmas Day was met with feigned incredulity and delight. We would, however, be expected to turn up for the final dress-rehearsal at two o'clock on Boxing Day!

The first night audience was as 'dazzling' as could be: half the government and half the House of Lords, with wives, seemed to be there. Yet they were as 'dazzled' by what they saw on the stage as the humblest occupant of pit or gallery. By cutting some of the Roman and battle scenes, Tree had shifted the stress of the play still more on to Egypt, the Eastern arch of the rangèd Empire, where Antony's pleasure lies. The

house lights were dimmed to the accompaniment of Coleridge
Taylor's mysterious music; a vision of the Sphinx appeared on
a front curtain, only to dissolve into gauze as the lights went
up on the stage; the evening ended with the reverse procedure.
There were a couple of splendid 'tableaux', based on descrip-
tions in the play, that showed the art of Messrs Harker and
Emden at its most spectacular. One such description is
Enobarbus's account of Cleopatra's arrival on the quayside in
Alexandria:

> The barge she sat in, like a burnish'd throne
> Burn'd on the water: the poop was beaten gold;
> Purple the sails, and so perfumèd that
> The winds were love-sick with them; th'oars were
> silver . . .
>
> > For her own person,
> It beggar'd all description: she did lie
> In her pavilion, cloth-of-gold, of tissue,
> O'er-picturing that Venus where we see
> The fancy outwork Nature: on each side her
> Stood pretty dimpled boys, like smiling Cupids,
> With diverse-colour'd fans . . .

Not content with allowing Lyn Harding to evoke the scene,
Tree could not resist the challenge of portraying it in minut-
est detail, to the accompaniment of stirring music and a
cheering crowd. At a dangerously late stage it was decided to
cut into the stage itself to facilitate the smooth running of the
barge. The 'scene' took fully five minutes to unfold. The other
tableau was based on Octavius's lines:

> I' the market-place, on a tribunal silver'd
> Cleopatra and himself in chairs of gold

Were publicly enthroned; at their feet sat
Caesarion, whom they call my father's son,
And all th' unlawful issue that their lust
Since then hath made between them.

This scene had the 'tribunal', on a diagonal upstage right, reached by a dozen carpeted steps; the golden throne was backed by a row of stout silvered columns; the backdrop depicted a view of Alexandria, with palm trees and large buildings in the foreground, the sea in the distance and the sky. Antony and his attendants were awaiting the arrival of the Egyptian queen. She entered, as Caesar puts it, 'in the habiliments of the goddess Isis', wearing a silver costume and crown, carrying a golden sceptre and the symbol of the sacred golden calf, followed by the screaming populace. To Connie's horror, Tree had also insisted on following Octavius's description to the letter and having her followed by 'all th' unlawful issue', which Tree had discovered amounted to no fewer than five children. Not only would the attention of the audience be distracted by the children, but the whole notion of Cleopatra as a passionate sensualist would be undermined. She pleaded, but to no avail: Tree would not sacrifice historical accuracy. Connie confessed that she would willingly have murdered the whole angelic brood!

The press was lavish in its praise. It was generally acknowledged that Antony was not one of Tree's better roles, but most thought that he had acquitted himself in manly fashion. One reviewer wondered how, managing a theatre and supervising such a production, he could be expected to act at all. Connie was universally praised for looking like everyone's idea of Cleopatra, though some felt that she sounded too modern, too much the Society hostess, too little the antique queen.

Once, soon after the New Year, conversation drifted on to

the subject of pantomimes and our childhood memories of them. Connie's were different from everyone else's. For years, every Christmas, in one town or another, her mother had played Dandini in *Cinderella*. I asked her about those provincial pantomimes and told her of my own childhood visits to Drury Lane. It turned out that Connie had seen many of them, too, not from one of the boxes, or even from the gods, but from the wings, privy to the workings of the machinery behind the magic, for one of her aunts had been wardrobe-mistress at Drury Lane. I wondered if they could ever be the same again now that Herbert Campbell and Dan Leno had both gone. Their deaths had occurred within weeks of one another, in 1904.

At the mention of Dan Leno, Connie looked as if she had seen a ghost. 'When did you last see him?' she asked.

I thought for a moment: it must have been the Christmas before Grandfather Sheridan died. 'Christmas 1900, *Beauty and the Beast*? He was Queen something.'

'Well . . . it would be two years later, in the New Year. I'd just joined Mr Tree in *The Eternal City*. We'd moved to a garret in Seven Dials, among all the tarts and gin palaces. One night, my mother and I got back very late. We'd been out to supper. It must have been about one in the morning. We went into the sitting-room and there, in the dark, lit only by the light from the window, was Dan Leno, sitting on the sofa! Next day, the maid told us how he had arrived at half past eleven and been waiting all that time. I couldn't believe my eyes! I had never met him and he was one of my idols. He took my hand and I could see that he was trembling with excitement. And those eyes! The eyes of a wounded animal . . . or a great tragedian! They looked as though they'd fill with tears at any moment. He started to tell me the story of his life . . . how he was the son of a Scottish marquis and a housemaid. How,

at nine years old, he had tramped up to London with his
mother, in bitter winter weather. Of course, we now know
that he was called George Galvin and was born in London, in
Walthamstow, and his parents were travelling entertainers.
Then he told me of his life of grinding poverty in London
until he began to be a success in the halls. All this time he was
holding my hand in an iron grip, almost hurting me. He had
seen me in *Ben Hur* and *Ulysses* and *The Eternal City* time
after time, sitting in the gallery, with his collar turned up, so
that no one would recognize him. He then talked about Henry
Irving. He said he had saved up enough money to fulfil his
life's ambition – he wanted me to sign a contract to play in
Shakespeare with him for five years. I could tell he was ill . . .
I said he must go and see Mr Tree in the morning and discuss
the matter with him. When we got downstairs, there was an
old coachman waiting for him. He went off quite happily.
Next morning, he was at the theatre when I arrived, the centre
of attention, everyone smiling and laughing. He had been
busy making up contracts with members of the company,
writing them out on bits of paper and signing them. I got a
message to Mr Tree that Dan Leno was here and that I
thought that he was very ill. After what seemed like eternity,
he was summoned to join Mr Tree in the stalls. For the next
half-hour, those two geniuses, the two greatest representatives
of music hall and serious theatre, sat there, talking, Mr Leno
explaining his plans, Mr Tree nodding excitedly. Presently
three men appeared – before summoning him, Mr Tree had
sent for Mr Leno's manager. Mr Leno shook hands with Mr
Tree and went off quietly. Afterwards Mr Tree said to me: "If
this is madness, what's the use of being sane? If he did play
Richard III, it would be the greatest performance we'd ever
seen." That, I thought was the end of it but, when I got home
that afternoon, there he was, waiting for me. He was holding

a jewel-case. He told me that Mr Tree had agreed to his terms.
All that was left was for me to sign the contract and he would
inform the papers. I didn't know what to do – I didn't know
that Mr Tree had warned the papers not to publish anything
about my future appearances. I had to tell him that I couldn't
accept his proposition. I have never seen such a picture of disappointment. "You don't believe I can play Shakespeare, do
you?" I tried to explain that this wasn't the reason, but it was
no good. He begged me to accept the jewels all the same. I said
I couldn't possibly do so. He left with tears pouring down his
face. He gave the diamonds to a barmaid on the way home.
She refused to return them when they tried to convince her
that he was not responsible for his actions. I should have kept
them and given them to his family. Two days later, he was
taken to a nursing-home. He came out and did one more panto
at Drury Lane and made a few more appearances in the music
hall. I saw one of them. The light had gone out of him. The
audience didn't laugh any more. He just looked bewildered.
He died a few weeks later. He wasn't even fifty.'

Once the run of *Antony and Cleopatra* got under way, we
settled into a routine. It would be a long run, brought to an
end only when the Chief got bored, began to forget his lines
and was thinking of another play. For weeks on end, with
luck, there would be no rehearsals. We could get up when we
liked and actually have some time to ourselves. Except on
Wednesdays and Saturdays, the matinée days, we had the
whole day free.

Meanwhile, Esmond showed little interest in anything. He
hardly ever read, even the newspaper. We still made love,
most days, though no longer every day, and it was beginning to
lose some of the charm, to become a release, rather than a
pleasure in itself. When I fucked him, I did so more aggres-
sively. Not that he seemed to mind; he seemed to prefer it, if

his groans of pleasure, delivered with ever greater conviction, were to be believed. Some days, after our late breakfast, he announced that he had some things to do, he thought he would call on X or Y. He might be back in the afternoon; otherwise, he would see me at the Theatre. I knew that he was bored and did not relish spending the rest of the day sitting around the house. I have never been bored in my life and find it difficult to understand boredom in others. For me, there was nothing pleasanter than sitting in front of the fire, reading, pursuing my thoughts, bringing my diary up to date, jotting things down in my notebook. Indeed I felt altogether more relaxed doing this when Esmond was not there, for I sensed his boredom. This boredom, I came to realize, never left him. He was not bored because he had nothing interesting to do. He was bored because nothing interested him. I tried to interest him in what interested me, but he would simply say something like: 'Oh, I'm not a clever clogs like you!' Either he did not like to risk engaging in such a conversation, or quite simply could not. I tried taking him to the National Gallery, the South Kensington Museum, the Tate Gallery, but to little avail. If his interest was aroused, it was no more than a momentary flickering, for no apparent reason. Only work distracted him, momentarily, from boredom – and, over the past few months, work had so dominated our lives that I had not noticed the subtle shift in him or in our relations. The truth was that Esmond had concluded that he would never be anything more than a very ordinary actor, scratching a living in small parts, but getting no satisfaction from playing them. He had set out, at school, as the star performer, playing Ellen Terry playing Lady Macbeth. With time and maturity, he might turn into an Irving. He now knew that he would never be a Lyn Harding, or even a Julian L'Estrange; he would not even rival his rival Reggie Owen, the Guildenstern to his Rosencrantz. So the one thing that had given his life purpose turned out to be not a guiding light, but an intermittent flickering. Once, with rare communicability, half asleep with drink, he declaimed these most celebrated of Shakespearean lines for all the world as if I might not know them:

Tomorrow, and tomorrow, and tomorrow,
Creeps in this petty pace from day to day,
To the last syllable of recorded time;
And all our yesterdays have lighted fools
The way to dusty death. Out, out, brief candle!
Life's but a walking shadow, a poor player,
That struts and frets his hour upon the stage,
And then is heard no more; it is a tale
Told by an idiot, full of sound and fury,
Signifying nothing.

I took his hand and said: 'It is and it isn't.'

'Of course it is. And the rest is just imaginings.'

'Possibly, but not to be despised for that, in the circumstances.' He shrugged his shoulders and would be drawn no further. He had already said more than he had ever said to me, even if he could only do it by using Shakespeare's words. In a sense, Esmond's situation was worse than the one evoked by the self-dramatizing Macbeth. In Shakespeare, it is generally the kings and queens who have such lines, yet the humblest member of the audience can identify with them. Macbeth was King of Scotland and his lines were spoken by Richard Burbage, the king of the King's Men, an actor playing a king seeing himself as an actor. At least Macbeth and Burbage could strut and fret their hour upon the stage. The likes of Esmond would never have the chance to strut and fret, and were on stage for only a few minutes; a few colourless lines and they had to beat a hasty exit. Esmond was speaking these lines only because he had seen himself as a future Irving, because the tuition of his devoted English master had got him to ADA, because his father had been able and willing to pay for his tuition, and because he was young and handsome. What would he be doing at forty, at fifty? Esmond's only claim to distinction was proving to be no distinction at all: it gave no present satisfaction and held out no prospect of doing so in the future. The only thing that did provide present satisfaction and arouse his interest in the prospect of it was drinking. Half-way through a meal, when a few glasses of wine were taking their effect, his mood would begin to change. He softened, relaxed, murmured a few polite words. As the effect increased, with more wine and the inevitable whisky, he would become affectionate, all tenseness gone. Sometimes, when he took himself off for the afternoon, he would arrive at the Theatre in just such a relaxed mood and I knew that he had been drinking. Then, later, towards the end of the run, he would arrive in a quite different state – not one of relaxed lethargy, but one of scarcely controlled excitement. He was uncharacteristically voluble and smiled beatifically like the cross-gartered Malvolio. I suspected, wrongly as I now think, that he had been to bed with someone. I should not have blamed him if he had: it would have given me an excuse to do the same. The reason for his elation, I later learned, was something else.

Great excitement was created in the Theatre when we learnt that Tree had received an invitation (the actual word used was 'command') from the German Emperor to bring his production of *Antony and Cleopatra* to Berlin. A fortnight later, we learnt that Tree had decided to take no fewer than five more plays. The recent revival of *Richard II* would be one. From the previous April's Shakespeare Week, he added *Twelfth Night*, *Hamlet* and *Merry Wives*. Then, for luck, he threw in his old faithful, *Trilby*. As if that were not enough, from mid-February rehearsals would begin for a double bill, *The Red Lamp* and *The Van Dyck*, which would open on 15 March, the day after the last night of *Antony and Cleopatra*! During the first three weeks of the run, we would be rehearsing the plays for Berlin. We would be leaving on 8 April and be back on the night of 20 April. The Shakespeare Birthday Week, with its six revivals, would begin two days later.

For the Berlin visit and for the Shakespeare Week on our return the entire cast of *Antony and Cleopatra*, and a few more, would be needed. Thereafter many would have to take their leave: the double bill required only some twenty actors – and no 'supers'. Many of the principals – Connie, Basil Gill, Lyn Harding, Fisher White – were included in the cast; so, too, were some of the *débutants*. Esmond, to his initial fury ('I see they've even given that little tart Cyril Sworder a part!') and to his later apparent indifference ('Cyril H. Sworder . . . A Servant! He's welcome to it!'), was not. His one-year contract had ended in January. No one had mentioned renewing it.

Soon after the cast list was announced, Esmond was summoned to Mr Tree's office. An embarrassed, but practised Chief began: 'I'm of the opinion that you have done some very good work in the Company. I particularly liked your Rosencrantz. However, I very much regret to say that I have been unable to find a part for you in the new show. But, then, you're obviously an ambitious young man and must look to the future – and I feel quite certain that you have a fine future ahead of you. What you need now is the opportunity of playing more substantial roles. To do that, of course, you will have to spend a little time in the provinces. I sincerely hope that you will come with us to Germany and do the Shakespeare Week. If you acquit yourself well, as I'm sure you will, I think you should approach Benson. I think he could find room for you in his Northern Company. I don't think I'm being indiscreet if I say that, with the right recommendation from me, you'll have no difficulty getting in. So there you are! A great opportunity awaits you! So, back to work!'

On Sunday 7 April, the entire company was invited to a send-off banquet at the Hôtel Cecil, attended by the Lord Mayor. The following evening, the forty or so actors, a mere dozen 'supers' (to be brought up to the required numbers in Berlin), a dozen other members of staff, the sets and costumes for six plays – there were ten sets for *Antony and Cleopatra* alone – were put on to a special train at Victoria. At Dover, the entire contents, human and material, were transported to a boat bound for Flushing, in Holland. The sea was very rough that night and the boat not particularly comfortable: many of us were sick. Another long delay ensued while everything was moved on to the Emperor's private train. At Hanover, we were met by local dignitaries and a deputation from our host theatre in Berlin. There were speeches, in which I could just make out such phrases as 'the brotherhood in art of two peoples'. Mr Tree replied in German, pointing out that Hanover formed 'a tie between our two countries'. Champagne was distributed and the ladies were presented with flowers.

We arrived in Berlin at the Friedrich-Strasse station. Inevitably, there was considerable delay as the enormous quantity of luggage was dispatched to our various hotels. Tree and 'Twig' went off to the Hôtel Bristol, in the Unter den Linden. The rest of us were accommodated in establishments of diminishing quality, according to status. Esmond and I found ourselves in a *pension* in Dorotheen-Strasse, a quarter of an hour's walk from the theatre, owned, I remember, by a Frau von Engelbrecht.

Next day, we turned up at the Neues Königliches Opern-Theater, formerly the Kroll Theatre, now the city's second opera house. Amid scenes of utter confusion, made worse by the fact that none of the resident stage hands spoke English and few of us, except the Chief, had more than a smattering of German, rehearsals began. An interpreter was requested, but he did not turn up until the following day. Fortunately, Tree had arranged for two 'London Germans', J. T. Grein and Max Hecht, adaptors of French and German plays, to be in Berlin with us. They acted as unofficial intermediaries with the German authorities and press. Lyn Harding's wife, who was German, also acted as an interpreter. Mr Digby, our electrical engineer, soon mastered the theatre's lighting system, while our conductor, Herr Schmidt, was entirely at home in the orchestra pit. That evening we were invited to a huge banquet at the Hôtel Kaiserhof, given by various writers' and actors' organizations. As we were standing around drinking champagne, someone touched my arm:

'And what is Mark Sheridan doing in Berlin?' I turned round. 'Don't you recognize your friend Harry Kessler?'

'Of course. I'm with the Tree company.'

'In what capacity?'

'I'm a walk-on, a supernumerary.'

Kessler laughed. 'For a moment I thought your father must have been moved to Berlin, without my knowledge!'

I introduced him to Esmond. 'This is my *ami particulier*.'

'Ah, yes. I thought so.' He giggled slightly.

'But he's a real actor – Rosencrantz . . .'

'Then I shall see you both in *Hamlet*. You must both come to a little party I'm giving after your last night.' He gave me his card, on which he wrote 'Thursday, 18th April'. 'Please forgive me, but I must leave you both. I know too many people here.'

We sat down at a table well removed from the high and mighty, but the food was no less splendid for that – the hotel kitchen, like those of the Cecil, the Carlton or the Savoy in

London, was obviously run by Frenchmen. Course followed course, wine followed wine; most of the company could never have eaten (or drunk) so well. Over coffee and cigars, the director of Court theatres proposed the toast: 'The German Emperor and King Edward!' Relations between our two countries were like a happy marriage. Tree spoke of his pleasure at finding himself among people – writers and actors – in whose midst he had spent his life. Thirty years ago, he had visited the city, full of boyish ambitions and daydreams, the dearest of which was to be realized that week – to act upon the stage of one of the great Berlin theatres. He praised the German state for supporting in Berlin alone two opera houses and two theatres. As a result, Berlin was now regarded as the theatrical centre of Europe: we English have much to learn from our German friends.

Next day, to the scarcely contained excitement of our faction, some sixty 'supers' turned up from one of the royal guards' regiments at Potsdam. Tree set to work trying to turn them into London citizens – and stage soldiers – planting his own dozen 'supers' among them. Our task was to direct their movements and to coach them in yelling such things as 'Long live King Harry!' At one point, we were standing idly by, as we often were, when I noticed two of the young Germans looking attentively in the direction of our group. I summoned them over and, in halting German, performed the introductions. The slightly taller, slightly older-looking one with dark hair was called Manfred, his friend, very fair of hair, blue of eye and fresh of face, Johann. Further investigation revealed that neither spoke English, but that Johann spoke quite good French. Neither was a professional soldier; they were doing their last year of military service before going to university. Manfred was a native Berliner and would be studying Law in the city; Johann was from the Rhineland and would be studying

'Humanities' at Heidelberg. They were twenty-two and twenty-one. They were both theatre-lovers and, learning of our company's forthcoming visit, had arranged to join the guardsmen: they had, they explained, influential friends in the High Command. They had been given a week's leave, so did not have to return to barracks each night. They were staying at an hotel that they often used when they came up to Berlin.

Our conversation took a rather laboured form: Manfred would say something in German, which I did not understand; Johann would then give me a much abbreviated French translation, which I would then pass on to Esmond in English. As the work of translation proceeded, there was much smiling. Indeed, our two German friends smiled a great deal, unlike most of their fellow soldiers, who seemed to take the whole business of appearing on stage very seriously, as if the honour of their nation depended on their ability to carry out orders. This had its advantages, from a theatrical point of view. But it also meant that the guardsmen found it difficult to behave as anything other than soldiers: they were better soldiers than citizens. Manfred suggested that, when rehearsals were over, we should go and have a beer together, and see something of Berlin. Esmond, who so far had shown only moderate interest in our deliberations, suddenly came to life. However, rehearsals went on late into the night. When we finally left the theatre, we agreed that we would postpone our tour of the city and go for a beer and a snack before retiring to bed. We found ourselves in the huge square in front of the theatre.

'Is this your first visit to Berlin?' I explained that it was, though I had been through Berlin twice, seeing the city from a railway carriage, usually at night. The Germans laughed: they would show us a little of Berlin by night another time. 'This square is the King's Square, Königs-Platz. That building opposite is the Reichstag, the Empire's . . .'

'Parliament?'

'Yes, that is right. Parliament.' We cut across the Tiergarten to the Pariser-Platz. 'This is the Brandenburg Gate. It is quite old – eighteenth century – a copy of the Propylaea in Athens. It is all that remains of our city wall; Berlin has got too big . . . The statue of Victory on the top was stolen by Napoleon to celebrate his victory over us. But then the English and Germans defeated Napoleon and Victory came back to Berlin. That is why we call this square Parisian Square . . . This is the new Hôtel Adlon – it is our best hotel, very expensive. And there, next door, the English Embassy.'

We proceeded up the Unter den Linden, a sort of Champs-Élysées, except that the four rows of trees were all in the central walkway, rather than in pairs at the sides. We sat down at a café terrace and ordered beer and a light snack. This, we were told, was the Café Bauer, one of the most famous in Berlin. As we were leaving, Manfred muttered something to Johann in German.

'Are you two friends?' Johann asked. The stress on '*Freunde*' and '*amis*' was clearly intended.

'*Bien sûr!*' I replied. '*Et vous, vous êtes amis, aussi?*'

'*Ah, oui, nous sommes amis!*' Laughter. Both clapped their hands on my back. We left our friends on the corner of our street, shook hands and parted.

Next morning, Manfred and Johann were there, but their fellow soldiers were nowhere to be seen. Apparently, the guardsmen had been confined to barracks. Further enquiries and protests revealed that the order was a bureaucratic error and that the soldiers would be arriving in the afternoon.

At the opening performance of *Richard II*, the Emperor, Empress, Princess Victoria Louise, the British Ambassador (Sir Frank Lascelles, father-in-law to my friend Cecil Spring Rice), most of the Embassy staff and much of the diplomatic corps were in the audience. Afterwards, the Emperor sent for the three crowned heads of the play – Tree (Richard II), his daughter Viola (Richard's Queen) and Lyn Harding (Henry IV). The Emperor told them that he had been 'very moved' by the downfall of the king. Some of us had wondered, in view of the naval rivalry between the two countries, how our hosts might take John of Gaunt's apostrophe to 'this England', with its reference to

> The silver sea
> Which serves it in the office of a wall,
> Or as a moat defensive to a house,
> Against the envy of less happier lands.

But there was not a murmur in the house, either because it was not understood or, if it were, the audience was too polite to object or considered such national sentiments as quite normal. We said goodbye to our two new German friends: we would see them again on Sunday morning for the rehearsals of *Antony and Cleopatra*. Next day, we saw that one of the reviewers found Tree's performance lacking in 'inwardness'. Many referred to the influence of the Meiningen theatre on Tree's productions, while disapproving of his attempts to 'improve' on Shakespeare, cutting the text and adding spectacle.

Saturday morning brought rehearsals for *Twelfth Night*: there were several changes in the cast from the Shakespeare Week performance. Esmond had been demoted to walking on, his own part of Fabian going to Cyril Sworder, though he was still understudying Basil Gill as Orsino. The press gave a warmer reception to *Twelfth Night* than it had done to *Richard II*, though it was noted that, at the end of the play, Tree had Viola interrupt Feste's song and sing one of the verses. I fully agreed with this criticism: it was an act of barbarism not to

end with the enigmatic, impersonal, curiously 'empty' figure
of the jester, with his melancholy, bitter-sweet songs, alone on
the stage. There was criticism, too, of the preponderance of
'incidental music', trying fruitlessly to vie with Shakespeare's
own music. Here, too, I tended to agree: I should have preferred no incidental music, leaving the songs, sung in their
original settings, to stand out all the more. After the play, Tree
invited some of his hosts, joined by members of the cast, to
supper at his hotel.

In Germany, as in France and everywhere except the
domains of His Britannic Majesty, the theatres are open on
Sunday – not, I am sure, that King Edward was himself a
devotee of Sunday observance. On that Sunday, a gala performance of *Antony and Cleopatra* was planned, preceded, in
the afternoon, by *Trilby*. However, anticipating difficulties
with the staging of *Antony and Cleopatra*, Tree had postponed
the *Trilby* matinée until Tuesday, thus allowing the whole day
for rehearsals. Tree's fears were justified, the main problem
being the stage hands: they were not used to rapid scene
changes and refused to be hurried. Compared with our own
highly trained men, they were undisciplined, unwilling to obey
orders – in a word, unGerman. Indeed they seemed to resent
our presence altogether. Certainly, Tree had no success in persuading them to abandon their two-hour break for lunch, and
was forced to adapt to them. As a result, rehearsals went on
longer than they would otherwise have done. In *Antony and
Cleopatra* there were some ten such scene changes, most of
them involving heavy, complicated sets. In London, as soon as
the curtain was down, an army of skilled hands would rush on
and, in the shortest possible time, transform a public square in
Alexandria into a hall in Cleopatra's palace. In Berlin, they
would reluctantly leave their mugs of beer, move slowly on to
the stage, trying to remember what they had been instructed

to do. If Cecil King, via his translator, tried to remonstrate with them, they would slow down even more. Meanwhile, Adolf Schmidt had to repeat the music intended to fill the time of the scene change and the audience grew more restive. On a 'gala' evening, the audience was not used to being kept waiting by those paid to serve them. In the Royal Box were the Emperor, wearing the Order of the Garter and the uniform of a British admiral, the Empress, Crown Prince and other members of the Imperial family.

Things began well enough. As the overture ended, the image of the Sphinx depicted on the gauze curtain faded to reveal a room in Caesar's house in Rome – not, incidentally, the first scene in Shakespeare's text, but his Act I, Scene 4: 'From Alexandria This is the news: he fishes, drinks, and wastes The lamps of night in revel . . .' The transition to the next scene was swiftly accomplished, since 'the room in Caesar's palace', with its circular pool surrounded by marble columns, was one of Joseph Harker's beautifully painted 'drops', which simply rose to reveal a room in Cleopatra's palace, the lovers lolling on a couch: 'If it be love indeed, tell me how much.' 'There's beggary in the love that can be reckon'd.' This scene was actually Shakespeare's Act I, Scene 1, shorn of Philo's opening description of 'this dotage of our general', which was moved to later in the scene and given to Enobarbus. As the play progressed, the gaps between scenes grew longer, Tree more and more agitated. The main interval arrived. Tree, trying to urge one of the stage hands to hurry, accidentally knocked the man's beer mug out of his hand. It was the last straw: the German stage hands went on strike. The next scene was Tree's great tableau of Antony's return to Egypt, set in the market-place. It was one of the most complicated of the sets, with very solidly built steps and rostrum. Grein and Hecht went off to appeal to the theatre management for help, while members of the cast set about erecting the set, rolling on the rostrum, fixing up the flats, lowering the backdrop, placing the furniture in position. The interval got longer and longer, with a distracted Tree pacing up and down, muttering 'My God!' over and over. An enquiry arrived from the Royal Box as to the reason for the delay. When the Emperor heard what had happened, he ordered stage hands to be sent from another theatre, but they arrived too late to be of any assistance. Suddenly, in the midst of all this feverish activity, the curtain went up, revealing English actors and German guardsmen in Roman costume playing the roles of stage hands. This got us our first laugh of the evening and, apparently, the Emperor was delighted by this unexpected piece of entertainment. No one could discover who was responsible for the rise of the curtain. Another half-hour passed before the curtain was ready to rise again. It was decided to play the rest of the play in the market-place, rather than delay the evening further. The disparity between Tree's intentions and what the audience saw on stage became especially obvious in the final scene, with the deaths of Antony and Cleopatra, supposedly in the queen's tower, taking place in the middle of an Alexandrian market-place. It was past midnight when the curtain finally came down. The stalls applauded politely, but with little enthusiasm; the younger section of the audience, largely students, in the cheapest seats, was openly hostile, shouting and booing. The German guardsmen were outraged by the behaviour of stage hands and students alike. Many came up to us and apologized for their compatriots: they were all *schmutzige Sozialisten,* 'dirty Socialists', we were told. Others described the trouble-makers as *Kommunisten.* Johann explained that Communist was a name adopted by the more extreme Socialists, that the trade unions, which they controlled, were now very powerful in the theatres and in many state-run organizations. They had imposed strict limits on what work their members were prepared to do and on how many hours they could work. How, I wondered, would Tree manage if ever the trade unions gained entry into His Majesty's? With much shaking of hands, we took leave of our company of guardsmen, who were marched off to the Friedrich-Strasse station, bound for their barracks in Potsdam, their Berlin mission accomplished.

The official who had given the toast at the Kaiserhof reception – Major von Hülsen, the director of Court theatres – came back-stage and explained that His Imperial Majesty had had to leave in order to catch a train and had instructed him to deliver presents to Miss Collier and Miss Tree. Viola was given a gold bracelet bearing the Emperor's monogram in diamonds; Connie received a similar bracelet with the Prussian arms set in sapphires. After which, Tree invited the entire cast to join him at a reception at his hotel. Make-up removed and costumes put away, we walked the half-mile round the Königs-Platz, through the eastern end of the Tiergarten, to the Unter den Linden and the Hôtel Bristol. There, in the hotel ballroom, we found a buffet supper and an already large number of guests awaiting us. Around one o'clock, Courtice Pounds was prevailed upon to give a recital of songs, English and German, after which there was dancing, accompanied by the hotel orchestra. We fell into bed at about three. Fortunately for some of us, the following day's play was *Merry Wives*, in which we didn't appear. We had already arranged that Manfred and Johann would call for us at about eleven and we would go off to Potsdam.

The twenty-minute train journey from the Friedrich-Strasse station, through the Grünewald forest, seemed to take us from one Germany to another, one century to another. Berlin was a sprawling nineteenth-century city, rapidly expanding into a twentieth-century one, with a population verging on three million. Though the capital of the province of Brandenburg, Potsdam was a small eighteenth-century township of some sixty thousand souls, seven thousand of whom were soldiers.

It was a bright April day, with a light, refreshing wind, and no showers. Indeed it had not rained since our arrival, which was just as well, since, later that day, the sets for *Antony and Cleopatra* were discovered stacked up, inexplicably, in the garden behind the theatre. We crossed the bridge from the station to the island on which Potsdam is built.

'This is the Brandenburg Gate. Yes, we have one in Potsdam, too. In fact, this one is older than the one in Berlin.' We were soon at the foot of the long flight of steps that lead up to the Sanssouci Palace. 'Our Prussian king Frederick the Great built it when he stopped being a soldier and he spent the rest of his life here. He is buried under the statue of Flora by the fountain. He said: "*Quand je serai là, je serai sans souci*".'

I translated, for the benefit of a clearly unimpressed Esmond: 'When I am there, I shall be without cares . . . carefree.'

'His favourite greyhounds are buried over there. He was a very good soldier, but he was also very studious – he loved French literature and music. He was a friend of Voltaire and invited him to stay here.'

In the palace, we inspected Voltaire's room, which contained a bust of the French writer. We saw the famous oval dining-room. The Gallery had some fine paintings, including some by Watteau. As we began to walk through the park, I asked Johann if he knew of a Chinese observatory that I understood had been set up in the park. He consulted Manfred. Yes, it had been erected a few years ago, but he had not seen it himself. Would we like to see it? I said that I should like to see it *again* and show it to them if they knew where it was. They looked puzzled: had I seen it before? On our way, I told them the story of the Kuan Hsiang T'ai or 'Watching the luminaries terrace'. This extraordinary collection of astronomical instruments was constructed in 1674 by a Belgian Jesuit, Father Verbiest, for the Chinese emperor. It was a time when the Jesuits were at the height of their influence in China. The observatory, placed on top of a tower built against the eastern wall of the Tartar City, was one of the many ways in which the Jesuits tried to convince the emperor of the superiority of things European and Christian. I had seen it when I was a little boy living in Peking. When I went back to Peking two years ago, it was no longer there: it had been removed and brought to Potsdam by the Germans who had led the rescue operation that ended the Boxer siege of the Legation Quarter in 1900.

'Yes,' said Manfred, partly, I suspected, in justification for the removal of the instruments, 'the Boxers murdered our minister, Baron von Ketteler.'

We found the 'observatory', reconstructed with meticulous care, together with an informative plaque providing a fuller history than the one that I had just given my friends and a detailed scientific description, scattered with such words as 'zodiacal armillary', 'ecliptic armillary' and 'aximuthal horizon', that I should have been incapable of giving them. There were six instruments in all, including a celestial globe, almost two metres in diameter, on which were marked all the stars known at the time. All were made of bronze, with an admixture of gold, and brass. They were so well executed that they still moved smoothly on their axes and pivots, despite being exposed to the weather for over three hundred years. They were also very beautiful objects, the decoration being Chinese in style, incorporating splendid dragons. After beer and a ham sandwich at a refreshment kiosk, we moved on to the 'New Palace', a large, wide, classical edifice, surmounted by a dome.

'King Frederick built this palace twenty years after Sanssouci. Perhaps he found that Sanssouci was not big enough. Nowadays the Emperor lives here during the summer.'

We hired a horse-drawn carriage that took us back to the station. On arrival in Berlin, Johann said something to Manfred, who said: '*Ja! Ja!*'

'Would you like go to our hotel?' Johann went on. 'We could have a few beers there, then go out and eat something.' I translated and Esmond agreed that it was a good idea. We crossed the Spree.

'This is the Kronprinzen-Brücke, the Bridge of the Crown Prince.' We walked on. 'This is the Lessing Theatre.' And further on: 'This is the Deutsches Theater, the German Theatre, our most important theatre. It was here that our most important *régisseur*, Otto Brahm, was director. They say that your Herr Tree was very influenced by Otto Brahm. He has now retired. The new director is Max Reinhardt. He has many enemies in Berlin – he is from Vienna and Jewish. But I think he is very intelligent. It is the new theatre. He does many foreign plays, many Shakespeare plays – *Merchant of Venice*, *Winter's Tale* and now *Romeo and Juliet*. You should see it, if possible.'

We entered a building that did not give any sign that it was an hotel. Once inside, it was obvious that it was run by fellow Uranians. We went up to the room and, after a few minutes a young man appeared with a tray bearing glasses and several bottles of beer. We sat down round a table. Johann explained that there were several homosexual establishments in Berlin that offered accommodation. It cost a little more than an ordinary hotel, but it was worth it. It meant you could do what you liked. I asked how people knew about them.

'Oh, word gets round. Then we have our own journals; but even the Berlin newspapers print advertisements that are perfectly clear to all but the most stupid.' Meanwhile, Esmond had given up trying to follow what was being said and just sat, rather lugubriously, staring into his beer.

Suddenly, Manfred got up and put his hand on Johann's shoulder. They walked over to the double bed. Johann began to undress. Without prompting, Esmond got up and did the same. I walked over and Manfred began feeling my crotch, smiling beatifically. I don't know why but, like most people, I regard sex as a serious matter, at least *in medias res*: smiling should come afterwards, if at all. I hazarded a half-smile and let my hand roam. Throughout, Manfred had been the prime mover and, though the oldest of the four, I suddenly felt inexperienced in comparison with our hosts. When in Berlin . . . Meanwhile, Johann was on his knees in front of Esmond. Manfred fell to his knees in front of me. After what seemed like a requisite few minutes, the two Germans rose to their feet and, as if obeying some unspoken rule of polite behaviour, Esmond and I knelt down. What I really wanted to do was get my hands on Johann. He had an almost hairless body, deliciously golden, unflawed skin, a long, tempting neck – and, I could hardly help noticing, a substantial cock. Manfred, hairy, thick of build and limb, I did not find attractive. I got up. Manfred picked up some lubricant from a side table, while Johann went over to one of the chairs and bent over. After applying it to himself and to Johann, he passed it to me – Esmond was already bending over one of the other chairs. Delivering loud slaps to his friend's bum, Manfred began to enter him, Johann emitting loud groans of pleasure. Within seconds, I was inside Esmond: I was finding the situation a good deal more exciting than I had found sex with Esmond for some time – no doubt he felt the same. After a few minutes,

Manfred withdrew from Johann and motioned me over to take his place. He then gestured to me to enter his friend with full force, which I did, almost coming in the process. Manfred gave a gesture of request regarding Esmond, I one of acquiescence and he moved over to him. I noticed that as each of us was fucking the other's friend, his eyes were fixed on what the other was doing.

We replenished ourselves with beer, then Johann went through a door, Manfred explaining that this was the bathroom. The remaining three of us got into the bed. When Johann came back, Esmond followed him and so forth, until, with some difficulty, all four of us squeezed into the bed. We rested for a while, then got dressed. Manfred suggested that we all go out to a tavern and get something to eat. With much smiling and display of affection, we went out into the street.

Unlike the hotel, which concealed its true nature from the passer-by, the tavern was quite evidently a tavern, though, once inside, it was clear that the *clientèle* was largely Uranian. Manfred ordered sausages, salad and beer, while Johann explained that there were many such taverns in Berlin, which were more or less entirely frequented by homosexuals.

'We also have cabarets, restaurants, clubs and Turkish baths where we can go with friends or make new friends. Do you have places like that in London?'

With some embarrassment, I explained that in England things could not be so open. I did not know of any hotels like theirs. I understood there were male brothels, but I didn't know of any clubs. There were Turkish baths, too, but they weren't just for homosexuals and you had to be careful. I suggested that things had perhaps got worse since the Wilde trial. Our German friends expressed horrified concern at our treatment of the great Oscar. It was strange, said Johann, because, in many ways, England was such a free country. And you have no military service! Berlin, they realized, was very special. It was not like this elsewhere in Germany.

'I think we are under the protection of the Court,' said Johann mysteriously. 'Everyone is talking about it. We hear about members of the government, generals, even friends of the Emperor. It is no coincidence that sixty members of the Garde du Corps were on the stage of one of the royal theatres. You remember Herr von Hülsen – he presented Miss Tree and Miss Collier with those bracelets last night – well, he is director of the Court theatres. He is like that –' he made the gesture of crossing two fingers '– with General Count von Moltke, who is military commandant of Berlin. There are others. People call them the *camarilla*.' It was, he said, a Spanish word: further discussion brought up 'coterie' as a possible translation. 'Potsdam is a veritable *bordel*. On one street, you can see ordinary soldiers selling themselves to officers. I suppose it was all started, like everything else at Potsdam, by the great Frederick – he, too, had his favourite guardsmen. Then there are the "champagne parties" in private houses, orgies . . . We are very fortunate. We have our own journals and now we even have an organization – the WHK.' There was some consultation between our friends, then Johann came up with 'Comité Scientifique Humanitaire'. 'It is campaigning for the abolition of what we call Paragraph 175, which condemns homosexual acts. It was started by a medical doctor who lives in Charlottenburg, in West Berlin; perhaps you have heard of him, Dr Magnus Hirschfeld? He is very famous in Germany now.' I admitted that I had not heard of him. 'In winter, we have great balls in which everyone puts on his best clothes – many *en travesti*, wearing splendid gowns and wigs. The ballroom of some large hotel is hired for the evening. It's all quite open. Plain-clothes police are there, but they don't bother anyone. They are there just in case anything illegal takes place.

We know this and so nothing illegal does take place – not there, anyway.' Knowing smiles. 'In summer, there are the beer gardens – and the Tiergarten . . .'

I expressed envy at their good fortune and compared what they had told me of Berlin with what I knew of London, Paris and Petersburg. Our new friends left us on the Friedrich-Strasse, the city's main north–south axis.

'This street will take you straight to the Dorotheen-Strasse, which is the second or third street you come to after the bridge. Keep a lookout for the name of your street. If you miss it, you might end up in Dresden. Dresden is much more beautiful than Berlin, but less amusing.' With much bowing and shaking of hands, we said goodbye to our German friends. They would be returning to Potsdam and their barracks next morning.

Merry Wives, we learnt, had been a great success: people had roared with delight. The Crown Prince and Princess summoned Constance Collier (Mistress Ford), Viola Tree (Anne Page) and Tree to the Royal Box, from which, to great applause, Tree made a speech of thanks in German. The press was as kind as the public. The scenery had been kept simple and unpretentious, with less tinkering with the text; Tree's Falstaff was declared to be unmatchable; the other actors were praised; there was a real sense of jollity on the stage and, supreme compliment, the production was deemed to be superior to Reinhardt's recent production of the play.

Antony and Cleopatra was less kindly received by the press. Tree had massacred the text in the interests of superfluous scenic effects (few of which had reached the stage, of course); his own performance was superficial and unconvincing (it had, indeed, been the poorest performance I had yet seen of one of his less successful roles); Connie was praised for her 'striking appearance' and her 'seductive charm'.

That day held two performances in store: the matinée of *Trilby*, postponed from Sunday, and, in the evening, *Twelfth Night*, for which we rehearsed most of the morning. I had seen *Trilby* three times, the original production in 1895 and twice since, always with Dorothea Baird in the title role. While still at ADA, Esmond had seen a revival, with Constance Collier. This time, much to Connie's chagrin, Viola Tree was to be Trilby O'Ferrall.

We decided that we would take the afternoon off and see a little more of Berlin. It was not, it seemed, a city of great age or beauty. If it was not, as one unkind member of the company put it, like a much bigger, much richer Manchester, with a great many more soldiers, neither was it comparable with Paris, Petersburg or London. Hearing the reference to Manchester, even with the addition of soldiers, Esmond was very tempted to abandon all exploration to me and watch Tree and Twig act out the strange world of Svengali and Trilby. Armed with Baedeker, I persuaded him that he could not leave Berlin without sampling its rich art collections. Half-way up the Unter den Linden, we stopped off at the Café Bauer and ordered sandwiches and large mugs of the excellent beer.

We crossed Schinkel's Schloss-Brücke, with its marble statues of warriors and Valkyrie-like goddesses, to the island in the middle of the Spree. To the right of the immense square was the Royal Palace; to the left, the domed mass of the Cathedral, like a fussier, more pompous version of St Paul's. The effect of the ensemble was not without a certain impressive grandeur, if lacking in grace and elegance. Like the Île de la Cité in Paris, the 'Museum Island' was the original site of the town. Following Schinkel's great plan, the five great museums are grouped together in the north end of the island. We had only a few hours, so I decided to eschew the riches of the Old Museum (mainly ancient Greek), the New Museum (mainly Egyptian), the new Pergamon Museum (though it contained a remarkable reconstruction of a huge altar from the second century BC, with a famous frieze) and the National Gallery (mainly German works, though, banished to its third floor, were paintings that I should like to have seen by Goya, Constable, Fantin-Latour, Monet, etc.). The Picture Gallery on the upper floor of the Emperor Frederick Museum seemed to have the best of the paintings. There we spent a couple of hours among the mainly Italian, German and Dutch masters. I particularly remember Jan van Eyck's *Man with Carnations*, Botticelli's *Madonna with Angelic Musicians*, and a pair of Watteaus, *Al fresco Breakfast* and *Open-air Party*. We then took a motor-cab back to our *pension*, where we rested for an hour, before making our way to the theatre.

After the performance of *Twelfth Night* that evening, the city's mayor announced that the Lord Mayor of London and fifty guests were to be invited to Berlin. The whole company then took itself off for supper in the foyer of the Kammerspielhaus, the small theatre next to the larger Deutsches Theater, as guests of Max Reinhardt. The reception was a much less formal affair than our hosts' at the Kaiserhof or Tree's at the Bristol, the guests being mainly members of the two companies. Looking around the room, I concluded that the average age of the Reinhardt company was older than that of ours – and that Uranians, or 'homosexuals' as Johann called us, were probably less in evidence in the Berlin company than in ours. This last hypothesis was very tentative: it could be that German, like Russian, homosexuals were more generally 'masculine' in demeanour, or simply less *désinvoltes*, less at ease, than those of London or Paris.

For much of our time in the foyer of the Kammerspielhaus, Tree was in delighted, animated conversation with Max Reinhardt, a shortish man in his mid-thirties, with a round,

amiable face and short, curly black hair. In another part of the
room, Connie held court, surrounded by a group of admiring
men. In yet another, I overheard an official from our host theatre and Jacob Grein explaining to some members of our
company how Reinhardt ran his two theatres. He operated a
repertory system in both, putting on each season seven or
eight plays in each house, roughly half of them being translations. Among these, they had already seen that season
productions of *Winter's Tale*, *Romeo and Juliet* and Gogol's
The Inspector General in the larger house, and of Ibsen's *Ghosts*
and *Hedda Gabler*, and Shaw's *Man and Superman* in the
smaller. (Some of us in the company had already arranged to
see *Romeo and Juliet* on Thursday evening, when *Merry Wives*
was being given again.) It sounded like a marriage of His
Majesty's and the Court, relieved of financial burdens by the
state – and this was only the 'second', more adventurous, of
Berlin's two 'national' theatres. Meanwhile, Tree and
Granville Barker were still pleading with the new Liberal government, more kindly disposed than the last, to set up our
own National Theatre.

Late next morning, we turned up for the dress-rehearsal of
Hamlet. This, and the performance that evening, went off
without hitch. Not only did Tree not have to organize sixty
theatrically inexperienced German guardsmen, but his *Hamlet*
was a production without scenery, which meant that he could
largely dispense with the obstreperous German stage hands.
Quite why this lover of stage spectacle had decided, in 1892,
to produce *Hamlet* on a stage decorated by no more than
'props' and curtains had been lost in the mists of time. But, on
the whole, the Germans seemed to like this unwonted auster-
ity and the subtle use of lighting that went with it, though
Tree was criticized for over-cutting of the text. Only Tree
himself remained from that first production at the

Haymarket – and the German critics tended to be less kind to his Hamlet than were the English ones. He was, they said, too old for the part (he was fifty-three). His performance was 'thin', 'sentimental', 'monotonous', 'ineffective'. They disliked such 'unwarranted innovations' as Hamlet returning after the 'nunnery' scene and kissing a tress of Ophelia's hair or, in the graveyard scene, coming back on to the stage and placing what looked like a florist's bouquet of flowers on Ophelia's grave. As Ophelia, Viola Tree won universal acclaim. Henry Neville, easily the oldest member of the company, was not Tree's first Claudius, but he was his second one and had played the part in every revival since. He was not my idea of Claudius. For one thing, at seventy or thereabouts, he was, quite simply, too old: the Claudius who kills his elder brother, then marries his widow should be in the full vigour of early middle age. Neville had the kingly bearing, but suggested none of the king's ambition and sensuality; supposedly a 'smiling damnèd villain', he seemed incapable of villainy and almost of smiling. In the Royal Box that evening were Prince von Bülow, the Chancellor, and the Prussian Interior Minister.

Next day, Thursday, brought our last night at the Neues Königliches Opern-Theater but, since Esmond, I and a good many others were not in *Merry Wives*, our last night had already passed. It was with some curiosity that we approached the Deutsches Theater to see *Romeo und Juliet*. It was a play that most of us knew well, though none of us had ever appeared in it. It was a strange sensation listening to a stream of German words, of which I recognized only the odd one, while inside my head flowed a stream of English words, Shakespeare's own. We were, I felt, in a privileged position compared with the unEnglished Germans in the audience. The handsome young Romeo, Alexander Moissi, who looked about my age, was clearly an actor of great talent and considerable magnetism. He was destined to become the greatest German Hamlet of his time. He was even more of an *Ausländer* than his mentor Reinhardt, who was merely Viennese and Jewish: Moissi was from Trieste, the son of an Italian merchant and an Albanian mother. He certainly looked more at home on the streets of Verona than anyone else on the stage, but some Berliners complained that he still spoke German with a slight Italian accent. Vocally, he had something of Forbes-Robertson's purity and beauty of tone, a light baritone of heart-melting emotional power. But he also had an instinctual vitality, a mercurial swiftness of reaction that the rather statuesque Englishman lacked. Camilla Eibenschütz was obviously a very fine actress, though, in person, she was not everyone's idea of Juliet: she was not pretty, rather plump of face and tomboyish. Reinhardt's production was less 'modern', less austere than his productions later became. Yet one soon noticed the non-naturalistic use of colour, a limited range of tones being used in any one set with a view to creating atmosphere, rather than verisimilitude. A street scene, for example, with narrow, cobble-stoned alleyway stretching into the horizon, flanked by houses, linked by a bridge and topped by tall chimneys, was dominated by a strong, bright red. As set followed set, there was, too, a continuing sense of unity, given by their underlying structure: they were triangular in shape, one side being formed by the proscenium, this the result of having as many as four sets on the enormous revolving stage at once. Reinhardt and Tree were both masters of crowd scenes, but here, too, the German producer strove not for naturalism, but for form.

We emerged into the Schumann-Strasse and piled into a couple of motor-cabs. As we crossed the Spree at the Kronprinzen Bridge and sped down the Königgrätzer-Strasse past the Tiergarten to Harry Kessler's, my head was buzzing with a confused mass of ideas about the theatre of the future. I knew that it was no use talking to Esmond or to any of the others about it: for them, dear souls, the theatre was just a matter of acting – and they had precious little in the way of words or concepts to discuss even that. I had felt similar things in Paris, at some of the Oeuvre productions; in London, after Craig's *Acis and Galatea* and Poel's *Everyman* and *Alchemist*; in Moscow, during the Art Theatre's *Cherry Orchard*. I was confused because none of these theatrical 'experiments' seemed to have any common denominator, still less a united approach to which one could lend adherence. One could not even say that they were united in a common rejection of naturalism, since the Moscow Art Theatre's approach seemed to be naturalism extended, not only to scenery, but also to the acting. Poel's approach seemed to be a rejection of visual naturalism, but a striving after a 'natural' form of acting. Reinhardt's actors seemed close to Poel's rapid, 'natural' way of speaking, but his productions departed from naturalism. Craig was calling for the most radical rejection of naturalism, so radical that he found it more and more difficult working with actual managements and actors.

To go from Reinhardt's theatre to Kessler's apartment was a change of scenery, the ten minutes' journey being the time required to change the sets. When I saw him in London, Kessler had warned me that he hardly dared step foot in his apartment since van de Velde had redesigned it for him. It was indeed like a stage set – for some modern play set in the apartment of a rich, artistic Berliner. One is used to rooms that are built and decorated to contain people and furniture. They rarely surprise: they are what one expects, given the social status and taste of the owner. If one is interested in such things, one may notice some item of decoration, a cornice, say, or a chimney-piece. One is not usually struck by a room as a whole, designed as a total, coherent entity, still less by a whole apartment decorated in this way. I thought of the Goncourt house: it had certainly been designed as a whole, or rather its mass of heteroclite contents had. But remove the contents and the house reverted to its earlier state, that of an ordinary house. I had been struck by how the Stephens' house in Bloomsbury had been 'decorated'. But that is not the right word, for what they had done, with white walls, bare floors and plain curtains was entirely negative, the absence of what was there before, rather than something new. In Kessler's apartment, what mattered was not the contents, but what had been done, in a positive sense, with the rooms themselves. Each had been 'designed' as a whole and in relation to the others, indeed each room seemed to flow into the next. They must originally have been rectangular cubes of various sizes, linked by rectangular doorways, but they managed, by subjecting the straight lines to curves, to give the impression of moving from one cave to another. Doors were higher on one side than on the other, floors may have been flat, but the ceilings were not; even the floors were often on two levels, linked by a curving step. Stairs leading to an upper floor were also curved, the banisters a riot of curving wrought iron, a post, apparently supporting the floor above, turned into a stylized tree, its trunk taking root in the mosaic floor of the hallway, itself a mass of swirls echoing those of the banisters. Throughout, the colours of walls and ceilings, there being no demarcation between them, were the greens and browns of nature. The furniture was all modern, clearly designed by van de Velde himself, and seemed to be organically linked to everything else, even, perhaps, rooted to the ground.

There were only a few guests there when we arrived: the *Merry Wives* contingent had not yet turned up. I made the

introductions and Kessler chatted to us about our visit. He
turned to Esmond and said, 'I thought you made a very dashing young student last night.' Esmond grinned, then blushed.
Kessler then took me to one side, leaving my friends in the
hands of three or four young Germans, who gallantly lavished
their attentions on Hilda Moore and Maud Cressall, though,
on the evidence of the odd glance in their direction, it looked
as if, after a decent interval, Esmond had become the centre of
attention.

'So you're going back to London the day after tomorrow.
Ah, a pity! I suppose your professional duties call.' Kessler
asked me why I had joined Tree's company as a walk-on, how
long I expected to stay. I could not really answer either question. 'Well, when you have time, you must come back to
Berlin – and I shall show you Weimar.' We talked of
Reinhardt, whom he knew well. 'The Emperor and the Court
don't like him at all – they think the whole thing is very sub-
versive. Too many foreign plays. The Crown Prince is a great
supporter, though he usually takes the precaution of going to
the dress-rehearsals, so it doesn't become an official visit.' We
talked of Craig: 'I introduced him to Reinhardt, who was very
interested in his ideas and asked him to produce a Shakespeare
play for him, but nothing came of it. I tried to get him to
come to Weimar and do something for us, but nothing came of
that either. Actually, I think he hates actors. He wants them to
wear masks. Now he's dreaming of a puppet theatre, where he
can do without actors altogether. A few weeks ago, he moved
to Florence. He says he's working on something for Duse . . .
A John o' dreams—' he paused.

I took up the challenge: 'Unpregnant of his cause and can
do nothing!'

'Exactly! Hamlet himself!'

'He played Hamlet once, though I never saw him.'

'Yes, I know. That is what is so strange. Stanislavsky and Reinhardt have ideas and theories, but they are both actors, practical men of the theatre. But then Craig isn't just an intellectual. He was an actor, too, and he is Ellen Terry's son! I really don't understand. Now Reinhardt is very clever, quick-witted. If Craig doesn't do something soon, Reinhardt will just take over his ideas and . . .'

'Ah,' I said, 'the actors are come hither.' And the cast of *Merry Wives* began to trickle in. Kessler took my arm and we went over to greet them, I performing the introductions. I rejoined the group around Esmond and was given an enthusiastic welcome by the young good-looking Germans, one of whom spoke quite good English and had been acting as interpreter. They were, I felt sure, part of Harry's personal entourage. Then there were the even more attractive young men moving discreetly among the guests distributing first champagne, then wine or standing behind a table serving food.

'Falstaff in Love' had again been a great success. Tree, Violet and Connie were summoned by the Crown Prince and Princess. Tree spoke from the Royal Box and then from the footlights, in German. There were plans, he said, for a return visit next year, when he hoped they would be able to visit Dresden, Leipzig, Munich, Cologne, Frankfurt, Hanover, Vienna, as well as Berlin. Tree's *hubris* was boundless. In the event, there was no German visit in 1908 – or in any other year.

Next morning, we did not rise betimes, arriving at the theatre rather late in the morning. Suddenly we had a whole day free and no one knew precisely what to do. In the end, we broke up into different groups, wandering rather aimlessly in the direction of the Unter den Linden. Those who had not yet visited the museums and had a mind to do so, I pointed in the right direction. My own group, for such it became, was content to wander the streets. About noon, it began to rain lightly. We made for the Café Bauer for a snack. More wanderings brought us back a few hours later to the same spot. We retreated to Kranzler's, the famous pastry shop, where we regaled ourselves with tea and cakes. After this, Esmond and I retired to our *pension* to rest. That evening, we were all invited by Tree to dinner at the Bristol. Next morning, we were seen off at the Friedrich-Strasse station by a delegation of officials. Our Berlin adventure was over.

We arrived at Victoria late that evening. Next day, Sunday, we were back at the Theatre rehearsing *The Tempest*, with which, on Monday evening, we would open the Shakespeare Birthday Week. There followed, on Tuesday, Shakespeare's birthday, *Winter's Tale*; Wednesday, my twenty-seventh birthday, was a busy day, with *Hamlet* in the afternoon and *Twelfth Night* in the evening; Thursday and Friday brought *Julius Caesar*, Saturday a second performance of *Twelfth Night* and *Merry Wives*. For Esmond, me and a few others, that *Twelfth Night* matinée was our final appearance on the stage of His Majesty's Theatre. Some of our fellows had already gone, others would follow shortly. Our revels now were ended, but these our actors did not melt into air, into thin air; they were not such stuff as dreams are made on, but men of flesh and blood, lacking employment. Esmond took leave of his friends, putting a brave face on his 'promotion' to Benson's North Company. (That week he had received a letter from Henry Herbert, who ran it, offering him a place. He was to go and see Herbert at Lincoln the following Friday to discuss the parts he would be playing.) I was asked if I were leaving, too, and I said that I was. No one asked what I should be doing with myself – it was assumed that I was no player, but a gentleman of leisure and no occupation. Esmond had to hang around until the evening to make sure that Basil Gill, a healthy Orsino in the afternoon, did not fall sick before turning himself into Fenton. Basil duly entered stage right as Fenton – never once had Esmond ever had to replace him – and we exited by the stage-door to the 'pub' on the other side of the road. Esmond had collected an envelope containing his week's wages of £3, and I left an envelope containing a letter for Mr Tree announcing that I was leaving the company and thanking him for giving me such invaluable experience. I had mentioned in my letter, by way of explanation, that I hoped 'to do a bit of writing'. The following week, a note arrived from Tree, wishing me good fortune in 'my new avocation' and hoping that 'if ever you think to recount your days at His Majesty's, you will report us and our cause aright to the unsatisfied'.

Esmond and I spent a curious weekend. I felt empty, drained, listless, not knowing what my life would bring, either in the short or the long term, wondering, too, what it would be like living without Esmond. He, on the contrary, had a clear idea what he would be doing for the next year at least – and was clearly terrified.

The following Tuesday, he went to spend a few days with his parents in Sheffield: he would go to Lincoln from there. He arrived back on Friday evening. Herbert turned out to be a man of 'about thirty', of diminutive stature, who had worked with Benson and was an adept of the brisk new Poel mode of speaking. He was not 'one of us' – at least he had a wife, Gladys Vanderzee, who played the leading female roles. Herbert's parting words were: 'You'll do, I suppose.' Esmond would be joining the Company in a week's time. For the first two weeks, he would do no more than walk on (and be paid £1 a week; when he started acting, his salary would rise to £4). Meanwhile, Herbert would rehearse him in his parts, beginning with Laertes, Sebastian (*Twelfth Night*), Lorenzo (*Merchant*) and Macduff; Orlando (*As You Like It*), Cassio (*Othello*) and Joseph

Surface (*School for Scandal*) would follow later. He was nervous, distracted, drinking more and at the slightest excuse. Next day, he muttered, without much conviction, something about having to see someone. He returned that evening in what was clearly a much more relaxed mood. Whatever the reason, it was preferable to the earlier nervousness and moodiness. It was not that he said more or less than before: it was rather a matter of what I took to be going on inside his head. Before, it was filled with a stream of thoughts: he was already trying, and failing, to see himself as Laertes and Macduff. Now nothing much at all seemed to be occupying his mind, worries for the future banished. Unfortunately, it also affected his concentration and ability to remember lines. He was at his best in the morning and every morning during that week I helped him with his future parts, reading the other parts, explaining the meaning of difficult passages, advising him on how his lines might be spoken – aware, of course, that Henry Herbert might have different notions as to how they were to be done.

I saw him off at King's Cross. We knew that he would not be able to come back to London until the end of the tour, which would be months away – Sundays would be spent travelling to the next town. I offered to join him for a few days if he felt that he needed my company. I knew that he would not take up the offer. There would never be enough time to see me. I returned to Smith Square saddened, but curiously relieved. Our enforced break had merely dotted the 'i's and crossed the 't's of a story that was nearing its end.

Late one afternoon during the following week, I happened to be in the West End and dropped in at His Majesty's stage-door. Rehearsals for a revival of *A Woman of No Importance* had just ended and the stage was being got ready for *Trilby*, which was being given a few performances before the Wilde play opened. Among the throng I saw Cyril Sworder.

'What are you doing here?' I asked. 'You aren't in *A Woman* are you?'

'No, and you aren't either. At least I'm still a member of the Company. What are *you* doing here?'

'Oh, just popped in to say hello.'

'Ah, can't keep away!' he said bitchily. 'Have you heard from Esmond yet?'

'No, no. He only went away on Sunday. Besides . . . I don't suppose . . . Things aren't what they were . . . Are you doing anything now?'

'Why, what have you in mind, kind sir?'

'Come and have a drink with me.'

We went to the 'pub' across the road, where we – Cyril mainly – launched into matters Majestic. I had known him from the beginning of my days in the Theatre. While still a student at the Academy, he walked on with me in my first Shakespeare Week. At the end of the run of *A Woman of No Importance*, he would be joining the company on a long provincial tour, lasting four months. We talked of friends: of Reggie Owen, now in the main Benson company; of Sidney Southgate, in whose coterie Cyril had been, now out of work; of Bob Atkins, a good friend of Cyril's, but not one of us. We talked of Esmond:

'He's a nice fellow, very genuine. Everyone likes him, especially the girls! The trouble is, he's not very bright . . . Not quick on the uptake, which, I'm afraid, you have to be in this business. If he was more of an actor, he could become a sort of Basil Gill. As it is . . . Not that I shall ever be that either. I know my limitations. And what am I to do with my dreadful name? What is your name, young man? Cyril Sworder, sir. Makes me sound like a snake. Should I change it? It isn't too late, is it? But that's enough about me. Esmond, yes . . . To be quite honest, I don't know what goes on his head . . .'

'I don't either. It's a terrible thing to say, but I sometimes wonder if anything very much does. He certainly has no intention of letting you know or . . . perhaps it's just that he doesn't know how to . . .'

'Talk? Not a very common fault in our circle, is it? Of course, he drinks a lot. Nothing unusual in that. The profession's full of drunks, but he's a bit young for it.'

Cyril was everything that Esmond was not. By no means an intellectual, he was quick-witted, witty, good company. On the other hand, he did not have Esmond's looks, his physical presence. He was twenty, attractive enough, in an unemphatic way: of average height, with mousy hair, eyes of uncertain colour, fresh complexion. I asked him back to Smith Square. It was a beautiful, mild May evening: we decided to walk.

There was no doubt what we both wanted, no need to go through the usual feints and civilities. I had no sooner got beers than we were kissing. Five minutes after crossing the threshold, we were in my bedroom, tearing our clothes off.

'O most wicked speed . . .' Cyril began.

'. . . to post with such dexterity to incestuous sheets!' we both continued, between giggles.

As I expected, he responded quickly, enthusiastically. I put my hands gently on his shoulders and he was on his knees. I propelled him to the bed and quickly went through my familiar routine, which would be more or less new to him at least. Before long, I was kneeling between his parted legs. The entry was unceremonious, unimpeded. I covered him with my body, my left hand on his throat, my right on his cock. The long thrusts began, the return movements coming to within an inch of an exit. I knew it would not last for long. It did not; when I finally exploded, he had already come.

We were a good, well-matched, well-contrasted pair. We pleasured one another, enjoyed each other's company, but found in one another none of the unfulfilled yearnings, the answering mystery, on which love is based. We walked back to the West End and dined at Romano's. Afterwards we got a cab and I dropped Cyril off at his digs in Lambeth.

Over the next couple of months, he called on me at Smith Square every two or three days. Sometimes he would spend the night with me, sometimes not. There was never any question of his moving in with me. I took him to the theatre. At Covent Garden, we saw Caruso in *La Bohème* and *Tosca*, *Traviata* and *Un Ballo in Maschera*. We were at the first night of *A Woman of No Importance*. At the Court, we saw the revival of Shaw's splendid *Man and Superman*, then, the following week, one afternoon, the first performance on the stage of *Don Juan in Hell*, the long, scintillating 'dream' episode from Act III of the play. It had always been omitted from performances of *Man and Superman* on the grounds of length. For Cyril, each outing, each play, each supper, was a fresh, apparently unexpected delight. Nothing was taken for granted. There was a feminine charm, ease of manner about him that Esmond lacked. Both young men were profoundly feminine but, whereas Cyril's femininity constantly bubbled up to the surface from the well-springs below, Esmond's was so deeply buried that it required the excavations of sex to bring it to the surface. With Cyril, the receiving was also a giving; Esmond seemed incapable of 'giving' anything, there appearing to be nothing inside to give, just an emptiness wanting to be filled.

One morning, leafing through *The Times*, my eye caught the headline: PRINCE BÜLOW AND THE COURT CAMARILLA. I remembered at once our conversation with Manfred and Johann on the subject of the *camarilla*, the coterie, its 'champagne parties' in Potsdam, its 'orgies'. Discussion of it had now reached the Reichstag. By *camarilla*, it seemed, the German Chancellor meant a group of friends who met at Prince Eulenburg's country seat, Schloss Liebenberg. (I noted the name: 'love mountain', not, it later turned out, a Venusberg, but an Adonisberg.) Without explaining why, the correspondent went on to remark that the affair was exciting enormous interest in Berlin. During the rest of June, hardly a day passed, but, turning at once to page 5 of *The Times*, I would find the heading THE BERLIN SCANDALS. It seems that, six months before, the journalist Maximilian Harden, in his periodical *Die Zukunft*, had made vague insinuations against certain members of the Liebenberg *camarilla*. As a result, Count Kuno von Moltke, Military Commandant of Berlin, and General Count von Hohenau, aide-de-camp to the Emperor, had resigned their posts. Of much greater account was the case of Philipp Eulenburg. A former Ambassador to Vienna, he no longer held office and could not therefore be stripped of it. His power and influence, we later learnt, did not, in any case, derive from office: he was nothing less than the Emperor's closest friend, some said his only intimate friend, the only friend with whom he used the familiar '*du*' form. They had met when Wilhelm was twenty-seven and still Crown Prince. They instantly became 'bosom friends', with undoubted infatuation on the older man's part. Although he had spent some years in the Garde du Corps regiment and later pursued a career in diplomacy, Eulenburg's main interests in life were artistic. At Liebenberg, he surrounded himself with like-minded friends. He invited the Crown Prince to these gatherings. There Wilhelm found what he had not found elsewhere: intellectual stimulation and a certain tenderness in male friendships. When, two years later, Wilhelm unexpectedly acceded to the throne, he came to depend more and more on Eulenburg's advice. In 1900, Wilhelm made the then Count Eulenburg a prince. It was at his instigation that the Emperor appointed one of his Liebenberg friends, Count von Bülow, Chancellor.

A week passed and *The Times* was speaking of 'grossest scandals' and 'alleged moral depravity' as well as 'political machinations', but still nothing specific. I remembered how the newspapers had reported the Wilde case and how difficult it had been to learn what had actually happened. Only after another week did the words 'unnatural offences' crop up, when Harden asked the Public Prosecutor to proceed against Eulenburg under 'Paragraph 175' of the Penal Code – ah, how could I forget Johann's impassioned plea against 'Paragraph 175'? The request was rejected. Meanwhile, Moltke brought an action against Harden for libel. Harden claimed that he was not interested in people's sexual activities. His motives were purely political: to draw attention to the deleterious effect that the *camarilla* had had on German foreign policy, especially on the Moroccan question. He referred to the presence at the 'Liebenberg Round Table' of the First Secretary at the French Embassy, Raymond Lecomte. The judge tried to get Harden to agree to a settlement. He refused: his entire purpose was to bring the affair before the public. Summer interrupted proceedings and we heard nothing more of Eulenburg and the Liebenberg *camarilla*.

Two weeks after Esmond had left, a one-page letter arrived:

Dear Mark,

I'm writing this back stage in Stoke on Trent which is blacker than Sheffield. Hamlet has just been sent to England. This time next week I'll be in Crewe waiting to go on and say What ceremony else? to the churlish priest and jump into my sister's grave. The fellow I'm replacing is leaving because he cant get on with Henry Herbert. Thats not surprising because Henry Herbert is a bossy little bastard. I cant get on with him either. The trouble is he expects everyone to speak the lines as fast as he does which is twice as fast as I'm used to. 'Do not mouth it!' he screams. 'Trippingly on the tongue!' The trouble is when I try to speed up, I cant always get my tongue round the words. I have to admit that he knows his stuff though. One fellow in the company says his tragedy is that if his head was another twelve inches from the ground heed be playing leads in London, instead of going round dreary little northern towns. Herbert's wife Gladys Vanderzee is a sweety she tries to make up for his tantrumms. The weathers quite good which is funny in a place like this. By rights it should be raining. I sometimes wish my clever clogs was here to give me a cuddle. Theres no Belmont up here. In such a night. I've made 1 friend here Ted Hodson. He tries to look after me. Means well. Hope your alright.

 Yours,

Esmond

Soon afterwards, a letter arrived from further afield. From somewhere in South Africa, Esmé Percy wrote to say that for the last six months he had been touring with Mrs Brown Potter's company, playing such roles as Orlando, Charles Surface and Armand Duval, to Mrs Brown Potter's Lady with the Camellias. He would be back in London, briefly, in July, before taking charge of Benson's Midland Company, 'playing Hamlet, Macbeth and Shylock in Northampton, Worcester and Father Giles's field'.

From 3 Gray's Inn Place, a letter arrived from Maurice Baring, inviting me to luncheon at the Cecil. It was eighteen months since we had last met – over just such a luncheon. He brought me up to date with his life. I asked him if he ever did move into an apartment with Constantine Benckendorff.

'Yes, I did,' he said, rather distractedly, as if wishing to give the impression that it was of no importance. 'We found a little place, just a two-room flat, in the Mwilnikov pereleuk . . . off the Bolshaya Konyushennaya.' I nodded. 'He's a dear, dear soul . . .' Soul? Was that all there was to it, then? '. . . my dearest friend. He's still there. I shall go back in July for a short while, then I'm off on a wonderful adventure. All the time I've been in Russia, I've never been to the South – west to east, but never north to south. So I'm going on a long trip down the Volga to Astrakhan and the Caspian Sea. It's the longest river in Europe, you know. I've given up being the *Morning Post*'s St Petersburg correspondent. I shall continue to write for the paper, of course.'

We talked of the political situation in Russia. Things were getting back to normal after the disturbances of 1905 and Russia seemed at last to be moving towards some sort of democracy but, being Russia, it was a slow business and he doubted whether it would get very far. Things would not move very fast, could not move very fast, given the invincible sloth, physical and mental, of those dear, simple people. He had reported on the two sessions of the Duma, last year and this.

'The Russians are very good at talking! They love talking. That is their charm. They so love their fellow men that they can never stop talking to them, asking them questions – and taking all day to answer them. That way, with a bit of luck, there will be no time to *do* anything. In Russia, the only people who do anything more than they can get away with are Germans, assisted by a few Scotsmen and Dutchmen – which is why they were brought in in the first place. I spent weeks listening to those windbags in the Duma discussing what was to be done. There they were, people who had never left Nizhni Novgorod or Veliki Ustyug, scarcely able to believe that they were sitting in the Tauride Palace, imagining that they were deciding the fate of Mother Russia. Then I'd get into conversation with some people on the train to Moscow – I always travel third-class, it's the only way to find out what people, the real people, think about things – and I'd ask them what they thought of the Duma. "Which Duma?" someone said. Someone else thought that Duma was the name of a town. Another said that nothing would come of it. "People won't go and vote. They know better." At this point, a guard appeared: "Shh, the government!" someone whispered.'

We talked of the plays that he had seen since his return. This led to Shaw: no, he had seen neither *Man and Superman*, nor *Don Juan in Hell*, though he had seen the former when it had been done last.

'I'm afraid I can't take Shaw any more. He's a monster, a dangerous monster. He has more power of invention than anyone else alive, yet what does he do with it? What does it all amount to? A world that, while sounding a little like ours, is entirely of his own invention. It bears no relation whatever to our world – any more than Wilde's does. He's just an empty clown trying to make us laugh. The rest . . . the ideas . . . are just claptrap. Now, compare this with Chekhov . . . There you have real people, with all their pitiful foibles. A few of them spout ideas, of course, but Chekhov makes us laugh at them. Unlike Shaw, he never lets us know what *his* ideas are . . . He's probably an unbeliever, but he's a Russian and so, whether he likes it or not, he retains a certain Christian spirituality. Oh, how I envy the Russians that. I am a very reluctant unbeliever . . .' (Two years later, having left Russia, Maurice Baring was received, not into the Russian, but into the Roman Church.)

I was taken aback by this attack on Shaw, coupled with an envy of those who had faith. At the time, I had no idea how to counter it. I said, lamely, that I could see the connection with Wilde, as with Sheridan and Congreve, and loved him for it. It was not the business of comedy to present real people and their foibles with verisimilitude – or that of tragedy either.

I asked Maurice if he had seen our friends Nikita Baliev and Nikolai Tarasov. He looked slightly pained, as if he would rather not be reminded of them.

'Once or twice, briefly, on visits to Moscow. Nikolai is usually sick . . .' He was intrigued by my year spent on the other side of the footlights, treating it rather as the whim of a naughty boy, something that I should grow out of. 'And what are you going to do now?' I said that I should spend some months in London, then travel for a while. Paris, Italy, Berlin . . . 'You want to go back to Berlin?'

'I don't know. What I saw of it seemed interesting . . .'

'Ah, I see! Germany is not a country I care for, though I'm a little German myself.' I asked Maurice what he thought of the 'Berlin Scandals'. He lifted his eyes to heaven and changed the subject. 'Aren't you tempted to go back to Russia? Your brother seems to be enjoying himself. My spies tell me there's a young lady . . .' Almost to counter his dismissal of Germany, I said that I had no wish to return to Russia. As for Matthew, he was like a familiar mystery. Maurice looked at me quizzically. 'Yeees, it sounds like a good definition of God.'

'I don't know about that. He probably feels the same way about me, probably more so.'

'He probably doesn't regard you as a mystery, you know. To arrive at such a notion a certain philosophical detachment is required, a habit of irritably reaching after fact, as Keats puts it in one of his letters. He probably just sticks with what he thinks he knows, believing there is no point in looking further, perhaps believing that one cannot.'

As we parted, he told me that he would probably be back in London in December and look for a house. His Russian days, it seemed, would soon be over. (In January 1908, he moved into a house in North Street, off Smith Square. We should have been neighbours had I not left Smith Square for ever the week before.)

A letter arrived with 'Berwick-on-Tweed' on the postmark, but the handwriting was not Esmond's:

Dear Mr Sheridan,

I am afraid I have some very bad news for you. Your friend Esmond is dead. It happened at the end of last week when we were at Newcastle. He fell off a bridge into the river and was drowned. I don't know whether he told you but I was his best friend in the company, I think his only friend. I was very fond of him. He was a nice lad, though he had a lot of problems. But I expect you know all about that. So I took the liberty of finding your address on a letter you'd written to him, which I enclose. I thought it better not to leave it around. You don't want the police asking questions. I know he was very fond of you. He often talked about you. I thought you ought to know what happened – no one else would have told you. Mr Savery, our business manager, has written to the parents.

After the show on Friday, he went out and got drunk, which I'm afraid he usually did. Afterwards he was had up by the police for soliciting. He told me all about it. It sounded horrible. They kept him in a cell all night and he was due to appear before the magistrates on Monday morning. Unfortunately we had to be in Berwick by then. He told me all about it after 'Hamlet' on Saturday night. He'd already 'died' once that night, as Laertes – I'd 'died' myself a few lines before – I'm he who plays the King. I'll always think of him coming and lying there next to me on the steps.

I'm sure he knew what he was going to do that night.

We went for a drink together, then went back to our digs. We shared the same room. I must have gone off to sleep very quickly, because I don't remember him getting up. He must have taken his clothes out of the room, got dressed and sneaked out of the house.

I think he was very depressed before all this happened. Henry can be very difficult. He's a perfectionist and expects too much of his young actors. He can be very sarcastic. I can't see him carrying on much longer. Anyway I did my best to buck Esmond up. It's all very sad. Not yet twenty. I hope you don't mind me writing to you like this out of the blue. I'm sure you won't. We have to stick together somehow in this harsh world.

Yours sincerely,
Edward T. Hodson.

Hamlet. Ted would always remember him lying beside him on the steps. At the end of 'our' *Hamlet,* he was no longer Rosencrantz but, like me, a mute and audience to that act, on the other side of the stage. It was strange that, in his letter, Esmond spoke of jumping into Ophelia's grave on a stage in Crewe. Off-stage, he had taken Ophelia's way to a watery grave. I was glad that he had not taken Anna Karenin's.

I was in a daze for the rest of the day. That evening, when Cyril arrived, I showed him the letter.

'Oh, poor kid! Poor kid!' he said. There were tears in his eyes: I had so far failed to bring any to mine – 'Too much of water hast thou, poor Ophelia, And therefore I forbid my tears.' He took me in his arms and we both began sobbing. We sat around drinking whisky – in Esmond's honour – then went out and continued our solitary wake over dinner.

At one point, Cyril said, 'Of course, you knew about the cocaine.'

I stared at him: 'Cocaine? . . . No . . .'

'He took cocaine. I suppose you've never had it.'

'No . . .'

'Well, you wouldn't understand, then. I started . . . once or twice, but decided I didn't like it. Sidney Southgate took it. Esmond got it from him, said it helped to keep him awake in the evening. Counteracted the alcohol, I suppose. I don't know whether he was on it the night . . . in Newcastle. How would he get it? Maybe that was the trouble.'

Cyril asked me if I should like him to come round the next day 'just to keep me company'. I said that perhaps it would be better if I just kept quiet for a few days.

Next day, I woke to a beautiful June morning, feeling as if I were recuperating from an illness, still feeling a little frail but, the fever having passed, clear-headed, relaxed. After breakfast, I went for a stroll round St James's Park. What I felt could not be called grief, for Esmond had 'gone' even before he joined the Benson (North) Company. In official parlance, he had committed suicide 'while the balance of his mind was disturbed'. Who was responsible? Our lawmakers, for interfering where they should not? The police, for acting so harshly to the 'offender'? Henry Herbert, for undermining what little self-confidence remained to a nineteen-year-old actor? Sidney Southgate, for introducing him to cocaine? His English master, for putting him on the path to a theatrical career for which he was not really fitted? His poor parents, for I knew not what? Others that I knew not of? I? Any of us? All of us, in varying degrees? Or Esmond himself, on the grounds that whatever set of cards fate deals us we alone can be held responsible for how we play them? I felt no guilt, but then I hardly knew what guilt was. Should I have felt guilt? Plato, Aristotle and the whole of moral philosophy were of no assistance in each particular case. I did not believe that we were 'free agents', deciding on 'moral' questions like gentlemen of education and independent means on the relative advantages of a new swimming-baths or public library. Given the overriding contingency of the world, we had precious little 'freedom of decision', some of us a great deal less than others. Yet, I tentatively thought, what little did remain, or at least seemed to us to remain, was ours, to be acted upon. Esmond may have needed the spur of having to plead guilty – for there would be no other course – before the worthy Newcastle magistrates, and the consequent shame before colleagues and parents, to get him out of bed that night and make his way to the river. He probably had to be sufficiently fuddled in the head to allow himself to fall, once he had managed to climb over the railing. But, deep down, and, with Esmond, everything was deep down, the decision that his life, sooner rather than later, would not be worth living was already taken, biding its time. He must have known that he would never be an actor, which was the only thing he had ever wanted to be. He knew that he was good for nothing else. In time, his looks, the one thing that he did have, would fade. Drink, almost his only consolation, would make him incapable of doing anything anyway, and would kill him before his allotted span was up. On balance, I preferred to think that, in his confused way, he had done it after the high Roman fashion. The theatre had at least taught him how to die, if not how to live.

Cyril began to call on me again and we took up where we had left off. At the end of July, he went to Portsmouth to spend a month at his parents', before going on tour with the Tree company. So I found myself 'alone' in London, 'everyone' having gone to sea or country, leaving the city to the millions whose means or occupations do not allow them to desert it for six or eight weeks. The Season might be over, the Opera House shut but, for those who did not mind their opera in English, Joseph O'Mara and his company were putting on a dozen different works at the Lyric Theatre well into September. There was other music to occupy evenings when I was not in thrall to more earthly pursuits. I attended some of Henry Wood's 'promenade concerts' in the Queen's Hall and recitals in the Bechstein and Steinway Halls.[1] I renewed my acquaintance with 'Jermyn Street' and 'Bartholomew's'. On the lookout for such suspicious-looking characters as plain-clothes policemen, I even frequented 'Dansey Place', with occasional success. Of the more memorable encounters, there was a French waiter from the Ritz met in 'Jermyn Street' and a shop assistant met in Jermyn Street, not in the baths, but looking in a shirt-maker's window. Even cultural pursuits yielded their quota: the clerk met in the bar of the Queen's Hall or the Oxford undergraduate I got talking to over the indexes in the London Library.

I read a lot of books, not always finishing them, especially the ones that I had read before. Without being entirely aware of it, I was seeking, not to escape, like the common reader, into another world, or even to arrive at a rounded, considered view, as a critic might, but rather to see how variously things might be done, to observe the craft of telling a story and describing the people in it. For this the work of one's own time is of greater use to the would-be writer. I read Conrad's *Nostromo* and James's *The Ambassadors*. James, I felt sure, must be one of us, though probably more in the breach than the observance. I read Morgan Forster's second novel, *The Longest Journey*, which had come out in April.

When I read his first novel, *Where Angels Fear to Tread*, I

1 The Bechstein, Wigmore Street, is now known as the Wigmore Hall – its German name was changed during the First World War. The Steinway Hall, in Lower Seymour Street, now also Wigmore Street, no longer exists.

marvelled at how that mousy Cambridge creature, that *Taupe*, as Strachey called him, that mole, had been able to create a world inhabited by people other than his Cambridge friends, a world, not only of women, but also of Italians. I did not know that Forster had attended Tonbridge School only as a day-boy and had been brought up entirely by women: clearly, that shy only child had spent his earliest years observing them. The 'English' side of the novel rang true to me, as did, too, the physical description of 'Monteriano', based, I was later to learn, on San Gimignano, where Pépé, Mémé, Matthew and I had spent a day or two during our Italian tour of Easter 1899. I was less convinced by the portrayal of the Italians themselves. They struck me as providing too pat, too schematic a contrast with the English of Sawston (a sort of Tonbridge). The spontaneity of the Italians, their 'naturalness', their emotional physicality seemed idealized, to spring – very Cambridge, this – from an idea, rather than from observation. That untutored, but basically uncorrupted 'animal', Gino, struck me as particularly idealized: Forster was probably more than half in love with him. It came as no surprise to me to learn that Forster had very little experience of the lives of ordinary Italians and had made the whole thing up.

The Longest Journey was more ambitious and less successful, I thought. Though Forster nowhere refers to it, the title comes from Shelley's 'Epipsychidion':

> . . . the beaten road
> Which those poor slaves with weary footsteps tread
> Who travel to their home among the dead
> By the broad highway of the world, and so
> With one chained friend, perhaps a jealous foe,
> The dreariest and the longest journey go.

We are all 'poor slaves' and the best that we may expect along life's 'longest journey' is to be chained to a friend rather than to a foe. For many of the characters, the journey is not so long, though death's frequent interventions are merely noted, never portrayed as tragic – how could they be, the lives being no better than those of slaves? One reviewer remarked that death carried off 44 per cent of the characters. The deaths, being usually neither plausible, nor moving, stand out in the surrounding naturalistic dreariness as melodramatic.

The novel is dedicated '*Fratribus*', to the brothers of the 'Society', and the opening scene is a gathering of Apostles in Rickie's rooms: '"The cow is there," said Ansell, lighting a match and holding it out over the carpet . . . It was philosophy. They were discussing the existence of objects. Do they exist only when there is someone to look at them? or have they a real existence of their own?' Rickie, the author's surrogate, is lame. Did this, I wondered, stand for all the inadequacies that Forster felt in himself, including his homosexuality? Not that there was any mention of the last – there was not even the slightest suggestion of the ambient homoeroticism of the Apostles and their circle. I found the light comedy of those early Cambridge scenes the easiest part of the book to digest. Once outside Cambridge, in the other two 'worlds' of the novel, 'Sawston' and 'Wiltshire', Forster has to depict the dreariness of the England that was not Cambridge. His chosen method is not comic hyperbole, but naturalistic 'truth', so the reader is left for long stretches in a suitably dreary mood.

Rickie has an illegitimate half-brother, Stephen Wonham, also his fellow slave, friend and foe. A rough son of the soil, Stephen represents the life-force, basically good, but lacking in the finer points of moral and social etiquette. He is an English version of Gino, a type that Forster obviously admires, I suspected lusted after, but did not (as yet) know. Stephen has the same schematic air to him as his predecessor, though his implausibility is more evident to the English reader, for whom Gino had to be taken on trust.

By the beginning of September, I thought that it might be worth trying to get in touch with Strachey. My letter remained unanswered for some weeks. A reply finally arrived. As I could see from the letter head, the Stracheys no longer lived at 69 Lancaster Gate, W., but at 67 Belsize Park Gardens, NW. Where could that be? I investigated and found that it was just south of Hampstead. The only person I could think of who had ever lived in that part of the world was Keats. Had the Stracheys sunk so low? It seemed as if the multitudinous Stracheys had always inhabited the vasty deep of 69 Lancaster Gate. What could have happened? Had I missed an announcement in *The Times* of Sir Richard's death? No, but the Strachey household was now much reduced and did not need such a large house. My letter had been pursuing Strachey around the country and had arrived a few days before he moved into his new abode. Would I be free on Friday 4 October? Somewhere within a quarter of a mile of Waterloo Bridge, northern end, naturally? I did not care for the roast beef and Olde England of Simpson's; Romano's might be too *bohème* for Strachey and the Cecil too stuffy for both of us. I hit on the slightly raffish *luxe* of the Savoy. But why the insistence on a restaurant on or near the Strand?

'Because, my dear, I am now employed full-time by *The Spectator*, the offices are round the corner in Wellington Street and I do have to be back at a fairly respectable hour.'

St Loe Strachey had taken him on to write regular book reviews. If I were interested he could probably get me a little reviewing, if I could bear the thought of taking bread out of the mouths of starving scribblers like himself. With rather uncomprehending fascination, he questioned me about my year in the theatre. He had seen several of the productions.

'I expect you got through those delicious young creatures one after the other.'

'No, only three of them,' I said, quietly. 'Are you still seeing your art student?'

'Ah, Duncan! I'm still *seeing* him. In fact, he's living quite near, with his parents, in Fellows Road – the Fellows in question being Eton's. The College owns all the land round us; there's also a Provost Road, an Eton Avenue and an Eton College Road. Duncan is such a tantalizing problem.'

I enquired after mutual friends.

'Poor Woolf is still in Ceylon. Moore and Ainsworth are still in Edinburgh, not for much longer I suspect.' (Strachey's prescience was borne out: a year later, they left Edinburgh, Ainsworth entered the Board of Education, married Moore's sister and the couple moved in with Moore at his house in Richmond. If Ainsworth had had a spare sister, no doubt Moore would have married her, and both couples shared the same house.) 'Sydney-Turner and Hawtrey are still in the Treasury. Keynes is still at his desk in the India Office. Meredith and Sheppard are both Fellows of King's now. MacCarthy has just started a new quarterly, which, with commendable originality, he is calling *The New Quarterly*. I shall be reviewing for it as well as for *The Spectator*.'

To Strachey's astonishment, I had not heard that Vanessa Stephen had accepted Bell's latest proposal two days after Thoby had died: apparently, they had married in February and were now living in the Gordon Square house. Virginia and Adrian had taken a house in Fitzroy Square and were about to revive the Thursday Evenings. I asked Strachey where he had been all summer. He had spent an idyllic week in Versailles with Duncan Grant, staying in a house once occupied by La Bruyère.

'I then spent an utterly boring month with three of my siblings, in a house in the New Forest. When I was not tramping the woods, I was reading French – Laclos, Baudelaire, that sort of thing. Oh, and, to transport Versailles to the New Forest, I got the London Library to send all three volumes of Saint-Simon's *Mémoires*. I wrote an article on Beddoes – you know Beddoes? Ah, you probably read *The Bride's Tragedy* in old Gosse's edition – pure Webster, out of Shelley. I'm convinced he was one of our sect. The same goes for Gosse, of course.'

'Gosse?'

'Oh, yes. In his younger days he was a close friend of Robbie Ross's. Ross is working on an edition of Wilde's complete works, by the way. And now the wicked man is Librarian to the House of Lords! Gosse, not Ross. Anyway, to return to Beddoes, he spent six months in Hamburg living with a nineteen-year-old baker's assistant. I was even wondering whether I ought to go over and enquire after a retired baker aged seventy-seven and get the full story. He spent most of his life in Germany and Switzerland. Practised medicine. In fact, he died in Basle – killed himself.' My heart missed a beat. 'Of course, you must have gone to Germany with Tree. Everyone seems to be going to Germany. There was a time when everybody was going to Bayreuth. Now everybody's going to Munich, Berlin . . . Morgan even spent six months in Pomerania a couple of years ago, so don't be surprised if a future Morganatic hero compares Sawston adversely to Stettin. Morgan, *par contre*, hated Berlin. Said it was ugly and full of unhappy soldiers. Was it ugly and full of unhappy soldiers?'

I said that Berlin was not Paris, that it was no uglier than much of London and seemed to me to be full of happy soldiers. I had met two, at least, who seemed to be having a very good time. Potsdam was one enormous male brothel. Hadn't he read about the Berlin Scandal? Lytton's mouth had fallen open, momentarily bereft of words.

'Of course, of course . . .'

'Speaking of Forster, what did you think of his latest?' I asked.

'Pretty dreadful, on the whole. I found the Cambridge bits quite amusing, though very unfair to the Society. Keynes and I tried to work out who was who. Rickie is obviously a rather cruel self-portrait. Ansell is made to look like Woolf, with his "lean Jewish face", but is really Hom – Meredith – though there's a lot of Ainsworth in him too.'

A few days later, leafing through *The Times* I stumbled on the headline: THE GERMAN COURT SCANDALS. So the German courts were now in session: the story of the scandal that had enveloped the Imperial Court would resume. Apparently, Harden's chief informant was Moltke's ex-wife, a Swedish countess of plain looks, but considerable fortune, who had herself instigated the divorce, early on in the marriage, on the grounds of cruelty. She had also provided Harden with copies of letters between Philipp Eulenburg and her husband, in which the correspondents employed exaggeratedly affectionate terms. For example, Moltke used the feminine form, 'Philline', when addressing his friend and the Emperor himself was referred to as '*Liebchen*' (darling). There were references to orgies at the Potsdam villa of a Major Count von Lynar. We learnt how, the year before, Prince Frederick Henry of Prussia had resigned his commission and suddenly departed for Egypt, and of the suicides of several young officers.

The trial proceeded. The German press, we learnt, went into a degree of detail that was not 'in accordance with English practice'. Unfortunately, *The Times* followed English practice. Witnesses included Moltke's ex-wife, the director of a Hamburg theatre, two medical experts (one being Manfred's

friend Dr Magnus Hirschfeld), two police commissaries, two
bank messengers, a wild beast trainer, a standard bearer and
several non-commissioned officers and soldiers of the Garde
du Corps. Prince Eulenburg was 'too unwell to attend': lawyers
were obliged to go to Liebenberg to take his evidence. We
learnt that Moltke had been Eulenburg's 'most intimate friend
for forty years'. Another member of the *camarilla* turned out to
be Major von Hülsen, Intendant of Berlin Court Theatres, the
very same that had addressed us in the Hôtel Kaiserhof and
presented the Emperor's bracelets to Misses Collier and Tree.
The judges of the lower court in which the case had been heard
acquitted Harden of libel. Moltke appealed. The Emperor, no
doubt grateful for the distraction, set off on a visit to England.
In November, a higher court reversed the earlier judgement
and found against Harden; an army investigation was set in
train and there were debates in the Reichstag on the appalling
state of the nation. And there, for the time being, the matter
rested. But that particular story continued a little longer than
mine. The following May, Prince Eulenburg was 'arrested' on
a charge of perjury. A motor ambulance took him from
Liebenberg to the Charité hospital in Berlin, where he was
moved to a police ward. He remained too ill to make a court
appearance and was returned to Liebenberg. When he did
finally appear in Court, in July 1909, he fainted and the case of
perjury was adjourned *sine die*. He and Moltke were described
as men of 'artistic tastes' and 'friends from childhood'; both
were exonerated of 'immoral and unnatural practices'. Moltke
emerged from the trial 'pure and untarnished, with no stain left
on him and his escutcheon bright'; he returned to the active list
and was given a high decoration by the Emperor. In a court
martial of the Garde du Corps, Hohenau was acquitted on the
grounds of insufficient evidence, but 'removed from the list of
officers, with loss of all decorations', while Lynar was found

guilty of 'abuse of authority' in six instances, two involving 'a breach of morals'. Harden was found guilty of libel and fined 600 marks (£30).

What, I asked myself, was I to do with my life other than amuse myself? The gods are unkind: in extremity, they kill us for their sport. Worship of Eros does nothing to appease the insatiable demands of Thanatos.[1] On the contrary, devotion to the one can hasten the arrival of the other. Not only the elderly die, or even the weak. A microbe invisible to the naked eye had with a little pin bored through the castle wall of that model of rectitude and health, Thoby Stephen. Esmond, in his own muddled way, had decided that life was not worth living. Was I under any obligation to make the best of it? I was well aware of my privileged position: I did not have to work to live.

I still wanted to be a writer, I told myself – though I had stopped telling others. But what if I turned out to be no better a writer than poor Esmond had been an actor? Would that make my life not worth the living? I thought not. I was too sensible, too practical, too balanced, too easily happy an individual to feel that. Perhaps for that very reason I should never be a writer of any consequence: I lacked the obsessive fascination with the workings of my own mind, the invincible belief in their importance for the world that creativity seemed to require. I should end up happier than the unchosen failed creators, but I should be happier, too, than the chosen few.

Most mornings, I worked at what I called my journal, a rambling amalgam of jottings about books and plays, descriptions of the places in which I had lived, the beginnings of short stories, comments on events, great and small. Its fragmentariness reflected the fragmentariness of my life. Most novels seemed to concern a small group of people, living in a

1 Greek for 'death'.

small number of places over a limited period of time. My life had lacked a stable context of place, a close network of relations, friends, neighbours. How could I, Wandering Jew that I was, assume a God-like view of such a community of souls, scient not only of all they did, but also of the secrets of their hearts and minds? How could I make sense of my life, give it a shape that could be narrated, turned into literature? Were I to attempt to recount it, the only unity in that concatenation of incidents and places would be the narrator himself. It could never aspire to the condition of fiction, but would remain stuck at the mundane level of autobiography. And who would want to read the autobiography of an unknown man in his twenties, who had not distinguished himself in any way? How could I use my life, a life that seemed to be little more than a series of unrelated incidents and adventures, as material for a novel? That was one problem, but there was another. Reading *The Longest Journey*, I had been struck by the evident short-comings of the narrator's omniscience: he knew middle-class Englishwomen and Cambridge men, the rest of humanity hardly at all. Nor did he seem to know much about how things happen in the world or seem very concerned about probabilities. He made up for this by resorting to melodrama to make the points that he wanted to make. Forster's novel may not have been the novel that I would want to write, but I would have been incapable of writing a tenth of it, even had I wanted to. I suspected that it was not entirely the novel that Forster would have wanted to write either, had he been free to do so. But how could Forster write about what really interested him? How could I? Moral and social conventions forced us to cheat in our writings as they forced us to cheat in our lives. What I wanted to write about was not only unrelated, but unrelatable, unpublishable. How could I write a novel that bore any real relation to my life and exclude *that*?

It is a truism that the aesthetic success of a work depends on the willingness of the writer to exclude material. Yet I still hankered after a form of fiction in which I could write about whatever took my fancy, my thoughts on art and life, as well as my *liaisons dangereuses*. At this time, I was reading, with great delight, Fielding's *Tom Jones*. This story of an attractive, full-blooded young man's amorous adventures, interrupted from time to time by the narrator's reflections on matters of a more general nature, seemed a more likely model for me than, say, *Eugénie Grandet*, *Middlemarch* or *Anna Karenin*. Indeed most novels prior to the fictional monuments of the nineteenth century seemed to consist of just such a sequence of adventures befalling the young hero, while the earliest prose narratives of all, dating from the third century AD, Longus's *Daphnis and Chloë* and the *Aethiopica* by Heliodorus of Trikka, for example, were collectively known as *erotikoi*. If only I could write my own *erotikos*, a Uranian *Tom Jones*! But when Fielding wrote *Tom Jones*, he was not my age or Tom Jones's, but a respectable, gout-ridden magistrate of forty-one with only five more years to live. Then, again, however much *Tom Jones* might appear at times to be an excuse to recount its hero's amorous adventures, it does follow the time-honoured pattern of comedy, ending in a marriage, hero and heroine living happily ever after. Could my adventures so end, with the narrator-hero settling down to a domestic existence with some male Sophia?

As the serious nineteenth century took over the novel, the episodic, hero-centred narrative, with other characters reduced to two-dimensional figures, did survive, not as a way of recounting amorous adventures, but as a philosophical exploration of the Romantic hero's coming-to-manhood: the Germans called such works *Bildungsromanen*, the French *romans de formation*. Could an Englishman, I wondered, summon up the native genius for mixing genres and create a blend of both kinds, one in which the hero is not only philosopher, but also philanderer, a lover of men, for that is what the Greek word means?

One book that might be called a *roman de formation* affected me deeply when I first read it. I came upon it quite by chance. One afternoon, a few days before we left for London that summer, I happened to be in my grandparents' study when Marcel Schwob was visiting. This short, fat, ugly, prematurely bald man was a polyglot, steeped in all manner of subjects, but a specialist in English literature. (He translated, among other things, Defoe's *Moll Flanders*.) He spoke German and English at the age of three; at fourteen, he published a collection of poems, at sixteen, a translation of Catullus into Old French. That afternoon, as always, the talk was of books, complimentary copies lying in haphazard piles on desk and floor.

'*Ah! Celui-là!*'[1] Schwob suddenly exclaimed, picking up a volume, then, switching into English, declaimed in sonorous tones and with only a slight accent: 'It was begotten by despair upon impossibility!'[2] Then, switching back into French, he went on: 'Or to be more precise, by *Zarathustra* upon my *Monelle*! A rare birth, I grant you, but not, I fear, one of my loves!' (Gide later told me that he had not, in fact, read *Le Livre de Monelle* when writing *Les Nourritures terrestres* but, having heard the charge of plagiarism from several quarters, though it probably had a single source, he did finally read the book and understand better why Schwob had been annoyed. I think Gide was being generous to an old friend: he would have been even more justified had he launched into a point-by-point refutation of 'influence'.)

1 'Ah! *Him!*'
2 From Andrew Marvell's poem, 'To His Coy Mistress'.

What Schwob had said about *Les Nourritures terrestres*
intrigued me so much that I decided to take it – together with
Zarathustra and *Monelle* – away with me on holiday. Matthew,
who had decided to read nothing but Balzac that summer,
spent a quarter of an hour leafing through the Gide book,
guffawing occasionally. He concluded that I was madder than
usual: in his eminently sensible way, he could not imagine
why, once I conceded that Balzac was greater, better, even
more enjoyable than this young André Gide that nobody had
heard of, I could spend time reading his books when I might
be savouring the delights of *Eugénie Grandet*. Indeed there
were times when I envied the quite evident pleasure Matthew
was deriving from his *Comédie humaine*: the Gide book was
certainly not remarkable either for humour or for recognizable
human beings. But that, perversely, was what I found intriguing, even attractive about it. Someone who had decided that he
could not write about marriages pending or flourishing,
people's obsession with money, the apparently insignificant
minutiae of social life, or report in exhaustive detail what
people looked like and what they said, someone, in other
words, like me, had decided that he would write novels nevertheless, books that would be about what interested him. He
showed me that one could be a poet and also write a book of
imaginative prose, whether or not one calls it a novel.

Les Nourritures terrestres puzzled and exasperated me, but it
fascinated me in a way that little else had done. I felt that I had
stumbled upon something by chance, as the result, not of a
recommendation, but of a pejorative judgement, a curious
charge of plagiarism. The book is a medley of aphorisms,
poems, journal, travel notes and moral reflections. In this it
much resembles *Zarathustra*. As in Nietzsche's work, there is
much travelling about from place to place, but, whereas
Zarathustra moves only from nameless cave to nameless

mountain side, Gide is very specific: various sections are headed Honfleur, Rome, Amalfi, Syracuse, Tunis, etc. The wanderings, though real enough, are also an assertion of freedom, freedom not only from all moral rules, but also from all attachment to things or ideas, places or people. Given this, it should not have come to me as such a shock when Ménalque declares:

> Families, I hate you! Closed homes; locked doors; the jealous possessions of happiness – Sometimes, at night, I stood, unseen, leaning by a window, observing . . . The father was there, next to the lamp; the mother was sewing; . . . a child, near the father, was studying; – and my heart swelled up with a desire to take him with me on the road. Next day, I saw him again, as he was coming out of school; the day after that I spoke to him; four days later, he left everything to follow me. I opened his eyes to the splendour of the plains . . . I taught him to detach himself even from me, to know his solitude.

I found this passage disturbing at first, then, on reflection, ridiculous. It begins in a way that suggests a horror story or an account of child molesting. The term 'child' (*enfant*) heightens the horror: Gide does not refer to a '*garçon*', though there is no doubt about his sex – and he is at least fourteen years old. Ménalque does not molest him, but 'persuades' him to leave his family and follow him. What 'child' would go along with Ménalque's Nietzschean phantasies? The truth is that not only the 'child', but Ménalque himself, is a phantasy figure, a kind of ideal self. Gide himself, as he freely admitted to me later, had no personal reason to hate families: his mild, self-effacing father died before he was eleven and though his mother was certainly over-protective, domineering even, her love for her only child was certainly reciprocated. It was also that same family and its accumulated wealth that has allowed Gide to do nothing all his life except write and travel. Nor was he, at the time of writing *Les Nourritures*, a free soul, taking to road and sea, unencumbered with friends or possessions. Unlike Ménalque, he never slept in ditches, 'on grass during the day, in barns at night', or in hammocks slung between two trees, or on ships' decks, but always in the best hotels. Moreover, at this time, he had just married his cousin, settled down at his family's estate in Normandy, even being elected mayor of his municipality, at twenty-six the youngest mayor in France.

Gide's would-be renunciation of all attachment even embraced the book that we, the readers, are reading. 'And when you have read me, throw away this book – and go out . . . from anywhere, from your town, from your family, your room, your thought. Don't take my book with you . . . May my book teach you to be interested more in yourself than in it, – then in all the rest more than in yourself.' For me, of course, there was no question of 'throwing away' *Les Nourritures terrestres*. For one thing, I did not read a book in order to have my life changed by it – enriched, perhaps, in which case it would remain on my bookshelves, a cherished possession, one window among others on to the world. Again Gide was advocating, through Ménalque, a course of action that he would never have dreamt of carrying out himself. When he was not writing his own – or spending hours a day at his journal, or penning countless letters – Gide was reading (and collecting) the works of others. That most prudent of men (at least where objects of value were concerned) would never have been so reckless as to 'throw away' a book. Through Ménalque, Gide seems to be advocating the rejection not only of this, the book the reader is reading, but also of all books, all knowledge that has not come directly from life itself. I found this admonition even more shocking than 'Families, I hate you!' I was too young, too recently acquainted with intellectual hunger, to have reached satiety. That would come later, when, after three years at university, I was overcome by a sense that I knew so much about books and so little about life. It is a false distinction, though a useful one at certain times in life.

If, despite such apparent incompatibility between book and reader, *Les Nourritures terrestres* held such fascination for me, it was because it was the first book that I could explore, argue with from a position of relative equality. It was the occasion of a quite new kind of intellectual excitement, one that concerned me and the world that I was about to enter. But, quite apart from the main arguments of the book, there were allusions, passages of a kind that I had read nowhere else. They concerned that hinterland of mind and body that we call sex. What was new in this book, to me at least, was the presupposition, expressed in the most natural, off-hand way, that sex was something one could, indeed should, practise with as many people as possible, male as well as female. Gide's nameless narrator speaks of *couches* – a more poetic term than *lits* (beds) – 'where courtesans awaited me; others where I waited for young boys'. There were passing moments so unobtrusive that one could easily miss them: the '*enfant*' who follows the narrator into the bushes of a public garden in Amalfi (there is even a reference to the boy's '*fruit*') or the postilion who shared his passenger's bed of hay. There was one passage that I could hardly believe had been printed in a respectable book (I knew no others): '*Mon coeur naturellement aimant et comme liquide se répandait de toutes parts; aucune joie ne me semblait appartenir à moi-même; j'y invitais chacun de rencontre, et lorsque j'étais seul à jouir, ce n'était qu'à force d'orgueil.*' ('My naturally loving and ready [liquid-like] heart spread out on every side; no pleasure seemed to me to belong to me alone; I invited

485

everyone I met to share it and when I came alone it was only out of pride.' I could not, in fact, have translated all of that sentence at the time. *'Jouir'* (literally, 'to enjoy') was the word used by French schoolboys; I did not even know what our English counterparts said. As usual in sexual matters, French is incomparably the better medium, so obviously enjoying sex in a way that English, possessing only a crude vulgar mode and a cold, technical-sounding one, does not.

I read *L'Immoraliste* when it came out in Paris in 1902. It was Gide's first book of any length that could really be called a novel: at first sight, it seemed a less extreme fictional departure than *Les Nourritures terrestres*. The hero had a marriage to relate and it was this that held centre stage: the Uranian side of his life was clear enough to those who had eyes to see, but was necessarily subordinate to the marriage and had to be treated with discretion. Rereading the book five years later, with much greater attention, I was struck by how obviously Uranian a book it is. Michel's recovery from illness begins when he notices that Bachir, an Arab boy, had *'chevilles charmantes'* ('charming ankles') and was *'tout nu sous sa mince gandourah blanche'* ('quite naked under his thin white gandourah'). Later, he notes that his gandourah has slipped, exposing his *'mignonne épaule'* ('pretty shoulder'). At Ravello, he is excited at the sight of young farm workers, with their *'belles peaux hâlées'* ('beautiful tanned skins'). Back on his Normandy property, he obviously becomes infatuated with the son of his estate manager, *'un beau gaillard, si bien fait'* ('such a handsome, shapely fellow'), who is seventeen, but looks only fifteen. Later, he has eyes for others on the farm: 'I pretended to supervise the work, but in fact I saw only the workers.' In Naples, at night, he waits for his wife to fall asleep, then gets up and slips out of the house, 'like a thief'. He walks the streets: *'Je posais ma main sur des choses; je rôdais'* ('I put my hand on things; I went on the prowl'). In Sicily, a young coach-man, *'beau comme un vers de Théocrate'* ('beautiful as a line of Theocritus'), praises his wife's beauty: he responds by praising the boy's. At Syracuse, *'la société des pires gens m'était compagnie délectable. Et qu'avais-je besoin de comprendre bien leur langage, quand toute ma chair le goûtait'* ('the society of the worst people was for me delectable company. And what need had I to understand what they said, when my whole flesh tasted it'). I could hardly fail to be struck by how much Gide had managed to get away with. I was struck, too, by the similarities and differences between Gide's and Forster's books. Both heroes share the same Nietzschean contempt for the weak, for 'respectable' middle-class life. Gide speaks of Culture, born of life, killing life. Yet how different the two books were – how different, too, must the two authors be. Gide was allowing the love that dared not speak its name to speak; Forster could only silence it, disguise it as physical deformity. When I last saw Lucien Daudet, he had looked at me as if I were mad when I asked if there would be anything 'indecent' in his novel. He clearly did not approve of Gide, yet, when he told me that Marcel Proust had had to abandon a long novel that he had started, I wondered if perhaps that was Marcel's problem: how could he honestly transpose his life into fiction, once he had gone beyond childhood?

On 31 December 1907 the lease on the Smith Square house would expire. Four years before, with the sale of the flat in the rue de Vaugirard, I had lost one of the two fixed points between which my life since the age of ten had moved. In two months' time, I should lose the other. There was a sense in which, with the absence of my Sheridan grandparents, who had made it what it was, I had already lost it when I came to live there two years before. At the time it had seemed like a new beginning. Joining the Tree company and living with

Esmond were part of that brave new world. As it turned out, there was a future in neither: they were both extensions of my life at Smith Square and had ended even before that life was due to end. As if to symbolize the terminal condition of that life, the square itself was disappearing at the hands of the new world of 'developers'; only our side, to the north, remained and half the houses there were already unoccupied, awaiting their fate. On the eastern side, hideous modern buildings had already gone up, while the southern and western sides were still building sites. It looked as though I was to be one of the last remaining residents of the old square built by Sir James Smith under the reign of George I.

I had decided that if I were to travel for a year or so, before taking a flat of my own, I might as well stay there as long as possible. I should probably go first to Paris, then spend most of the winter in Italy, perhaps even in North Africa. Greece, too, called, but the fate of Thoby Stephen was not encouraging. At some point, I should return to Berlin and explore its attractions further. Other times, other places.